Praise for Doublesight

"Lately fantasy rarely surprises and seldom delights, but Terry Persun's novel *Doublesight* does both and more. Richly textural, complicated in character, and presenting a world unlike any other, this debut imbues new blood into the genre. It is a stunning fantasy for the new millennium."

—James Rollins, bestselling author of *The Eye of God*

"Persun's captivating new fantasy raises the art of shape shifting to a new level. Enter the world of *Doublesight* where man and animal are one. A fresh adventure awaits!"

—Janet Lee Carey, author of *Dragonswood*

Doublesight
Book One

by Terry Persun

I'd like to thank Catherine for giving me space to write, Nicole for keeping me on-task, Terry and Mark for their encouragement, and Richard Mandel and Ken Davis for their editing skills. I would also like to thank Mark Mandell for looking over several beginnings to this book before I got it right.

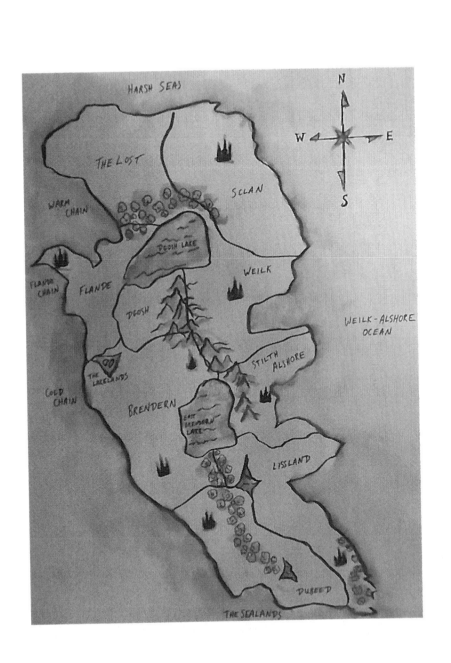

1

The morning was perfect. The crescent sun pulled itself over the peaked mountains and lay gold across the branches of the trees. Leaves quaked in the slight breeze. Members of the crow clan, loving sunrise, perched in the trees. In human form they had made a great haul the day before, stealing more than usual and escaping the village at night, unnoticed in their multi-colored caravan of wagons.

A low fog settled in the valley and along the Lorensak River several miles away where only the tops of the trees were visible. On the hillside the air felt crisp and clear. Songs and chatters of other birds also rose to greet the sun, but Zimp heard only the cawing of her clan as though they could drag the sun up the sky with their voices.

She hopped to the end of a branch and ruffled her feathers, leaned into sound as it dragged through her throat. Zora, her twin sister, perched beside her. The cawing rose as over the distant mountains the sun, no longer a crescent, broke loose full and round, a blazing orb. A wave of crows lifted from behind Zimp and flew closer to the wood's edge, landing in the cottonwoods, aspen, and pines around her. Zora left her side, glided to a nearby branch, landed, and held fast.

The air snapped with a start. Zimp didn't see where the sound came from, but many of her clan lifted into the sky, a black wave. Another snap and thwang brought an arrow into a branch in a cottonwood to her left. Zimp turned toward the sound. Two-dozen men stepped from behind a grove of trees not a hundred yards away. Another six arrows slid into the sky, one hitting a crow flying overhead who attempted to warn the clan. Zimp heard a wing snap.

The crow paused midair for a moment. Its wing grew fingers, which then pushed into the open sky as a spindly arm, then two arms, then the lengthening of legs. The body of her cousin Lim dropped, still alive, flailing to grasp something to stop his fall. The arrow must have produced enough pain to tear him from his crow image. The fall would surely kill him. There was nothing she could do to help.

Before long three more clansmen shifted into human form and fell from the sky. Cawing mixed with human screams. The sight shocked her into immobility. She felt her crow instinct push forward. She couldn't allow her crow image to take over her mind completely or there would be no turning back. She shook her head. The screaming became louder as more clansmen were shot from the sky, shifting to human form as they fell earthward. Then she heard a familiar voice.

Zora let out a moan.

Zimp glided to the branch where Zora perched. The tip of her wing shifted into a slender human hand. Strong fingers held to the thin branch as legs formed and her torso took shape.

Zimp placed a wing over Zora's hand and began to shift along with her sister. She held tight to Zora's hand as her body changed and gripped the branch they occupied. More screams filled the sky. A rain of human bodies plummeted, some crashing through branches, some getting tangled in the trees, others hitting the ground with the clear thud of a dead body. The sky grew black with another wave of crows as a flurry of arrows launched.

Zimp completed her shift, then wrapped her legs around the rough corrugation of the branch. Her red cloak fell to one side, and her chin drove into the branch. She saw that the arrow had hit close to her sister's heart. She stared into her own face: the high cheekbones, the thin slanted eyes, the full, lightly parted lips. The branch bent with their combined weight. "Hold tight,

Zora. I'm right here." Zimp slid forward and let one hand slide down Zora's arm for a better grip.

Another arrow pierced Zora's neck. Her eyes shocked the air with a show of pain. Her grip weakened. A sliver of blood trickled from the corner of her lips, and she released her grip on the branch.

Zimp held fast. Then came a loud crack and they fell with added momentum. They slammed into the tree trunk, freeing the branch from between Zimp's legs. Her grip failed and Zora fell toward the ground, the broken branch beside her.

Zimp rolled onto a larger branch, slamming her back, knocking the wind from her lungs. Arrows sang to her left and right. She threw a leg over the branch to bring her upright and breathed in tree dust.

Zora's body lay crooked below her, partially hidden in the underbrush. The small limb they had held to, first as crows and then as humans, lay at Zora's side, a twig next to Zora's human form.

The archers stood to the side. Zimp slid down the branch, stayed close to the trunk of the tree, and shifted into her crow image. An arrow grazed the trunk above her head. Many of her clan still held to branches in their human image, wounded or dying, trying to hide from the archers. Some of them had shifted back into crow image. Others were already far in the distance, flying toward the Lorensak.

Zimp glided closer to the archers, her flight taking her behind a large cottonwood where it would be difficult for them to see her. She landed, heart racing, fear building.

She had little time. The fight against instinct was great. She knew that if her fear continued to escalate she might remain in her crow image permanently, losing her natural human image, her whole human life. She couldn't allow her survival instinct to push her that far.

She peered at the men and saw that they were dressed similarly to those in the village they had robbed. Another man, unarmed except for a broad sword and differently dressed, stood back from the others. She shook her head. Her fear was winning. She had to either shift or retreat. She chose to retreat.

Zimp pushed straight up into the thicker part of the pine, dodging the close-set branches. She broke into the sky and headed into the valley. She felt unbelievable sorrow for her sister. Even as a crow, love crept through as a human emotion. It was so strong a sensation that she nearly shifted. She dove and tried to release the human feelings growing inside her. But then, another thought came unbidden. Her grandmother. Another human attachment. Too many human thoughts came at once. She was losing her personal battle not to shift.

Zimp plunged to the ground and landed in a patch of tall grass halfway down the hillside. She shifted into human form, allowing the thoughts to rush into her mind. Planning and thinking were best done in human form. She needed a rest. To better hide, she removed her red cloak and tucked it under her arm while she hunkered close to the ground.

"Zimp?" A whisper came toward her from within the grass to her right. Noot crawled into view. He wore a brown vest and brown shirt. His green pants had a patch of red spreading over them. He looked at it. "A scratch. I was so scared I had to shift before I stayed in crow image. I didn't know what was happening for a long while. I got hit in the middle of shifting, then landed in some underbrush and crawled out."

"You crawled all the way down here?"

"No. I shifted and flew part way." His hands shook as he spoke.

Noot had always been the more timid one in the clan. Zimp crawled over and sat next to him. "We need to check on the others. Oro, especially."

"What do you think happened?"

"Someone knew we were doublesight," she said.

"How do you figure?"

"I saw a man standing back from the archers, trying to stay hidden. I couldn't make out his facial features, but none of the villagers would have guessed what we were. They were human only. I saw no other doublesight during our raid."

"He must have been hiding somewhere," Noot said.

"But why would another doublesight do that?"

Noot laughed. "We're not the most loved of the doublesight.

Perhaps a longstanding enemy?"

"Perhaps." Zimp touched his leg. "Can you go with me?"

"I'm sure the others circled around and returned into camp." Surprise came to Noot's face. "Unless the villagers attacked there too. Do you sense anything?"

Zimp closed her eyes and took a long breath. Her first sensation, sadness toward Zora. She fought that emotion and dug deeper, to a calmer place, where she could sense the world outside herself. "It feels safe there." She opened her eyes and looked into Noot's. "But I'm not really good at this yet. Not as good as..." She stopped. "Oh, to the Gods, to the Gods."

"Zora?" Noot said.

Zimp reached out and held him, more for her benefit than his. "She's dead, Noot. I held her hands as we fell. They killed her."

Noot placed a hand over her head and let her rest against him. "Go ahead. It's okay."

Zimp heard cheers coming from the grove of trees where the archers had appeared. "They made their kill," she said.

"We'd better get to camp. Check on everyone."

Noot was right. Zimp pulled away, wiped away her tears. "Can you shift and fly?"

"It's not that bad. I'll be fine." Noot cocked his head as his arms and legs shortened. His legs thinned into bird legs, his arms fattened into wings, all happening while his head squeezed into itself and his nose protruded and became a black beak.

Zimp followed suit and felt her bones shift and her body shrink. She became physically lighter and could feel the hollowness of her own bones as she changed. As crows they flew low over the tall grass in the valley. At the lifting fog, they rose up and flew north where, a short distance off, they had made camp the night before.

On approach Zimp noticed guards had been set out. Seven wagons stood at various distances from one another along the river. Zimp shifted into her human image, then searched the group for her grandmother.

Oro sat on a stool in the midst of the clan.

Zimp rushed to her and bent down. She took Oro's hand

and stared into the old woman's eyes, afraid to speak. She lowered her eyes.

"I know, my dear." Oro touched Zimp's face with a wrinkled and shaking hand.

Zimp lowered her face into the old woman's lap. "What happened? Why didn't you see this? Why didn't I see it?"

Oro said nothing in response to Zimp's questions. She took a deep breath and placed both hands on Zimp's head.

"We'd better break camp," the distinct voice of Arren said. Zimp turned to face him.

He stood tall and lean. His arms were laced with muscle and he held a sword as though ready to fight at any moment. He waited for Oro's approval.

The old woman pushed against Zimp's shoulder and rose to her feet. "Come, my dear. Arren is right. We must move on. The council will not meet without us."

"It's the council that has us moving in such a large group. If it wasn't for them, this wouldn't have happened," Zimp said. "If you had gone to the council meeting alone as always, you wouldn't be detected."

Oro shook her head. "We chose to enter the village in force. Perhaps that was the mistake. A small band could have gone in."

"You don't seem to care about Zora. What about her death?"

Oro turned to Arren. "Prepare to move." She turned back to Zimp. "Have you thought that perhaps Zora volunteered to leave this plane of existence?"

Zimp opened her mouth to speak, to scream, but no words came.

Oro nodded and reached for Zimp's hand. "Help me back to the wagon."

2

The air had chilled with the humidity of early morning. The trees dripped with dew in the low fog of the forest. Silence broke, disrupted by the soft paws of thylacines pattering back home in the dark. Brok loved it when the family went out together. And an early morning return meant a hearty breakfast and a short, sound sleep for a few hours. Bringing up the rear, Brok could hardly see his father ahead of them.

Fremlin stepped into the clearing and shape-shifted into his human image to unlock the door to the family cabin. He smelled something unusual just before he shifted, but lost the scent. Lina, Brok's mother, was next, and his brothers and sisters followed her. They shifted more slowly into human form and joked while following Lina and Fremlin into the clearing. A night of fun and play brought them home later than usual.

Fremlin fumbled with the door for a moment as though it were stuck. Then it suddenly slammed open. A massive man wider than the door itself jutted across the threshold, knocking Fremlin to the ground. His sword high over his shoulder, the man leaned toward Fremlin and swung, removing Fremlin's head in one stroke. Brok heard the cracking neck bones and the gurgle of blood.

Lina screamed and turned, ushering the others back into the woods.

Brok's sister Keena, swung around but arched her back and

fell forward, a dagger in her back. Rem stumbled and kneeled to the ground near her, a dagger protruding from his neck.

Lina hesitated so that she could help her children. Her body doubled and crouched toward the ground. Her hands shifted into paws and her legs bent, molding into the legs of a thylacine, one of the most ancient of the doublesight, half wolf and half mountain lion. She scurried while shifting, her gaping jaws letting out a loud, warning growl.

Three more men came from around the cabin. Two of them rushed Lina, swinging their swords violently as they approached. She collapsed, her back severed.

Brok, his younger brother Therin and youngest sister Breel, shifted and ran into the woods. Brok led, but the three of them halted long enough to look back as Lina went down completely. Brok noticed Therin's body jolt with the blow to his mother's back, and two subsequent blows to her head and body.

Brok and Breel continued into the woods, but Therin stood motionless.

Breel barked to get his attention. Something was wrong.

Brok turned to go back and motioned for Breel to go on. He sprinted to Therin as the men rushed closer. Brok bit into Therin's tailbone and dragged him backwards.

Therin growled and yelped, but turned and ran after his brother.

It was easy to gain distance from the men once the thylacines were in beast image.

The three marsupials ran deep into the woods. They ducked under and through brush, leaped over fallen trees, and swerved so that they would look as though they disappeared within the fog. There was a meeting place near a hollowed tree where they had all planned to meet if anything were to ever go wrong. They would regroup there.

Brok panted with fear. The images of his father, mother, and siblings flashed through his mind. Their human forms helped to keep him conscious of his true form. Instinct had forced them to run.

At the hollowed log deep in the Brendern Forest, Brok took his time shifting into human form. On his knees, breathing heavily, he spit into the crisp leaves in front of him. He could see Breel and Therin in his peripheral vision. Neither shifted.

Rays of sunlight filtered through the thinned canopy of trees. The fog had become transparent as it burned off. The black trunks of trees held onto the night for as long as they could, even as the leaves turned brilliant with color.

Brok stood and rubbed the back of his head and neck. "Shift, you two. We need to plan." He waited a moment. They were both still panting.

Breel arched her back as though shifting was painful.

Brok ran to her to make sure she hadn't been cut or stabbed. He saw nothing. A small sound like a whimper escaped her mouth. Drool slid from her canines. Her legs shifted first, always her choice since she was small. Then her torso changed shape and finally her head. Breel fell into Brok's arms and cried.

He held her. There was no use in telling her that everything was all right or that they'd be fine. He knew better. His family had been murdered and the three of them would most likely be hunted down.

Brok turned his head and saw that Therin had not shifted. "Therin. Shift."

Therin sat on his haunches and cocked his head.

Brok teared up. "Therin?"

Breel pushed from Brok and leaned toward her little brother. "Oh, no," she said.

Brok grabbed Therin by the fur and shook him. "Therin," he yelled. "Therin." Hearing their human name was the strongest pull to return doublesight to their human form, but it wasn't working. Therin was young and nervous. He had always been the most vulnerable and Lina had been over protective of him because of it. So now, Brok feared the worst.

Breel slapped Therin across the jowls and yelled his name. "Shift," she said. "Shift, Therin, shift."

Therin turned to leave.

Brok grabbed hold of the fur along Therin's back and pulled him into a sitting position. He knew the signs. Still holding his brother, Brok sat back and stretched his legs outward. He dragged Therin onto his lap and held him.

Breel reached out and stroked her brother's head. "Why did this happen?"

"I don't know." Brok answered both questions at once—about Therin's permanent beast image and about the murder of his family. He reached one arm across Breel's back. "We've got to hide somewhere for the day so we can sleep."

"There's nowhere to go," she said.

"Dad always felt this was safe enough." He looked around the area. A mound of leaves and dirt rose a few hundred feet from them. He nodded.

Breel stood up and ran to it. "The hollow log's over here."

Brok strolled over to her side. Therin followed obediently and nudged Brok's leg once he stopped. Brok reached down and scratched his brother's neck. "We'll have to shift and sleep that way."

"I've never done that before," Breel said. Her eyes were wet and her brown hair hung in tangles near her shoulders. Her shirt matched the black striped coloring of her thylacine image, but her pants were brown like her hair.

"If you wake up disoriented, shift to human form for a few minutes to get your bearings. Don't stay that way long though; your skin can't handle the ant and spider bites like your beast image can." He raised his eyebrows. "Okay to do this?"

Breel pushed her lips together so that they looked like a straight line across her face. She nodded, but didn't look all that convincing to Brok. Then she burst into tears again.

He reached for her, but she waved him away. "This will be difficult," she said.

"I know." He scratched Therin's head and looked up at Breel. "It already is." As the oldest sibling, Brok had been trained to fend for the family. Just recently Fremlin had indicated that he felt there was reason to feel unsafe, even though their whole lives had been fine up until then. He told Brok only a few days ago, "The doublesight are not trusted and have been under siege more than normal lately. None of the villages know we're doublesight, but we must be more cautious than ever." Fremlin had told his son that they were lucky to live in the Brendern Forest near Stilth Alshore because the Three Princes of Crell

who ruled Stilth Alshore were friends to the doublesight. Brok
wondered how true that was now. Had things changed?

He and Breel trudged over the rise and shifted into their
beast images. Brok made sure that Therin scooted into the log
between them. Before crawling in he looked around to get his
bearings. Which trees lay to the north? If they had to leave in
the night, he needed to know in which direction to run first.

Brok curled his tail close to his body and put his nose near
Therin. He could feel the log shudder a moment and knew that
Breel's sadness would make sleeping difficult for her. He let
himself mourn, mentally, as much as possible without dragging
him back into his human image. The doublesight were once
revered, even worshipped. Why they had become feared was
a mystery to him. "History," his father had told him. "Where
instinct drives the decisions for beasts, fear drives decisions
for humans." But his family had hurt no one. They kept to
themselves.

The images of Fremlin being beheaded and then of Lina
being sliced flashed through Brok's mind and he felt himself
begin to shift. He pushed the images from his head. Strange
that those same experiences would cause enough fear in Therin
to keep him in beast image.

3

Scouts returned with news of the dead. The village archers were gone, returned to their village. Crow clan members were sent to retrieve their wounded brothers. All morning the camp rushed into activity. The sunshine warmed the gravel shore of the Lorensak. Horses whinnied as they were tacked up and harnessed to the wagons. Footfalls crunched against stone. Voices rose to a low murmur over the rushing sound of the river. Each wagon endured a rigorous check for sturdiness in expectation of rough travel.

Zimp caught brief conversations concerning those who had died. She recognized a variety of family members and distant cousins. Tears were shed for lost children. Still, at Oro's command, the camp gathered its sorrows and prepared to go.

Arren came around the rear of Zimp's wagon to report to Oro that he had sent scouts north along the Lorensak and that all was clear to continue upriver to the crossing point.

Zimp sat motionless on a wooden bench near the rear of the wagon, her red cloak pulled close to her body, her head tucked into her shoulders, unlike her usual self.

Arren placed a hand on her knee. "I lost my brother and closest friend. We are all sad."

Zimp did not acknowledge his comment. She brushed his hand away.

"In a few days, at the council grounds, we'll celebrate the

deaths." He nodded toward Oro before he turned to leave.

"Help me to lie down," Oro said to her granddaughter.

Zimp uncoiled her body from the cloak and stepped closer to Oro. The sun came through the trees overhead and penetrated the multi-colored canvas that lay over the wagon. A display of red, yellow, and blue spread over both cots and the floor. Zimp held the old woman's hand and guided her to her bunk.

Oro sat for a moment, then allowed Zimp to lower her onto the cot and to lift her feet into place. Oro reached out and grabbed Zimp's wrist before she could turn away. "Talk with her," she said.

"I can't. I'm not that far along. It's still difficult to hear Mom's voice."

"Zora was your twin, dear. There is a bond there. A greater bond than with a parent." Oro let go of Zimp.

"I'll try," Zimp said.

Oro turned toward the canvas side of the wagon. "This will be quite a ride today," she mused aloud, "for these old bones."

Zimp returned to the rear bench so that she could see out the canvas opening. There was no mention of Oro's intuitive abilities or why she hadn't sensed the potential for attack. Zimp went limp with regret that Oro was getting old and perhaps not able to sense such dangers any longer.

As the horses began to move forward, the wagon pitched to the left and right, shifting over increasingly larger stones, heading toward the edge of the tree line that bordered the river.

Zimp grabbed for the edge of her seat and held on. She leaned against the rear corner post to help steady her body. Although gregarious at times, and often social, Zimp also needed privacy and quiet. The ability to appear playful or shy made her a good pickpocket and thief. Yet now, she relished the sense of being secure and cozy, tucked away in the wagon.

It was Zora who had wanted to command all the time. If she were alive, Arren would be taking direction from Oro through Zora.

Zimp didn't mind the limelight, but retracted from the responsibility. Zora had craved it.

The northbound caravan followed animal paths along

the plains and as close to the river as possible. The creaking and rattling wagons frightened small herds of elk and buffalo that were chased from one grazing area to another. Where animal paths meandered down near the river, Arren lead the way making his own wider pathways. The hope was to avoid contact with humans, whether in villages or traveling the main roads. As Arren guided the caravan into the edge of the field, mounds of dirt, varmint holes, and ground-bird nests all made the traveling unsteady.

Zimp bounced and bucked in the back of the wagon. She heard Oro moan when a great jolt pitched her to one side or the other.

The sun rose to Zimp's right and burned against her cheek. She squinted. The golden and green grass around the wagon wheels tangled in the spokes and tore from the ground creating a clearing of tracks and a haze of floating seeds. The new pathways would make it easy for the villagers to follow, although that wouldn't be very smart. Six archers were a small number against a hundred or more crow clan. They had been surprised once, but that wouldn't happen again. All those deaths for very little in jewelry and utensils.

"All those deaths," Zimp heard. She raised up from her seat and stuck her head outside to look around. The wind caused the field of grass and weeds to ripple and shift. The breeze came from the northeast. "Hello?" Zimp said.

Oro rolled onto her side. "Zora is speaking to you."

"No."

"You should not be surprised," Oro said.

"This soon? She'd try to contact me this soon?"

Oro let out a long breath and waited for a moment. The wagon pitched forward and to the left. "We forgot our ritual this morning," she said.

Zimp turned in question.

"You wonder why no one noticed the sneak attack. Perhaps a moment of quiet and a call to the other realms would have caused a shudder in our ritual," Oro said.

"We were excited for the morning," Zimp said.

"Birds love morning sunrise."

"That's what we are."

Oro grunted. "We are human with bird images. Human first. Have you forgotten as well? Morning satisfied Zora's need to rush into a decision and abandon her gifts." Oro reached for Zimp to help her sit up.

"Just lie there. I'll come to you." Zimp rocked with the pitch of the wagon as she crawled to Oro's side and sat on the rag-made carpet over the floorboards. She held Oro's hand.

"You will make a better leader," Oro said.

"Arren can lead."

"You don't mean that. We both know that Arren is angry and demanding. He may be able to lead an army, but you will lead a people. Now that Zora is in the next realm, your advanced training begins."

"I'd rather be in the backgroun, invisible when necessary. Let someone else lead. You have many years in you. Watch the clan. Select a better candidate. It doesn't have to be family."

Oro smiled at her granddaughter and shook her hand. "What did Zora say to you?"

"All those deaths," she told Oro. "She repeated my thoughts back to me." Zimp looked away and said, "Perhaps I was hearing things."

"Perhaps," Oro said.

In a few hours, the wagons halted. Zimp leaped from her seat and greeted Arren, who stopped promptly in front of her as though he knew his place. "I thought we'd stop, eat, and then cross the river just ahead," he said.

"You know best," Zimp said looking up at his eyes. "Oro's resting."

"How is she faring?"

"She's not that old," Zimp snapped.

"I meant nothing."

She nodded. "I know you didn't mean anything but concern for her. Well, she's doing fine. This route isn't the smoothest for any of us."

Arren continued to stand in front of Zimp.

"Anything else?" she said.

"It's allowable for us to camp here for a meal?" he said.

Zimp raised her hands and opened her palms as if to say that it was his decision. "If you say it is," she said.

Arren grimaced, then turned on the balls of his feet and stepped away abruptly, off to announce the plan.

"That was awkward and strained," Oro said from behind Zimp.

"Zora..."

Oro shook her head. "Don't want to hear it."

As the sun passed slowly overhead, the clan gathered in a great circle. Oro dragged Zimp into the center of the circle with her. At a makeshift altar made from a wooden bench encircled in pine branches, Oro placed two candles. She lit one and spoke a prayer for the lost members of their clan. "The next realm," she said, "has called to us. It has pulled many numbers from the lottery. It has selected the best and the worst for its own plan. The next realm has begun gathering together its own army for a battle and it needed our help." Oro pointed for Zimp to light the other candle.

With her hands shaking, Zimp poured some powder onto a twig. She cracked two flints together and the powder caught fire in a flash. She lifted the twig and lit the second candle. Before she could shake the twig's flame out, the candle snapped and spit sparkles into the air. Zimp jumped. Sparkle candles were for special purposes. What special purpose did Oro see in their lunchtime prayer?

Oro opened her arms to include the wide circle of doublesight who sat around her. "We come into the circle in sorrow and in pride. We are saddened for our loss and joyous for their gain. Our friends. Our families. All who have moved on will be there to help us. Today we celebrate their lives and deaths." She pinched each candle out by licking her fingertips and lightly squeezing each wick.

The emotion of the clan had changed in that short time. They held to Oro's words, accepted them, acted on them. Zimp held to them, too. She helped Oro collect her candles and stand up to go back to the wagon. The altar would be taken care of.

"A brief goodbye," Oro said.

"And a joyous dance," Zimp added the saying of their clan

whenever someone died. There was more to the saying: A tear and a laugh. One realm leads to the next. Life leads to life. An eternity in time. Infinite in distance. We all walk the same road homeward.

Back at the wagon, still in thought, Zimp helped Oro return her sacred items under one of the benches. "It wasn't my place to light the candle," she said.

"It is your right," Oro corrected.

"I was not selected. Zora was."

"And Zora was needed elsewhere. Now, you are selected."

"Why?"

Oro placed an arm around Zimp's waist. "No more questions. It is time to accept."

Zimp helped her grandmother to the side of the river where the clan met for a quick bite to eat. She lowered Oro onto a fallen tree trunk, then strolled farther down river before she sat down.

Zimp watched the water slip past as though it were oblivious of the hundred or so doublesight along its shores, oblivious of the trees and the sky. She wished she could ignore everything and everyone and just flow easily through life.

"Zimp?" Arren held a piece of pan bread with dried fish paste spread over it. He thrust the bread toward her and sat on the stones next to her feet once she took it.

"I am not your favorite cousin," he said. "I know this. But I will say what I must. You don't appear to be strong enough to lead us." He lowered his own pan bread and let it rest on his thigh. He looked into Zimp's eyes. "Although my allegiance is to Oro. I trust her completely." He appeared to be thinking. When he looked up again, he said, "You probably couldn't tell, but she had selected you from the start. Zora was a front while you were being trained in the dark arts."

"That's not true," Zimp said.

"I wish it were not true, but I am not mistaken. I can see clearly when it comes to warrior training."

"I don't want it to be true."

Arren picked up his bread and stood. "Should Oro die, you can choose another," he said before walking off.

Zimp watched him go. He hated her, she thought. He'd

listen to Oro as long as she was alive, but he had already begun to take over. Once the clan recognized him as surrogate leader for Oro, it would be a small thing for him to continue in the lead. Zimp didn't want to expend the energy it would take to expunge Arren's apparent need to command. The intuitive arts took silence and a softness of spirit. How did Oro balance the external demands of energy necessary for leadership with the meditation and quiet needed for communication with other realms? Zimp wished that Oro would choose someone else.

After eating her pan bread, Zimp sat with her legs stretched toward the Lorensak River as it licked at the pebbles in front of her. Not far from the shore the river current raged southward toward City Raldern, the economic center of Brendern. The water appeared to run smoothly, but Zimp knew that had she stepped several feet into the river from where she sat, the undercurrent would drag her violently down to a rocky bed and most likely drown her before delivering her downstream. That, she thought, was what Oro possessed. Even the thought of trying to maintain such a character exhausted her.

4

Near the mouth of the Lorensak River, at the Brendern Eastlake spill, many tributaries spread over almost a mile of shallow swamp interrupted by mounds of dry dirt and stone outcroppings. Only one wagon got stuck while crossing the River. It took an hour of digging, shoving, and dragging to separate it from the bottom silt. Dozens of men and women lay on the ground around the wagon, resting for a moment. The sun blazed horizontally in the shimmering distance, still hot in the clear sky.

"We're ready," Zimp alerted Oro.

Oro rolled to her side and glanced down at Zimp standing outside the wagon. "I don't like camping in the open. We need trees so that our guards can perch high and see far."

"I'm sure Arren will feel the same way," Zimp said.

"Arren has taken more than his share of command today," Oro responded in anger. "Go and tell him that we will camp at the edge of Brendern Forest this evening if we have to travel several hours into the night to do so."

Zimp jumped from the wagon. She knew where to find Arren. At the head of the caravan. Up the hill. Zimp pushed forward into a jog.

Arren must have seen her coming. He waved two of his brothers away as she approached. He stood firm.

"Oro said that we travel to the edge of Brendern Forest

before we stop. Even if we travel through the dark."

"I was just saying the same thing," he said.

"You didn't send anyone to Oro?"

"Anyone would have made the same decision. I didn't need her approval for what was obvious." A strained smile crossed his face.

"We camp when we reach the forest," Zimp said before leaving.

A short distance from him, Zimp allowed her body to begin a shift. She knew that Arren's eyes stabbed her in the back as she stepped heavily downhill. She needed the lightness of her crow image. Focusing on change itself, Zimp kept her head up even as her legs shortened and the grass appeared to rise. She turned her hands out and arms up to catch the wind. She could sense her bones hollowing and contracting, her head thinning, and a beak growing outward from her nose and mouth. Then for just a moment before she left the security of the ground, Zimp heard a familiar voice.

"Tonight we dance," Zora said.

Were the words coming from her head or from the wind? The last moment of a shift were often still, empty. The final metamorphosis from human to beast or beast to human could not be conceived on any level. When the Gods created the doublesight to remind humans and beasts of their grotesque interbreeding, there had to be a place of complete oneness with The Great Land. Fleeting as it was, that moment also reminded the doublesight of their connection to both human and beast, to the physical realm and the spirit realms. Zimp felt that euphoria at the exact moment she heard Zora's voice clearly dance into her mind. But a moment later, in full crow image, doubt set in. She couldn't dwell on the possibility. Too much human thought would cause her to shift back.

Zimp kept her human thoughts just behind her crow instinct. She recognized the humans below her, but did not place memories or emotions too closely with any of them. She glided over their heads for a moment longer, then lifted into the sky to get a clearer view of the distant lake. Making a great sweep around the wagons and people, Zimp turned from the sun and dived, homing in on her own wagon. Thinking momentarily that Oro would be there, Zimp glided while letting her entire body—legs, arms, torso, and head—change at once. She shifted and landed just outside the wagon.

"What are you thinking?" Jessant asked as he watched her land. He stood a short distance away getting into his wagon.

"There is no one around but our own scouts," Zimp said.

"Did you see any of them?" Jessant wanted to know.

Zimp didn't answer.

"Did you forget what happened this morning? We are not safe if anyone knows we are doublesight."

"We have already been found out," she said.

Jessant shook his head and continued to climb into his wagon. His wife, Soonta, peered out the back of the wagon at Zimp for a moment and shook her head. Zimp knew that she disapproved of flagrant image changes in broad daylight and in the open.

The wagons proceeded away from the mouth of the Lorensak. The edge of the sun approached the horizon and the reflective mass of Brendern Eastlake. The wagons made long shadows across the grass. Brendern Forest treetops lifted into the sky several miles ahead of the clan.

Zimp didn't say anything to Oro about her unprotected shift. And now, she felt embarrassed about doing it so blatantly in front of Arren. Shifting was an intimate act. Even though the crow clan was tight-knit, traveled well together, and often shifted en masse, a single purposeful shift like the one she did was like stripping down in front of someone. That private act showed her arrogance, something she wasn't proud of. She lowered her head and peered out of the wagon.

Of the seven wagons, Oro's was in the center, the best protected. It was tethered to the wagon in front of it so that no driver was needed. Less than twenty-four hours ago, Zimp would have been arguing with her sister about something, or they would be laughing. Oro would be sleeping as she was now.

Zimp crawled along the carpet to her sister's cot, the closest to the front. She lay down and rolled onto her stomach. She smelled Zora and buried her head into the soft fabric of the rolled blanket. With a long sigh and a sad heart, Zimp allowed herself a moment of tears. Her sister had only crossed over into the next realm. She had not left The Great Land forever. Of all the people of the crow clan, Zimp knew this fact best. There were moments when Zimp spoke to her mother's spirit. She had heard Zora's voice twice already.

She could feel herself shifting, but not a physical shift from human to crow. This shift was less familiar and made her unsure of what she might do. She tried to relax into the feeling, but a sharp anxiety pulsed through her. Fear grew in her, but it was a familiar fear, even though she didn't recognize its origin. Zimp tried to open her senses and when she did, something was wrong. She sat up and crawled back to the bench at the rear of the wagon. "Something's wrong," she whispered to her grandmother.

Oro stirred. "What is it?"

"I'm not sure. Should I go see?"

The wagon stopped.

"It looks as through you're about to," Oro said.

Voices approached the wagon from the front of the caravan. Oro reached for Zimp, who helped her grandmother sit up. Three of the scouts came around the side of the wagon and stood just outside. Sunlight struck them from the side. Black hair drew in the light and created white streaks where the sun lay full on them. "Doublesight," Zerran said. "We saw them coming from the edge of the lake toward Brendern Forest."

"Are you sure?" Oro said.

Crepp spoke up. "We're pretty sure. There was a man and a woman along with a thylacine. That's not something you'd see too often."

"Oh, to the Gods," Zimp said. "I hate thylacines."

"That is odd," Oro said. "A thylacine would rip a human apart. Although I've heard of using thylacines for protection, I've never seen such a thing."

"Arren suggested Zimp might come with us to make sure." Zerran spoke with an unsure voice.

"Arren does not make those decisions," Oro said.

Crepp said, "That's why we came here."

Oro nodded in approval. She turned to Zimp.

"Should we fly?" Zimp asked, but Oro didn't have to answer. In a moment Zimp perched at the edge of the wagon. Zerran, Crepp, and Storret all shifted at the side of the wagon and soon all four were in the air.

The caravan began to move again once Zimp and the scouts were on their way. Zerran led the group in haphazard twists and turns, depending on the updrafts and side winds. In the distance, Zimp saw three figures crouched down and slinking through the tall grass toward the forest. They didn't have packs or weapons, which appeared very odd. She forced from her mind the impulse to analyze her observation.

Zerran dipped toward the three strangers and circled around toward the edge of the forest.

Zimp followed and landed in the top of a tall evergreen. She could still see the two humans and the thylacine. The scouts took positions in other trees while Zimp hopped toward the tree trunk where she could shift without falling.

A slow shift was the most painful to execute. Being part human and part crow meant that bones were either expanding or contracting unnaturally. Zimp let one wing turn first and reached to hold onto the tree as the rest of her body grew and reshaped. To humans the change would look gruesome and frightening, but to other doublesight it could be a beautiful transformation.

As human, Zimp could focus more intensely. She made sure that she felt secure against the tree, then waited for the odd threesome to get closer. Zimp could see another being's ethereal body if she concentrated. Many doublesight and humans alike could see auras, but only the well trained or the intuitive could tell if there was a second shape just beyond the first. The ethereal body would not be that of a human.

Zimp breathed deeply the strong, sweet odor of the tree. Her small fingers pushed into the deep ridges of the bark. She relaxed into her senses. Her legs hung over a thin but safe branch high in the tree. She squinted her eyes and focused her attention at the edges of the body. The young man was tallest, so she stared in his direction. She instantly saw his aura, a mixture of green and brown, red streaks of anger coming from his heart chakra. She held to the image without trying to interpret what she saw. All he had to do was turn his head and there it was: the shadow of his ethereal beast image, moving slower than his human aura. It just glided into view.

At first, she saw only the shadow of his beast image, but with time and more movement the shape became clearer. He was a thylacine doublesight, all right. A shiver went up her spine. At least he was doublesight.

Next she tried to focus on the thylacine that walked with them, but couldn't even make out an aura with the tall grass in the way. So, she focused on the girl and found that she, too, was a doublesight.

Zimp shifted as quickly as she could without losing the sense of being human, which she held in check while in crow image. The others saw her take off toward the caravan over a small rise. Storret followed her, while Zerran and Crepp stayed at their posts.

In a moment, Zimp and Storret were at Oro's wagon with the news.

"What do you think happened? Why are they out without weapons or packs?" Zimp said.

"They are in danger," Oro said. She turned for a moment and placed her hand to her head. Her lips moved but no sound came out.

Zimp and Storret waited.

When Oro turned back around, there were tears in her eyes.

"What is it?" Zimp asked.

"Great emotional pain," Oro said.

"I know. There is a lot of healing going on. I noticed a green glow to his aura. But it was muddied in many places, blocking the healing," Zimp said. "And there were deep red streaks of anger like lightning coming from his heart."

"Take ten helpers. Stop them. Let them know that we are safe. They camp with us tonight." Oro waved a hand to indicate that she was through and for Zimp to take care of the job.

"I'll let Arren know," she said.

Oro snapped her fingers and pointed at Zimp. "You'll tell

him what you are doing and you'll go. Arren is to continue on toward a campsite."

"But I hate thylacines. They scare me."

Oro looked her squarely in the eyes. "They are doublesight. You must welcome them to stay with our clan tonight. No other can do this but you." Oro was finished.

Zimp turned to Storret and told him to gather eight others for the trip. She delivered Oro's message to Arren who jutted his chin but said nothing. He would obey.

When Zimp returned there were ten crows perched on the top of her wagon. She ducked into the wagon, kissed Oro on the cheek, and shifted in private. She flew from inside the wagon, out of the opening, and into the sky.

The sun was beginning to enter the lake.

5

The trip from The Lost, over Lake Ernwood, through the forest area of Dgosh, and southward into Brendern Forest had taken much longer than Lankor would have liked. Yet it wasn't often that he got to travel with his father, mother, and brother. Mianna acted as though the trip was the grandest time of their lives and doted over her sons while Rend navigated the journey, including the sailing trip across Lake Ernwood.

Rend kept the purpose of the journey secret, although Lankor caught him talking with Nayman from time to time and feared that a secret was brewing. And why would Nayman need to know information that Lankor didn't know? Why was his older brother favored, when it was Lankor who could run faster, fight more fiercely, and think more clearly?

Mianna reminded him one evening, before the final leg of their journey to the council compound of The Few, that both he and Nayman were special. "Your brother, you'll recall from the stories, saved your uncle's life. That is how his foot got crushed. And that is why your uncle chose to make the ultimate sacrifice and remain in beast image forever."

Lankor hung his head and glanced over at Nayman and Rend who talked outside of camp, the firelight playing across their backs like spiders. "How might I be special?" he asked Mianna.

"You have great power," Mianna said. "We all recognize

that in you."

"Then why is Father so hard on me?"

"Great power must be controlled by great strength. Rend has that strength and is imparting it to you. Some day you will have to control your strength alone."

Lankor picked up a stick and threw it forcefully into the fire. Sparks scattered in every direction. The wood hissed. Coals leaped into the air.

Mianna jumped up. A hot coal landed on her arm and burned her skin to a dull red. Rend and Nayman turned and ran to her aid.

Rend checked his wife's hair and body for other embers.

Lankor brushed coals from his cloak and pants. Nayman shoved him away from the fire, then turned and brushed Mianna's clothes with his big hands.

"Don't shove me," Lankor said, and came at his brother from behind to pull him around. Set in a fighting position, Lankor urged Nayman on by backing up slowly and weaving from side to side. He glanced to his right to locate his staff and sword, but Nayman didn't take the bait.

Rend stood with his arm around Mianna's shoulder. "Stop it. Your mother is fine. Now, what was that about?"

"Nothing," Lankor said.

Rend looked to Mianna for an alternate response. She turned squarely to Lankor. "Learning to control his power," she said. "He just found out what too much force for the situation feels like."

Lankor tightened his lips and let his shoulders fall. A breeze pulled at his long hair. He said nothing. He just nodded and turned away from his mother's glare, toward the woods, and walked away. Behind him he heard Rend say to Nayman, "That is what I was talking about."

So they had been talking about him. What other things did they say to one another? Did they discuss his temper? His recklessness? He could hear them now, mocking and laughing at him. But just because they were willing to stay trapped in the barren lands of The Lost didn't mean that he was willing to stay there as well. The doublesight council didn't frighten him.

Nor did the hundreds of other doublesight clans. He knew the history. He knew their fear. So why did Rend and the rest of their clan go along with what The Few ordained?

Lankor took a circuitous route through the woods and reentered the camp after an hour's walk. "I hate being boxed in," he announced, waving his arms in a circle to indicate the trees that held space around them.

Rend glanced up and shook his head in dismissal. He, Mianna, and Nayman sat around the fire, keeping the moist, cool night air from them. "We are late getting to the council," Rend said. "As soon as we arrive, the council will meet with The Few, and we'll be back on our way home."

"I wish to go home now," Lankor said. "Somewhere I can stand on a hill and see for miles, not in this Godless canyon of greenery."

"I thought you wanted adventure, travel," Rend said.

"Not here. I want to go to Sclan, where we once reigned."

"The Sclan Dynasty is over. Ruins lay where castles were built. King and Queen Deetem rule over a handful of fishing villages, nothing more," Rend said.

"You never want to return? To rebuild our ancestors' homes?" Lankor asked.

"No," Rend said. He looked at Mianna for approval and received it.

Nayman stood. The movement stilled the conversation. "I have slowed everyone down. It's my fault we're late."

"We all knew what time it would take. We started out late and we'll arrive late," Rend said. "We have the farthest to journey. The Few are well aware of that fact."

"Why couldn't we shift and fly there?" Lankor said.

Rend turned on his son. "Would you like to be crucified before we arrive? Would you like to have someone in one of the small towns we've passed send men to The Lost and hunt us down?" He waited for an answer, and when none came he said, "We stay human as long as we can." He nodded to himself, and Mianna nodded in response even though not asked to do so.

"One month," Lankor said. "If we don't change in one month, we'll be human forever. Would you like to have that happen? After all we've been through? After Uncle Dellin's sacrifice?"

"It won't happen," Rend said. "When the time comes, you'll know it and you'll have to make a decision then. You'll feel the need. It could be a month. It could be two. I've heard of doublesight who learned to stay in beast-image for several months and still return to human form. And the opposite, although that is never recommended."

"We'll see," Lankor said. "This trip will put us very close."

"Exercise control and restraint," Rend ordered.

Nayman hobbled to his brother's side and slapped Lankor on the shoulder. He led Lankor into the circle of firelight. "This one," Nayman said, exposing his brother, "turned two nights ago while he thought everyone slept."

Rend glared at his son, but it was Mianna who spoke. "Would you put us all in jeopardy so that you can please yourself? Do you think dragons are invisible?"

"Quiet," Rend said. "This forest could have doublesight anywhere. We must not even say the word."

Lankor burned with shame and defiance. "We must stop hiding."

Mianna shook her head. "You are frustrated. I know, but we'll show ourselves in due time, my little one, in due time. But now is not that time. Your father has been a member of the council for many years. The Few will make the suggestion, the council will vote on it, and then we'll emerge and reintroduce ourselves to the greater doublesight community. My suspicion is that it will be at this meeting. Why else would entire families, instead of just council members, be requested to attend?"

"I disagree," Lankor said. "Something else is up. I can feel it. What if it's a trap?"

"You may disagree, but you may not disobey," Rend reminded him. "You will not turn again without discussing it with me first. Do you understand?"

"No one saw me."

Mianna and Rend looked at Nayman.

"He's right," Nayman said. "I saw his footprints and heard his flight, but I did not see him shift."

"It is shameful to shift in front of anyone you do not wish to know intimately. Unless you are doing it to shock those you've met, as a strategic move, you keep it to yourself," Mianna said.

Rend added, "You know that once you shift in front of another doublesight. . ."

"They can always see your true nature," Lankor finished.

"Do not mock my words, son."

Lankor nodded in respect. "I merely remember them, Father."

Nayman put an arm around his brother and the family appeared to relax.

"We should eat," Rend said.

Mianna stepped around her sons and rummaged through their packs for the provisions they carried.

The breeze through the woods picked up and the depth of the moist cold air drove the family closer to the fire. Rend stoked the coals. Lankor shoved another log across the flames. Sometimes in such light, Lankor saw himself in Rend like a mirror to the future. Rend's long arms matched Lankor's. They were both tall, almost equal in height, over six and a half feet. The resemblance didn't always please him. The roughness around his father's eyes, the calloused fingers. He glanced at Nayman, who had the softer look of Mianna. Nayman was the good-looking one.

Mianna prepared a small feast of fish they had caught and dried while sailing Lake Ernwood, of leaves she had gathered while walking through the forest, and of roots and mushrooms Rend gathered while collecting wood for the night fire.

The sounds of wildlife drew near as the evening pressed on. Lankor heard shuffling and running. He heard the soft movement of wings. At one point, he heard growls, low in tone, and evil. The sound came to him as though it had to first pass through a mouth filled with saliva and drool, a gurgling growl, a focused threat. He shivered in the night, rolled over, and went back to sleep once the animal moved away.

By morning, rested and eager to go on, Lankor got up to pack.

Mianna woke and stretched her arms. "We should eat

breakfast before we leave."

"I have eggs," Rend said appearing from around a large oak. "Spotted them while I was out gathering last night."

"Wonderful." Mianna took the eggs from her husband. "These will do nicely."

Nayman brought out the pans and readied them. He stoked and fed the fire without having to stand. His crushed foot was bare and looked like a boneless sack of skin, red and swollen, the toes misshapen.

Seeing his brother's foot, Lankor imagined how it must have been for Nayman to run into an avalanche of rock to save their uncle Dellin. Lankor doubted that he would have done the same. He valued life too much and wanted to live more of it. Wanted to live more freely, to travel and explore without the threat of being hunted down.

A light fog rose from the ground. Moisture penetrated their packs and their sleeping blankets as well as their clothes and hair. Mianna clasped her arms around her shoulders for warmth as Rend built the fire higher. "We could have stayed in an Inn somewhere," he said. "Perhaps that would have been better."

Mianna shook her head. "I like being on our own. This is an adventure we don't normally have together."

"If you say so, Mother," Nayman said with a laugh. "But sleeping on the ground in the cold would not be my first choice for adventure."

Rend laughed, then offered, "Soon we'll be in the compound and can build a full camp, collect bedding, errect tents for privacy."

Lankor asked, "I thought we were going to listen to the council and leave?"

"We'll see when we get there," Rend said. "You are in such a hurry to have it over."

"It won't hurt to socialize a little," Mianna added with a little bow and dance step.

"These people persecuted us." Lankor said.

"Not these people," Rend said. "And only some of their ancestors. We had allies. Besides, most of these people don't even know we exist," Rend said. "To them, we are just another doublesight clan."

"Most?" Lankor asked.

"The Few. They know. And there are intuitives who are well aware."

"Intuitives? How can you trust them? Perhaps it's a trap. They'll all be there waiting. They knew we'd be last to arrive. And if the intuitives told the rest that we existed?" Lankor said.

"It wouldn't be the same as it was in the past. We've all changed. Those horrible times haven't existed for centuries. It's nothing like you're saying." Rend reached down to grip the frying pan with his hand wrapped in a shirtsleeve and flipped the eggs through the air over the fire.

"Fear and hatred are not easily overcome. Not even in centuries. That is what we are taught in school. That is why we must be careful. That is why we continue to live in The Lost," Lankor said.

"You are the one who turned. Did this fear strike you then?" Lankor hung his head.

"My son, you will learn that we can only teach what came from the past. We must create the future as it occurs. What you have been taught has nothing to do with what we will find when we get to the compound of the council. I agree with your mother; this may be a very special time for us."

Nayman poked his brother with his disfigured foot. "Relax and enjoy the adventure. When have you ever been outside The Lost? It might be cold and closed in here, but it's a new experience."

Lankor shoved a hand against Nayman's shoulder. "You may just be smarter than you look."

Nayman kicked Lankor again, and they both laughed.

Mianna appeared to be grateful for their easy spirit. "The evening we arrive, let us be in the best of moods," she said

Rend cut and delivered the eggs and they all ate in relative silence, discussing only which of them would carry what bundle of supplies when they cleaned up camp, and what sounds were heard during the night. In an offhand comment, Rend asked Lankor if he covered his tracks when he turned two nights before.

Mianna gave Lankor a stern look that he interpreted to mean that he should be polite to his father. "I did."

Mianna nodded and Lankor finished his breakfast.

By the time they had cleaned up and warmed their bodies for the last time around the fire, the fog had lifted quite a bit. The forest floor stood intermittently bare and cluttered with underbrush. Animal paths led in several directions, but the road they traveled lay before them as the easiest route.

They had run into very few travelers once they entered the Dgosh woods. The only people who appeared to travel the roadways that went through the woods were those who headed from one village to another or those who lived deep in the forest and away from other people. Hunters and fur traders. With spring upon them, most settlements in Dgosh would be preparing their fields, repairing their homes after a hard winter, or generally getting ready for summer. Spring was also the time for many of the festivals celebrating the end of winter and the dawning of new life. Lankor wished that he were home to celebrate as well.

Rend took the lead, but continued to watch Nayman peripherally to make sure he wasn't in too much pain. Mianna often walked beside Nayman, talking quietly and pointing things out. The rest of the time she walked beside her husband.

Lankor had watched this go on before, and especially on this journey, how Mianna favored the other two men. Lankor was glad to take up the rear, meandering, falling back, then racing to catch up. It was the only way he could continue to stay interested. Their progress, or lack thereof, annoyed him. He tried to stay interested in their surroundings, but found it difficult to do so. They were surrounded by trees, every one like the next. The dense foliage overhead blocked his sight of the sky much of the time, which truly unnerved him. In some areas, the underbrush and close-knit tree growth closed him in. A pair of horses could hardly pass without one getting off the road altogether. Lankor wondered if a wagon could make it through without breaking branches and tearing out new growth.

He sped up and encroached on Mianna and Nayman. "How far do you think it is from here?"

"Several days," Rend said from in front of them. "They know we're coming."

"They should. They sent for us." Lankor said.

"I saw two night hawks circle over. They were the sentinels and messengers."

"Will the council meet right away? Do you think The Few have already talked with the other clans? Has our arrival already been discussed?" Lankor asked.

"Too many questions, and I can't answer any of them," Rend said. "What I can tell you is that no one will know our identity until we arrive. The Few would never do that."

"What about the intuitives?"

"They are the most trustworthy of all," Rend said. He held up his hand for silence. "We'll rest for a moment here."

Nayman sat on a rock that lay at the side of the path. He let out a loud breath and stretched his foot in front of him.

They had stopped at a wide section of road, which meant that they were probably close to a village or clearing with a few more houses than the occasional lodge.

Rend sat cross-legged on the ground. "Gather around," he said, and everyone sat with his or her attention on him. "There are many mysteries in the world and we are only one of them. How one species dies off and another returns from death is in the hands of the Gods, not ours. The council of the doublesight has grown in and out of many of these changes, but only The Few, the three chosen ones, know all the clans. To become part of the council you must show yourself to The Few."

"Willingly?" Lankor said.

"Yes, and every individual who is the clan's representative, who is part of the council, must do the same. Your great-grandfather had to show his beast image, your grandmother showed hers, and then me. One of you will be asked to do so when I stand down, or if I should die and one of you goes in my place. It is the first thing you must do." Rend looked into Lankor's eyes. "No one attacked me or tried to kill me because of what I was."

Lankor lowered his head and nodded. "I can see now, but should I be convinced that all the members of all the clans feel the same way?"

"No, you should not. But you should know that The Few are highly respected and that they are safe." Rend took Lankor's hand in his, then reached out and took Nayman's hand as well. "One of you may be asked to show yourself to The Few."

"Are you standing down? Is that what this is about?" Nayman asked.

"No. This must be something more important. The Few have never called such a meeting. I just want you both to be ready for whatever might happen."

"Nayman is the oldest," Lankor said.

"And you are the fittest," Nayman responded, pointing at his damaged foot.

The two young men looked at one another. Rend shook both of their hands and then let go of them. "We will see."

"The intuitives?" Lankor said.

"All intuitives must restrain from seeing your ethereal body. Some can't help themselves. They just know. You'll meet her, though. And you'll instantly trust her just as I do."

6

Eleven crows flew toward Brendern Forest. They circled three unsuspecting doublesight and landed in tall grass. Zimp shifted to her human form and stood first.

The thylacine jumped and let out a little yelp. The two other doublesight stopped. The man reached down and grasped the thylacine's scruff behind its head, which appeared to calm the beast. The young woman immediately reached for the man for protection. "Leave us alone," the man threatened.

"We're here to help you," Zimp said. She glanced around. The other ten people of the crow clan rose from the grass, encircling the three strangers.

The thylacine growled. Its mouth hung open and saliva dripped from its lower jowls to the ground.

"Easy, Therin," the man said. His shoulders relaxed as he glanced around at everyone. "You weren't here before, were you?" He brightened with recognition. "I saw crows."

Zimp was satisfied that he didn't say the word. Something had happened to them that made him careful not to offer too much information. "We came to help," she repeated. "We are doublesight like you."

The woman smiled and looked at her partner. "Brok?" she said. "Is it true?"

He stepped toward Zimp. "It's all right, Breel. For now." He kneeled next to Therin and stroked along the underside of the thylacine's neck. "It's safe. Just sit for a moment."

Therin sat and Brok stood with Breel. She held to him with both her arms wrapped around one of his. Her hair fell in tangled brown curls. Shorter than Brok, Breel appeared younger as well, and slight. Her tan clothing was soiled and tattered at the edges.

"Stay with Therin," Brok said. He slipped from Breel's grip and took a few steps closer to Zimp, who took an equal number of steps toward him.

Zimp's heart raced. She saw how Brok's wide mouth could easily match the enormous gape of Therin's. She had never been that close to a thylacine before, let alone a thylacine doublesight. She thought that she could feel heat coming from Brok's body.

A breeze kicked up and blew Zimp's red cloak to the side. It snapped and fluttered. Her black hair twirled around her face. She reached around with one arm to hold the cloak close to her side. Staring into Brok's eyes as they both took one cautious step after another, Zimp noticed that the color of his clothes matched the grayish-brown of Therin's coat. His vest even bore the same dark brown stripes of the thylacine. She feared that he wore a thylacine pelt. How barbaric. Did they purposefully kill the animal that bears their own beast image? What would be the reason? Once the beast became extinct, the doublesight would no longer exist, either.

She stood fast for a moment and Brok mirrored her stillness.

The sun shook to her left, behind the heat waves lifting from the lake. Halfway into the lake and appearing to sink faster every moment, the apricot-tinted light cast a strange glow over the three thylacines. Shadows sliding up hill grew longer as the doublesight stood and talked.

Brok cocked his head toward Zimp as though sizing her up. He turned slightly to the left and right.

Breel, kneeling next to Therin with her arms around his neck, let one word slip from her lips. "Brok."

He spun around, crouched like an animal. Several men from the crow clan had closed in on Breel. "Therin," Brok said.

Therin burst toward the men who had surrounded them, knocking Breel back onto the ground. He made a sickening cough-like bark as he advanced.

"Wait," Zimp said. She yelled to the men, "Stand down. Open space for them to leave."

Brok turned back and resumed his former position. "How do you plan to help us?"

Zimp's hands shook and her breathing was uneven. "I don't know exactly. I am the messenger. I was instructed to ask that you camp with us this evening and to let you know that it was safe." She pointed toward Therin. "Safe for you. I'm not convinced that it would be safe for us."

"He's protecting his sister, that's all." Brok's eyes narrowed. "But don't rest long. We are hunters." He opened his arms as if to indicate that he had no weapon. "We may look unarmed, but we are not vulnerable."

"You don't need to threaten us," Zimp said. "It's an offering." The other ten with her were regrouping near Zimp where Brok could see them. "See," she said. "It is safe."

Brok motioned for Breel and Therin to join him. "Who sends the message if you are the messenger?"

"Oronice the Gem," Zimp announced.

Brok turned and smiled at Breel who looked confused. "I know of The Gem of the Forest," Brok said, as he turned back around. "She is old. My father thought that she had died."

"Oronice is very much alive." Zimp advanced a few more steps and held her arm out toward Brok. It was difficult to hold steady. Her arm waved like a branch in a wind. "Then it is agreed?" she said.

Brok reached toward her forearm. "We have never killed a crow. Not while in human or thylacine form."

"But you are predators and capable of such acts," she said.

"We are very capable," Brok said.

They held one another's forearms. "Brok Taltost," the man said. "My sister Breel and brother Therin."

"Zimp of Lissland," Zimp said.

"You are a long way from home," he said.

Zimp shook her head. "We've been traveling for years. I'm not sure we have a home."

While still holding each other, they each made a single

motion downward with their arms before separating.

Zimp turned her back on Brok in a forced attempt to indicate trust. Her spine tingled and several of her men looked surprised. She indicated the tops of wagon canvases that could be seen cresting the hill, then motioned toward the sun. "We'll walk with our guests to the forest and meet with the rest there."

"We just came from the forest and were heading south along the lake," Brok said.

Breel, now beside him, said, "We were ambushed at our home." She pointed toward the forest.

"We have scouts. It's safe." Zimp stepped toward Breel. Her energy felt softer than her brother's, but still made Zimp feel jittery and nervous. "We were ambushed too. Trust me, it's safe to camp near the forest. It's not far and you can be on your way tomorrow."

Breel smiled broadly, an unnerving act to Zimp, but she returned the smile.

The sun made its last glimmer of direct light and the air thickened with gray. It would be dark soon. Zimp yelled to Storret, "Take five men with you and penetrate deeper into the forest. I want no trouble from beast nor man." Ordering Storret felt strange to her, but she had to show her command to Brok. She felt little respect coming from him, only anger, and anger can set off like a flame instantly.

Storret and five others slumped into the grass and a moment later flew out of it on crow wings. The sight always made Zimp want to fly along with them. She sensed her body become lighter even as she watched.

Therin followed Brok and Breel closely. Any time someone got too close to either one of his siblings, he growled a warning.

Zimp noticed that her companions were also uneasy around the thylacine. Yet, curiosity caused them to stare and migrate near the strangers, especially the one in beast image.

The nine of them walked in an uneven line toward the forest. This meant that Zimp could not focus on Therin to see if he had a human ethereal body. Later she may have the chance.

Darkness crept into the air around them. The edge of the forest shown bright compared to its depths. Wind built from behind them, from across the lake. Cold and damp, it pushed at their backs. The grassy hillside leading to the forest leaned in the same direction the crows and thylacines trudged. The caravan of wagons appeared one by one over the ridge ahead of them and to the left.

Brok plodded up the hill at a slower pace as four, then five, wagons came into view. Zimp sensed his concern over their numbers and eased closer to him until she heard the quiet growl of his brother. "Oronice has assured your safety. Even if you do not trust me, you must know that anyone who is part of the council is true to their word."

"My father was part of the council," Brok said.

"Then you must know that what I say is true."

He nodded and picked up his pace.

The wagons arrived at camp first. By the time Zimp and her fellow travelers made the forest edge, the wagons had been settled just inside the trees wherever space allowed. Several fires had been started, large pits scraped open, and blankets placed over the grass all around the pits.

The camp felt familiar already to Zimp. "Come with me," she said to Brok and his siblings. "Noot!" she yelled to her cousin. "My wagon?"

Noot looked up and pointed to the tallest tree. "At the base of that tree. But she's not there, as you can tell."

A dark bird-shaped shadow perched at the upper tip of the tree that Noot had pointed at. The moon rose to one side. The shadow hopped into the light that illuminated the edges of the limbs at the top of the tree.

"What is she doing?" Breel said.

Zimp didn't speak right away. How could she explain an old woman's urges? She took a deep breath and turned her head back to ground level, turned her eyes to Breel. "Flying," Zimp said.

"But she's not flying," Breel said.

"When your body is that light and sitting on a branch that could never hold your whole weight, it feels like flying. Oro is resting for a moment." Zimp smiled at the woman. "Come with me and I'll find clean clothes for you."

"No," Brok said.

Breel and Zimp waited for more.

"We, thylacine, that is, are nocturnal. We may not even be here in the morning."

"You need not return the clothes," Zimp said. "But if you want to wash what you have on and replace them sometime in the night, you may choose to do so."

Breel stood until Brok answered with a slight nod of his head.

"Noot, help Brok with something, too," Zimp said.

Therin stayed with Breel, to Zimp's disappointment. The two of them followed Zimp to her wagon and waited while she pulled some clothes from her own compartment. Zimp thought to use Zora's clothes, but then changed her mind.

"You can change inside and your brother can wait here," Zimp said.

Breel lowered her head and sniffed. She brushed the back of her hand along the side of her face, catching a tear that had slid from her eye.

Zimp automatically stepped closer to Breel, placing the clothes across the back of the wagon first.

Therin made a low groan, but Breel pointed at him and he stopped. The young woman turned into Zimp and shuddered along her shoulders. "I'm sorry. I'm sorry," Breel said.

"No. Don't be sorry. I understand." Zimp held her, but sensed a curious rejection while doing so.

In a moment, Breel quit sobbing and shoved Zimp forcefully away. "Enough," she said.

The aggressive act surprised Zimp, but she let it go. "Well, then," she said. "I'm going to make sure Oro is all right. Can you meet back at the center fire when you are through here?"

"Of course," Breel said.

Zimp stepped to the front of the wagon and shifted peacefully into a crow. There was a pace at which minimal pain and maximum elation could be reached. Only occasionally was a doublesight able to reach that point. Something allowed Zimp to be there this time.

She flew almost straight up and landed near Oro. The moon

sent a glow over the canopy of the forest, which appeared to be a single rolling softness of green, the yellow green of early life, of spring. A fresh smell lifted into the sky, the fragrance of life, the perfume of growth, of new birth.

Oro let go of her branch and glided toward the plains they had just crossed with their wagons.

Zimp followed her as she weaved back and forth along the way, turning toward the lake and then back around and up toward camp.

Oro penetrated the blackness of the forest, circled around, and landed near her wagon. She shifted into a bent old woman.

Zimp stood in human form beside her and took Oro's arm to help her walk into camp.

"You needn't help me all the time," Oro said.

"I want to."

"Did you welcome our guests or did you ask Storret to make the greeting?" Oro said.

"I did it, just as you asked."

"Good. It wasn't so difficult, was it?" Oro said.

"For who?" Zimp asked. She shook her head. "No, it wasn't bad. But I still don't like thylacines. And, I'm not sure what happened, but they were ambushed and the one brother, Therin, is still in beast image."

"Did you look to see if he had a human's ethereal body?"

"I couldn't. Either he was too low in the grass or we were walking together. There was not time. I fear that it's permanent, though." They walked farther together. "That's got to be awful."

"The yearning never stops," Oro said. "For the rest of his life he will get close to human thought and expect a shift, but nothing will happen. You've seen animals that appear to be almost human? Well, often they were. The inability for a human to shift back from a beast image can drive one insane. It's a yearning that can never be satiated."

"There's nothing you can do?"

"There are no herbs to cure a permanent shift. The poor boy. He must have experienced something terrible. It takes a lot for a doublesight to remain in either beast or human image. Something just clicks inside the ethereal body, something gruesome and frightening happens and *snap*." She snapped her fingers. "We must accept what has occurred."

7

Fireflies blinked in the cool evening air outside the reach of the firelight, deep inside the woods and well into the field. Their presence added a magical quality to the night. Zimp and Oro came from the wagon into the camp area. Festivities had already begun. Stalks of grass had been collected, bound, and placed all around the fire for when they wished to feed the fire into a high blaze. Early spring flowers had been collected and set around the camp. The women wore flowers in their hair. The men had gathered wood and made the fires wide so that they could cook near the edges and let the flames reach up above their heads.

Looking at the smiles on the faces, even those with bandages from their wounds, would confuse anyone who knew of their morning travesty. Oro motioned where she wished to sit near the center fire, and Zimp led her there and helped her to sit on a bench that had been brought from someone's wagon.

"Oh, the freshness of the air," Oro said.

Zimp had mixed feelings as she stepped over to Brok and his siblings, who had been brought to the center fire to wait for Oro's arrival. Zimp reached for Brok's hand, but he refused to take it. Breel and Therin stood silently beside him. "Let me introduce you to Oronice the Gem," Zimp said.

Brok nodded, Breel curtsied, and Therin sat with his bottom jaw hanging and saliva slipping from his mouth.

Oro pulled a candle from her pocket and leaned onto her knees to light it in the fire. She let a few drops of wax fall onto the ground and placed the candle into the wax.

"I am…" Brok began, but Zimp stopped him with a lift of her hand.

Oro whispered something while staring at the candle, as though she were talking to it. She took a small amount of powder from her pocket and threw it into the fire. A green smoke rose quickly then dispersed into the night air. She placed some of the same powder over the candle flame and it created a red smoke. She looked up at Brok. "You are here in our care. You are safe as long as we are alive."

Zimp indicated that it was time for Brok to speak.

He lowered his head farther than the nod he had given at first. His curly hair fell around his dark brown face obscuring it for a moment. When he lifted his head he threw his hair back with a twitch of his neck. "I am Brok Taltost," he said with pride.

Breel reached for his arm. Tears were in her eyes.

"This is my little sister, Breel Taltost." His head lowered to include Therin, "And my brother, Therin Taltost."

Oro smiled brightly. "Oh, oh, oh. Then it is my personal honor to be in your company. For we are blessed to be sure." She looked at Zimp. "We are in the presence of the children of Fremlin Taltost." Oro placed her hands together and bowed to the three thylacine doublesight siblings.

Zimp cocked her head.

Arren, who stood just outside the circle of seated crow clan, spoke up. "Fremlin Taltost once stood as High Guard to the Three Princes of Crell. He held Crell Center almost single handedly against the attack from Southern Weilk, then known as Stilth."

"That was before the Three Princes of Crell joined with Stilth to make Stilth Alshore," Brok said. He appeared pleased that someone knew his father.

Hearing the story, Zimp recalled her history lessons. "It is my pleasure as well," she pulled her cloak around her and bent at the knees and lowered her head in respect. When she stood and looked over at Oro, the woman was motioning with her head.

"Your candle," she said.

Zimp felt her face turn flush. "I didn't bring one."

Oro reached into her other pocket and pulled an orange candle from it. She stretched it toward Zimp. "Never be without the proper sacred tools again. You are heir to the leadership of our clan and you will act appropriately."

Zimp took the candle from Oro and noticed Arren's glib smile. Her blood rushed faster to her face, but she stayed collected. With the candle, Zimp turned toward the thylacines and kneeled so that she could light the candle from the fire. Like Oro had done before her, Zimp let some wax fall to the ground and set the candle firmly into it. She placed her hands together over the flame and spoke into the candle so softly that she hoped no one could hear her. "To this sacred moment and to this sacred place, I acknowledge my shame in not being prepared. I place in the hands of the other realms my future. And, I accept that Brok, Breel, and Therin are here for some purpose that I may not yet know. To the Gods."

She looked up and Brok reached out to help her stand. She shook her head to get him to back away.

"Sit, my honored friends," Oro said. "Tell me how you came to be here. Tell me how your parents are, the rest of your family?"

Breel burst into tears and Brok placed a hand over her shoulder. Therin buried his head into her lap.

"They are all dead," Brok said straight out, as though there were no other way to get the information from his memory than to let it gush from him. "Attacked while we returned from an evening outing."

"There was a big surprise that Daddy wanted to tell us about," Breel said through sobs. "He made us wait. We were celebrating." She coughed into her hand.

"A short trip for the family, perhaps?" Oro said.

Brok stirred noticeably. He looked as though he wanted to stand in anger, in surprise. Zimp couldn't tell which it was.

"How would you know?" Brok said.

Arren stepped forward and closer to the fire where he could

be seen. "We are all going."

Oro cut him off. "You," she said, pointing a finger at him, "will not speak at this moment." Noticeably angered, Oro turned back toward Brok and let her entire demeanor change. She became soft.

Zimp watched her grandmother with amazement.

"The Few have called a council meeting of all the clans of the doublesight," Oro told them. "They have asked us to bring our families. Our immediate families," she said. "Although, you can see that we travel in larger groups than that." She indicated Arren and the rest of the camp. "They will wait outside the encampment of the council until we are through."

Brok pulled his sister close.

"You, my young man, will now attend with us. You and your travel mates," Oro said. "You must go in your father's place. I would be honored to announce your arrival and personally introduce you to The Few."

"We can travel alone," Brok said. "We were going south."

Breel pulled back to look at his face then pulled on his arm. "Alone," she said.

Oro reached for Zimp to help her get off her knees and sit on the bench once again. "As the son of Fremlin, you may choose to do what you will. But the council of the doublesight has called to your family. Your father must have imparted to you the importance of such a request." Oro waited for a moment.

Breel whispered, "Please," into Brok's ear.

There was silence for a long while. Zimp didn't know what to do but felt that Oro was waiting for her to say something. She rustled around for a moment and all eyes turned toward her. From her belt hung a small deer hide pouch. She pulled it around so that she could open it. She reached inside and removed a beautiful ring too large for her fingers. The blue and white stone sparkled in the firelight. She threw it to Brok. "A peace offering," she said.

Brok caught the ring in one hand. "It's my ring," he said. "You stole my ring. How? You were never close enough."

"Closeness has little to do with it," Zimp said.

"You stole my ring, my grandfather's ring, from me, and

now want me to accept it as a peace offering?"

Zimp stretched tall and clenched her teeth. She glanced at Oro, offended by Brok's response. Under any other circumstances, that ring would have been as good as gone. Disappeared forever. Thieves do not return stolen items. Never. Her act was one of respect and humility and he acted upset? How dare he?

Oro laughed and they all looked at her. "Our ways are different than yours," she said to Brok. "We keep what we take. If you do not hold it close it becomes ours. Exposing herself to you is not only honorable, but thought to be an act of blessing and respect. It is like saying a prayer for you every day for a year." She stopped and looked into the fire for a moment, trying to remember something. "I know. It is like the honor you place on a beast-only, on a permanent thylacine if you find it dead. You wear its pelt to honor its existence. Having the pelt, or a tooth or claw necklace, is a reminder that you as a doublesight could not change shape if that shape did not also exist wholly as a beast."

Brok didn't look very convinced. "Do not steal it again," he said, appearing to be more of a threat than a statement.

"She won't," Oro said. "Not without returning it willingly. Once an item is returned in such a way, like this ring, it can only become the piece in a game, never again as an item to be stolen and kept."

"My father wore it. He passed it to me several days ago." To Zimp he said, "Do not take it again."

Breaking the seriousness of the conversation, the orange candle Zimp had used popped and spit and burst into flames, throwing a fireball straight into the air. All around the camp a cheer went up. Drums began to be pounded and people got to their feet to dance.

Oro threw her hands up and let them slap onto her thighs. "That was the only extra candle I had with me." She smiled brightly at Zimp, a flash of elation took over her face. "I suppose we dance and welcome our dead into the next realm." Arren advanced into the circle and reached for Oro's hand. She took it, to Zimp's surprise.

"I don't know if I can do this tonight," Zimp said.

"Your sister needs to speak to you," Oro said.

"But she has spoken to me. I can't say goodbye. Not yet. I don't want to celebrate her passing. I'm not ready."

"Very well, my granddaughter. You can postpone your dance, but you can hear from the sound of the drum that the rest of the clan cannot wait. Go, then. We begin to travel early. I hope to be at the council grounds late tomorrow evening."

Oro bowed to Brok and the other two thylacines. "You may do as your custom suggests. You will answer our invitation by morning. If you wish to leave, we'll supply food and weapons." She took a breath. "I am sorry about Therin. I am truly sorry. You will have to watch him closely as his instincts may become much stronger than you can imagine."

Breel rubbed Therin's forehead and the thylacine whined in pleasure.

Zimp followed Arren and Oro as they rounded the fire and headed toward the field where the dancing had already begun. Before she peeled off to head for the wagon, Oro took her wrist.

"I sent you to welcome them as guests and you steal his ring?" Oro said.

"That is what we do, Grandmother. Had it been anyone else you would have been proud."

"It was not someone else," the old woman said. "And I sent you to keep them safe."

"He threatened us."

"And you stole from him. Then, too," she said with a nod, "it was a pretty jewel."

Zimp kissed Oro's cheek. Perhaps the last comment was an acknowledgment that Zimp had made a wise choice, perhaps it was the only concession Oro felt she could offer at the time.

That evening, Zimp lay face down in her cot. The wagon cover muffled the sound of joy and song. She heard the rising wail of the celebrants, and the loud sizzle when the bound grass was thrown onto the fire. She listened to the drumbeat climb and fall, and imagined the rise of elation and fall of sadness that the clan would go through. She lay in the dark, letting her chest heave with the rise and sink with the fall of her own emotions as they moved through humiliation, distrust, and fear. Brok openly disrespected her. His arrogance grew stronger when Arren recognized his father's name and recalled Fremlin's history. Even though she tried to understand that Brok might not know of her traditions, there was something about the way he carried himself, always ready to act, that felt dangerous to her. The anger in his aura when she first looked at him oozed from his character like sweat from the body.

"Collect the herbs to stop the bleeding," she heard in a whisper. She held her breath and listened closely, discarding her previous concentration.

"First thoughts, then words, then symbols, then actions," Zora said. "Yes."

"Why did you die?" Zimp said into the blackness of the inside of the wagon.

"So you could hear," Zora said, "and now you don't." Zora laughed until the sound of her voice faded, as though her physical body escaped through the top of the canvas, traveled into the woods, and disappeared.

8

Darkness fell quickly under the tightly woven canopy of the deep Dgosh forest. Lankor held onto his staff with his right hand. His ears perked at every sound outside his family's steps and movements. He could see ahead that Rend, too, had his hand on his broadsword. Mianna gripped Nayman's arm, as though her presence was essential to keep him upright.

Rend halted. Mianna and Nayman stopped but one step afterward.

Lankor trudged on to see why they had stopped. When Rend's hand went up, Lankor halted his own movements, began to breathe in shallow breaths, and listened for unnatural sounds. But it wasn't sound that arrested his attention. The passing odor of human sweat lingered for a moment. He checked in with his body. He wasn't sweating. The air stood still, thick. Perhaps it was Nayman. He worked hardest. But Lankor knew his brother's smell. He lowered his grip on his staff and lifted the weapon off the ground slightly. He leaned toward Mianna and Nayman. "I smell humans," he whispered.

Rend motioned behind him for them to retreat.

Before Lankor could register the sound, the whoosh of an arrow broke the silence. It sped through the air, only to be interrupted by Rend's quick reflexes as he lifted the blade of his broadsword.

Mianna pulled Nayman to the ground as another arrow

skimmed a nearby tree and sang over their heads.

Lankor could hardly see in the dark and wondered how their attacker could see well enough to aim an arrow. He advanced to where his mother and brother kneeled.

Nayman's sword was drawn and being used as a shield. Mianna had removed her pack and drew it in front of her facing the direction from which the arrows came.

Rend, in an unbelievable movement, altered the path of yet another arrow.

"How can he see?" Lankor asked.

Mianna motioned for silence and Lankor realized that Rend couldn't see well in the dark, but that he listened for the arrow cutting through the humid air, and let his reflexes do the rest.

Rend backed slowly until he was close to them. He lowered onto one knee, "They can't see well enough to aim perfectly." His voice was almost inaudible. "Arrows are only coming from there," he pointed before them, "one at a time. They must have been coming toward us and were surprised by our presence. Boys? Flank them. They can't be more than a few hundred feet given the speed of the arrows and this dense part of the forest. Mianna, take my pack." He slipped the shoulder straps down his arms, careful to have his sword ready. "Back up and get behind the biggest tree."

Nayman, despit having a crippled foot, moved more quietly than a cougar. Lankor matched his brother's stealth in the opposite direction. He heard another clank.

Thick shadows darkened the area. They were not only difficult to see into, they provided places to hide for their attacker. A sliver of moon rested in the sky overhead; its light fell as if through a canvas bag. When Lankor noticed a glimmer of white, it was often moisture that had accumulated on a leaf and not the ricochet from the point of an arrow. He circled wide until he caught the scent he noticed earlier. He kneeled behind a tree and waited. He and Nayman had no way to indicate to one another when they were in position. On bent knees, Lankor slipped from behind one tree to a neighboring tree, all the while straining his eyes for movement, sniffing the air for the tart scent of body sweat.

"Hey," Lankor heard someone say. He stopped mid-step.

"Got 'em," another man said.

Lankor heard them take a few steps and then stop. How many were there? He continued behind one tree and then the next. He rested his hand against the rough bark and placed his face along the tree trunk as protection. In very dim light, Lankor observed three shadows, the only shadows that broke off at human height and moved. Standing still, he heard the strings of a bow screeching softly as it was pulled back. He took a deep breath then heard the trill of a morning bird. Nayman.

"What was that?" The arrow did not fly. The bow relaxed.

Lankor pushed off with all his strength. He leaped, then took three full steps and swung his staff across the head of the archer, cracking him hard enough to throw him to the ground.

Nayman was already swinging his broadsword across the shoulders of the man closest to him.

The last of the three fell to the ground with his arms protecting his face. "No! I beg you," he screamed.

From where Rend and Mianna hunkered down, came the strength of a powerful voice. "Don't kill him," Rend said.

Nayman yelled back, "There were only three."

"I'm coming."

Lankor heard Rend trot through the woods, Mianna at his side. "Good work, you two." He appeared in the dim light, a dark figure, tall and broad like his sons.

Lankor and Nayman flanked the man on the ground, who sat in silence.

"Why were you trying to kill us?" Rend said.

The man cowered and hesitated.

Nayman said, "He's trying to come up with something."

"No. I'm wondering if you'll kill me anyway."

"We should," Nayman said.

"But we won't," Rend said.

The man looked from Nayman to Lankor and back. "They might."

"Not without my saying so," Rend assured him.

The moon, on its walk across the sky, entered a position where light settled more fully over them. The man chewed his lower lip, attempting to size up the situation before he spoke. "There's a war brewing," the man said.

Rend looked puzzled. "Between who?"

The man shifted to sit more comfortably. Lankor placed the butt of his staff against the back of the man's head. "I don't like that," the man said to Rend.

Rend nodded to Lankor, who drew back the staff.

"Might I say without injury?" the man bargained.

Lankor watched as Rend considered his answer. If the decision were up to Lankor, he'd knock the man out and leave him there.

"Your name?" Rend said.

"Dig. That's what they call me." He nodded toward Rend. "I have two boys of me own. In the village ahead."

"Why would you attack us?"

"The doublesight," Dig said.

"What of them?"

"The evil ones are back. They attack at night and steal children."

Rend laughed. "A tale to keep children from running off."

"It's true. All around Brendern, Kurstom the Great is hunting the doublesight down. He announced that there would be no more raids on his people."

"What's this got to do with a family traveling in peace?"

"You're traveling at night. Only doublesight, a nocturnal doublesight, owls or thylacines, or cougars, travel in the dark." Dig swallowed. "Unless you are one of Kurstom's army. Your swiftness is like that of an animal, might I say. Like that of a doublesight."

"I don't know these woods, and hoped that we would find an Inn soon," Rend said. "We will be more careful from now on. Where's your village?"

Lankor braced himself when Rend lied. His father never lied.

"To the East."

"We wouldn't have passed through. We are going almost due south." Rend got to one knee in front of Dig. "We'll let you go and you will wait for your friend here who was knocked out.

He'll have quite a headache. The two of you will return home with your dead friend. We won't pass through your village and you won't follow us. You can see that we are nothing but a family traveling away from your home, not toward it."

Dig nodded his head. "We'll go home. I'll tell them not to worry. Shall I say you are a soldier?"

"You do that." Rend stood. "Is there a clearing up ahead where we might camp?"

"Several. Maybe a mile for the first one."

"We'll post guard. You'll leave us alone."

Dig hid his face and answered, "Yes."

Lankor noticed the grief in Dig's face and thought that the dead man must be a brother or friend.

Rend turned to go and Mianna followed. Her sword flashed as she placed it back into her sheath. Lankor wondered if she were as quick with the blade as Rend. As he and his brother stepped away from Dig, the man crawled to the dead man and rolled him over, probably in the hopes that the wound was not mortal. Lankor knew better. Nayman had been trained, as were they all, by Rend. War made up much of their history, as they were used by Sclan as fighting machines before Sclan turned on them. This long history of fighting was in their blood even though few battles had occurred in The Lost the last few decades.

Away from Dig, Rend repeated, "Great job tonight," as he helped Mianna with her pack.

"Do you believe Dig?" Nayman asked.

Rend looked serious. He swung his pack across his back and slid his arms through the straps. "I don't want to believe him. Kurstom the Great fought beside Brendern."

"The Holy Man?" Lankor asked.

"The doublesight Holy Man. Brendern was a thylacine. That's why Brendern Forest is overrun by the animals." He helped his boys with their packs. "Most of the thylacines are animal only these days. There are doublesight and humans living throughout the forest, mostly fur traders. They live side by side, but I'd guess that the humans don't know which are which. In fact, I'd bet that many of the doublesight don't know which other families are of their kind. Regardless, Kurstom has always been a friend to the doublesight, knowing that we are the most peaceful. We revere life as neither the humans nor the animals do."

They began to walk. Mianna said, "You are both well aware of the reason for that fact."

"We are, Mother," Nayman said. "But we did not bless the dead back there."

"I blessed him silently," Mianna said.

"And I," Rend said. "Had we performed a complete blessing, Dig may have figured us out."

After a few minutes of walking, Lankor asked, "What brought us back into existence after the slaughter by the Sclan armies?"

"A mistake of the natural world," Nayman said. "Great Grandfather was born doublesight."

"I know that story," Lankor said. "I just didn't know how he was born that way."

"No one knows," Rend said. "A throw-back to another time." He stopped and turned toward his family. "It was supposed to be impossible. He ran from his village and hid out for many years before taking a wife." He pointed into the darkness that surrounded them. "Let us stop talking about this in the event that others are out there listening."

"There doesn't seem to be many thylacine in this forest," Lankor said.

"Dgosh means left-behind," Mianna said. "For some reason the thylacines stayed in Brendern Forest. Few migrated this far north. Close to Lake Earnwood the weather gets pretty harsh, but farther south along the boarder of Dgosh and Brendern you'll find a few strays."

"Have you traveled this way before?" Lankor said to his mother.

"A long time ago." Mianna touched Rend's shoulder.

The sliver of moon lighted the path before them. It lay directly overhead. A clearing spread to their left and Rend headed for it.

"Won't we be conspicuous?" Nayman asked.

"We'll look friendly and unthreatening," Rend said. "And we'll take turns walking the periphery. Lankor first."

Lankor nodded. Nayman needed to rest his leg if he were to travel the next day at all. And Rend would not sleep soundly anyway. He'd protect the campsite while Mianna slept beside him.

"Leave that staff and hold your broadsword ready," Rend said.

"I like my staff," Lankor said.

"I know, but I want you ready for anything."

"Do as your father says," Mianna said. "And put on your cloak. It will be cold out there."

Lankor threw the staff down and pulled his sword and handed it to his mother to hold until he retrieved his cloak from his pack.

Moss and mushrooms covered the clearing. Nayman and Rend kicked the mushrooms from a space where they were going to lay their blankets, and dredged the moss so they could build a small fire. Lankor felt the space becoming comfortable already, but he wouldn't get to experience the soft ground or the warmth of the fire for a few more hours. He leaned his pack against a sapling, removed his blanket, and spread it from the pack toward the fire pit. Anyone who happened by would see that a guard had been posted and would be more careful about his actions.

Lankor lumbered into the darkness, keeping an eye on the dim glow of moonlight over the camp. In a few minutes, the fire will provide even more light. They had not eaten in hours and the acid in his stomach churned. He leaned against a tree and let the odors of the forest seep into his lungs. The smells were exotic, filled with musk and earth, the scents of a strange place in a land he had never walked nor seen, but had only heard of. If he thought of the trees closing him in as a cave or canyon, it eased his mind. But if he allowed the vast dark of the forest to assert itself, he felt closed in as if the trees were the thick bars of a cage or a maze that was impossible to exit. At the moment, he couldn't see more than a few hundred feet in any one direction and that unnerved him.

He concentrated on the caves of Sclan. Exploring them deep into a mountain, those caves grew tighter to his sides and close overhead, yet he always knew his way out. Once he learned this forest, would it be less frightening to dwell here?

The fire pushed light farther into the forest and Lankor extended the periphery he chose to walk. As quiet as he could be, he knew that Rend could hear the occasional snap of a twig, or the whoosh of a branch let go. Lankor chose to stop and listen to the night every few hundred feet. He concentrated on staying just outside the firelight. It would be days before they reached the council grounds. He wondered what they would find there.

9

Brok sat against a tree overlooking the plains to the south of Brendern Forest, his sister sitting and his brother lying on the ground beside him. Off to their left, the crow clan danced, drummed, and sang for their dead. Much of the time the dancers appeared to be joyful, which caused Breel to react in the opposite. Her tears sopped Brok's shoulder. Her quaking body could hardly be contained. Occasionally she mumbled words that he could not understand. Her thin fingers disappeared into the thick fur around Therin's neck. When she finally moved perpendicular to Therin so that she could lay her head across his stomach, Brok climbed to his feet and stood beside her.

The moon lay directly overhead and placed a soft glow across the plains. In the distance, Brok thought he saw buffalo grazing. He walked into the tall grass nearby. He needed to consider Oro's invitation, but the strength of vengeance coursed through his blood like acid. He opened his hand. His father's polished sodalite ring gleamed in the moonlight. He felt peaceful while looking at it. He relaxed.

Brok turned to see that his siblings were asleep. They were in the open and still felt safe. There would be time enough to decide their path. Casting the worry from his mind would be good for him. Let the memories fade for a while.

Brok pushed the ring onto his finger. He bent at the knees and placed his hands on the ground. He crawled into the field until he couldn't see the dancers, only the fires sizzling higher and higher into the night sky. In a slow, thoughtful, and painful process, Brok shifted into his beast image. Immediately his olfactory senses kicked in and he could smell the buffalo a few miles away. His eyesight cleared to the point of being able to see details, an increased contrast between blades of grass, stones, mounds of dirt. And yet, the color of those same objects became dull and muted. His smell was in color, thousands of tiny odors mixed in the grass. There were rabbits nearby, and moles. Worms poked their heads out of the ground at night and created a new odor, different than the odor present during the day.

The sound of crickets clattered in his ears. The air around him was warm, close to the ground and amidst the grass. He moved farther from the campsite until he knew he wouldn't startle anyone with noise. At the moment he felt distant enough from the others, he burst into a full run, leaping occasionally to view where he was. His strong body leaped and turned as he ran full speed. He didn't stop until he stood on a small grassy knoll where he could see the buffalo herd grazing and sleeping. Strategically placed sentinels watched for predators.

For a moment, as a thylacine, Brok had the urge to charge them. But his human mind encroached and he sat. One buffalo snorted, and a few walked off and grazed. The ground had been trampled and eaten into a clear area. Brok shifted into his human image. As all doublesight must do, he longed for both images, but could have only one at a time, the human image being the most natural.

He listened to the crickets. Fireflies blinked all around him. The moon had shifted slightly and shadows lay across the ground, adding bulk to the buffalo, causing the animals to look larger than they were.

Brok wondered what it was like to live that way, completely animal, with literally no human side. Did they yearn for more? And he wondered equally about those who were human-only. Did they want an animal side, physically? He had heard that it was their oneness as a human that caused their sanity to slip, that humans could be more ruthless because when their minds slipped into an animal state, there was no control, no coming back. Was that to be the fate of Therin?

His shoulders and back tensed with the sorrow he felt suddenly for the death of his parents. As much as his face muscles tightened and his eyes welled up, he could not cry for some reason. His thoughts would cut him from the sorrow and connect him to images of vengeance, not against all humans, but against the ones who murdered his family and left only three of them to fend for themselves.

In human form, Brok focused on his own thoughts, and the sounds and images faded at different degrees, dependent upon his emotional state. In deep sadness the entire plain could have been invisible, while in thoughtful openness to the sensibility of the buffalo his senses were more acute on the lumbering animals, but still oblivious of the plains around him. It was during a time of anger, with his eyes closed, imagining the deaths of his enemies that someone was able to creep up on him. It was the jump and snort of a buffalo that alerted him. He turned and saw a shape encroaching.

"Don't be alarmed," the shape said as it approached.

Brok looked around and reached for a rock.

"It is Arren of the crow clan." The man stepped closer until Brok rose to his knees in a ready position. "I thought you might want company. You might need to talk. Caring for your brother and sister can be an arduous task when you are going through a lot of emotions yourself. There is hardly time to consider your own choices."

"All the more reason for me to be alone," Brok said.

"Would you like to tell someone what happened?"

The buffalo moved away from the two in a calm manner. Brok knew that the animals could sense the lack of danger in their presence. The sound of Arren's voice broke the silence in a strange way, like the slow cutting of a long cloth—even, yet somehow destructive.

"Why the interest?" Brok asked.

Arren ignored the rock in Brok's hand and crouched next to the thylacine doublesight. "I lost a close friend in the attack on my people early this morning."

"Yet you celebrate tonight."

"Our ways are difficult for others to understand. You see, all crows are intuitives in some small way. My friend, all our relatives step into the next realm. None of us truly die."

"His body is gone, being picked apart at this very minute. How can you say he didn't die?" Brok let the rock slip from his fingers. He sat back and crossed his legs.

Arren turned his eyes to the moon. "He doesn't speak to me. At least I can't hear him if he does." He made a fist. "But I feel his presence. Feel it with my whole body. He...he touches me." He opened his fist toward Brok. "And you, my friend?"

"Memory."

"Clear? Sharp memory?"

"Horrible memory. I close my eyes and I see my father's head severed by some monstrous human, my mother's back slashed as she tries to escape, my sister stabbed in the back while running toward me. The images are stuck in my head."

"How ruthless humans can be when they are fearful," Arren said.

"Fearful? Of what? Doublesight are the least dangerous among them. And in Brendern Forest? You'd think of all places for the doublesight to be safe it would be here, especially thylacines. I think these humans came from another place. Sclan perhaps, or Weilk. Much of Weilk are warriors from the Sclan battles. There is still much trouble along Torturous Road leading between Castle Weilk to the Weilk Stronghold."

"Doublesight have not always been so peaceful. There was a time when you and I may have fought to the death," Arren said.

"We are both predators and prey," Brok said.

"We are, I admit. Do you wonder if the doublesight are having an uprising? Are The Few behind any of this? Why else would humans from another land come into the Brendern Forest? Wouldn't Kurstom have his own guards planted?"

Brok huffed. "You may be right."

"About the guards?"

"About the fear." Brok searched Arren's eyes for the reason the man visited him. "Thylacines can be frightening animals if at every turn you run into one. Have you ever seen a thylacine take down a deer? A bear? If so, you wouldn't want to allow your children to run free."

"These men knew you were doublesight. It sounds as though the attack was planned to me," Arren said. "If I were you, I'd want to avenge my family's deaths."

"I thought you believed they didn't die?"

"I said, 'If I were you' that's what I'd do. You are the one haunted by the images."

"What about avenging your clan? How many died?" Brok stood above Arren. "Twenty? Fifty? They may have changed realms, but they are not here. Even you admit that you can't talk with your dead. You can't put your arm across his shoulder. Don't you want revenge against your attackers?"

Arren reached out and gripped the stone that Brok held a few minutes ago. He slammed it into the ground, and a few buffalo jumped and trotted farther away. His teeth clenched and his jaw set. "Yes, I'd like to see them dead. Does that surprise you? Doublesight are the peaceful ones, it is said, but that does not mean that we are dead inside. That does not mean that we must sit back and accept whatever fate befalls us." Arren stood to meet Brok's gaze. "Oro is getting old. Zora was reckless. The way she wanted to run the clan would have us all dead. And Zimp." He stopped and looked away. "We were not well organized. We set no guards most nights. The warning signs were everywhere."

Brok remained silent. He waited for Arren to say what he came to say.

"The crow clan needs a warrior leader, not a sensitive woman too weak to look you in the eye," he said.

"But Zimp has powers."

"She turns them all inside. She forgets tradition. You saw that she didn't even have a sacred candle with her. And then, to mock our dance by not participating? If she loved her twin, she'd welcome her into the next realm. No. Zimp is a danger to us all. She would have us all killed with her lack of concern for anyone but herself. No different than her sister." Arren took a deep breath. "If she were only gone."

"Killed?" Brok said.

"Just gone. I don't care how."

Brok tightened his brow and stepped back. "You want me to kill her?"

"No, no, that's not it at all. I just want her gone. Oro will be unable to lead. She's unable to lead now. Zimp can't lead. If you challenged her, showed everyone that she doesn't have it in her." Arren quieted. "I'm not proud of this. But we're vulnerable. Do you feel safe with us?" He turned to leave, then swung back and said, "I would be your greatest asset in finding the people who killed your family. All Oro is concerned with is the council and the call of The Few. They are not so important to me."

Brok said nothing. There was nothing to respond to.

Arren had said what he wished to say. But then Arren turned one last time. "Think it over." Arren walked into the grass and bent down to hide from view. In a moment, a large crow entered the sky like a shadow. The silhouette glided low over the plain and cut east so that it did not enter the camp directly.

The blazing fires had died down; only a glow existed to indicate the campsite. The night temperature placed a cool hand against Brok's body. The drumming had silenced. He hoped that Breel and Therin were still asleep.

A breeze pushed his curls along his neck. Chills ran up his back. He closed his eyes and opened his arms to the light of the moon. He considered Arren's proposal, and Oro's. He wished on his own life that he could hear Fremlin's voice as Zimp must surely be able to hear her sister's, and how Oro, he guessed, could hear the whole of the other realm. What should he do? What was his duty to his family? To the doublesight and The Few?

Brok set his intention on making a decision before morning. He took in the plains and the buffalo, turned and stared at the forest, his home. He pulled in the night air until his chest expanded to its limit. Long and slow, he exhaled as his body shimmered and changed, as fur appeared to burst from his skin, as he felt his head elongate, the colors dim. Forced by the shifting shape of his own body to drop to the ground, Brok let out a small whine. His teeth felt wet with saliva, cold against the night air.

He sniffed the area where Arren had been. The scent of fear lingered still. The thylacine let his mouth hang open and pulled in the scent as deeply as he could, pulled it up and through his nasal passages in the hopes that in human image he would remember the smell. After scouring the area, he turned to the buffalo and burst into an angry run. At one point he imagined the bodies of his family and almost shifted back into human image. But he continued on, casting the thought aside. Once the buffalo ran, he turned to run back to the camp.

The woods, in its darkness, calmed the beast. His animal sight brought clear edges and unique details to the trees and underbrush. He heard the caw of a crow and shifted into his human form. The bird clucked and Brok wondered if that was a signal for a false alarm. He touched the trunk of a nearby spruce and traced its bark with his fingers. Returned to his human form, the darkness had closed in, the sparse moonlight the only illumination.

Brok sneaked up on Oro and Zimp's wagon. At the entrance he stopped and placed his hand on the side pole. He tensed to pull himself into the space as quietly as he could.

10

The wagon's center of gravity shifted and Zimp knew that she had company. She lay still and held her breath. A chill scurried like a mouse up her back and into her scalp. She held back from shaking it off. A floorboard squeaked and the intruder hesitated before advancing another careful step. She let her breath slip out and turned as if in sleep. A knife, located along her feather mattress, found its way into her hand. In a more ready position, Zimp allowed her arm to stretch in the dark at the exact pace as the advancement of the person in the wagon with her.

"Zimp?" a voice broke through. A moment later a hand reached to touch her shoulder.

Zimp opened her eyes and in the deep darkness of the wagon picked out the body mass of Brok. She turned her wrist in a very slow movement to indicate to him the position of the knife she held. It pushed against his solar plexus until it met resistance. She pulled back.

"You were awake," he said.

"Never try to surprise a thief." She sat up onto her elbows and let the knife slide back into place along the mattress. "What are you doing here?"

"I shifted and took a run into the valley tonight."

"You are free to do what you wish. Why tell me?"

Brok rested his knee on the floor. "I had a visitor."

"Go on."

"Your clan is not as tight as you might think. I am afraid that someone tried to use me, thinking that my anger would be easily sparked into the flames of hatred. Thylacines are predators, but so are crows." He stopped.

"This is a warning, then?"

"More than a warning. You are not the only one in danger."

"Oro?"

"It appears that your captain does not trust you or Oronice. He suggested I dispose of you." Again, Brok stopped speaking.

Zimp quieted and checked in with her own emotions. So much happened during the day that she wasn't sure what she felt. "If you mean Arren, he's loyal to the clan. He may not believe that I am the right person to lead, but he wouldn't harm me, either."

"He may not, but who might he solicit? When might he choose not to protect you? He is a man who does not do his own dirty work. Such men are the most dangerous."

"Why should I believe you? You haven't liked me from the beginning. I can see how you look at me."

"It is treachery like this that killed my family. Perhaps once the doublesight fought amongst themselves, but my father has always said that those days were ended, that the doublesight would be wiped out if they did not protect one another."

"I see." Zimp reached out and touched his hand. She sensed calm in him. Either he hid his hatred or he had none in him at that time. "I will admit feeling uneasy around you and your family. The power you have within you frightens me. But I can tell that you mean me no harm."

"We are taught how to hold our aggression so that we may spring it upon our prey."

"Then I am thankful that I am not your prey," she said.

"You would not know until it was too late," Brok said.

"Another warning?"

"Arren may be right about your inability to lead, but it is not for him to decide, nor is it for me to decide. I have heard great things about The Gem of the Forest and I believe my father would have given his life to protect her. I am offering the same."

"You are an honorable young man," Oro said from outside the rear of the wagon.

"Grandmother? You were listening?"

"I noticed young Brok was off on his own and became suspicious, I am afraid. I felt no deep fear, but I am old and don't always trust myself any more. The other realms have their own needs, their own battles, and the voices I hear do not always want what is best for this world. Remember, my dear, we can be tricked as easily by other worlds as we can by this one."

Zimp felt the weight of responsibility being shifted from Oro's shoulders to her own. "If you can't rely on your senses, how can I ever learn to do it?"

"Your sense of the other realm delivers only half of any decision. You must draw the other half from your own beliefs."

Brok pulled his hand from Zimp's touch and addressed Oro. "I am sorry you had to hear this," he said. "You need not worry about it." Brok let his head drop into a respectful bow.

Zimp tried to make literal sense of what was happening. A natural enemy, a thylacine, and one who admittedly disliked her, just announced his loyalty and protective services, while a fellow clan member became exposed as her enemy.

"Help me into the wagon," Oro said.

Brok quickly crawled over and extended a hand.

Zimp, still dressed for the ceremony she had skipped, pushed the blanket from her lap and sat with her legs next to Brok's.

With Oro in the wagon and seated on her cot, Brok bowed once again to both of them, stepped out the back and onto the ground. "I should check on my brother and sister," he said.

"If there is a way I can thank you..." Zimp said.

"I will let you know," Brok said.

Zimp felt another obligation settle on her shoulders.

Oro settled back on her cot. "You have made a mistake not taking part in the Ceremony of the Dead. Your clan must know that tradition is as important to you as it is to them if they are to trust your leadership. There was much talk about your absence."

"But you said I could do as I pleased," Zimp said.

"And you can."

"Riddles." She flopped onto her back. The darkness suddenly felt heavy and smothering. Her eyes welled up with the confusion she felt inside. Who could she truly trust? Brok, even while warning her about Arren, made it clear that he was not trustworthy, either. Must she suspect everyone? "Anyway, there is more to be concerned about than mindless tradition," she said.

In a sleepy voice, Oro said, "Tradition is never mindless unless you act in a mindless manner."

More riddles. Zimp let the tears seep from her eyes and run down her cheeks to tickle her ears. She squeezed her eyes shut in frustration, as though she could block out the world she now lived in. It was all she could do to hold back the pressure that originated from inside her. She tensed her muscles. She could not move, had no will to move. The distinct sound of Therin as he crawled under the wagon to lie down relieved some of her concern for Oro. Brok had kept his promise and set his guard. Zimp allowed her mind to wander until she faded off into sleep.

She awoke to the sound of birds chirping. Her head and neck ached with the stiffness of a tense sleep. Prior to opening her eyes, Zimp checked her thoughts for a dream, but remembered nothing more than her last conversation with Brok. Everyone appeared to be against her, even Oro. Arren thought her weak; other clan members felt she didn't adhere to tradition. Even Oro asked that she make decisions that Zimp felt were beyond her ability. Zora may have loved the chance for all the attention, but Zimp did not. She had her difficulty with Arren, but he was a trained soldier—better trained than she was. So, why wouldn't he make a better leader than her? He wanted the post. Let him have it.

She rolled to her side. "Did you sleep well?"

Oro sat with her legs on the floor. "I feel rejuvenated."

"That's better than how I feel." Zimp stretched her arms. "That thylacine slept under the wagon all night."

Oro smiled. "What a comfort."

Voices that were at a distance and lost amidst the morning

chirping came closer. Zimp recognized Brok's thick whisper. He and Breel appeared at the wagon's rear opening.

"You're up," Brok said. He did not wait for a response. "That favor. We are not far from our home. We would like to enact our own tradition and, while there, pick up some supplies and weapons. Can your clan guard the area while we are there?"

Zimp looked to Oro who did not return her gaze. "Well, Grandmother?" Zimp said, urging a response.

"I sense that you already have the answer to that question rising inside you, my dear."

Defiantly, Zimp turned to Brok and said, "No."

Brok raised his chin to let her know that he'd obey her words. He took a deep breath and swiveled on his heels to leave.

"Wait," Zimp yelled. She crawled to the rear of the wagon and swung out. She reached back and gripped her cloak. It fluttered almost weightless above the ground. "Your request is granted." She felt her face redden. She didn't want to disappoint Oro. She glanced at her grandmother, who nodded approval. "I will let the camp know of my decision."

"Thank you," Breel said. Brok took his sister's hand and led her away. Therin squeezed under the rear axle and followed them.

Zimp turned to Oro. "This means that I've altered the plans for the entire clan. What will they think of such a decision?"

"Your first answer to young Brok was weighted with the fear of change. How will the clan feel about you if you change their plans for the day? Your second answer bore the fruit of a true decision." Oro reached for Zimp's help. "This morning we must perform an opening ceremony."

Zimp helped Oro from the wagon, then excused herself to find Noot. She decided to make him her personal courier.

Breezes swept toward Brendern Eastlake as the sun pushed shadows across the dew-wet plain. "I am honored, my cousin," Noot said after Zimp made her offer, "but shouldn't one of Arren's brothers be asked before me? Might they be angered by such a decision?"

She wanted to wave his worries away with a sweep of her hand, tell him just to announce the new plan; but first she stopped, looked him square in the eye, and placed a hand on his shoulder. "I need someone I can trust. You are the one I choose."

It was obvious to Zimp that Noot was surprised by her strength and conviction. She alone knew how difficult those words were to force out. "Now, let each wagon know that we will perform a daybreak ceremony before we leave. Breakfast is to be eaten while we travel to the thylacine home, where we wait until the children of Fremlin perform a death ceremony for their family. Afterwards, we go to the conference grounds to arrive in early evening, if we are lucky."

"Some of the clan won't want to wait for the thylacines. Whether prejudice or hatred, grudges are still held from the time the doublesight fought one another. There are those who hold that thylacines are not to be trusted. Can those clan members go on ahead?"

"That would be Arren's choice, regardless of the reasoning." Zimp focused on the pressure she felt building inside her. She closed her eyes and willed the tingling in her face and ears to stop. "We act together. And we shall travel together. Oro must be the first to enter the conference grounds. We will need a driver for the remainder of the trip. You, Noot, after the thylacine ritual. Will your family be all right without you for the last hour or so of travel?"

"It will be an honor to escort Oronice to The Few," he said. With a shaky snicker and smile, Noot said, "I will break the news to the others."

The daybreak ceremony could be long or short, and often no one knew until Oro got started. She appeared near the edge of Brendern Forest. The entire clan except for scouts and guards stood before her. She motioned for the drums to begin, then one member of each of the seven wagons and one member of each of the walking clans began to chant a low mantra of their own. The combined sound could frighten wild animals with its low and scratchy resonance. The words, undecipherable and repeated, sounded like an incantation from a body of witches. Oro lifted her hands and each clan member sang out an individual mantra, raising the incantation to a dangerous level. Zimp spoke her own words and turned to face the sunrise. Oro chose not to speak that morning. The sound of voices rose, drowning out all other sound including that of the wind through the trees, the distant snort of buffalo, the chirping of birds. At a natural and familiar peak to the harmony all went silent, and the outer sounds rushed in with magical clarity. Zimp rose with the ceremony like never before and now felt the power that it created, felt the strength in their numbers.

Oro's voice and movements appeared to be stronger this morning.

The clan members rushed back to their wagons talking among themselves.

Arren stood outside the ring of sound and glared at Zimp. He stood, an arrogant pillar, in her peripheral vision. She turned away and held Oro's arm to help her return to the wagon. Zimp twisted around and looked to see if Arren had left, but he stood firm. He waved and smiled when she looked at him. The sneer on his face was gone, but she still saw it in her memory.

11

The wagons stayed to the wider road through the forest. Some of the walking clans spread to parallel paths worn visible by animals or hunters. Once the caravan got close to the thylacines' home, Brok indicated a place where the crow clan might wait. He heard Zimp speaking with one of the scouts who brought news of strange happenings in some of the smaller villages. Bands of assassins were on the move. Some appeared to look like soldiers from various borderlands.

"I do not wish to place your clan in any danger," Brok told Zimp. "We can do this alone if you would like to continue toward the council grounds. We can easily catch up."

"You make this very difficult for me," she said. "Oro is right. The decision has already been made and it is the right one. I can't leave you three here and vulnerable. Five of us will go with you so that you can perform your tradition in peace. The others will wait with Noot and Oro."

Noot stood by her side. "I'll sit with Oro in my family's wagon."

"You may not wish to watch our ceremony," Brok said.

Zimp told Noot to gather Arren and two of his brothers, Dail and Felter. Arren's other brother, Kal, could stay with their families. The fifth member of Zimp's troop would be Storret, the scout who had brought the warnings.

Brok led his sister and brother into a dense part of the woods.

A narrow path opened up and the three of them moved along it single file, followed closely by the five crow clan members.

No one spoke. A few hundred yards down the path, Brok turned to Therin and bent down to receive a wet nuzzle from his brother. "Hey, Therin, listen." Brok held his brother's head between his hands. "Go see if it's safe. Let me know, all right, Therin? Let me know." He released his brother to run ahead.

"I hate that we have to talk with him that way," Breel said.

"So do I, but I don't know how conscious his human mind is. Until we settle into camp at the council grounds, it will be difficult to test."

"He's better than we think," Breel said.

Brok accepted her assurance. "I believe you."

The party took a few more steps before they heard the terrible sound of growling and barking. Brok recognized Therin's cough-like bark and leaped into action. He made a quick turn off the path to be out of view. Several strides and he slipped into the mindset of a thylacine. Several more and his body tumbled onto the ground partially shifted and uncoordinated at first, but soon he ran like a cat. Brok burst onto the scene just behind Therin.

A female cougar squealed out its wild cry, standing near the bodies of Fremlin, Lina, Keena, and Rem. Two younger cougars flanked the first.

Brok noticed that part of his mother's leg had been eaten. The bodies had been dragged closer together. His father's head appeared to be missing, but as soon as Brok noticed, he immediately pushed the thought aside. He could smell that the cougars were afraid. He and his brother curved their bodies away from one another and stepped around the dead at an angle. The two smaller cougars retreated closer to the female, their mother. Breel, now in thylacine-image, broke through the underbrush, growled from deep in her throat, and crouched on her legs ready to attack.

The mother cougar fought against her fear. The scent of open flesh appeared to strengthen her commitment. Blood stained her muzzle and the muzzles of her young.

Brok waited for the mother's tense and ready muscles to

relax.

There.

He leapt over the human bodies as if they were not present. The mother cougar toppled backwards from his weight as he bit deeply into her shoulder. The mother rolled and tucked her legs under her and propelled Brok off her. He righted himself, created powerful springs from his bent legs and leaped back onto her before she could gain balance. Another bite, this time closer to her neck. His wide jowls and enormous gape were almost lethal as they closed down. The cat let out a squeal and scratched at his belly and foreleg. Claws penetrated his skin, but he held on. The weight of another thylacine landed on the cougar and she went down. Brok let go of her neck and backed away. Breel had severed the cougar's backbone just behind the neck. Therin appeared next to his sister and helped her drag the animal into the woods and out of sight. They then returned for the smaller cougars.

Brok bled from the shoulder. The wound was tender when he walked, but he regrouped with his siblings nose to nose. Immediately they rotated around, stepping sidewise in one direction for a complete revolution, then in the other direction for a complete revolution. At the finish, the three of them backed away. The two larger thylacines then crouched down as though they wished not to be seen.

*   *

Zimp had never witnessed thylacines in battle. It was as if they had no fear of death. The cougars didn't have a chance. An unbelievable power overcame the three doublesight and that power increased tenfold as they attacked simultaneously.

She stood with her mouth open, and her arms crossed over her chest for protection. The almost audible pounding of her heart was noticeable in the pulsing veins of her neck. She wanted to, but could not, turn away.

When Brok and his sister kneeled close to the ground, Zimp did the same. She motioned for the other crow clan to respect their privacy as well. Arren and his brothers turned their heads away. Storret looked at his own feet. Zimp could not see totally over the bodies that lay between her and the thylacines. She could not turn away. What she could see was a head lift up, and the ectoplasmic collapse of a thylacine nose, the clay-like flexibility of the reshaping of that material into a human face. She heard one of them cry out as the reshaping took place. When they rose from the ground, red soaked Brok's shirt, which hung in tatters along his side. He favored his left arm.

Breel reached for him, but Brok stopped her. He whispered something that Zimp could not hear. The two of them entered the small cabin.

Therin stayed behind. He sniffed around the bodies. He nuzzled his mother's cheek. He sat back and just stared at his dead family, his head turning back and forth as though he tried to remember them as human, and perhaps remember himself as human.

There was something about the way in which Therin stared at his parents' bodies that caused Zimp to want to cry. She could never understand what it must be like to be shocked into a permanent image.

Brok and Breel came from the cabin with loaded packs. They dragged swords with them and their clothes bulged with additional items. They let all their items drop to the ground, and Breel stepped back inside and came out with a large carving knife in her hand. She approached the corpses and kneeled next to Fremlin's headless body, a grimace across her pale face.

Brok reached inside the doorway and brought out a painted staff of many colors. On either end of the staff hung a strip of pelt that looked like it came from a thylacine. It was the same dark brown color with black stripes. In the center of the staff a silver-colored metal had been wrapped around the smooth wood. At either end of the silver ring, leather strips dangled down, bearing several blue and yellow beads knotted in place. Tied at the ends of each strip were feathers: hawk, owl, and crow. As Brok walked over to stand behind Breel, the beads attached to the leather strips clacked together.

Therin sat upright next to Breel. Brok began to shake the sacred staff. He and Breel hummed and produced nonsensical sounds. "Na-na-nu-we. Lo-si-wa."

Zimp did not understand the words, but thought they may be from an older language. She could see that Brok's wounds seeped steadily as he shook the staff with both hands firmly clasped over the silver center. What she did not expect was when Breel placed the carving knife over her father's chest and dug it into the flesh, dragging it down as though she were going to gut him like a wild animal.

Another cut across the corpse's chest and Breel set the knife aside, reached down with both hands, and separated the skin. She pulled out Fremlin's heart, which glistened in its own blood and juice whenever the sunlight fell on it directly.

Zimp stepped backward into the woods and almost fell over a fallen tree. She regained her balance as she watched the gory ceremony proceed, unable to take her eyes off Breel's movements.

Breel reached over the body to lay the heart on a stretch of clothing. She scooted around Fremlin's feet on her knees—a good choice, Zimp thought—and stopped next to her mother's body.

Brok followed her movements and never stopped chanting or shaking the staff. Therin crawled alongside his sister and sat beside her once again.

Breel used the knife to slit her mother's chest open and pull out the heart.

Zimp wondered if the crossed cuts Breel made in her mother's chest had any meaning, or were merely to make the job easier.

The two hearts sat together on the cloth. The ceremony was not repeated for the siblings.

Zimp watched as the hearts were placed side by side.

Breel stopped chanting.

Brok continued to chant at an increased volume as he threw the staff high into the air where it turned slowly above him and dropped back into his hands. His face twitched with pain, but he held fast.

Breel sliced through both hearts, creating three equally sized pieces of each mass. She separated the pairs then crouched close to the ground. Brok set the staff behind him on the ground and crouched down.

Zimp knew they would shift and was afraid of what they would surely do next.

As thylacines, the three stepped up to the cloth, sniffed, and reached out to eat their parents' organs. When finished they stood back, heads arched toward the sky and whined. The sound dragged with it unexplainable sorrow and grief. The woods around them cracked with the pain. A small wind came up.

Zimp found herself crying without knowing why. Was it the horrific tradition she had witnessed, or the sorrow that reached inside her, that entered her soul with the sound the thylacines made? She could not decipher or explain how she felt. Whatever the reason, she saw that Storret and Dail cried as well. She could not see Arren and wondered about his spirit. Did it go out to the thylacines? The crying filled her mouth with saliva and Zimp let it slip from her lips onto the ground. The feeling of her mouth filling again with moisture and the momentary thought of what just happened before her made her wish she could vomit. Why had she watched the ceremony through completion?

When Breel and Brok regained their human image, Breel ran to the side and threw up. The hearts would remain with the thylacine image. Only her breakfast came out.

Zimp envied Breel's ability to be disgusted by her own actions. It must have taken great control and power for Breel to remain in thylacine image throughout the ceremony.

Brok lifted the sacred staff and shook it and sang one of his chants. His face looked hard, like stone, and set with anger and fire behind his eyes. He walked back to the cabin and removed a long pouch from his pack. He slid the staff into the pouch and tied it at the top. He dragged both packs over to his sister and lifted one.

Breel wiped her mouth and slid her arms through the straps. Brok kissed her head, a moment of vulnerability and tenderness, and turned to go back through the woods.

"That was horrible and wonderful," Storret said from behind Zimp.

She stopped and stared at him, but didn't speak for a long time. "We'd better follow them back. Someone needs to tend to Brok's shoulder."

12

Zimp heard the guards cawing, and pushed past Brok and Breel on the path to run ahead. Therin took to her heels and followed her, which made Zimp kick up her pace. After what she had just seen him do, she felt less comfortable with him in their camp.

The clan scurried to get weapons and create a wall around the wagons. Zimp clasped the shoulder of the first person she ran into. Arealie was a distant cousin. She had a strong back and plain face. Reliable. Capable. "Take Brok to Oro. He's hurt."

Arealie handed a short sword to Zimp and reached for Brok, who was emerging from the woods. The woman kept her eye on Therin, Zimp noticed, and appeared very reluctant to actually touch Brok, but she did it anyway. Zimp was surprised that he let Arealie help him when he held his sister at bay.

Breel followed close behind her brother until she reached Zimp. She stopped and asked, "How can I help?"

"Stay with your brother. He may need the comfort of his family," Zimp said.

Breel glanced down at Therin. She looked around the camp at the crow clan. Another crow cawed a warning. "Forgive me. You are the host. But truthfully, I can outfight most of the men in this camp. My brother was not threatening you when he said that we could be dangerous. He was telling the truth." Breel reached down to touch the hilt of her sword. The slender handle had been formed perfectly for her fingers, for her grip. The way she stroked it unsettled Zimp. Breel slipped the pack from her shoulder. "Have someone take my supplies."

Zimp motioned and a young boy ran over and hefted Breel's pack into his arms and lumbered off toward the center of the camp.

"Therin," Breel said, and her brother stepped to her side. "Let's go see who's coming."

Zimp had the suspicion that the passion of the thylacine's ceremony still filled Breel's body with power. The young woman pulled her sword, intensely alert, unbelievably smooth, and undeniably strong. A worthy opponent, as Breel said, for any of the men in the crow clan. Zimp led.

Crepp met Zimp as she crossed through camp. "There are only a few of them, but they have armor. We're not sure what to think. There are several small ones with them, but that may be a ruse. They drag a two-wheeled cart that's making a lot of noise as though filled with metals."

"Stand ready," Zimp said, "and follow me." She looked around for Arren, then closed her eyes for a moment to regain her own strength. She had to do this herself or she would let Oro down. Arren couldn't help her stand strong. He could only offer her a way to be weak. Regardless of that, she noticed Arren and Felter pass through the wall of crow clan to her right. Dail came through on her left. Storret and Crepp followed her. Breel and Therin were at her side. "Let's go," Zimp said.

"Not far up this path," Crepp told her.

About two hundred yards farther and Zimp, Breel, and Therin stopped. The others caught up.

A large, heavy-built older man held tight to long-poles attached to the cart Crepp had mentioned. Flanking him were two men, both rather thin and small, but wearing breastplates with the Flande Emblem of a blue, three-leafed clover. Two horizontal red lines were crudely painted beneath the clover.

What were Flandeans doing this deep into the Brendern Forest? Zimp stepped forward.

The big man set down the long-poles. Off the back of the cart two little boys hit the ground and ran around to see what was happening. "Hold it, boys," the man on the left said.

Around the left rear of the cart stepped two other men in breastplates and two women, one of which bore the Flande breastplate as well. The one wearing armor reached for the hands of the little boys, but only one relinquished and held to her. The other boy reached for the sword hand of one of the men, who seemed likely to be the boy's father.

Zimp noticed that the father took the boy's hand and she relaxed somewhat.

From the right rear of the cart walked another man in a breastplate and a woman, obviously pregnant.

"My lady," the big man said. He bowed slightly and motioned behind him to the others. "We are traveling peacefully."

"Then why the armor?" Arren said. Zimp turned toward him and set her jaw.

The big man looked from one to the other questioning who he should speak with. Arren's lips flattened and his eyes hardened, but he backed up two steps to allow Zimp space to address the travelers.

The big man must have understood the small conflict and held his empty hands up toward Zimp. "To answer the question, my lady. These woods have been wild with action these past months. We are with our families, and although we travel in peace, we must be cautious and ready to protect our loved ones. You would do the same, no?"

"And have you run into trouble?" Zimp said.

"Only once."

"The poor bastards," the man on the right said.

The big man turned his head slightly and the man behind him quieted.

Zimp recognized the tension in the family interactions, just as the big man must have seen it between she and Arren. A smile crossed her face for only a moment, but the Flande soldiers noticed and she saw their shoulders fall. The man on the left holding to his son shook the boy's hand.

"The name's Brull Willenstock," the big man said. "My sons," he pointed to the ones on the left first. "Raik," he said of the man holding the boy's hand, "and Cis." Both men nodded.

"And here," Brull turned, "are Galwit and Bennek." He stopped. "And the women: Raik's wife Eena and my wonderful lady, Nebbie. With child is Bennek's bride Idune." Brull smiled and said of the little boys, "The one holding tightly to his father is Ka, the other, Zip."

Zimp went to one knee, set the point of her sword into the dirt, and bowed her head. She stood and placed her sword into its scabbard, motioned for the others to do the same. One at a time, she introduced her people and then the thylacine doublesight, without mentioning Therin, as though he were only a pet.

Ka turned to his brother and said, "Zip, I told you it was a girl's name."

Raik bent down, "Shush. She said Zimp, not Zip." He looked at his other son, the younger one holding to Eena. "Zip is a warrior's name," he said, and the boy's face brightened.

Brull pointed at Therin. "Those are dangerous pets. Who might be the trainer?"

Zimp looked around. She wasn't sure it was wise to say just yet.

Idune, the pregnant woman, spoke out. "The brown-haired woman," she said.

"Do you recognize her?" Zimp said, suspicious of the woman.

"The animal touched her leg with his muzzle and she didn't flinch," Idune said.

Breel reached down and touched Therin's head.

"Very aware of your surroundings," Zimp said.

Brull slapped his breastplate. "We are of the Flandean Guard. It is our duty to be aware of our surroundings."

During the great wars when the doublesight fought along side the humans, Flande had a great army. The High Priest of Flande was a horse doublesight and hated war. He felt that the humans and doublesight should live together in peace. The Flande way of battle was to count coup rather than kill their opponent. That didn't mean that the Flande army didn't kill, only that it wasn't their first defense.

Zimp recalled Oro telling her how the army maintained

the highest standards of training, even though The High Priest asked them not to fight to the death. And here were some of them begging peace. She accepted and believed Brull. "We are camped nearby, but will leave soon."

"I don't think we'll bother you," Brull said. He backed a few steps, lifted the long-poles, and began to pull the cart.

Zimp turned and waited for them to pass, then motioned for her clan to follow.

Arren stepped close to her, "What do you think?"

Zimp slowed and the others slowed with her. She squinted and focused around the bodies of the Flande group. Flashes of etheric bodies came into view, almost like an aura, shapeless but moving. Shivers ran up her spine. She focused from one to the other, but didn't receive the same sensation from each member of the party.

"What is it?" Arren must have noticed something odd.

"I don't know. Maybe," she said.

"What?"

"They're true Flandeans," she decided. "Some are human and some doublesight."

"That's disgusting," Arren said. "How could that be? For generations it has been forbidden to mix blood."

"I don't know. But that's what's coming through."

"Zora, does she say anything?" Arren said.

Zimp turned to him, but noticed that the others were listening. "You trust the dead over me?" she said, an edge creeping into her voice.

Crepp looked as though he was going to support Arren.

Zimp stopped. "Go on, then. Go. I will try to ask her."

Arren acted more than satisfied to lead the others away, and arrogantly stepped to the front while Zimp remained where she was.

Breel and Therin held fast, like loyal subjects, to their positions near Zimp.

"Thank you for waiting with me," Zimp said.

"You are the Chieftain. The others should have stayed, as well. It may not be my place to say this, but I would watch my own people closely." Breel looked around as though wary that someone might be listening. "It is through the most common activities that alignments happen."

Zimp sat on the cool, damp ground in the center of the path. In only three deep breaths she dropped into meditation and opened her third eye. A blue haze appeared around the pure white center of her mind where she focused. She expanded her hearing inward. She opened her senses as though she had stepped into a world unlike any other, a world in which she needed to be cautious.

"Enemies and brothers. Liars and thieves," came the whisper of Zora's voice. "One man holds sanity in a tortured soul."

"Clearly," Zimp implied without using words. An unexplainable movement occurred. She thought she heard clicking sounds, a soft drumbeat. Zimp held to the pure white center.

"Who are the liars and thieves? Who are enemies and brothers?" The questions faded. Zora cawed and Zimp felt the soft wind of a wing flutter near her cheek. Again, a voice. "Watch your clan. Varied in their beliefs, unsure of their positions. Watch your traveling companions, they are varied in their beliefs."

Zimp questioned Zora one final time, her voice diminished, weak. "What of the Flandeans?"

"They are varied in their beliefs," Zora repeated.

Zimp rose back into the physical world through three more breaths, and looked up. Should she tell Breel that the crow clan was splitting their alliances? That Zora said Breel and her brothers were split? "I gained little on them. There were other things Zora said that I cannot tell you. She repeated herself. I am not so good at this yet."

"As you wish," Breel said.

"She did say one thing early on. She said that one held sanity in a tortured soul."

Breel reached down and rubbed Therin's ear. "Could that be my brother?"

"I don't know," Zimp said. "But that would make sense."

The three of them hurried down the path to enter the camp just as Arren led the Flandeans into the crow clan circle as though invited.

"Some army you have yourself," Brull noticed.

"It is no army, I am afraid," Arren said. "We are but entertainers. We travel to villages to sing and dance."

That is what they did, too, Zimp thought, sang and danced and stole what they could. She let Arren settle with the Flandeans for the moment and went to look in on Brok.

Breel followed Zimp with Therin at her side. At the rear of the wagon, she stood beside Zimp and peered through at Brok and Oro. Her brother sat with his back against Zimp's cot. His head leaned back on her pillow, which was stuffed next to his shoulder. Oro closed up the man's shirt and began cleaning a small bowl onto a piece of waste-cloth.

"What did you do?" Zimp asked.

"Only what I could. I did not have the proper leaves or roots. It is mostly just pressure and something to sooth the pain."

"I should have told you that Zora whispered that I should know how to stop the bleeding."

Oro continued to clean the bowl. A small white candle flickered. Oro bent to blow it out, then changed her mind. "We'll just leave this for a while. Good energy," she said to Brok.

"I will go and get what you need," Zimp said.

Oro shook her head. "I heard that you met up with Flandean Guards. It appears that you let Arren lead once again."

"I told him to bring them here while I stayed behind and checked them for doublesight."

"And now you wish to leave and collect herbs for your wounded friend," Oro accused.

Breel placed her hand on the small of Zimp's back and rubbed it gently. Zimp let her embarrassment slide away into Breel's gentle motion. "Should I stay with the Flandeans and ignore my duty to you, ignore the wounded?" Zimp hated that she didn't know what to do.

"The entire clan is yours to protect. Can I not help your friend without you? Can I not rely on the clan to look after me?" Oro wrapped the waste in the cloth and tied a ribbon around it to close it off. "What would you want of a true leader?"

Zimp hesitated, but the answer to the question didn't come

to her. She knew that what she had done was evidently wrong in Oro's eyes, but what was right? "And he," she pointed at Brok, "is not my friend."

With that, Zimp felt Breel's hand retreat. "I didn't mean you," Zimp said, turning toward the woman.

"We must disgust you. Our ways and our beast image." Breel stared into Zimp's eyes and would not turn away.

Zimp held her breath. Her shoulders crushed against the muscles in her neck and her head ached. "I am sorry," she said before she walked away.

13

Lankor followed the flashing light from a small bug, curious what it might be. In a clearing, there were many more flashes of the same light, many more of the insects. Amazed at the sight, he sat amidst them with his sword across his lap. He couldn't help smiling as he watched them rise and fall, their tiny moonlights pulsing. One landed on his leg. Its light stayed out. Lankor bent close and in the dimness of the real moon's light saw two orange stripes, one on each wing from its head to its rear. The bug opened its wings and lifted into the air. The light opened and closed in an easy rhythm.

He rose to his feet. What magic was this before him? What God made such kind and pleasant insects? They did not bite or sting, but danced through the air creating a lamp to light their own way. A breeze wound through the clearing and pushed Lankor's cloak behind him into a soft flutter of sound and motion. He turned and watched the insects as they created a spell around him. His breath matched the easy rhythm of light until he wondered which way he had entered the clearing. Had the bugs truly placed a spell on him? Suddenly he felt sure that he had been led away purposefully by some witch or warlock of the night. That the insects would soon turn into large stinging bees, or heavily armed assassins.

Lankor turned in each direction, searching for something familiar. The magic place had obliterated the real world and taken him away. His family. What of them? He must find his way out of the clearing and back to his camp.

Lankor swung his sword as if to wipe out the bugs, but appeared to miss them. He scurried into the dark woods away from the clearing, far away, before stopping. His heavy breathing made it difficult to listen closely. Had he been followed? He held his sword ready. Forcing himself to take shallow breaths, he heard a twig snap at his right. His hand became sweaty and beads of moisture appeared across his brow. The thick air entered his lungs slowly. Oxygen-starved, Lankor took a long breath to fill his lungs to full capacity. His eyes darted from side to side, searching the darkness. His ears focused on the possibility of a footfall.

From behind, something large and hairy and black pushed him over. He rolled to his back, bringing his sword up in a great slash through the air, slicing a branch from a nearby sapling. It fell, the leaves brushing his arm and face as though alive. His eyes widened. He pushed along the ground with his feet to get away from the form that shoved him over. His eyes focused on two large black bears. Both stepped closer as Lankor tried to scuffle to his feet. As he gained balance and got to one knee, he pulled his sword in front of him and slid it back and forth in the air. He turned it as he moved from side to side, pointing it at one, then the other bear.

One of the bears stamped forward with a little hop as if in play, while the other one dropped and rolled into the darkness.

His legs trembling, Lankor rose to his feet, the sword still moving, but his ears perked and listening.

From the space where the black bear entered the woods stepped a handsome young dark-skinned man. He began to laugh and said, "Put down the sword, my friend."

The other black bear slipped behind the first to block him from full view. He made no sound as he shifted his image. They looked to be brothers. Twins, perhaps.

Lankor maintained his ready position. "You are wizards. You cannot trick me."

The brothers looked at one another and laughed. "Wizards?" The one on the right said, "Wouldn't that be fun?" The other one laughed and patted the first brother's shoulder. "Would it be that different?"

"Who are you? What do you want from me?" Lankor said.

The brothers calmed and simultaneously examined Lankor from where they stood. Their eyes appeared bright as though they could see in the dark, even in human form. The first one to shift said, "You called us to you. You entered dreamtime and opened yourself. When you became scared, you called for help."

The other brother said, "And here we are." He spread his arms.

"I didn't call for help," Lankor assured them.

The first to shift lifted a hand into the air, palm out as though he was indicating that he had no weapons. "My name is Mammadoon. My bother," he pointed, and his brother said, "Mammadeen." Then they both laughed. Mammadoon said, "We are dreamtime followers. And you most assuredly did call for help."

"What is a dreamtime follower and why would I call you? How would I?"

"I shouldn't be surprised that you don't know," said Mammadoon.

"We spend much of our time in dream. Dream is but a space between each realm. The immediately departed often go there to speak to the living," Mammadeen said.

"If you wish to talk with the dead," Mammadoon said.

"You were there, playing with the fireflies," Mammadeen said.

"Fireflies? That's what they're called? They were not your sentries?"

The brothers laughed. "Our sentries. We need no sentries."

Lankor began to understand. "I felt lost."

"You are still lost, my brother doublesight," Mammadoon said very seriously.

Lankor stared at him.

"Put down your sword. It is beginning to make this less fun," Mammadeen said.

Lankor lowered his sword. "Did you come to help?" he said

suspiciously.

"We did," Mammadoon said.

Lankor cocked his head. "Do you know what my beast image is?"

"That is a curious question, my friend." Mammadoon stepped forward until he apparently noticed Lankor's body tense. "You are a curious stranger to this place that was left behind. Where do you come from, and who are you?"

"Lankor is my name. I come from The Lost."

The two doublesight bears laughed for a long while, then stopped. "You do not look as though you could last a month in The Lost," Mammadoon said. "Not that I've ever been there, but I've heard it is a wasteland, an empty place left barren and cold after the Sclan wars."

"It has changed."

"Well, it must have." Mammadoon took another step toward Lankor. "To answer your other question, we do not know what beast image you are. Neither your aura nor your etheric body shifted while you were dreaming. We saw in them that you were not entirely human. That is easy to do in dreamtime. But unless you shift while you are there," he shrugged his shoulders, "we wouldn't know."

"I shall remember that when I dream."

"Enough talk," Mammadeen said. "You probably wish to get back to your family." He led the way back through the clearing. His brother stepped up and closed in next to him.

Lankor, so he didn't get left behind, followed.

Twenty feet outside the clearing a few fireflies still blinked. Lankor kept his distance to the brothers.

"Your mistrust of us is exhausting, brother Lankor. We truly mean you no harm and you were never in any harm with those insects, for sure. Fireflies are the blessed sparks that flew from the fingers of the Gods while they were creating the beasts of The Great Land. We like to think they are the closest to our own creation since we have a light into multiple worlds," Mammadoon said. He stood smiling at Lankor. "Down there, about fifty steps." Mammadoon dropped to the ground behind a bush and leaped out as a black bear. Mammadeen dropped behind his brother and shifted as well. They both made a honk-like barking sound toward Lankor, then ran off into the woods. Lankor hurried through the woods where they had indicated for him to go, and practically rushed into the camp in his haste. He stopped short, but noticed something wasn't quite right. Fear struck him for the second time that evening.

"Were you lost?" Rend said.

Lankor turned to him. "I ran into some doublesight. Bears."

"I heard nothing."

"Back there," Lankor pointed into the darkness. "They were strange. They said something about dreamtime."

Rend placed a hand on the back of Lankor's neck. "Bears, eh? Dreamtime... Well, if you truly met with bear doublesight, I suppose dreamtime is as good a place as any."

"No, you don't understand. I was staring at these blinking bugs and getting caught in their magical ways. They were like embers of a fire floating through the air. I slipped into a dream for only a moment, then ran away. The bears said I called them. They led me back here." Lankor felt his father's grip tighten. "Were they intuitives?"

"There are many varieties of intuitive doublesight. Bears live much of their lives in a space between worlds. They call it dreamtime. I don't know much about bears, but I've heard that they can change your dreams while they are in there. I've heard that they can play with your soul." Rend pulled his son closer to the fire. "I'm not so sure I trust having bears this close to our camp. Mianna I know is strong enough to hold onto her own dreams and not let them be manipulated."

"But Nayman," Lankor said, "and me?"

"Sit by the fire, son. Recall your trip, our destination. You'll be fine. It sounds as though they were being helpful. Let us rise early and move on."

14

After the Flandeans passed through camp, Zimp approached Arren. "Did you learn where they are going? They weren't heading toward Brok and Breel's cabin, were they? Suspicions might rise quickly if that were to happen."

Arren pointed to where the Flandeans had exited the camp. "They went northwest. They're Flandean Guard, so it doesn't matter what they say. Even that direction is most likely a false lead."

"Did you learn anything from them that might be reliable?" she asked.

He gazed at her out the corner of his eyes. "I got the sense that they have not been together during their entire trip. It's like they came together recently to follow some mission together. One of them wore a wristband that looked like it was made in City Raldern. That's quite a bit south."

"What gave you the sense?"

"I am crow clan too, young Zimp. I trust my feelings, as dark as they might seem to you." Arren lifted the wristband from the pouch he carried on his belt. He turned it in front of Zimp. "Care to hold it for a moment?"

Against her feelings toward Arren, Zimp had to laugh. "You stole it?"

Arren softened too. "What else would I do? I'm surprised that you didn't steal it. Or that ulexite ring the pregnant one wore."

"I didn't want them coming back or following us." She pulled the wristband from Arren's fingers. "Something you didn't think of." Zimp closed her eyes, but her pulse rushed too full and with too much power for her to get any image from the piece. "Let's see what Oro gets."

Arren snapped it back from her. "We'll go together. How is the heart-eater doing, anyway?"

"He's fine. Let's be careful with our language though. They are in our care for now."

"For now," Arren agreed.

At the wagon, Arren presented the wristband to Oro. Brok rested against Zimp's bed.

"You said they were from Flande? Guardsmen?" Oro said.

"That's what they claimed," Arren said.

Oro held the wristband and closed her eyes for only a moment. "I don't like the feel of this. Who wore it?"

"The man with the two sons. I forget his name," Arren said.

Oro waved him off. "Get the others. We need to know the man's name." Once Arren was out of view, Oro leaned toward Zimp. "You must begin to take charge. We don't want the Flandean Guard to come looking for this thing. And if they do return, I wouldn't want them looking to Arren for answers."

"Yes, Grandmother." Zimp leaned against the wagon. She lowered her eyes.

The old woman ignored Zimp's reaction, and closed her eyes again. She cupped the wristband in both hands. "I see many deaths, many people killed." She took a breath. "And many lives saved." Oro opened her eyes and studied the wristband. "Fairly new. From City Raldern. A lot has happened since this wristband was purchased. Many miles have been traversed."

"Should we be concerned they might return?" Zimp asked.

"I don't know. Unless this was stolen from the body of a dead man, the bearer of this wristband is a powerful warrior," Oro said.

"That's hard to believe. Whatever his name, the man was small in build, not the powerful warrior type," Zimp said.

In a groggy voice, Brok said, "Never underestimate a man

or woman's power. Passion and energy have more to do with battle than raw strength."

Oro smiled. "Smart man. You should listen to him," she said to Zimp.

"Learned it from my father. His strength grew like magic when he needed it. An amazing thing to witness," Brok said.

"And he is a part of you now, young Brok. You must never forget that. Fremlin is a great man, even now."

Zimp was struck by the kindness Oro extended to Brok. She obviously knew of the details of the ceremony, and was comfortable with them. Perhaps the mixture of cultures among the doublesight at the council had much to do with Oro's knowledge of the world and herself. Nothing seemed to bother her. That is, except Zimp's reluctance to lead.

"Raik," Arren said, jogging toward the wagon. "The man's name was Raik. Breel remembered. And I have to say that she's rather creepy."

"That's my sister," Brok said.

"Sorry. There's just something about her," Arren said.

"I like her," Zimp said.

"Is this necessary conversation?" Oro demanded. "Let us leave. The ceremony is complete and we need to reach the council grounds by nightfall." She looked at Zimp and Arren. "Go!"

Noot drove Oro and Zimp's wagon. Brok lay across Zimp's bed and Breel sat next to Zimp on the floor. The thylacine doublesight had her arm on the bed near her brother's leg, her head resting on her arm, her body turned away from Zimp. She slept much of the day in that awkward position.

Zimp let her head fall back against Brok only once. She felt the man's solid arm under the back of her head and jerked upright. There was something about the energy that came from Brok that annoyed her. Perhaps it was the same energy Brok spoke about when he talked about Fremlin. Magical. She knew that magic came in many forms.

Zimp could still see the ceremony in detail in her mind. She pushed the images aside and tried to imagine what the council grounds would be like. She had never been there, but had heard stories from Oro for years. Even when Zimp's mother and father were alive, Oro would sit and tell Zimp and Zora stories about the doublesight.

The road through the Brendern Forest thinned out in places, but there was always space for the wagons to pass. Branches laden with leaves or needles scratched across the canvas. Noot kissed and clicked to the horses, and used the whip only when needed. The traveling was smoother in the woods than it had been through the plains. The air temperature dipped colder, though, and Zimp missed the warm sun. She suspected that the thylacines enjoyed the cool air of the forest since that was their home.

She lifted up and could see that Therin pranced behind the wagon like an obedient dog. She had to remember that if they passed anyone on the road, to have him hide from view. Having a thylacine pet would appear strange to anyone. She should have been more sensitive to that when she went out to meet with the Flandeans. She glanced over at Oro, eyes wide, staring into the dim light passing through the canvas cover. Zimp wondered what Oro thought about. "Teach me," she whispered to Oro, to the air inside the wagon, to Zora, or any entity who might be listening at the time.

Oro turned her head to peer directly into Zimp's eyes. "What angers me is that you already know and will not listen."

"But I don't know anything. I seldom listened when Zora attended training."

"Zora attended nothing you did not attend. She asked about spells. She asked how to make certain candles," Oro said.

"Candles are simple to make."

"For you." Oro breathed deeply and reached out to take Zimp's hand. "Tell me, child, what plant could I use to have stopped Brok's bleeding sooner?"

"I don't..."

"You know. Now tell me. What is the first stalk or leaf you saw in your mind, even as I spoke the words? Before the words left my mouth...or could you feel the root of the plant? Could you smell its fragrance? What?"

"Okay, okay. Sherpurse. That's what we were taught."

Oro shook Zimp's hand. "What did you see?"

Zimp teared up. She squeezed Oro's hand. Her breathing became shallow. "To the Gods with you," she said. "I felt the spiky stems of horsetail."

Oro smiled. She made a smacking sound with her lips. "Horsetail," she affirmed.

"Horsetail is poisonous," Zimp said.

"Not in my hands."

"But in mine," Zimp said.

"I don't believe that." Oro let go of Zimp and closed her eyes to rest.

The wagons made significant progress. The horses pulled as though they were heading to a stable for feed. They were as determined as the clan to end the trip. About a mile from the council grounds, the caravan stopped. Noot woke Oro and helped her to the front of the wagon to sit next to him. The wagons were rearranged so that Oro entered the doublesight council grounds first. She forced Zimp to sit next to her as the caravan began to move again. At a Y in the road, a thinner path jutted to the left toward the center of Brendern Forest. Oro motioned for Noot to take that path. She turned to Zimp and said, "You must meet The Few with me."

Zimp expected a natural oasis of openness, but found a series of clearings recently excavated for the purposes of setting smaller camps. Tents had been set up intermittently along the roadway as though they were guards leading into a palace, but no palace lay ahead. She caught a glimpse of Therin running deeper into the woods around the clearings as though he knew not to be seen.

A tall, thin man stepped into the middle of the road and raised a hand. His arms and legs appeared out of proportion to his torso. A great long sword hung from his waist, the length of which would rival any Zimp had ever seen. Upon seeing Oro, he bowed. Zimp noticed a long black pony tail swing over his shoulder. He approached the wagon with knees bent. "Oronice, welcome. It is good to see you again."

Oro patted Zimp's leg. "Wallenstat, meet my granddaughter, Zimp of Lissland."

The man bowed to Zimp. "You are very beautiful, Zimp of Lissland. Whatever you may want, just ask." He rose to full height and reached out to her.

Zimp began to reach out to him in return, but Oro stopped her.

The man let his hand extend to its full length and then bend at the elbow until his fingers touched his breast where his heart would lie. Upon completion of his salute, the man explained to Noot how to arrive at the locations set aside for the clan's campsites. The clearings were close, but separated by trees. Oro's site, Noot was told, would be the closest to the center of camp.

"I didn't realize," Zimp said.

"Just the initial greetings. The formalities will relax as we are here longer," Oro said.

"You are that important to the council?" Zimp urged.

A tiny smile emerged from Oro's lips. Her chin lifted slightly. Zimp sensed pride from her grandmother.

As the clan separated, parked their wagons, and began to set their individual camps, Oro held onto Zimp's arm and led her down a recently worn path.

At a great parting of trees, she stopped and stared up. "To the holy order of Gods," Zimp said.

Canvas stretched from tree to tree to tree, lifted and held by ropes draped from a height of twenty-five or thirty feet to the ground. She could not see the full width or length of the tent from where she stood, but judging from what she could see, the tent stretched over a distance of two hundred yards or more.

The evening had darkened but the moon shed light across the canvas, causing it to emit a dim glow that filled the space with more light than what was available had the tent not been there.

Oro pulled Zimp's attention to the right of the council tent. They walked into the woods to where a smaller cabin stood tucked between several great old growth aspen.

Two young boys guarded the cabin. One sat on either side of the door. They stood simultaneously as Oro and Zimp approached. "The Few will not take visitors until the morning," one said. He had rehearsed his small speech and delivered it with an even tone.

"Very well," Oro said and she began to turn away.

Zimp leaned into her and said, "Tell them who you are."

"If The Few are taking no visitors then they are taking no visitors," Oro said as though it was a simple matter. "Come, we will celebrate our arrival. The night is just settling upon us."

Zimp helped Oro back to camp. People wandered around on the paths and in clearings along the way. Tents, lean-tos, and sometimes blankets alone signified a family's campsite. Zimp wondered what animal image each person could shift into. The sense of having all these doublesight in one place excited and terrified her. Years had gone by, but the doublesight history told of great battles between clans. To have them all here and in one place felt wrong in many ways. "Grandmother," Zimp whispered, "how am I to learn when to assert my power and when not to? Like back there, at the cabin?" she asked.

"Back there?" Oro said. "That was respect. The Few were not exhibiting power, but were requesting time alone. Had I insisted, I would have been viewed as arrogant, as though my power overruled their request for peace and quiet."

The people Zimp and Oro met on the path didn't appear to know who Oro was, which meant that they were family members and not part of the council. Zimp slowed at one point on the return walk and tried to envision the auras of a few people sitting together building a small fire.

Oro poked her in the side with an elbow. "That would be rude here and at this moment," she said. "Allow these people their secrets for now. All will be revealed soon enough."

Noot had done a great job of setting camp for Oro and Zimp. Brok leaned over a small fire he must have built, and Breel stood over him. Zimp noticed the strength in Breel's arms as she had removed her shirt and wore only what appeared to be a thylacine pelt vest like the one her brother wore. Her sword stretched down along her thin leg. Something about her posture, her stance, made Zimp respect her.

"Brok, my young friend, how are you feeling?" Oro reached for him. Brok rose to his feet and extended his hand to her. She leaned in close and hugged him.

Zimp was shocked to see Oro so close to the thylacine, but the look on Brok's face was even more shocked and, at the moment, amusing. Oro appeared to have caught him off-guard.

15

Three days wandering the camp, eating some meals inside the enormous council tent, and attempting to act civil with all the other doublesight proceeded to get on Zimp's nerves. "I have an urge to know what image each holds. I've already begun to guess, and am sure that I'm right much of the time. That family to the east of where The Few have their cabin, for example. Hawks."

"And what gives you that idea?" Breel asked, sitting cross-legged on the ground near Zimp. Therin had reentered camp that first night and slept much of each day away. His head, at the moment, lay across Breel's lap like a tamed animal. Yet, if anyone came near, Therin's body stiffened with awareness and great globs of drool would begin to slip from his open mouth.

"They wear cloaks, first of all. Doublesight with flying images tend to wear cloaks. I believe it is the fluttering sound that makes us comfortable. Then there is the way their eyes appear to be always looking into the distance. It's as though we can see better from several hundred feet than from up close." Zimp took the twig she twirled between her fingers and threw it into the fire. Smoke rose in a stream from the twig, then it snapped in two and spit tiny sparks toward her. "A layer of smoke, a spitting of fire," she said.

"What does that mean?" Breel asked.

"Probably nothing. Oro has been pounding things into

me since we've arrived. I have to notice everything out of the ordinary and speak instantly of what it might mean."

"Why are smoke and sparks from a stick you threw into the fire not ordinary?" Breel said.

"The twig should have just caught fire slowly and burned. This one didn't do that."

"What does this teach you?"

Zimp looked around the camp. "I'm not sure," she said. They both laughed.

Noot ran into the camp and motioned for Zimp. "Come with me. You won't believe it."

Zimp jumped up, Breel at her side. Therin stood, but yawned as though not fully awake. "What is it?" she said while following Noot. To Breel she said, "Finally, something is going on."

Noot led them through the woods and around a few turns. The arms of trees reached for Zimp's cloak and pulled at its tattered edges. Noot headed toward the entrance to the council grounds. When he stopped suddenly, Zimp bumped into him. Breel stopped dead in her tracks and, like a dancer, shifted her weight onto her toes and stepped smoothly around Noot to his other side.

The Flandeans dragged their cart up the path. Wallenstat followed, talking with Raik, the father of Zip and Ka, and the man Arren stole the wristband from. Brull threw down the long-poles and advanced in great strides. "Idune was right all along. You were doublesight." He stopped in front of Zimp and looked back and forth from her to Noot and to Breel. "Like that thylacine vest," he said to Breel. He looked into Zimp's eyes. "But you're no thylacine."

"You don't know that she is," Zimp said, motioning toward Breel.

Brull yelled over his left shoulder. "Bennek, bring your bride here."

Bennek and Idune walked forward and stood beside Brull. Nebbie came around the other side of the cart and stepped next to Brull to take his hand. In a sudden strike, she reached with her head and kissed Brull quickly on the cheek.

Zimp got shivers up her spine at the motion.

Idune said, "Yes."

"What's your sense about these three?" Brull said.

Idune lifted a thin arm and stretched a long finger toward Zimp, then Noot, then Breel saying, "Crow, crow, thylacine."

Brull shrugged his shoulders. "There you go."

"An intuitive," Zimp said.

Bennek laughed and stroked Idune's arm gently. "She is nearing birth," he said as though that was answer enough.

Brull reached out and hugged Zimp before she could react. His arms wrapped around her as he pulled her tight against him. He let go and did the same to Noot. With Breel, he hesitated, then placed his hand at her head and let it slide down along her hair. His fingers stroked a few strands clear to their ends below her shoulder. He backed and turned to retrieve the cart.

"There is something terribly strange about these people," Zimp said.

"What do you notice?" Breel tested as though she were Oro.

Zimp smiled at her. "Seven trees behind them. The wind bends each in a different direction. They are each a different type of tree."

"That is strange, to be sure," Breel said. "Perhaps they do not hold the same image."

"Exactly," Zimp said.

"That's not normal," Noot said.

Breel glared at him. "Thylacines traveling with crows. And that's normal?"

"But they are one family," Noot said.

"I knew what you meant." Breel reached for Noot's arm and walked into the woods holding it. "That wouldn't be so bad, a mixed family, would it?" she teased.

Noot pulled his arm loose. "You're not funny." He ran on ahead. "I'll inform the others."

Zimp laughed as Noot ran by. "I'd like to see you do that with Arren."

"He wouldn't run off, I'm afraid. I'm the one who would feel slimy. He brushed against me the other day, on purpose, attempting to feel how solid my stance was."

"How do you know that?" Zimp said.

"In thylacine image, we play like that. Pushing and shoving, trying to mow one another over. It's fun." She got quiet for a moment. "It was fun."

Zimp slowed and turned toward Breel. "I'm sorry about your family. I've never said it out loud, but I've been sorry."

"You lost a sister," Breel said. She began to walk again, shrugged her shoulders as though death suddenly made sense. "What happened to your parents?"

"When I was young, we were in Crell at Westlake on a southern trip. Crell at Westlake is a beautiful city if you haven't been there. I still remember the sparkling beaches, the miles of shells and colored stones. It was magic. We danced and played music nearly every night and the people loved us. But they didn't know we were stealing from them. We could have taken anything. And we did. But there is only so much time we can spend in any one city before we are noticed, before someone finds out. We stayed too long. Oro had made the warning known and gathered up Zora and me. My mother moved on with us, but a half-day's travel south, we got word that a battle had broken out and she flew back for my father. We waited three days before moving on."

"The townspeople never came after you?"

"Oro said that Crell hated and feared the doublesight. All that had to happen was for several of our clan to shift image and the people of Crell would have fought in fear."

"Fear makes a warrior a difficult opponent," Breel said. "Do you miss them? Did you blame Oro?"

Zimp laughed. "Oro channeled our mother so well that it was like she was there with us for years. She channeled our father, too, but he moved on to another realm, and then another, until Oro lost track of him. Our mother eventually followed and we slowly became used to having only Oro."

"But you are an intuitive," Breel said. "Couldn't you channel your own mother?"

"I did for a while. I suppose I resented her, too. For returning to Crell and getting killed. Zora maintained the link much longer than I did, even though my connection had been stronger at the beginning. I stepped away from contact."

"Zora was an intuitive, too?"

"All crow image doublesight have an intuitive side. In crow image especially, we can see into at least two realms, if we wish. As human, there are a wide variety of levels of intuition stemming from a sense about something to full channeling like what Oro is capable of."

"She's a wizard, isn't she?" Breel said. "I've seen her behind the wagon mixing things, looking into a cup filled halfway with tea leaves. She had a small sack last evening and dumped it onto the ground. There were leaves, buds, sticks, stones, shells. She stood over them a long time moving her lips. She read them."

The two of them were almost back at camp. "She's been teaching me, too. Some of it is impossible to learn. Oro sees so much more than I do. But I'm learning. I hear Zora more that ever, now. I've relearned how to listen. There is a sort-of trick to it."

In the clearing, Oro sat next to a cold fire pit. "Where have you been?"

"Those Flandeans are doublesight," Zimp said. "But there's something strange about them."

"Strange?"

Breel nudged Zimp, "Tell her what you noticed."

"What did you see?" Oro said.

"Seven trees behind them. The wind bent each in a different direction. They are each a different type of tree," Zimp repeated.

"Flandeans are known for their mixing," Oro said. "Perhaps only seven are doublesight. How many are there?"

"Ten," Zimp said.

"Three humans. Don't tell me one is Brull Willenstock." Oro pushed her hands to her knees and stood.

"He's a council member?" Zimp said.

"It's difficult to say for sure. Once a year the council meets. He comes to the council once every several years. Not that I blame him. He must feel terribly uncomfortable." Oro reached out and gripped Zimp's forearm with one hand and Breel's forearm with the other. "He's human, you know. Human only. There is a hunger in him to be a doublesight. That is the way of many people from Flande."

"He hugged me," Zimp said.

"Rude. That's him." Oro looked away as though thinking back. "He is a fake. He tries too hard to be part of the doublesight. We need humans to understand us. There could be many Flandeans who would be more worthy to represent the humans. I never understood why they would pick Brull."

"So they are mixed," Breel said.

"Oh, you don't know the half of it," Oro said.

16

Brok scratched his shoulder where the wound had been. Little was left of it but the itching caused by the healing of the final layer of skin. He thought of the carcasses left behind. Nothing had been buried. He hoped that thylacines fed off his family, nourishing his own kind in some small way. He had taken to sleeping under one of the wagons and often woke up, like this morning, with Therin and Breel by his side. He rolled from under the wagon. This time it was Arren's wagon, which nestled between two cedars nearest the edge of the council grounds.

"Slept in?" Arren sat with his back against a tree several feet away.

"I could have slept longer."

"I don't doubt it. You were all up last night, roaming the forest out there." He motioned beyond the camp. "What do you do all night? Kill?"

Brok bent at the waist and stretched his arms to the ground until his fingers brushed the dead leaves and needles that lay at his feet. When he returned to an upright position, he cracked his neck by bending his ear to his shoulder on one side, then to the other. "Kill," he said. "Not often. Only when we're attacked by another animal. Of course you'd like to think that I kill on instinct, without regard for the life I take. Like an animal. Perhaps you're hoping that I performed a kill for you?"

"You're not funny, little man. I should have known you couldn't do it."

Brok sauntered over to Arren and looked down at him. "Of all people, you should know what it's like to be in beast image. I don't know about you, but we play. We relish in the senses of the beast. Sometimes, when I'm human again, my memory allows me to catch a scent that illuminates within me. A scent with color and texture, a trace of my beast image memory." He bent down to Arren's level. "I couldn't agree to anything for you that evening. When I shifted, I smelled your fear. It stunk of weakness. I could never do the dirty work for a weak person. That would only make me weaker than you."

Arren turned his head away. "What you did, your ceremony, was disgusting. You could do that. You could eat the heart from your own parents." He wrinkled his face.

"You could ask a stranger to kill for you, so that you can falsely step into a role you are not yet able to perform. Being in front of the line of wagons does not make you the leader."

"You'd align with her?"

Brok laughed and rose so that he could look down at Arren. The man tensed as though he thought Brok was about to strike him. "I align with no one unless I have chosen to. I am simply grateful for the hospitality your people have shown me. It must be difficult having such a predator inside your own camp. I notice most of you step aside when we come around. Some place a hand over the hilt of a sword or knife when Therin's near. You think we don't notice?"

"Do you blame us?"

"My father once said that fear alone can make someone kill. He meant fear of any kind. Fear in the face of death, fear of not being heard, fear of losing something precious. For you, it is fear of your true self. By controlling others, you don't have to face who you are."

"A Godless philosopher." Arren spit on the ground next to him.

"Fremlin also said that all doublesight had one thing in common." Brok rotated on the balls of his feet.

"What thing is that?" Arren said.

Brok walked into the woods toward the council tent. He touched the bark of some of the trees as he passed them, felt the deep gouges of one and the smooth surface of another. The bark of the aspen crumbled under his fingers. He tried to take a different path toward the council center each time he walked. On this day he circumvented the larger area of the camp and entered from due north. He wandered near small open places, observing other doublesight as he slipped past. Each day the entire camp waited. One family had yet to arrive. On his walk he was reminded of his own family, how they would take long walks through the woods, shift into their beast images, and play in a fairyland of intense odors and sounds no human could sense. Why had the humans not tried to attack the council grounds? They must have known of the meeting.

A crow cawed deep in the woods and startled Brok. He instantly grabbed his sword handle and crouched ready to spring into action. He listened and heard breathing and running getting closer, and realized it was Therin tracking him down. His brother came out of the woods and over to him. Brok bent down and stroked the thylacine's head and patted its body.

"I am sorry. I should have waited before I sent a warning," Storret said as he stepped from behind a tree.

"Your job is to guard the camp," Brok said.

Storret bent down and stroked Therin behind the ear, rubbing it gently. Therin leaned into the scout's hand.

"You're not afraid of him?"

"Should I be? You forget I was witness to your ceremony. How could anyone not be compassionate after that?"

"It didn't sicken you like it did some of the others?" Brok found his own curiosity as interesting as Storret's ease around Therin.

"Sure it did. That was a bit emotional to watch. But a sacred ceremony takes on a unique level of awe as it is performed. It takes much more time and focus for me to draw from the depths of my intuitive nature. I go there much easier while in crow image, but I could sense the compassion, the sadness." Storret lowered his head and shook it. "You've never watched our dances. You've not been witness to our unique ways yet.

Wait until you are exposed to us, or to the bear doublesight, hawk doublesight, or even horse doublesight. I've been all over The Great Land and have learned that every sacred ceremony is based on some deeply felt emotion, often tied to a belief." Storret patted Brok's shoulder. "Here's a tip for life: never try to change a belief that someone else has. Beliefs are the deepest elements of a person and often chart their entire lives. You can only change your own beliefs."

"I'll remember that."

"Mind if I walk with you? You are going for something to eat, are you not?" Storret led the way.

"You don't have to go back to guard duty?"

"There are others. Come on, we'll talk."

Brok spent the morning with Storret. At the council tent, other doublesight stepped back to give them room as long as Therin stood at his brother's heels. Brok and Storret had fun with it for a while, edging near a table of fruit or eggs, and giving each other the eye as other doublesight stepped out of the way. Finally, Brok asked Therin to lie down near the edge of the tent and wait for them. Brok then brought back the cooked leg of a boar to Therin, who ate the meat and then ground into the bone all the while Brok and Storret talked.

A strained discussion broke out at the table just as Brok and Storret sat down near Therin.

"Everyone's on edge. This waiting is not helping us get along with one another," Storret said.

"One family, right?" A man with large brown eyes said. "Why can't we just have this big meeting without them? What if they aren't coming?"

"Oh, they'll be here late tonight. I heard it from one of the hawk doublesight," a woman said.

"Who are the last family? How many are there?" Brok said.

"What are they, you mean. I don't know," the man asked.

"They must be important," Brok said.

"We're all important," Storret said.

"You've been to these meetings before?" another man said.

"Not at all. Unfortunately." Storret stared into Brok's face. "I love being here though. After you've seen what I've seen, something changes inside you. You want to see more, know more. A curiosity sets in. I've envied Oro's coming here. I can't wait to see what her real function is. You don't get called The Gem of the Forest for nothing." He smiled as a memory appeared to cross through his mind. "I've escorted Oronice several times, only to wait well outside the campgrounds until she was through. I heard a lot of chanting and drumming, a lot of talking, but never enough to satisfy my curiosity. But look, now we're here, and we're a part of it." Storret stuffed a piece of apple into his mouth. He turned to Brok. "Tell me about your father. I've only heard of him. What was he really like? Was he difficult to live with?"

"He was fun. He loved life and people, everyone and everything, it didn't matter. He was the greatest fighter and warrior around at one time, but he never wanted to harm anything."

"And you are the same," Storret said.

"I'm not the same. All I want is to kill the men who attacked us. I only came here because I thought that my father would have wished it. These council meetings were of the highest importance to him and I never truly knew why. After tonight, after the council meetings end in whatever time that takes, I'm going after those men, and I'm going to kill them."

"You can't avenge a death," Storret said. "Death is but a shifting of another kind. There is no such thing as true death."

"Your belief, not mine."

"Many of us can talk with the dead. So, they can't be dead. They're in the next realm," Storret said.

Brok wiped his mouth with his hand. "So I've been told. But thylacines can't talk with our dead. I've never known a thylacine intuitive. Perhaps it's all in your heads. You just think you speak to the dead."

Storret shook his head. "Sorry. It's true. They go into the next realm."

Brok and Storret talked all through the morning before Brok strolled back to camp and Storret shifted and flew back to his post. Brok decided on taking another nap to while away the day. He had been up late. He woke once, briefly, when Breel asked if he wanted lunch. He declined.

Storret woke Brok later that day. The early evening chill had settled into the area. The air smelled fresh. Seeing Storret's face, Brok asked in a partial daze, "Are they here?" He had to talk over the sound of drumming and chanting. "I'm surprised that noise didn't awake me."

"Your body is re-energizing," Storret said. "The others have not arrived yet, another hour or so. Just before sundown I'm told," Storret said.

"Then what is it?"

"Zimp is dancing. You must see this. You must witness our ceremonial dance and you will better understand us." Storret pulled at Brok's hand.

Brok lifted to his feet, Storret still holding to him. He followed the crow doublesight through the woods and into the clearing at the far side of Oro's wagon. Drumming pounded through his eardrums and he placed his hands over his ears. Breel sat in front of him and Therin lay beside her.

Zimp held her cloak in each hand and lifted it into the air and around her head. She danced what appeared to be particular steps, some slow and some quick, but each precise and practiced.

Brok heared the cloak flutter as it twisted through the air. Was the sound that loud or was it so distinct that it pierced through the drumbeat? The tattered edges of the red cloak flowed on the air, a series of tails to the distinct shape of the cloth itself. Deep within the sound of the drum, the low chanting, and the flutter of Zimp's cloak was an additional sound, a jingling of bells. Smoke from the fire intensified the sound with the thick odor of sage. Brok saw that Oro sat near the fire and threw something into it that made it spit and spark. Zimp's movements shifted and peaked with the licking tongues of the fire. She and the flames were in a synchronous motion, dancing and snapping, the cloak and the fire, whipping the air.

Although it would not be dark for hours, the dense forest held back the full sunlight. Shadows from the fire blistered the ground and leapt against the trees. More of the crow clan arrived and encircled Zimp as she danced.

Brok stood mesmerized, staring at the exotic movements, letting everything around Zimp and her cloak and the fire go blank. Focused and hypnotized by the motion, the shifting body, the rolling fire. He saw a blackness enter the dance that he couldn't explain. It drew him in even deeper. A wing, but that was impossible because just as he saw the wing he also saw both of Zimp's hands. The curve of a feather, the sharp point of a beak drew his attention back into the movement. There was something dancing with her, a crow.

He saw it clearly now. It flew into her cloak, then over her head. The crow clucked and cawed. Zimp chanted and sang. The glistening white of her tears blistered the air. The black soul of the crow's eyes looked through Brok and he blinked and lost the image for a moment. Zimp danced lower toward the ground, scooted around the fire, leaped into the air. Zora followed, flying into the cloak and between Zimp's legs.

The chanting became louder and Brok noticed that it came from all around him. The drumming speeded, the dance became a blur, the feathers of the crow whisked the air, the body of the crow lifted above Zimp until she leaped higher into the sky than she could humanly have done. She became as light as a bird. Her cloak, thrown above her, flew in slow motion over the head of her sister…her dead sister.

Brok feared he was seeing an illusion, but Zora was there, her wings held open as her black body turned below the arc of the cloak. And as the cloak fell in slow motion it spread out above them both. It lowered toward the ground, toward Zimp, as Zora tucked her wings and dived into the fire. Embers exploded into the air. The drumming ended abruptly. The clan silenced their chants. The cloak floated down to settle over Zimp's head.

Brok jumped when Storret touched his shoulder.

"You see?" Storret said.

Zimp remained under her cloak as the clan departed.

Brok stood with Storret, staring in disbelief. His heart and head felt light. "Was I placed in a trance?" he asked Storret.

Oro turned and motioned for one of them to help her. Storret and Brok came to her side, each taking an elbow. She motioned with her head for them to step away from Zimp. "There was no trance placed upon you except the one you may have accepted for yourself," she said.

"But, what I saw—"

"Was a manifestation. Zora is in another realm, her physical body is gone, but her etheric body lives on, her subtle aura lives on. You, my young man," she poked an elbow into Brok's side, "shift into a thylacine and think nothing of it because you assume that both are in this world at the same time. The ectoplasmic body of your thylacine manifests into a solid body."

"Doesn't the ectoplasmic body of Zora die with her physical form?" Brok said.

"It becomes more difficult to hold to. The other realm does not need the physical. It is not of the physical. Zora cannot project ectoplasm of any form from there to here. But Zimp..." Oro silenced for a moment. "How do I say this? She loaned Zora her ectoplasm. What she did took tremendous energy and focus. I am very proud."

Brok and Storret helped Oro to her wagon where she collected a few herbs and candles. "Just in case I need them," she said.

It was time to gather at the council tent. Oro instructed Storret to double the guard. "Make sure the new arrivals are not followed."

A fluttering occurred behind them, and Brok saw Zimp in crow image lift into the sky.

"Let us go," she said to Brok after Storret's departure.

The paths through the woods were filled with families sauntering to the council tent. Brok wished he knew what beast images some of them had. He did notice that he felt comfortable being close to some of them and uncomfortable around others.

Oro had hold of Brok's arm. Breel and Therin ran up from behind. Breel said, "You've become quite the helper."

Brok grimaced at his sister.

Oro patted Brok's hand. "Your brother is a very special person, my dear. Your teasing indicates that you have noticed something different about him."

"I have," is all Breel said.

From a distance as they neared the tent, Brok noticed Zimp at the apex of the glowing mass. She appeared surreal, a young woman wrapped in a red cloak against the chill of the oncoming evening. She perched atop the giant tent, no apparent way to reach the place where she sat. The red cloak, a lump of color from this distance, ruffled and shifted, shrunk, turned black, and sprouted wings, an intimate gesture had they been closer. Zimp flew down to the side of the tent, out of view, and stepped around it in human image to meet them.

17

"It may be dark by the time we arrive." Lankor slapped a tree trunk with an open hand in frustration.

"My fault," Nayman said. "My foot has been bothering me."

"I told you we should fly there," Lankor mumbled under his breath.

Rend stopped dead in his tracks and turned on Lankor. He stood silently in front of his son. "This trip is not about making your life easy. It is about something greater than that."

"Like what, Father? You don't know. All you know is that you were summoned and asked to bring your family, instead of making this trip alone."

"And that makes it important," Rend said.

"Not to me. I don't know The Few or the council or anything about the doublesight except what I've been taught. I've never seen anyone shift except my own family." Lankor stared as though into a mirror, only the mirror had put on years, had wrinkled across the brow and under the eyes. The mirror had a mouth that turned down into hardship, no doubt from living off the barren lands of The Lost. Lankor felt love and pity for his father at that moment.

"The Few does not take the survival of the doublesight lightly. If you paid attention to your schooling, you would know that."

"Maybe it's just a changing of the guard. Maybe one of The

Few died and they're selecting a successor," Lankor said.

Nayman stepped close to them, "That could be, but the summons said urgent."

"He knows?" Lankor said.

Rend turned away. "He is the oldest. His learning is naturally beyond yours. Now, let us move on. We must make the council this evening."

Mianna touched Lankor's shoulder. "You must be patient, young Lankor. All things will be revealed in time."

Lankor stepped away from his mother and lifted Nayman's arm over his shoulder. "Lean on me," he said, and began to forge forward through the forest.

Rend led the way, speeding his walk to accommodate Lankor and Nayman's enlivened pace.

The deeper they traveled into the forest, the less underbrush they encountered. In places, the canopy blocked most of the sunlight, not only darkening the woods, but also holding in the moisture. The scent of loam lifted into the air. The movement of small animals kept them alert. The forest became a noisy world where each sound came from something hidden under leaves, overhead, or behind a tree. Most of the sounds were unfamiliar to Lankor, so he made up animals that crawled, flew, and scurried. This kept his mind busy while he helped his brother traverse the road toward the council meeting.

Over a knoll, a small opening in the woods fell before them. A large tent stretched high along several trees. Small camps were visible around the larger tent and within the woods beyond the council tent. Fires blinked and small figures wandered. Lankor imagined many other camps tucked all around the spreading cedars, maples, aspens, and other trees that grew freely in Brendern Forest.

Nayman took a deep breath. "Not much farther," he whispered into his brother's ear. "Thank you for helping."

Lankor often felt more affection for Nayman than he did for Rend. He squeezed his brother's side close to him. "You would do the same."

Rend and Mianna held hands as they hurried downhill into the compound.

Nayman slowed Lankor's progress for a moment. "Look. These are the clans of the doublesight. They are like us. To stand here, you would think The Great Land was made of only doublesight, but we are a small number by comparison to human only or animal only. Tonight, though, we are many."

"And yet, my brother, I wonder which of them were the ones who crucified us? Which joined in the great war, the slaughter, against us? Which have deceived our clan?"

"By deceived you are speaking only of the history of the doublesight. Whatever is going on here is about our present time, not our history." Nayman considered for a moment what Lankor said, then responded, "Or are you suggesting I deceived you by not telling you what father passed to me in confidence?"

Lankor looked at Nayman with a small grin. "Perhaps both, but mostly I wonder about the doublesight down there."

"Father is wiser than you might think. If he says that the doublesight gather now for a single purpose, then it is fact."

"We'll see. We'll see." Lankor pulled his brother along as he descended the knoll into the compound.

Nayman said, "Are you planning something? Please, say that you are not. If you can't think of Rend, then think of Mianna."

Lankor remained silent as he forged down the hill into the growing crowd outside the council tent.

In the compound, Rend appeared to know a lot of the people who had gathered for the council meeting. He clasped palms and gripped the shoulders of many men and women. He hugged and kissed the cheeks of some, as well. He had warned his family how each clan greeted one another in their own way, how each had their own way of showing friendship and affection. That, as part of his family, they would need to go along with whatever they encountered.

Bending to the ways of others, rather than having them bend to his ways, was yet another annoyance for Lankor. When an old woman came close to hug him, Lankor stepped back and nodded. He didn't even notice her name as Rend introduced her.

Rend shot him a concerned look; while Mianna stepped in to alleviate the discomfort, which Lankor had created in the situation by hugging the woman closely.

Unused to large crowds, Lankor and Nayman stood back a little more than what they were asked to do. Nayman apologized once again for not telling Lankor more about the urgency of the trip, but added, "That is the only information you didn't have." He assured his brother that he didn't know why the meeting was urgent, and that he didn't think Rend knew either.

Mianna, the perfect wife, stood beside her husband, listening intently, and mimicking the greetings of whomever she met.

"What's that?" Lankor said, pointing to a doglike creature prancing into the group on its toes.

Rend turned to him and whispered, "A thylacine."

"A doublesight with a pet? Is that normal?"

"It can be," Rend said. "Some people like animals around them, some do not. It must be so, since it is suggested that we do not shift while at a council meeting."

"Why is that?" Lankor said.

Rend glanced back and forth between his sons standing together in the crowd. "It is no different here than at home. Privacy is respected. Seeing another's true self is a privilege not taken lightly. You know that."

"Is it based on respect and privilege or fear?" Lankor said. "The bears showed themselves."

Mianna turned to Lankor and grabbed his arm firmly. "Do not mock our ways. You've been taught all this. Why can't you stop agitating your father for once? As for the bears," she said, "you may have been dreaming."

"Is that what you think?" Lankor said.

Mianna squeezed her son's arm, hard.

"Yes, mother." Lankor shrunk under his mother's stare.

Rend ignored their interaction. "We made it just in time. I understand they were going to begin the council meeting tonight whether we showed up or not. They expected us earlier, based on their sentinel's report on our position."

"Do they know we came from The Lost?" Nayman asked.

"Many of them know," Rend said as he led his family under the large tent.

* * *

Zimp had taken over for Brok so that he could be with his siblings. Standing near Oro, she noticed the tall family arrive and watched as her grandmother moved to hug the younger one who rudely stepped away. At least the mother was kind to Oro, and the father appeared friendly enough. Zimp would have interfered had she not arrived late and still a little dazed from her dance.

She reached for Oro, and noticed that the older son of the last doublesight clan arrival had a disfigured foot. Perhaps he got hurt on the journey and that was why they were late. Too bad. Such a journey should be done with pleasure, not pain.

The tent filled with families Zimp recognized from the last few days of wandering the camp. The human, Brull, and his mixed doublesight were there. Had Oro not asked her to refrain, she would attempt to see their beast image. Now would be the perfect time to do so, with her heightened connection to the unseen realms. She waved to those she knew in an attempt to be friendly. She nodded and smiled to Breel, amused at how distant others stood from her and Therin. As Zimp scanned the group, she paused on the newest arrivals, who had stepped to the side to allow other families to enter. She nodded to them in welcome. Each acknowledged her except one, the youngest, who turned his head away as though he did not see her at all.

Zimp pulled at Oro's arm and edged closer to the latest arrivals, thinking she might find a way to teach the younger one a lesson. The four of them appeared to take up more room than other clans who stood close-knit. As she neared, she sensed a definite force, like an energy surge that surrounded the clan. Oro, though, didn't appear to notice.

The crowd quieted and on a platform built for the occasion, Hammadin, Wellock, and Crob, The Few, stepped up to speak.

Hammadin began, "We wish to apologize for our silence and absence. There has been much for us to consider and plan. We have heard that there have been mutterings this past week. Concerns about the rising attacks on the doublesight. Let us now verify your concerns." He bowed to the rumbling crowd, then turned and acknowledged Wellock and Crob in the same way. They bowed in return.

Hammadin's voice rose above the crowd, "Many ages ago, all living creatures on The Great Land could mate and bear children. This freedom caused a horrible time in our history. We are reminded of our past at the temples in the cities. Statues of birds with crocodile heads stare out at us. Human torsos attached to the hind quarters of a horse are still symbols in our skies." He paused. "All nature of creatures were present in those times. Some were searched out for their strength, their ability to fly, their ability to breathe under water. Ultimately, as humans and beasts bred, they gave birth to horrible anomalies that could not live." His voice rose as though appalled at what his own words were announcing. "Parents, horrified with what they had done, destroyed their own deformed children. Children killed their parents." Hammadin breathed a great sigh. "The Great Land became a place of great sorrow.

"The Gods themselves became saddened and angry. They came down from the sky and ended inter-species mating because neither humans nor beasts of The Great Land took responsibility for their actions. Yet, in their kindness and compassion for all living creatures, the Gods allowed those who had been most responsible to be gifted with doublesight. Each human could choose one animal that best represented himself and his family. These chosen ones were then given the ability to shift."

Zimp saw the young newcomer turn to his older brother. She heard him whisper, "We came all this way for a history lesson?"

The mother reached out and poked her son in the side. When he turned, she gave him a stern look to keep quiet.

Upon the stage, Wellock stepped forward and continued with the speech. "Even this gift was abused by many in the human race. Power and control became the order of the day. As oppression heightens, there is no other retribution but revolt and revolution. This history is taught to every doublesight to remind us of our duty to one another. You know that a long war rid the land of the most powerful doublesight. Gryphons, dragons, centaurs, gargoyles of all types were destroyed forever. With bloodletting comes more bloodletting, and even the doublesight turned against its own to hunt down and murder those most powerful beasts. They were wiped out for fear of their potential, not their choices. Another dark time in our past." Wellock paused before going on. "We have reason to believe that perhaps this part of the history lesson is not true."

The crowd became still. Zimp noticed that some people looked frightened while others appeared curious.

Wellock nodded to Crob, whose turn it was to continue to address the expanded council. "It was during war that the life on The Great Land became separated. Fear of exposure, fear of the true self, and fear of the Gods turned individuals against their own natures. Choices were made. Some doublesight became beast-only, while others became human-only. The true doublesight diminished in number. Knowing the beast-image of an opponent puts one in a superior position to take advantage. Knowing the beast-image of a neighbor does the same.

"A great enough fear, a great enough depression, a great enough inner turmoil or confusion will force any living thing into a stable state where a doublesight in beast-image will remain a beast and a doublesight in human-image will remain a human." Crob paused for a long moment. "Forever," he said with disdain and force.

"During the dark war time, fear of the great beasts spread across the land, forcing many to make a single choice. Some say the Gods had a hand in this change as well, but somehow the doublesight lived through even this. We are few in number now."

Zimp put her arm around Oro and leaned in to speak into her grandmother's ear. "They are not announcing a war, are they?"

Oro shook her head and shrugged her shoulders.

"But you have a feeling," Zimp said.

Oro looked around them to point out to Zimp that she was disturbing others.

Hammadin said, "We have learned to live together as one, we doublesight."

"And there are great things we must still learn from one another," Wellock said.

And Crob put the story straight. "There is a great pressure

to reject all doublesight in the land and to exterminate us by forcing us to choose singlesight. Or be killed," he said. "We have reason to believe that one of the powerful clans have not died out, but are still living on The Great Land."

Again the stirring of the crowd stopped.

Zimp heard the young clansman say to his brother, "We are back to the beginning again."

Zimp saw that the mother and father of the clan to arrive last reached for each other. The mother then touched the shoulder of the nearest son, the oldest, the one with the hurt foot, while the other son took a step away from his family. She watched him closely out the corner of her eye, as he raised the hood of his gray cloak to hide his head.

Hammadin stepped forward again. "We have reason to believe that there is a rogue dragon in the land."

The crowd began to mumble.

"Silence," Hammadin shouted. "We don't know what is happening, but we do know that this beast is setting humans against the doublesight. We are already in small numbers." He spoke louder to get over the din from the council gathering. "We still have allies among the humans. But they are few. And while we do, now is the time for us to find what is truly happening in our land and to stop the perpetrator. Care must be taken. All over the land humans are killing doublesight." Wellock and Crob had their hands in the air to keep the crowd quiet. Hammadin went on to say, "We have taken days to select the search party. After this brief meeting, we will enter into the camps of the chosen ones. You will get special instructions and information. Tomorrow you set out."

The young son turned to his father and sneered. Zimp heard him say, "We were supposed to be late, weren't we? An urgent message? A lie. The Few wished to make their selection before we arrived? To exclude us?"

The father turned his face away from the son and looked over at Oro and nodded to her. Oro appeared to know more that she had let on, as well, and Zimp felt anger rise inside her.

Hammadin held his arms high. "Silence!" The din decreased, but did not end. "Silence!" Another decrease. He spoke over the remaining whispers. "Return to your camps. We will send someone to collect our choices. All of doublesight is at risk and we must begin our quest soon."

Zimp turned to Oro. "Will this be a suicide mission? Small attacks have been going on for years. They have recently increased. Our own clan…" She stopped.

Oro shook her head and shrugged, once again to avoid an answer, Zimp thought.

The crowd began to leave. Conversations resumed among individual families. Each intimate group appeared not to be cognizant of those nearby.

Zimp sensed a change in the dynamic of the new clan. When she looked toward them, the younger son hesitated while his family turned to leave. The boy faced The Few and purposefully walked toward the small stage.

As if he could feel a change coming, the father spun around to yell at his son. "Lankor, no." The mother and older son turned around too. Several other clans nearby looked up to see what was going on.

The younger son, Lankor, untied his cloak. He lifted it quickly with both hands and threw it from his body, high into the air. Under the cloak, Lankor shifted. Zimp stared as his human form was projected with great force away from the beast forming beneath it. Shrugged off with violence, his human image arced behind him, an opaque, skin-only form that then fell weightless toward the ground as it became transparent, and then was gone.

Simultaneously, the young man's feet shifted into thin ugly appendages with four claws at the end of each. Lankor's arms cracked as they stretched twice their length and turned to gnarled bone, a double claw on the end of each, and thick, canvas-like wings with knuckled boney supports hanging in disarray below them. Lankor's face enlarged and crushed into a huge beak, sharp and curved like a predator. The sides of his face grew spikes, long bones in the position of whiskers. Then there emerged an armored and spiked tail, with a wide wing-like expanse several feet before its sharply pointed end. The tail wing, an evolutionary appendage used to stabilize his huge body while in flight.

Zimp held onto Oro, her arms wrapped around her grandmother to protect her.

The scent that emerged from the change reeked of the residue of fire, the strong smell of ash and burning flesh, as though he had burned his own body away, instead of merely discarding its image as Zimp knew she did when she shifted to her crow-image.

Lankor's head shook with a gross violence that allowed a thick mucous to scatter in all directions. He opened his mouth showing the bright red meat of his cheeks and tongue. For only a moment, he turned both wing claws in toward his face and stared at them as if he didn't believe the change, as if he had to be sure, reminded that he was no longer human but was now in dragon-image. It was a curious motion.

Zimp watched as the father grabbed hold of a tattered wing and Lankor turned on him. The older man stood his ground and shook his head back and forth in disapproval and appeared to reprimand his son like the rebellious young man he was.

Lankor looked beyond his father, though, to his mother. Then he looked over the heads of those in the room. He had grown to almost twice his original height and several times his width. His own head lowered and he appeared to implode. His mouth opened as though in pain, but no sound emerged. His dragon-image shriveled and shrunk smaller, as his human-image appeared to rebuild itself around the dragon's frame. He returned fully to his human-image with equal fanfare. He bent to pick up the cloak he had thrown off.

The closest clans encircled the dragon family as if to hold them at bay.

"Stop!" Hammadin stood with his hands out in a pleading gesture, his old body noticeably worn down from all his screaming. He spoke loudly, "An unfortunate display of anger. But I might say that I cannot blame him. These doublesight have been represented here for years. All you council members know Rend. He, and his family—in fact, all of his clan—are doublesight." That was all he said.

Zimp watched as the hesitation of the clans around the

dragons subsided with each council member acknowledging Rend and then turning to their own family showing acceptance. The Few had spoken. Those who had closed in on the dragon family parted to allow them to leave peaceably. The whispers of surprise began with fervor.

Oro pulled Zimp with her as she rushed over to Rend. "My friend," she said. Rend, still holding the arm of his son, smiled at Oro. She reached for Rend's hand and he gave it willingly. She then reached for the mother's hand. "Mianna," Oro said to her as she pulled Rend and Mianna's hands together where they clasped. "A word to you both?"

"Of course," Rend said.

Zimp felt uneasy in the presence of the dragon family. Her initial reaction was to stand back, but her pride and her trust in Oro kept her in place. Zimp did grip Oro's shoulder in surprise when Oro reached up and touched Rend's cheek. "He not only has your look, dear friend, but he has your spirit. Remember how it was for you before you decide on his punishment."

"I am angry at the moment," Rend admitted. "I will wait to choose punishment, as you say." He nodded. "But I will not wait to reprimand."

Oro patted Rend on the shoulder, and to Zimp's pleasure, stepped away and let them pass.

"Cute act," Zimp said to Lankor as they backed away. She looked above his head and could see the dragon image, like a fog around him. It stirred and she felt its power emerge. "I don't think this whole meeting was aimed at you," she said, fighting the fear that shook her.

Once the dragon clan was out of the tent, Oro said, "You need to be reprimanded as well."

"What did I do?" Zimp said.

"Agitate," Oro said. "Unnecessarily."

"I'm sorry, Grandmother. I didn't mean to upset you."

"An unkind reaction to what happened," Oro said.

Zimp said, "That shift into dragon was the most frightful thing I have ever seen."

18

"You knew," Zimp said to her grandmother. "And if you knew, how many others have known about them for years? I can see why they were wiped out. They're frightening, arrogant, and they smell."

Oro didn't answer. She kept her pace, Zimp holding to her arm, but being pulled along rather than helping her grandmother. Before they stepped into the clearing, Brok, Breel, and Therin appeared magically beside them.

Brok said, "I don't trust him."

Oro dragged Zimp the last few feet to a stool that sat near the fire. She settled onto the stool and took several deep breaths. Zimp began to open her mouth and Oro raised her hand for silence. "No," she said. Another breath or two and Oro pulled a small cloth from her shirt and wiped it across her forehead. She coughed into it, replaced it, and kept her hand in her pocket searching for something. She removed a candle.

Zimp recognized a flicker candle when she saw it. "What are you doing?"

Oro handed the candle to Zimp. "Light it."

Storret flew into the clearing and hopped behind the wagon. In less time than it took Zimp to light the candle, Storret stepped around and into view.

Arren burst into the clearing followed by his three brothers. Several others from the crow clan entered the circle the firelight spread into the night air.

"This can't be true," Arren said, "I just heard that—"

"It's true," Zimp told him.

"We've got to do something. We can't let them—"

Oro stood and cut Arren off.

"You've known all along," Arren said. "And you said nothing. What about the welfare of the clan?"

Oro's voice sounded thick and coarse when she spoke. "The dragon clan has suffered enough. Hundreds of years. They are doublesight and we will respect them like our brothers and sisters."

"With respect, Oronice," Storret said, "but didn't The Few suggest that it was a rogue dragon who might be behind the recent increase in doublesight killings?"

She looked at Storret with surprise.

"I listened from outside," he said.

"Are there not rogue crow doublesight?" She turned to include Brok and his siblings, "And rogue thylacine?" Oro reached for the lighted candle. Dark red swirls curved around the candle's circumference and the flame appeared to change color at times. "This family, I assure you, is a friend to the doublesight. They are as horrified to find out about the rogue dragon as you are."

"How can you say that when he did what he just did in there?" Brok said in a forceful and angry voice. "Could they be turning us over, one clan at a time?"

"Not this family," Oro said.

"They won't help us," Arren said. "If they did, they'd be helping to destroy their own existence. No doublesight can exist without both its animal and human counterpart."

"He may be right," Brok said.

"It is true." Arren rushed in and slapped the candle from Oro's hand. Wax flew toward her face and she backed to get away from it, tripping and beginning to topple.

Breel leapt smoothly to the side and caught Oro before she could fall backward.

Zimp sidestepped the action, seeing that Breel needed no help. Instead, she clawed at Arren's hand a second too late.

Brok was quicker. He tackled Arren at the knees, bringing him down. The candle rolled away. Arren's brothers, with looks of shock on their faces, jumped onto Brok's back to pull him from Arren.

In a split second, Zimp glanced over at Oro, Breel's face next to her grandmother's cheek. Oro blew into the air. Zimp imagined that she could see her grandmother's breath in one long, thin stream of smoke, arriving just as Zimp inhaled. Something energetic coursed through her body. She didn't know what had just happened, but she knew what her duty was now. Her duty was to the greater clan of the doublesight. She fought the idea only long enough to be overwhelmed by the responsibility. "Enough!" Zimp allowed her body to straighten, no longer in movement, no longer reacting to the situation.

The brothers peeled off Brok.

Brok sat back onto the ground and rubbed his once-injured shoulder.

Arren stared defiantly into Zimp's face. "What do you think you can do for anyone? A shy girl does not shift into a warrior woman." He spat on the ground.

"Remove him," Zimp said.

Dail, Felter, and Kel helped their brother to stand and walked him into the woods toward his own wagon.

"Are you all right?" Zimp asked.

Brok nodded. "I could have handled it," he said.

Zimp suddenly didn't know where her words came from but she said, "I did handle it." She swung around and clasped Breel's forearm with her hand. She gripped firmly and reached around to embrace the girl. "You are a true friend to our clan. Your brother I'm beginning to tolerate," she added with a slight smile.

Brok retrieved the candle. "What is this supposed to do?" He relit it from the fire.

"A prayer candle usually, but I don't recognize the color. What herb is this?" Zimp asked Oro.

"It is blood."

Zimp stepped back. She had never heard of a prayer candle using blood. The crow clan didn't use blood in any ceremony.

Without thinking she glanced over at Brok.

"Now that," he said, "is ceremony I can understand."

Breel had to laugh as she helped Oro sit near the fire.

Zimp set the lighted candle onto the ground.

Oro whispered a few private words over the candle. She threw cedar into the candle flames. "Join me," she said.

The three thylacine doublesight, Zimp and Storret kneeled next to her. Other crow clan stood outside the clearing to witness the ceremony. Each would provide a blessing to the prayer, strength to whatever it was that Oro whispered into the flame.

Zimp jerked when the candle spit fire nuggets at them. It flickered weakly next to the campfire.

Oro threw a handful of leaves into the larger fire and it roared, flared up, and danced as though the wind had changed. "Speak after me, my children," she said. "Let these days of peace."

"Let these days of peace," the group said.

"Stay true in our hearts."

"Stay true in our hearts."

"As battles before us."

"As battles before us."

"Plan to tear us apart."

Zimp looked over in surprise as she repeated the words along with the others. The candle spit again and a terrible odor rushed into the air. She wrinkled her nose.

"The doublesight must know," Oro proceeded.

The chorus rushed like a wind behind her words.

"To protect one another."

"To protect one another."

"For the ability to shift."

"For the ability to shift."

"Dies with our brother."

Brok raised his head and gave Zimp a look as though he didn't want to believe what Oro was saying, that as one clan dies out the rest become weaker. But he murmured the words as he was asked to do.

Therin whined and laid his head across Breel's leg. "Not you, Therin. You haven't caused any problems for us." She scratched behind his ear and he nudged her leg as though he understood what had been said.

Oro reached out and snuffed the candle flame between her fingers.

"That smell," Zimp said. "It's the same smell that he gave off."

Oro took a deep breath. "Every time a dragon shifts they are burned by their own internal fires. It only happens from human image to dragon image. The return, I understand, is sweet and inviting. But then, instantly, the hunger for pain, the hunger for the dragon image returns."

"He must have been angry," Breel said.

"Frustrated. Perhaps hurt, would be my guess," Oro said.

Brok stood and brushed leaves and pine needles from his pants. "The prayer. Is it true? Are we weakening every time another small family is killed?"

"The whole of doublesight is in danger," Oro said.

Brull wandered into the clearing followed by two of his sons. "Life is not destroyed, only the doublesight. I'll tell you, being human-only is not so bad."

"Brull. You might say it, but you do not believe it, my friend," Oro said. "Even I can sense the longing inside you. That is why you married a doublesight, to be close to your hunger."

"My sons," Brull said, turning to each in turn. "Bennek and Raik." He walked forward and they paced him. "Can you use your wondrous senses to tell me which is the doublesight and which human only?"

Zimp stepped next to Oro. Without thinking, she said, "Raik is the doublesight."

Surprise crossed Brull's face. His jaw clenched. "Lucky guess, young one. I thought Oronice was the intuitive."

"We're all intuitive in some way," Zimp said. "In our clan we don't have to be pregnant to open to other realms."

"You mock us?" Brull advanced and Raik and Bennek pulled their swords.

Therin leapt several feet from where Breel kneeled to just in front of Zimp. In an instant Breel stood next to Brok.

"Enough," Oro said. "We must work together."

"You don't mean work," Brull said, indicating for his son's to put their swords away. "You mean battle. And I've heard that the doublesight brought this onto themselves."

"You would fight us, knowing that your own family could perish?" Zimp asked.

"No," Brull said. "I am angry. The doublesight have kept themselves separated, not the humans."

"Persecuted, segregated, mistrusted," Oro began.

"Not by everyone," Brull said. "The High Priest Orn of Flande," he reminded her.

"And the Two Sisters of Lissland, where we come from," Oro said.

Three young boys burst into the clearing, jumping as though chased by something fierce. They stopped dead in their tracks between the two families. The boys appeared nervous but obviously had a duty to perform. "Wonder of wonders, several at once."

"What is this about?" Zimp said.

"You," one boy said, pointing at Zimp. "And you," he said to Brok. He turned and lowered his head as though Brull's boys were difficult to see in the dimmer light from the fire. "Oh, and you, Raik," the boy said with a smile. "To The Few. To The Few." The three of them ran back toward the woods but stopped at the edge of the clearing and turned completely around. The speaker of the trio cocked his head. "Someone not hear me?"

"What of Bennek?" Brull said.

The boys huddled together and brought up their heads. "Not today."

Zimp looked to Oro, who nodded approval.

Breel stepped in and said, "I'll care for Oronice." She hugged her brother, "Be well."

Brull motioned for Raik to follow the boys. "Be careful," he said.

The three boys spoke to one another in whispers. The speaker pointed, "Is that Therin?"

"He is," Brok said.

"Oh, then he must come along too," the speaker said. Again, the boys jumped into the air and onto the path.

The four doublesight followed quickly with no time to think about their argument.

When the boys turned to a separate path, Zimp, who was out front, followed them. The boys stopped and swiveled around in unison. One shook his head. "Where are you going?" He pointed back to the other path. "To The Few," he said leaning into the words and letting them out slowly as though she might not understand them.

"This way," Raik said from behind her.

Zimp nodded to the boys and spun around to follow Raik. She heard the boys scurry along the other path.

Zimp sensed that Brok waited for her to be close before he spoke to Raik. "It appears that your father has very strong opinions about the doublesight," Brok said.

"He does," Raik said.

Zimp felt extremely intuitive that evening. Her dance and her openness to Zora had overwhelmed her and kept her in the mid-zone between realms. She didn't know how she knew that Raik was the doublesight; she was merely positive of the fact. She hoped that she could see Raik's etheric body easier, too. She squinted and peered over Brok's shoulder.

"But your father is not a doublesight," Brok said.

Zimp almost instantly saw Raik's shifting aura, which moved smoothly over his physical body, sliding rather loosely back and forth. It had little shape, no ears that she could notice, and no snout. She tried harder, but thought it might be their movement through the woods, the shifting shadows caused by the moonlight, that kept her from seeing clearly. It could have been the adrenaline from the argument.

"My father is human," Raik said. "But he will fight for the doublesight. He is loyal to The High Priest Orn of Flande."

"And if The High Priest is against the doublesight?" Brok suggested.

"Then Brull will battle to save his own family," Raik said.

"I'm not so sure," Brok said.

Raik spun around, pulled his sword, and coiled his body in a position to strike.

Brok stopped and reached for Therin's scruff to hold him

back. "Not now, brother."

Just as quickly as he turned on Brok, Raik put his sword in its sheath and swung around to continue down the path toward the cabin of The Few. His body slid into motion as though it were fluid.

Zimp became suddenly aware of her own walk, which bounced her along the ground, her head bobbing as she walked in an almost hopping motion. Brok, too, she noticed, bobbed somewhat as he walked on his toes, just like a thylacine. She reached out and clasped Brok's shoulder. "To the Gods," she whispered. "They are snakes."

19

"That was the most arrogant thing I have ever seen," Mianna said.

Lankor lowered his head and let his shoulders slide forward.

"What in The Great Land do you think you were doing?" She bent toward him.

Rend still held his son's arm firmly.

"They were accusing us," Lankor said.

"They were stating a fact," Nayman said. "There are still dragons in The Great Land. These doublesight didn't know that until now."

"They made the announcement only when dragons posed a threat. That implicates us." Lankor turned to his father. "You knew about it. We were supposed to be late. You walked us into the middle of a potentially dangerous position."

Mianna slapped Lankor on the back of the head. "You will not talk to your father in that way."

Rend indicated with a nod of his head for Nayman to find a clearing and set up camp.

Lankor stood on the path and between two large cedars beside his father. Mianna acted angry, where Rend only appeared to be disappointed.

Rend shoved Lankor off the path and onto the ground. They sat opposite each other. Rend took a deep breath, closed his eyes for a moment, then lifted his head and stared into his son's eyes.

Lankor suddenly felt an unbelievable power come from his father, a power he had never sensed before. He had often been aware of what he considered his father's weaknesses, but never his strength. At that moment, the power grew so overwhelming, striking him in the chest and head that Lankor turned away from Rend's eyes.

"Look at me," Rend said.

Mianna stood behind her son. Her quiet voice entered Lankor's ears. "Listen. You are about to learn a great lesson."

Lankor did as his father and mother requested. He met Rend's stare with his own squinting and angry glare.

"You have been taught to sit in silence? To meditate?" Rend said.

"To calm myself before sleep or to control my anger," Lankor said.

"No," Rend said. "To harness and focus your power and strength. Your brother has already learned this lesson. Now I offer it to you. You must do as I say. Explicitly."

"Why would you wish to teach me now after what I did?" Lankor said.

"So it doesn't happen again," Mianna said.

Lankor felt Rend's power decrease once he began to talk. The focus averted. "What just happened?"

"Close your eyes," Rend said. "Focus on shifting, but stop short of entering a shift. Once you begin to create ectoplasm, you cannot stop. The best way to stop the shift is to open your eyes at precisely the right moment, bring your focus to the other person, and hold the feel of the shift."

Lankor closed his eyes. He allowed his mind to drop into his dragon consciousness. He began to feel the burn and opened his eyes with a start, stared into Rend's face. But it was too late. His arms cracked and spread to his sides. His face pushed into a beak and grew spikes. The pain caused him to groan and call out. As his torso felt enflamed, it grew, and pushed against the tree behind him, sliding him across the ground toward his father. His sight shifted. Colors took on a strange appearance. The dark, which spread all around them, took on its own hue. There was no black, only color. He felt the flame inside him.

Lankor drew a winged claw close to his face to be sure that he had changed. It struck him that he had failed his father's lesson. His anger would not let him stop short of the shift into beast image.

A quick, logical focus and he began his shift back to his human image. At the crown of his head Lankor felt the tingling sensation of a gentle massage. The sensation rolled down his neck and hovered over his shoulders. He relaxed and let the muscles reform into their natural shape, all tension released as they changed. He took a deep breath. The darkness fell in around him. The black shadows obliterated what was once there to see. "I failed," he said.

Rend appeared satisfied by the event. "Now try again. Remember, just before the burn."

Lankor focused inward in search for the very beginning of a shift. His determination heightened, but his control did not. His dragon image thrust off his human image as it transformed into existence. As he returned to his human image, he felt tired. "I failed again."

"We will practice more. Do you sense any difference?" Rend asked.

"Little. By the time I notice the shift, it is too late to stop it."

He tried again. Once he shifted into his dragon image, a gasp came from the path. Lankor turned and three boys huddled together. "The dragon," one said.

"Yes?" Rend said to the boys.

"He is summoned to the cabin of The Few."

Rend nodded and the boys ran off faster than they had arrived.

Lankor shifted back into his human image. "What is going on? Are they going to banish me?"

"Never," Rend said. "The Few have only the doublesight in mind." Rend stood and held out his hand.

Lankor stretched his arm up. His father had a strong grip. Rend leaned back and Lankor lifted to his feet.

"Oronice was right. I may have done the same had I been in that position," Rend said.

Mianna stepped around Lankor and pulled close to Rend.

Lankor sensed a bond between them he had never noticed before.

"You must practice, my son. Practice every moment you can. With a partner, if possible. You'll find that you can control a conversation or situation merely by increasing your human energy toward shifting." Rend patted Lankor's shoulder. "I'll walk you to the cabin of The Few."

Mianna kissed her husband's cheek.

On the way toward the cabin, Rend said, "It is said that when your beast image is larger than your human image, others can sense it. To many people, you already feel powerful, larger than what you appear to be. Do you see?"

"I think I'm beginning to."

Rend changed the subject. He laughed and said, "Oronice knows me as well as I know myself."

"Were you that angry when you were younger?" Lankor said.

"Frustrated and trapped. I know what it's like not being able to show your true nature. Even when people tell you that it's all right to do so, they don't mean it. Except Oronice. Before I learned her beast image, I used to think she, too, was a dragon."

"What image does she hold?"

Rend placed a hand at the back of Lankor's neck. "One of the most amazing animals I know of."

"A bear?"

"No, although bears are magical in their own way. No, Oronice is a crow image. And among the crow clan, she is the most powerful. That's why she is part of the council," Rend said.

"Then you are the most powerful of the dragon clan."

"There are so few of us to choose from. I am merely in line to represent the clan. I have to admit that I am surprised to learn that there may be more of us. Perhaps your uncle…"

"Maybe he saved two clans of dragon," Lankor suggested.

With the cabin in view, Rend stopped for a moment. "Listen, I don't like what's going on here, either. I trust the council. I trust Oronice The Gem. There are other, unfamiliar faces. What I'm saying is, not all of these people are council members. Watch your step."

"Will you wait for me here?" Lankor asked.

"No. You'll be fine. I have to be sure Mianna and Nayman are all right." He patted Lankor's shoulder. "Now go on. You can find your way?"

"I think so. The path winds a bit, but that's all."

The three boys sat on a log near the doorway to the cabin. They stood and backed away as Lankor approached. Two of the boys shoved the other one forward. "Is your skin hot? Can we touch it?"

Lankor stepped toward them and said, "No."

The boys backed away, stumbling over each other and forcing one to the ground.

Lankor opened the door and stepped into the cabin.

Two small benches sat on either side of the door. Hammadin, Crob, and Wellock stood against the wall in front of him.

"Close the door and sit," Hammadin said.

Lankor looked to both sides. The woman who stood with Oronice at the council meeting now sat with the man who had the thylacine pet. On the other bench sat a small-built man. Lankor sat next to him.

Hammadin stepped forward to address the five of them. "The doublesight are in need of information if we are to battle and win against an enemy none of us have seen and we are only guessing exists. We have heard most that the hatred stems from Castle Weilk, that this crazed doublesight is killing humans systematically. We ask that you five travel together. The doublesight attacks have increased in number and in severity, so you must hide your identities. Your journey is only to gain information. You will travel in peace, but that does not mean there will be no danger. I cannot promise that in these troubled times. Do what you must to survive and return."

Lankor looked from side to side to size up the others.

"Brok, please stand for a moment," Hammadin said.

Both Brok and his pet stood, Lankor noticed.

"I am sorry to hear of your father. Fremlin was a great and loved man, highly admired by the council. We hereby honor you with his post on the council. Do you accept this honor?"

Brok lowered his head. "I accept."

Hammadin motioned to the others. "These doublesight and we, The Few, witness this acceptance. You are to give your life for the doublesight no matter what they may bear as a beast image, no matter what they may appear to do or say in your presence. There are longstanding feuds even among our kind. These feuds must end now. You must swear to abide by this rule. Will you abide?"

"I will," Brok said. He nodded to Hammadin, then turned his head toward Lankor.

"Every doublesight," Hammadin said.

Brok's jaw tightened. "I understand."

Hammadin then got down on one knee and reached out. "And do you speak for Therin as well? Will he, as long as he is able, abide by this rule with you?"

"I will speak for my brother. He will abide," Brok said.

"You may sit," Hammadin said. He pointed at the woman who had stood with Oronice and, saying her name, asked her to stand. Once again he said, "We hereby honor you with a post on the council. Do you accept this honor?"

"I accept," Zimp said. "And I will abide by the rule of the council and The Few to give my life for the doublesight."

Hammadin smiled. "You need not be so eager to hurry this along. Your sincerity might be questioned."

"My word is my sincerity," Zimp said.

"Very well." Hammadin asked the man next to Lankor to stand, saving Lankor for last.

One moment the man sat next to Lankor and the next moment he stood opposite Hammadin, but Lankor had trouble connecting the two positions together with any movement. It was as though the man had been standing the whole time. For a moment, Lankor felt similar to how he felt around the bear doublesight Mammadeen and Mammadoon. He thought it interesting that the speaker for The Few's name was Hammadin, and wondered if he, too, might carry a bear image.

"Raik," Hammadin said, introducing the man as he repeated the short ceremony.

Lankor noticed that while Hammadin spoke, Raik slumped

easily in his own body, almost as though he stood ready to escape
the human flesh at that very moment and shift into his beast
image. Raik's stance indicated a lack of respect for The Few.
Obviously, Raik was not impressed by Hammadin's position.
Even the man's answers were slow in coming and direct. Raik
stuttered slightly when he spoke, as though he wasn't quite
sure of his answers. Lankor liked him already.

When it was time for Lankor to stand, Hammadin stood
before him for what seemed like a long time. He sighed. "Please
stand, Lankor."

The bench creaked as Lankor's weight was removed. He
stretched to his full height, above Hammadin's by half a foot.
"Rend has been a loyal member of the doublesight for many
years. Do you feel you can honor him if we accept you as a
council member?"

Lankor felt the blood rush to his face. So he is to be
humiliated first, he thought. "Can I trust that the council, The
Few, and these newly appointed council members will, as you
have asked them, die for me as a doublesight council member?
After all, my father's beast image was unknown to many of the
doublesight for years. Was that out of fear of what they might
do? Should I carry that fear?"

Crob and Wellok stepped closer to Hammadin, apparently
for strength.

"Your question: does it come from a lack of trust in your
fellow council members or do you mistrust all life except those
in your own image?" Hammadin asked.

"I question that allegiance to the death can be acquired in a
ceremony of words. I have seen no actions to tell me that I am
safe to travel with these doublesight."

Zimp stood. "And we have no guarantee that you won't
burst into anger and turn on us, not after what you did this
evening."

"Stop," Wellock said. "Perhaps we should choose another
way if you cannot swear to our..."

Raik, like the motion of water, took a position next to Lankor.
He slid his sword from its sheath and lifted it so that the point
almost touched the ceiling of the cabin. "I wa-wa-would protect

this man to my d-death, and any other doublesight whether a council member or na-not. It is my word. The word of the G-Guard of Flande."

"And, I too," Brok said while standing.

Hammadin asked Zimp, "And you?"

"If he accepts the honor and swears by the rule, I'm in," Zimp said. "Well, big boy?"

Lankor studied the faces of the others. "I will honor my family and my life as a doublesight by accepting the council and living by the rule of the doublesight as one clan and not many," he said, finally. Lankor wanted to add that he would do so only if they did, but held his tongue. Hope in the sacredness of the ceremony suggested that those in the room could be trusted, and that he had little choice but to trust in it as well. His father and mother placed their lives in the hands of The Few and the council. He could do the same.

"Then you are all hereby council members," Hammadin said. "For the night, go to your families. In the morning, meet with your family in the council tent. We will explain the assignment details at that time."

The meeting was over. Hammadin, Crob, and Wellock turned around and clomped into a back room.

The five new council members turned toward each other, but didn't appear to know what to do next. Lankor thanked Raik for standing when he did, and then nodded to Brok. When he went to acknowledge Zimp, she turned her head and said, "You're welcome. Now, let's get out of here. I need a good sleep before this morning meeting. I have a feeling about it."

20

"I can't believe this," Brull said to his son. "What are they thinking? The doublesight can't win a battle against the humans. It doesn't matter what beast image they carry, there just aren't enough of them. Why can't they remain what they are?"

"And what's that?" Raik said.

"A symbol of our past mistakes, of what went wrong," Brull answered while pacing their small campsite.

"We are all m-mistakes?" Raik said. "Then why would you m-marry one of us?"

Brull calmed. "You know that's not what I'm saying. The High Priest Orn of Flande has been a friend of the doublesight since the beginning. I believe in that friendship. And the Three Princes of Crell have always welcomed the doublesight."

"As long as the d-doublesight are passive," Raik said. "As long as we are a novelty, an intuitive, a sh-showman of some type."

"You are one of the Guard of Flande, my son. Do you not take that position seriously? That is not a novelty."

"Do you not take your council position seriously, father?" Raik said.

"And which loyalty would you have me take first? My family, the High Priest, the doublesight? Which would honor and be loyal to me over the others?" Brull said.

"Which do you b-believe in?" Raik said.

"I just think that your band of peaceful infiltrators should include at least one human." Brull took one step closer to his son, his voice rising. "Someone who might know how humans think."

Raik backed away. "Would you suggest Bennek in my stead?" he retorted. "Or C-Cis? Or perhaps yourself? Should The Few trust humans while they turn and k-kill anything more powerful than they?"

Brull lifted his fist, as Raik slid to one side in response and removed his sword.

Nebbie screamed out, "No. Why must you two always fight?"

Raik lowered his weapon and glanced over at his mother. To Bennek he said, "I'm sorry for my words."

"I understand," Bennek said.

"Do you trust yourself?" Brull asked Raik.

Raik felt the point of his question. "I must."

"That is not an answer I would suggest you take on this journey of yours. They don't know anything about you." Brull turned his back and ducked into his tent. Nebbie followed right away.

Bennek closed the space between he and his brother. "You have to understand him. I know how it is to stay awake and wonder why your body won't change, why you feel like an animal sometimes, but can't quite reach out far enough to shift. And you, so powerful and so weak."

"It's a c-curse being like this. Why doesn't he try to understand m-me?" Raik responded. "You've seen my boys. What would you suggest I do about them? Zip will k-kill Ka one day."

"Doublesight must be provoked to be aggressive when in beast image, you know that. And with your sons, family bond will stop them from harming each other," Bennek said.

"I'm not so sure. The Great Land is ch-changing. Don't you worry what Idune will produce? What if your own son or daughter b-bites you one day? Humans are afraid of us. I've heard you talk with Idune about the potential p-problem. I'm surprised you married her."

"Look Raik, I'm not our father. You aren't either. Have you ever tried to kill any of us? Have you had that thought?" Bennek said.

Raik's wife Eena poked her head from one of the tents. "Please, Raik, the children can hear you."

He replaced his sword. "I've had the thought, but have done n-nothing about it. Perhaps you're right about family."

"Even the doublesight are human first. Try as you might, that is a bond you cannot break easily. Of all people, the doublesight know that war brings the potential for nonexistence as a race. Your human image will never go away. That's what you are. It's what you return to when you die." Bennek strolled over to Raik's side and placed a hand on his brother's shoulder. "Let us walk a bit."

Raik followed Bennek's lead. "I wouldn't be able to s-sleep anyway," he said.

They walked on the moss cushion that lay over the forest floor in some areas, once they got off the winding and crossing paths between campsites. A few days before, on their way to the council, their family group crossed a small creek. Raik longed to be there now. The ripple and tinkle of slowly moving water as it folded over itself relaxed him.

"You may shift for a while, if you like," Bennek said.

Raik stopped walking and bent forward to listen, his hand held up to quiet his brother. "I hear others talking. We are too c-close to the camps." He smiled and paced forward again. "I'm easier to talk with after a shift. Is that why you suggest it?"

"It's only easier after the right kind of shift. But, no, that wasn't what I was thinking. I just wanted you to have the opportunity to roam around tonight, nocturnally. I thought you'd appreciate it."

"I wouldn't be much help in the m-morning, though. It will be difficult enough for me to sleep tonight." Raik said. "I couldn't meet tomorrow unless I shifted t-twice. That w-would take hours."

"Why don't you give yourself equal time between images? It's like you ignore a part of yourself. It gets the minimum amount of time you can give it, and during those few hours, you hide away. I've been with you then; you're not so bad. In fact, you're quite pleasant much of the time," Bennek said.

"I'm not pleasant, I'm afraid. I'm angry. And I'm easily persuaded. That's the t-time when I am most apt to do something wrong, something against my n-nature. That's when I hate myself the most. Th-this life I live isn't right. I would w-wish it on no one."

"That's not how I see it," Bennek said.

Raik pounded his chest. "You are not in h-here. You do not have to b-battle yourself." He turned around and Bennek followed. "Let's go back. I am afraid someone might overhear our conversation."

"See, it's more difficult talking intimately with you now, yet this is when you are most willing to talk." He went quiet until they were almost to their campsite again. "At least you can shift."

"Not at will. Not like all these others. After I s-shift, I must wait hours before I can do it again. It scares me when I'm unable to change. These doublesight shift back and forth like they are blinking their eyes. Don't you see, I don't fit in here and I don't f-fit in with humans? I'm as unique a creature as the dragon image doublesight, Lankor."

"You fit in more than I do. Staying here is uncomfortable for me. There are just too many doublesight, and they all look at me like they know I can't shift, like I'm a freak of nature, like the gargoyles of the past. I can literally feel all the different energies around me, all the different beast images just waiting to snap into existence. It scares me like you wouldn't know."

"And h-having me scared with you would help?"

Bennek shook his head. "I don't think having you scared would help so much as having you listen and understand my vulnerability. That's how you feel, isn't it? Vulnerable?"

"I feel as vulnerable around the doublesight as I do around humans," Raik said. "At the m-moment I am at my strongest and most able to participate. Eena understands that about me and likes me this way, before a primary shift."

"Even the way you talk about shifting is exclusive, primary and secondary. I might suggest you switch the two," Bennek said, "and learn a bit more about your other half." Bennek grabbed Raik's arm. "We both know why Eena likes you closest to your primary image. I wonder if she has ever been a threat. And one more thing before we enter camp again; I suggest you consider how you will explain your double image to your new travel partners. You might consider letting The Few know as well. I would like to see you return, my brother, regardless of our differences."

"Do you fear they will kill me rather than the dragon traveling with us?" Raik said.

"The dragon is a weapon to be used against another dragon. He must know that. But you are truly different. You know how some people are with something they don't understand. Consider a separate meeting with The Few. Let someone know. That's all I'm suggesting."

"I'll think about it," Raik said. He pulled his arm loose from Bennek's grip. He pointed at the soft glow of moonlight that lay across the clearing where their tents were set. "I should s-sleep if I am to leave in the morning. Eena will wish to have time with me, t-too."

"And Idune will need my warmth this cool evening," Bennek said. "I want you to know that we argue about the sex of our child as much as the possibility of it being doublesight or human only. Add to that the possibility of a variety of images, and we've had a few battles I'd wish on no one. But still, she is the woman for me."

"She is that," Raik said.

21

Zimp recalled Zora's warning that the Flandeans were 'varied in their beliefs, unsure of their position,' and that they were 'enemies and brothers' and 'liars and thieves'. She had to wonder if the thieves mentioned were her own clan, which would mean that the Flandeans were liars. But did Zora mean all the Flandeans? Apparently not, or they would not be varied in their beliefs. The problem she faced was which of the warnings included Raik, now that she would be forced to travel with him.

A wheezing sound came from Oronice as she slept.

Zimp lay awake, waiting for the sun to draw out the call of the birds, robins in these woods. The mental thickness of deep sacred meditation from the evening before had slipped from her mind. The memory of her meeting with The Few and the other four doublesight shifted inside her as though she were making some of it up. The meeting may have been cut short by Lankor's questioning. If The Few changed their mind about including him because his actions proved him volatile, she would feel safer.

She rolled to her side and smelled the fresh scent of the forest wisp through the wagon. The loose canvas hanging over the end flapped in a soft breeze. Silence stood all around, beyond where she lay awake. It was possible, she thought, that all the doublesight had packed up and moved on, leaving only her wagon. She felt the presence of no other person except Oro, lying in her bunk. Zimp rolled to her back, then to her other side. Something wasn't quite right with the silence. She could sense morning as her own instinct kicked in. In a slow, easy motion, Zimp drew her blanket from her body and slipped into her clothes. After tying her shirt, she smoothly tumbled from the wagon and landed soundlessly onto the ground. Her arms stretched from her sides. Her ears picked up a soft crunching of leaves and she turned to see Breel stepping with caution from behind a nearby tree.

Breel came close. "It's too quiet."

Zimp nodded.

"Your guards?" Breel said.

No sooner did she ask than Storret stepped from the path that led toward the council tent. He rushed to Zimp and Breel. "There are humans advancing from all sides."

"Why didn't you send a warning?" Breel asked.

Zimp turned to her and answered for Storret. "They would have attacked and we would have been unprepared. We must alert everyone in quiet."

"Their weapons are not pulled. They believe they are being stealthy," Storret said.

Breel smiled. "I'll go around the east side with Brok and Therin."

"I'll go west," Zimp said.

Storret reached to stop Breel, his hand brushing her gently, almost affectionately, Zimp noticed. Once he got her attention he said to them both, "Zimp, Brok, and Therin must meet with The Few immediately at the council tent." He smiled and touched Zimp's face. "Take Oronice with you. She must be protected."

Zimp nodded.

Breel looked as though she was about to cry. "Why both of my brothers?" She asked no one.

"I'll watch over you," Storret said.

Zimp appreciated her cousin's gentleness in the situation. If she had not known him as well as she had, she would have thought that he felt deeply for Breel.

"Go," he said. "I'll travel west. Zerran and Crepp will alert us if things change." He rushed toward the path and disappeared in a moment.

Breel took Zimp's hand and squeezed it. "May your Gods be with you and ours be with my brothers," she said. Then she let go and slinked off down the easterly path.

Zimp rushed toward the wagon to wake Oro, but her grandmother waited, sitting upright on her bunk.

Oro handed Zimp three bundles. "Take these."

Zimp strapped the bundles to her waist. When she reached up again, Oro handed her granddaughter a sword and a dagger. Again Zimp tucked the two weapons on her body, one around her waist and the other inside her boot. After that, Oro allowed Zimp to help her down from the wagon. The two scurried off as quickly as they could.

The activity level increased as they approached the council tent, but the people remained silent. Zimp had an eerie feeling from the activity, which included flashing blade, knives, staffs, and anything that could be used as a weapon. Children were ushered along the path toward the council tent. Zimp met with Eena, Raik and their two boys. Bennek's wife Idune was with them, but Bennek was not.

Eena answered Zimp's unasked question. "The men are warriors and guards. They will fight."

"Except for me," Raik said from her side. "I'll hide with the children."

"You must not be seen," Oro said, almost breathless.

"We've got to trust The Few. We are part of the council now," Zimp said. "Remember your oath?"

"You need not be concerned with my memory," Raik said.

Eena pushed against his side to quiet him. "He didn't sleep well," she said.

When Zimp and the Flandeans entered the tent, Brok and Therin greeted them. Lankor showed up only a moment after Zimp and Oro. The Few ushered the five of them out a side exit. Before letting go of Zimp, Oro said in a soft voice, "Listen for me." Zimp noticed the want in Eena's eyes. Raik held her for a long time, then separated and followed The Few down the path and into the cabin where the door closed behind them.

"We wait until we are signaled to go," Hammadin said.

"There is always a weak point." He looked at Lankor, "Or a weak point is created."

"Why look at me?" Lankor said.

Zimp knew the answer to that question. "Your family will create the weak point," she said.

"Correct," Hammadin said. "Now, for quick business." He motioned for them to circle him. "You are now one body and one soul. Your differences must end here." He didn't wait for acknowledgement, but kept talking. "We have provisions in the back, and horses. You are travelers, but what kind of travelers is something you may have to adjust as you go. You are young. No one will suspect you are on a mission. If we sent men of arms, they would be attacked and killed out of fear for their purpose. You should be safe as long as you are careful."

He spun around when he heard the cawing from outside. He didn't have to say what the sound meant. The noise picked up around them, metal on metal. "You must shift, when it is safe, for your comrades. You must be able to see each other's aura and," he looked at Zimp, "etheric body. This will allow you to truly know one another whether in beast image or human image." He swung around to Lankor. "We have agreed that you are to be wary of your temper. The lives of your fellow travelers and the lives of your family and the lives of all the doublesight rest in the hands of you five for now."

"Not by the sounds of it," Lankor said about the noise outside the cabin.

Hammadin gave him a great grin. "To surround us, they had to thin their small party to near breaking point. Just before you arrived, we got word that the humans are mostly villagers. They are poorly prepared for battle. We have already slipped past them and nearly surround them as they believe to have surrounded us."

"Will you kill them?" Raik said.

"Not at all. We are not the animals that humans are. We'll merely hold them until you can leave quietly, then send them back to their homes with their wounded." Hammadin appeared to be satisfied with that answer.

A knock came to the door. Crob opened it. The noise had

subsided considerably.

Breel stood in the doorway. "They are bargaining for their lives already. I was told that the northwest passageway is cleared for you." She reached for Brok's hand and he stepped close enough to grasp it. Therin rubbed against her leg. "Hold dear the heart of my mother. Hold dear the heart of my father," she said.

Brok nodded. "I will return."

Breel turned to go and disappeared into the woods.

"One last thing." Hammadin clapped his hands together. "Zimp will act as your leader."

"Not *my* leader," Lankor said.

Hammadin turned on him. "You can stay if you like. Our decision that you go was marginal."

Zimp saw Lankor's eyes narrow and his jaw set. He nodded to Hammadin, then turned to Zimp. "Where to, my lady?"

"Good," Hammadin said. "One more rule." He looked Lankor in the eye. "You, son, will be the last to shift into your beast image."

And with that, the five of them were ushered out the back of the cabin. Bundles of food and bedding were brought straight away. Zimp recognized the bedding from her wagon and asked about it.

A thick man with strong arms and dark skin said, "Your families helped us select your gear." He pointed to Brok, "Except for him. We brought everything he owned."

Zimp saw the sheath that held Brok's sacred staff sticking up from its place strapped to his pack.

Lankor gripped his staff and raised it into the air as though hefting its weight to be sure it was his.

Another short man stepped from the path with five fully packed horses, saddled and ready to go. One bore nothing but provisions.

The two men strapped each traveler's pack onto the packhorse.

As the doublesight prepared to mount, Zimp realized that Lankor had never been on a horse. The two men had to help him get into the saddle. His ride appeared uncomfortable with the unbalanced Lankor on its back.

22

Lankor gripped the saddle horn and stiffened his legs. When he squeezed his thighs to keep his balance the horse speeded up, and he bounced like a child riding on his father's knee.

"Relax your body," Raik said from behind.

"I'll fall off," Lankor said.

"You'll sit the saddle and flow with the horse," Raik said.

The narrow path would not allow Raik to ride next to Lankor. Turning around in the saddle to look behind him, Lankor felt less safe. So, he kept his eyes forward and watched Brok ride while listening to Raik's instructions. Upon relaxing his lower body, Lankor began to allow his hips to move with the trotting horse under him. He noticed Brok's upper body bending and flexing and tried to copy the movements.

From behind, Raik said, "That's it. Feel that? Much b-better."

Lankor still didn't feel completely safe atop the horse. Flowing with the animal's movements took a lot of concentration. He felt lucky that he didn't have to control the horse's direction. It followed Brok's horse, which followed Zimp's. Northwest was the direction of Weilk. Of all places for an opening to occur that was a lucky break, except that much of the region consisted of settlements made of small armies, warriors from one battle or another. Time had passed, but each area created its own laws, its own tight community. They didn't like strangers and they were always suspicious who might be trying to invade their land.

Lankor had heard all about Weilk, for it had held the borders from the hordes of warriors coming down from Sclan when Sclan had the strongest and most ruthless army in The Great Land. Since that time, Sclan had been destroyed from inside. It now lay barren and broken. Lankor had never been to Sclan or Weilk, but he knew the history of The Great Land, and wasn't sure he wanted to head into those harsh territories.

His ears were ringing from the tension he held in his head and neck. As the group slowed down to a walk, Lankor's shoulders relaxed. He felt tired. His stomach had been holding itself tight and he let out a long breath as his whole body slumped in the saddle.

Raik brought the head of his horse near Lankor on the left. "You were catching on, but you kept t-tensing up in the turns and when we slowed. See how you feel now? Feels good, doesn't it? That's what you w-want while the horse speeds up."

"I don't think that's possible," Lankor said.

"It'll have to be or you're going to be body sore and so will your horse at the end of this first day."

"I'm ready to rest already."

"No d-doubt," Raik said.

A few hundred feet more and Zimp stopped to wait for the rest of them to ride into a clearing.

Lankor's horse stopped and then began to back up.

"Be easy on it," Zimp said.

Raik came up next to Lankor and reached over to slap his shoulder. "You're doing fine."

Lankor had not noticed Zimp's face during their brief meetings. Her high cheekbones and oval eyes made her look as though she'd come from a far, far land. The light filtered by the trees played over her hair, and he could see streaks of red from time to time. Her red cloak could have been causing the illusion, though. She pushed herself up using her legs and leaned on the saddle horn. She had strong arms and hands. Before she spoke, Lankor noticed a slight hesitation.

"We travel over the Yellow Hills and along the mountain north toward Castle Weilk. A few days at best," she said.

"We'll have to travel parts of Torturous Road," Brok said.

Zimp sat. "I know."

Brok said, "Have you thought that possibly a path was not opened by the doublesight, that our escape may have been planned? We may be riding into a trap waiting on the other side of the hill."

"I've thought of that," Zimp said. "Before we reach the crest later tonight, I'd like you to send Therin ahead."

Brok lowered his head. "Done."

Lankor wondered what connection there was between Brok and Zimp that he would take orders from her so readily.

"Tonight we show our beast images to one another," Zimp said flatly. She reined her horse around and proceeded at a walk toward the Yellow Hills.

Numerous paths — some animal and some human — wound up the side of the hill toward the top. Lankor wondered why Zimp selected one particular route over another. At one point he followed as those ahead of him rode horizontally along the hillside for a thousand feet and then turn nearly vertical. The horses groaned as their bodies pushed themselves and their riders up the embankment. Raik, who had the packhorse tethered behind him, had a more difficult time getting the two to climb simultaneously. Lankor learned to lean forward over the saddle horn and let his horse find its own foothold at whatever pace it wished. Trying to slow the ride only caused his horse to lose its footing.

Several times during their ride, Lankor noticed Therin burst down the hill. Once he leaped from a rocky ridge and tumbled toward Brok's horse, frightening the animal into leaping sideways. The thylacine appeared to be having fun in its beast image. It was obvious that no one waited to ambush them.

Because they rode toward the top of the hill, they eluded an early sundown, gaining on the sun as it slipped slowly over the hill and into the distance. Along the ridge, Lankor stopped, expecting to see a valley vista; but only a western stretch of Brendern Forest lay before him. The hills rolled into the distance a green and yellow hue in the fading light.

A crow cawed and Brok asked Zimp if it had followed them.

"No. We're alone. He warns others of our arrival." She slid

from her saddle and bent her legs. "Quite a ride," she said. "I'm not used to traveling like this."

Brok dismounted and held out his hand. Therin ran from the north trail to greet him.

Lankor feared that his legs wouldn't work properly once he got off the horse. He had not eaten the whole day, except for the bread that was handed him. His body felt exhausted.

Raik threw a leg over his horse's neck and jumped to the ground. He stamped as though making sure the earth was real. "This is where I belong," he said. He walked around his horse and reached for the bridle of Lankor's horse. "H-hop down."

Lankor wasn't sure whether to swing his leg behind or in front of his saddle like Raik had done. When he pushed into the left stirrup and began to lift his leg, the horse shifted its rear to the side in a swift motion, which caused Lankor to fall. He heard a few snickers. "So I am not a horseman…" He stood and brushed himself off.

Raik led the horse away. "I'll care for the horses. This w-was a long trip for them, t-too."

The ridge area Zimp had chosen lay open to the approaching night sky, already exposing stars that hid throughout the day like invisible watchers. Rocky outcroppings pitched over long drops. Dirt and stone packed the rough ground. Scrub grew in odd patches here and there. The ridge ran north and south, and in both directions looked fairly open, bare of the thick forest they just left. The hills shrunk in the southern direction as the ridge turned west. Followed far enough, the ridge would drive them due west along the north side of the lake toward Stilth Alshore. Higher ground stood north of them. Yellow Hills drew closer to the sky, colder, and more dangerous to travel. A great tower had been built near the peak. It was said that around Memory Tower stood stone images of the most gruesome combinations of animal and human that ever lived. Lankor had never been anywhere near Memory Tower. He would have liked to see if his dragon image was set there in stone.

"Beautiful view," Zimp said.

Lankor glanced over at her and put his hands on his hips. "Better than having trees all around. I felt closed in. Trapped.

Not here though."

"My concern is our position," Brok said. "We're in the open. If we make a fire, it'll be seen for miles."

"That's what we want," Zimp said. "We don't want anyone to take us as criminals slinking through the forest, looking for our next take. We're just a band of happy travelers, out to see The Great Land and all it has to offer."

"I'll collect firewood," Brok said. He and Therin stepped off into the woods from where they had just emerged.

"Can you make a fire?" Zimp asked, then burst into laughter. Her hand flew to her mouth and her face reddened. "I'm sorry. I said the words before I thought about them. You know what I mean, though, don't you?"

Lankor shook his head. "I'll take care of it."

As Zimp walked off to check in with Raik, Lankor created a beautifully tiered fire pit. Brok dropped armful after armful of wood next to Lankor, who placed the pieces strategically for maximum heat and minimum waste. Already the wind along the ridge had chilled. It would be a cold night up there.

Before long, even the haze from sunset disappeared and darkness fell over them. The stars provided an evening tapestry of light. The moon would rise later in the night to cross above them. The fire pushed enough warmed air into the area for them to huddle around. After a quick meal, Zimp suggested now might be the time for them to shift in front of one another. That would allow each an awareness of the other's beast image while human, and human image while beast.

"My brother has given my image away," Brok said. "I should go first."

"Or me," Lankor said. "I've already made the mistake of changing before many of you." Lankor pointed at Raik, "And you, my little friend? Would you not volunteer?"

"I am afraid you may not like traveling with me once you know the truth," Raik said.

Lankor laughed for the first time since their morning. Laughing made him aware of how sore his stomach muscles were. And his shoulders hurt even though it was his butt that held fast to the horse all day. "Did you see me shift last evening?"

"No. I was looking away at the time. I couldn't see over everyone when I did turn around."

"I saw it," Zimp said.

"So you can see my image even now? Or do you sense my beast another way?" Lankor said.

"I see it if I choose to, but also sense it another way," she said. "I'm an intuitive, remember?"

"I can smell it," Brok said. "Once I've witnessed the change, I can smell it all over the person, or beast. I just know who they are, what they are."

"Therin?" Lankor asked.

"Yes. So far," Brok said. "I've only heard of doublesight remaining in their beast image, I've never witnessed it myself. Breel and I are afraid that Therin will lose his human sense as he slips deeper into the beast image only. He understands me now, but how long that will go on, I don't know."

"Could he become dangerous?" Zimp asked.

Brok stroked his brother's head. "What do you think, Therin?"

The thylacine shook his head as though answering Brok. "It appears he is saying no."

Brok didn't look as convinced as he sounded.

Lankor looked to Zimp and to Raik. Each had their own challenges and here they were thrown together for a mission Lankor felt was vague. To bring back information so that The Few could decide how to handle the problem. What information? How would they decide to resolve a problem that they didn't understand?

"My feeling is that Brok will know what to do with Therin and when to do it," Lankor said.

"You may be right, dragon boy," Zimp said.

23

Brok stepped to the edge of the ridge, surrounded by a clutch of blinking insects sparkling like lost coals from the fire. He turned and looked at his companions, "Watch me shift."

Zimp felt a surge of fear run through her body like nothing she had felt before. Secretly, she didn't want Brok to be first. Each time she watched a shift, the image became easier to see, more permanent. She and Brok were not on the best of terms, and the ability to see his thylacine at all times would be tempting, yet horrible. She had no choice in the matter.

She stood and motioned for the others to stand with her. Shifting would become a sacred act they would do for one another, not just in front of one another. "Wait," she said.

She felt that Brok understood immediately what was about to happen. She reached down and pulled a blazing branch from the fire and lifted it over her head. "The crow clan has no ceremony for such an event. I am sorry. But know this," she swallowed and let words come to her, "that with this flame, in this dim light, we are here to share in your shifting. We are here to accept your beast image, and will forever respect and care for you as our brother." Her heart pounded. The words, her words, as though they were coming from another realm, touched her soul.

Raik placed his hands together as though praying. He bowed.

Brok looked over at Lankor and waited. Zimp pointed to the fire at another branch, cold on one end and aflame on the other.

Lankor reached down and pulled the flaming wand into the air with an awkward motion. He touched it to Zimp's. "Together, we bring more of the light of understanding." He mumbled the last word. "Ah, greater strategic brilliance and tenfold fire power to our plight."

Raik shook his head. He reached down and grabbed a branch with little unburned wood showing. His hand fell dangerously close to the flame and when he placed it next to the other two branches and the flames joined and leaped higher, more brilliantly into the night sky, Zimp was sure that his fingers burned. But he did not flinch.

The three of them stood side by side.

Brok spread his arms wide then pulled them in front of his body. His face elongated and spittle dripped from his mouth. His eyes burst into flame from the reflection of the fire the three others held. He shook his head as if trying to will the transformation into being. The sound of a moist mouth and clattering teeth filled the air. His head stopped shaking. In a low howl, he fell to all fours and barked a horrible and painful noise at them. The transformed Brok turned, the stripes along his back and the marsupial tail flashed briefly before he was gone into the woods.

Raik threw his stick into the fire and blew on his fingers. "That was an amazing thing to d-do," he said.

"Thank you." Zimp found herself respecting Raik for his tremendous self control.

"We must make it a tradition as each of us shifts," Lankor said.

"I felt silly," Zimp said. "There is no ceremony that I know of, yet I felt like we had to do something. Preserve the moment in some sacred way."

"It creates a bond," Raik said bluntly and with conviction. "At first I didn't know w-what to do. In war we would toast or cheer. Your instincts are good."

Lankor dropped his flaming branch into the fire. "Should

someone go out and bring him back?"

His words brought back the reality of the situation for Zimp.

"No," she said. "Give him a moment. He'll return shortly."

"He appears pretty independent to me, pretty cocksure of himself. He may decide to stay out all night," Lankor said.

"She's s-sure." Raik said.

Zimp and Lankor sat down near the fire. Both gazed into the flames watching them twist into the air as Raik lifted his chin and stared at the sky.

The loud scream-howls of the two thylacines pierced the air. Other squeals and barks burst into the camp as well. Yelps broke through the noise of the crackling flames. Death cries. Fear had struck.

"Wolves," Zimp suggested.

"They don't sound very happy," Raik said, laughing.

"It sounds like Brok and Therin know how to fight," Lankor said.

"As a thylacine, perhaps. We'll have to see what he can do in human-image," Zimp said.

Raik winked at her and she felt eerily penetrated by his stare.

Just beyond the ridge, the woods behind them became a blackened wall, visually impenetrable. The cool scent of the forest still prevailed in the air around the camp, mixed with the smell of the raw cold from the northern mountains.

"It is beautiful here," Zimp said.

Another bark spread over them, this time falling into silence much too quickly.

"Something died," Raik said. He turned to look over at Zimp. "And in such beauty."

She felt acknowledged, but not comfortable, with him listening so attentively to her heartfelt message. And then to twist her sense of beauty into a story of death. Was it sarcasm that he delivered?

"More greens and yellows than I'm used to," Lankor said. "Too closed in."

"I've never been to The Lost. Is it as barren as they say?" Zimp tried to ignore the howls and cries that interrupted their conversation from time to time. She noticed that Lankor listened closely to the far off battle, too, appearing impatient and frustrated with having to just sit and listen.

"The Lost is poorly named. My home is as alive as this place, but as different as it could be. Rocks grow instead of trees. The flowers are pointed, bristled with danger and poison – some of them. The game doesn't always have fur like here. There are cold-bloods everywhere, and insects that bite and leave huge welts on your arms and legs."

"Why would anyone live there?" she asked.

Surprising them both, Raik spoke to answer her. "It's wide, filled with sky. There is little humidity." He looked into the air over the fire. "There are as many b-browns and reds in The Lost as there are greens and yellows here. A different b-beauty, b-but beauty just the same." Raik lowered his gaze to meet Lankor's eyes. "Does that explain it?"

Lankor nodded. "If you own a dragon as beast image, I am afraid I do not recognize you. But, my little friend, you have stated the truth about my land."

"Not a dragon," Raik said. "I've traveled to a lot of places. Training. All over The Great Land and well into The Shallows, even on the Sea."

"The Flande Chain?" Zimp asked.

"The Cold Chain and the Warm Chain of Flande, yes. And the Sealands. I've been north to the Harsh Seas beyond The Lost." Raik lowered his eyes and looked into hers.

"The noise has subsided," Zimp said turning to look away. "I wonder if Brok and Therin will be back soon."

Lankor began to rise. "I'll check."

"No, you won't. What do you think those angry wolves would do to your human image?" Zimp said.

"I can fight them," Lankor said, but his action was to sit back down.

"I know, big boy, but you'll have to wait to show off. It's Brok's night to be free."

"I hate waiting," Lankor said.

Raik sat upright, pulled a dagger from his boot, and began to scratch into the dirt near his leg. "That is what will make you a b-bad warrior," he said to Lankor. "Hammadin was smart not to p-put you in charge. Your lack of patience would be harmful to the rest of us. I could train you to hold back for the right moment."

"You can't kill in any battle by holding back," Lankor said.

"And what experience have you got?" Zimp said.

Lankor remained quiet.

"Exactly," she said. "You might do well to listen to Raik."

A rustle from the edge of the woods brought two scuffed-up and bloodied thylacines into camp.

Zimp had to focus to see which was Brok. As she did so, the beast image on the right began its metamorphosis into human form. The jowls shriveled first, which disgusted her, and she turned her head.

Lankor pointed for Zimp to continue looking. "Shifting happens both ways. This is an honor."

He was right. Brok could have shifted in the woods and stepped into camp in human image, but he chose not to. Zimp began to stand again, but Lankor placed a heavy hand on her forearm and she sat back down and just watched as Brok shifted. His tail shrunk. His stripes faded. As his paws became hands he began shaking his head again. Zimp wondered if there was much pain involved in his transformation.

Brok coughed a few times, wiped his mouth with the back of his hand, and stood to his full height. "Thank you for leaving us alone," he said.

Zimp recognized Brok's sincerity. "No real help to send you."

"We f-figured you'd let us know if you needed us," Raik said. His easy tone was that of confidence. Zimp recognized that Raik would be the first to know if help was needed.

Therin sat and looked up at his brother. His black eyes were a doorway into the dark of the night. He cocked his head. Brok put his hand down and Therin stood and placed his muzzle into his brother's open palm. Brok smiled and stroked Therin's nose. "They didn't have a chance."

Zimp's stomach turned at the thought of what Brok and Therin could do to a wolf once it was caught in those huge jaws.

Lankor broke the silence when he said, "Who's next, Captain?"

Brok pointed at Zimp. "I've seen your kind, but have not seen you change. You had might as well give us intimate knowledge."

Zimp hated the idea of being intimate with Brok or Lankor on any level. The idea that she could see Brok's beast image any time she chose to was enough for one night. Now, to let him see into her? That felt disgusting. "I'll wait, thank you."

Brok turned his attention to Raik. "Would you like us to guess?"

"Y-you couldn't," he said.

"What are you nervous about?" Brok said.

"Leave him alone," Zimp said. Her feelings toward Raik had not yet jelled. She knew so little about him.

"I'm not doing anything. I'm only asking." Brok picked up a twig and threw it into the flames.

Regardless of his stutter, Zimp saw that Raik didn't appear to be bothered by Brok the way that she was. She felt out of control in the situation and didn't know why. Brok, having just come out of beast image, could be throwing his weight around: one battle won, another underfoot? She didn't want to believe that, but that's what occurred to her. "Do what you want, Raik. There is no pressure to change."

"Except that you said we'd do it tonight," Brok said. "Are you changing your mind?" Brok leaned in closer to the fire. He kneeled and sighed. "The doublesight are being destroyed. There are more attacks every day. The Council sent us on a mission. You know that we need to be able to sense one another's beast image or human image in order to work together efficiently, right, Captain?" Brok said to Zimp. "We may find more trouble than just humans on the rampage against doublesight, you know. There are doublesight all over The Great Land who are fanatics about their power to shift. They believe only in their own clan. They would be happy to help the humans rid them of predators, for instance. It may have been a wolf image clan who killed my family."

"Is that what you think? Is that why you and Therin attacked those wolves tonight?" Zimp questioned. Night birds hooted and sang as though calling to her.

"He's right. Has this not been part of your lesson in history?" Lankor said. "Why else would the dragon clan stay hidden to this day?" His statement was delivered in an even, quiet tone.

"The Few knew about the clan," Raik said.

"And many of the Council members. Oro," Zimp said.

"You have been isolated long enough," Raik said. "I'm sure you've been taught your own history, your own life story. What the doublesight did in the past was done out of fear of power. We are no longer in the past. If The Few knew about you, the *existence* of dragons should have been out in the open long ago."

"The existence of dragons," Lankor said. "You make it sound unbelievable. I know nothing else but the existence of dragons. I had never even seen a thylacine." He looked from Brok to Zimp. "How can I be of help to anyone?"

Zimp sensed his desperation. She sensed that Lankor knew what his purpose was, and her heart went out to him. The four of them were to become a tight pack in their own right, yet they all knew that Lankor was there to battle for the rest of doublesight. He was the only one who could battle another dragon. She knew that Lankor was to be used as much for bait as for warfare.

Zimp gazed at Lankor. "Do you want to shift? It is time that we became our own party of five." She included Therin.

"Six," Brok said. "Your sister."

Lankor and Raik sat up to look around. "Who?" Lankor said.

Zimp felt a gush of sadness and choked back a tear. She gave a brief explanation of her intuitive connection with Zora. "The rest is for another day," she said. "Now, we are on a mission. No one else is here any longer. No one controls how we interact or operate. To truly become one we must separate from The Few and the Council of the Doublesight."

"Here, here," Brok stood. "I'm with you, Zimp. We are the ones in danger. It's time to make our own decisions."

Zimp turned to Lankor. "So, would you honor us?"

Raik stood. "Please, you two. I know it can be good to

change the rules, but I'm a military man in many respects. Can we not break the rules and stay true to them all at once?"

"How?" Brok said.

"Lankor shifts last."

The emotion Zimp felt coming from Raik and his beliefs, the sadness from Lankor, the courage from Brok, all overwhelmed her and she burst into tears of affection for them all.

Brok gave her an odd look, but Raik took her tears in stride. Lankor reached out to her with a long arm and she let him wrap it around her.

"You are all so unbelievable. I had no idea," she said.

"You do now," Raik said. "Watch m-me."

They all stood, and with tears streaking her cheeks, Zimp reached to the pile of twigs, branches, and dead logs that sat near the fire. She stuck the thin end of a short branch into the fire and it burst into flame. She raised it. "I don't remember what I said before," she admitted.

Brok took a stick and plunged it into the fire. "Together we bring greater light and greater strength to one another," he said.

"Thank you," Zimp said as Brok touched his fire to hers.

"May my little friend show us his true self, knowing that we are his brothers, his family," Lankor said as he, too, held a lighted branch to the others.

Their words were awkward, but Zimp cast that thought away. She knew that in their disjointed way each of them had been truer in their hearts than at any clan ceremony she could remember.

Raik suddenly looked unsure of himself. Zimp wished she could help him, but she waited. After all, it was Raik who had voiced the virtues of patience.

The thin, wiry body of Raik pulled into itself, forming a single tight muscle. His head squeezed into the shape of a triangle. His eyes closed and then opened to indicate vertically elliptical pupils. He fell heavily onto the ground. There came a series of loud cracks as if every bone in his back were breaking. It pained Zimp to listen to the sound. Then Raik literally snapped into the shape of a snake of enormous size. Almost eight feet of writhing muscle curled into striking position before their eyes.

Raik raised his head into the air and swayed back and forth, his tongue flicking in and out, testing the air. His body color was between pink and brown, with reddish-brown cross bands that spread over his back in narrow strips that widened at his sides. His head color faded into a dull copper hue.

Zimp reached out and grasped Lankor's forearm. She was the weakest of them, the least terrifying. Brok was the oldest, Raik the best trained, and Lankor the most powerful. Why had The Few chosen her as leader?

The snake's head shifted, creating a threatening and horrifying image. This huge snake with Raik's head. But the snake image could not hold the human head for long. Shifting cannot stop mid-change. It can only be slowed. Raik's human head became heavy and fell with a loud thump onto the ground. There was no snapping sound this time, but for a moment Raik's human image appeared to have no bones in it at all. He flopped around and with difficulty sat upright. "Ahh," he said, in what sounded like complete relief. "You," he said to Zimp.

"I don't know."

Brok threw his stick into the fire. He took the branch from her fingers. "It's all right. We're here. We'll hold the space for you."

His words only made matters worse for her.

Lankor stepped away from her, threw his twig into the fire, and grabbed another stick from the pile, which he lighted and held into the air.

Raik picked up a stick, touched it to flame, and raised it above his head. "I acknowledge you as the leader of our band of warriors." He seemed quiet as he spoke, his energy drained from his own change.

His words thrust through her with their sincerity and loyalty. They gave her courage. She stood tall and stepped back from them.

"I trust that you have been chosen as our leader for a reason that we do not have to understand. And, I too, accept you." Brok placed his burning stick to Raik's.

Zimp, even in her heartfelt state of surprise, noticed Brok's delivery as being guarded. Did he feel slighted for not being named their leader?

Lankor echoed their sentiments and touched his fire to the others.

Zimp could not see what they saw. She could only feel herself become lighter. She saw them rise in her point of view, as she must have sunk to the ground. Often she leapt into change so that she could fly off, but here she must change with ease, before these three men who now knew more about her than she often knew of herself, if only they'd choose to gaze into her true nature. Zimp knew the moment she changed. She flapped her wings. The three men in front of her, their faces twisting in the light of the fire, were in black and white. She had but a memory of color. She hopped around to get farther from the heat of the flames, then shifted back into human image. She looked to her companions for support.

"B-beautifully d-done," Raik said.

The ritual was repeated for Lankor. This time, he changed without anger, and Zimp recognized the difference. His dragon image was still frightening to look at, but softer at the same time. He appeared to have heart. That was the only way she could explain it. Like what she would expect from Breel, frightening, but with a softness, as well.

After he changed back into human form, the three others threw their flames into the fire, which grew higher and brighter than it had been when they began their exposures.

The four of them came together and hugged one another. Therin rushed over as well, and for the first time, Zimp kneeled down and pulled him close to her. Something had changed in the last hour, but she wasn't sure what it was. She felt naked and empowered at the same time. She felt love and sadness, courage and fear.

As they separated and moved to sit around the fire, Zimp sensed a further change in Raik. He appeared nervous and pained. Unsure. He sat for a moment, then crawled over to one of the larger packs and curled next to it.

"What is it?" Zimp asked.

Lankor and Brok must have noticed as well. Lankor began to get up to go over to Raik.

"There's something more you need to know," Raik said in a quiet voice, a weakened whisper. "I lied."

"About what?" Zimp gazed at him, opening to the image of a snake around him. "Oh, to the Gods be damned."

Lankor stood still. "I don't understand. What happened to the image? Where is the snake?"

24

The image was gone from Raik. His aura appeared shapeless. Lankor refused to step any closer to the man. "This makes no sense." He tried harder to see Raik's beast image, but to no avail. A shiver went up his spine. He turned around and glared at Zimp. "What have we done here?"

Zimp did not speak.

Lankor looked from her to Brok, the elder of the group. A breeze spread over the ridge, shifting the firelight into snake-like shapes. A vast, cold, and earthen scent entered his nostrils.

Brok began to speak, then quit before a word could be formed.

Lankor urged him on, but Brok didn't proceed.

Raik lifted his head. He shook briefly then raised a hand toward them as if to keep them at a distance. "I'm sorry. I am not the warrior you believed I am. I can only cause harm to come to you."

"What are you saying?" Lankor overcame his own reluctance to advance. Raik had tried to help him ride properly. Raik had been the only doublesight Lankor felt comfortable around. What could be so wrong? "Hammadin said that you would teach us to fight, and now you say that you cannot? Well, I'll tell you now that it doesn't matter. Hammadin is not with us. This night we have made our own pact."

Raik curled into a tighter ball. "Y-you're scaring me."

Zimp got up and stepped close enough to touch Lankor's shoulder and draw him away from the frightened Raik. She removed her red cloak, unfurled it, and kneeled to place it over Raik's shivering body.

"I lied," he said. "That is what happens with me. I am no good. I can't fight. I am fearless and fearful, courageous and cowardly."

Lankor heard Zimp whisper, "You are with friends. If we must, we will protect you. We will teach you to become a warrior."

Raik gritted his teeth and turned. Zimp's cloak fell away. "Will you keep them away?"

"They are your protectors as well," she said. She motioned for Lankor to step back. She helped the small man to his feet.

His body appeared less coordinated, jerky in its movements. The fluidity of the snake was gone.

Raik stumbled closer to the fire while gripping Zimp's hand. His eyes turned down and looked away from Lankor and Brok.

"We have given you a promise of our allegiance," she said. "Trust in that."

Raik nodded reluctantly. He glared directly at Lankor and Brok as though he mistrusted them. His lips shivered and grew whiskers. His hands fidgeted, thinned, and shortened. He shifted more quickly, as though he were afraid to stay human any longer.

Lankor immediately fell to his knees and tried with all his will to be small and harmless.

The small, adult mouse that sat before them shook in its own fur, its tail twitching.

As Zimp lifted it into her hands, the mouse stepped forward and rose on its haunches as though ready to fight.

Lankor spoke to him. "You are safe, my little friend." Almost before he finished his words, Raik began to shift back into human image. Zimp set him down quickly.

Sitting next to their crow leader, Raik lifted his head and spread his arms open in a bold motion.

Around him, like a haze of transparent matter, moved the copper head. Raik stood. "Do you see now what I am?" Angry with himself, he rushed toward the other men, then stopped short and lowered his head. "I am a freak of nature. I am at once the prey and the predator."

"How is this so?" Lankor asked.

"I don't know," Raik said. "My parents have tried to rationalize it by suggesting that I am a throwback from a bygone era. That the ability to shift into any animal was still in our heritage."

"Any animal?" Zimp asked from behind him.

"Only two. The two you've seen. I couldn't stand any more than that."

"How does it work? Why can't I see the mouse image?" Lankor said.

"You will see it when it is time for the mouse to emerge. Now that you've seen both shifts."

Brok shook his head and turned to walk away. "I don't understand this."

"Wait," Zimp said, "let us hear him out." She turned to Raik. "Go on."

Brok crossed his legs and sat down, raising his chin toward Raik. "Yes, do explain." He leaned back on his arms, feigning relaxation.

Zimp shot him a glaring look.

Lankor felt curious about Raik and truly wanted to understand what had happened. He approached Raik with his hand out. Raik took Lankor's forearm and Lankor took Raik's forearm. They stood for a moment, shook once, and each put his free hand on the other's shoulder. Lankor disengaged and stood off to the side.

"B-Briefly," Raik said. "I have two beast images, as you saw. I also have two human image p-personalities that go with them. I continually try to balance the two, but it's difficult. I alternate between the images as I s-shift. But that's not the bad p-part."

"The bad part?" Lankor said.

"There is something about the timing of it all. If I am in snake image for several hours, then I must be in mouse image nearly as long before I can shift back into human form. And if I hold onto mouse image longer, which I can do, then I am forced to hold to snake image for a longer time. I am not so bound while in human image. Once human, I can shift at any time."

"Impossible," Brok said. "If that were true, the shift times would become longer and longer until you would be in beast image for years."

"There is a realignment period. I don't understand that either."

"How long?" Zimp asked the question on everyone's mind.

"A single day. After that, it's back to the beginning."

"Sunset to sunset in beast image?" Lankor said.

Raik nodded. "I just completed a whole-day shift recently. That's how I was able to shift so quickly from one to the other."

"But you can stay in beast image longer, can't you?"

"Oh, yes. Like the rest of you, I can stay in beast image for quite some time without remaining there. I don't know about you, but I can feel the pull back to human, at which time I must choose."

"There is no such pull toward beast image?" Lankor asked.

Raik twisted his face into a look of questioning. "Is it so with you?"

Lankor looked around and realized that he was the only one who felt the pull toward beast image, another way in which he was different than his companions.

Zimp shook her head in answer to Lankor's unasked question. "I have a knowing that change needs to happen in order for me to hold my shifting ability. A knowing. Not a pull or an urge in any way."

"Not me either," Brok said. He nodded toward Lankor. "It must be a survival instinct," Brok said. "Without it, dragon doublesight would disappear from The Great Land. Again."

"There is a lot to learn here," Zimp said.

Lankor noticed Brok becoming irritable. Perhaps there were too many oddities in their group, too many unfamiliar possibilities.

"Lankor's urges are up to him. They're his problem and affect us little," Brok said. "But what are we supposed to do with a snake or a mouse for a whole day while waiting for him to shift back into human form?"

Zimp shook her head and paced a short distance away. Lankor watched her enter her own mind as though searching for something not yet whole. He wondered if she were talking with her sister. He wondered how that might work, and if it worked how it could help them on their journey.

Zimp raised a finger into the air. The blackness of forest behind her, her body haloed with blinking white-light insects made her look more magical than he felt she was in truth. So many things were happening that he did not understand, that he needed to remain open about. He stood in awe, his eyes wide, waiting for her to speak.

"We will learn to use this anomaly as a strategy. Perhaps we can sneak Raik into a dangerous city as a mouse." She shook her finger and pierced Lankor's glare with her own, then turned that intense stare on Brok, who leaned back as though poked at. "Inside the city, then, Raik becomes the snake warrior and leads our forces."

"Great," Brok said. "What dangerous city? We are to gather information. The idea of us traveling together is so that we don't run into problems. We find the source of conflict and report back to The Few."

"That's not the mission. You know that," Zimp said.

Lankor felt the strike of her blunt words. No, he thought, he was the mission. He had to fight even if none of the others did.

Zimp must have noticed his thinking, or read his thoughts, because she looked into his eyes and said, "You are not alone in this either."

He acknowledged her words with a lowering of his eyes.

No longer the center of attention, Raik moved toward Brok. "Let us rest so that tomorrow we ride with renewed energy."

"He's right," Zimp said.

They took their places beside the campfire. The horses had been quiet through the entire shifting session. Raik checked on them one last time before rejoining his companions, taking a seat next to Lankor. "I am sorry for what appeared to be a deception."

"You don't need to apologize. You and I are equally outcast even from our own kind."

"For some reason, my m-mousey human image is nothing like the m-mouse itself," Raik went on in a whisper.

"It must be difficult," Lankor said.

"Sometimes I feel as though the s-snake is waiting to eat the mouse. Every time the m-mouse is my next beast image, I imagine the snake hidden somewhere inside me, ready to strike, killing part of my very s-soul as it does so."

Brok laughed briefly. "Maybe then you'd be like the rest of us."

Raik looked across the fire squarely at Brok. "I'll n-never be like the rest of you."

Zimp spoke in soft tones. "I can only image what it was like in The Great Land when there was complete freedom between beast and human. How horrible. Just like our history says."

Lankor waited before saying what was on his mind. "Do you think that is part of the fear about dragons?"

"What would that be?" Zimp asked.

"That if one species is back, that perhaps others will be, too. And that we might be going back to the way we were? A cycle?"

"Look at me," Raik said. "If I'm any indication where our kind might be headed, no wonder those who are human-image only are afraid of us. No wonder they wouldn't want us to evolve. What would The Great Land turn into?"

"I don't know," Zimp said.

Lankor didn't feel that she was being honest. For her, the situation wasn't personal. Her entire clan wasn't at jeopardy. It would be impossible to rid The Great Land of crows.

Zimp leaned back and looked around for her cloak. Seeing this, Raik crawled back and grabbed it from where he had been earlier. He balled it up and threw it to her. Zimp spread it out next to her and rolled onto it. She placed her arms behind her black hair.

In the firelight, Lankor watched her face shift with the shadows that swept over her. The wind stressed the fire, which in turn created stress in the fine curves of Zimp's cheeks, lips, and chin.

"We need sleep," Zimp said.

Brok drew a blanket from within his pack. Therin sauntered

over and lay down to sleep next to his brother.

Lankor drew on his seriousness and leaned toward Raik. He jerked his head up to indicate that he wished to take a walk. Raik stood as Lankor did.

"Don't be gone long," Zimp said. "Especially you, dragon boy. You'll need all your strength just to ride tomorrow."

Neither of them answered her, although Lankor felt the sharp edge of her ridicule as he followed Raik along the northern ridge near the edge of the forest. They were some distance away when Lankor first spoke. "You are no different than I am," he said.

Raik stopped and lifted his head to the stars and the sky. "Each of us is unique. I'm just doubly so."

"Why us, do you suppose? What is it that we five have to offer The Few or the doublesight, that they couldn't have gotten through another means? We don't even know one another well enough to be strategic, as Zimp puts it."

"She'll pull it all together," Raik said. "Trust her. I have been around many leaders. There is something in her that is natural and will show itself soon enough."

Lankor looked at the sky. "How many more of us are out there? How many doublesight?"

"There are but thirty-seven clans left in The Great Land. We are a dying race. The human singlesight are strong and many. They have learned to control many animals and make them fight for them, work for them. Our problem is that we still respect the beasts, being half beast ourselves."

"I eat animals," Lankor said.

Raik laughed. "Yes, as do I, but I respect them as I do so."

Lankor laughed with his friend, a hearty, free-flowing laugh. One that he needed. He slapped Raik on the shoulder and looked out over the rolling hills to the west. "How far does this go on?"

"As far as we choose to travel, my friend. As far as we choose. That is if we run into no bandits out here."

"Bandits?"

"Look out there. The world folds in on itself. It rises and falls, shifts and turns. You can't see the river valley from here. It looks like one endless forest, but it's not. There are many places to hide out there. You'll see," Raik said.

"Is it always windy up here?" Lankor said.

Raik pointed to the north. "Colder air is pushing in. Yes, after the sun goes down, the wind picks up. But look, we may have rain by morning."

"There are almost no clouds."

Raik pointed to the west, shaking his head. "Do you see any stars over those trees?"

"I hadn't noticed," Lankor said.

"I'm sure you have the same thing happen in The Lost, only the wind comes from The Harsh Seas."

"Seasonally."

"You need only train your eye using different colors, my friend." Raik turned to go back. "I need sleep. The chill is getting to me."

Lankor followed him back, noticing that the smooth movement of his body was back in place. So far, he liked Raik best.

Before they reached camp, Lankor heard a loud crack and a distant boom. A brightness flashed out the corner of his eye.

"It's coming," Raik said. "Let's hope it rains in the valley and leaves us alone up here."

25

The rain never came that night, but the wind swept the crest in a fury, bending short mountain pines and drawing dirt and stones into the air like small tornadoes. The dog-like howling of the wind woke Zimp before sunrise. She pulled her cloak closer to her body and tucked her head into it like a turtle under attack. She opened her eyes into a sliver. A dark shape sat near the edge of a rock ledge. She grabbed her dagger and coiled into a ready position, then sprang from under her cloak. The shadowy shape did not stir, but she recognized it anyway. Lankor sat on his haunches, his arms wrapped around his legs and his hands holding his knees. He appeared as the statue of the man she met only two days prior.

Zimp walked over to where the silhouette perched. Her hair blew back from her face. The chill morning air tightened her skin in bumps. "Did you sleep?" she asked when she was close enough for him to hear.

"Yes. Several hours." Lankor said.

"It's going to be a long day," she said. "And with your riding ability…"

"I'll survive. You needn't remind me of my limitations so often."

She strolled closer. The hard, angled features of his face became more defined. His hands were strong and his body thick with muscle. She ignored his comment. "You're not afraid you might fall from this height?"

"I could shift before I hit anything dangerous."

She leaned over to look down. "That would be a fast shift for a beast of your size. Wouldn't that be painful?"

"Not as painful as death," he said. Lankor turned his face toward her. "Are you concerned for my health?"

Zimp drew her eyes away from him and forced herself to glance over the edge of the ridge toward the rolling hills. She placed her dagger back into her boot and felt Lankor's eyes watch her movements. She wasn't sure, for the moment, whether she liked his stare or felt threatened by it.

"We'll be traveling down into the forest again for the next few days," Lankor said. "I wanted to be in the open for as long as I could. I wanted to see the morning light illuminate the trees in the distance. Watch it glide over them a little at a time. The expanse makes me feel homesick, but good."

"A romantic thought about your homeland," Zimp said.

Lankor stood and his knees cracked. The ends of his boots extended past the rock he stood upon. He leaned dangerously forward.

Zimp stepped closer in an automatic motion meant to rescue him if he should slip.

"You couldn't save me," he said.

"I'd try."

He turned on his heels and came down from the rock. He stood next to Zimp. The sun began its rise behind them. A shard of light darted into the distance. "Mornings are beautiful," he said.

She felt his eyes as he studied her profile. She thought to say something, but words didn't come. The morning light and his stare were all she could take for the moment. She didn't like how she felt. Her mind churned, muddled and thick.

From a nearby tree bending in the slowing wind, Zora whispered, "Care for your safety."

Zimp swung her head around toward the voice.

"What is it?" Lankor asked.

"Nothing," Zimp said. "We should get ready to go on."

Zimp left Lankor at the ridge and woke the others.

They rustled around camp, collecting their packs and getting the horses ready. Lankor appeared sluggish, but active all the same. Morning birds sang the sunrise alive. Several crows entered the sky and flew south. The doublesight group had a quick breakfast, each eating from their own pack's breads, dried meats of various kinds, handfuls of nuts and bark. The fire pit had already been put out and roughed over, the extra wood scattered.

"Everyone, before we leave," Zimp said motioning for them to come to her. Zimp lighted a candle of green and gold. As she placed it onto the ground, she reached out to indicate for them to make a circle around the candle. She closed her eyes. "We thank the Six Shapeless Gods for creating all life on The Great Land. We thank them for returning and separating man from beast when we could not control our own minds. And we thank the Six Shapeless Gods for allowing the doublesight to know the truth of shapeshifting. We now urge them to protect our lives on this journey. To the Gods."

"To the Gods," they each said.

"You know the Shapeless Gods were just playing and didn't know what they were doing when they created us?" Raik said.

"Even as children, the Gods were able to create life. They saw how they had made a mistake and corrected it. Have we ever done that? Have the beasts or the humans ever done that?" she said feeling anger rise in her.

"It doesn't make the Gods right. It only makes them our creators," Raik said.

"And they could destroy us if they chose to do so," she said.

"It is my belief that they will never return," Raik said. "They don't care what happens to The Great Land or the doublesight. We have become an old toy, discarded and broken."

Zimp stared at Raik for a long moment. "You may believe what you wish. As long as we travel together, I'll have morning blessings if we have time to do them."

Raik nodded a reluctant, slow approval and acceptance of her directive.

"Now, let's ride. Brok, could you have Therin run ahead and sniff out any trouble?"

"Done." He bent down and talked with Therin, something that continued to look strange to Zimp. It was difficult to tell if Therin understood his brother. The thylacine's jaw dropped and drool slipped out and onto the ground. Its dangerous mouth looked hungry.

Zimp recognized the same wide, sweeping mouth on Brok that his brother exhibited. The eyes were similar too, dark and difficult to look into. She blew out the candle and slid it into her pack. Concerned for Lankor's ability to ride throughout the day, she decided to take breaks whenever she could. She rode back and asked Raik to keep an eye on Lankor as well.

"I would have done that anyway," Raik said, an edge in his voice.

Zimp shook her head. Raik must have taken their disagreement to heart. She wondered how she was to manage all those men with their individual annoyances.

Brok waited for her to ride to him several hundred feet from the other two. "I don't trust either of them," he whispered.

"They took the oath," Zimp said.

"So did we," Brok said.

"I should not trust you?" she asked.

He turned his horse and led the way.

"Do you know where we are going?" Zimp wanted to know.

"Down," Brok said. "Therin's tracks will show us the easiest descent." He turned in his saddle to glance at her. "Or would you like to find our way?"

She wondered how she had managed to anger each of them in a single morning, then checked her own feelings of anger. But it wasn't anger so much as a sense of vulnerability. As a woman and as a crow clan member, intimacy was not such a threat for her as it might be for the others. Still, not wanting to give in to Brok, she said, "I trust your brother."

He laughed as he swung forward and squeezed his horse into movement. He rode with an easy sway as though he were part of the horse itself. His curly hair glided over the back of his neck.

Zimp had never seen him cry over the death of his parents. In fact, there had been very little show of emotion whenever she was around. Breel, on the other hand, had the feel of being more human in nature. She joked and talked. She asked questions and openly cared for people. Brok appeared cold, except when he addressed his siblings. He hugged and kissed his sister, held Therin across his lap. There seemed a definite split in his feelings for his family versus all others. Yet he never cried over his parents, and that still felt odd to Zimp.

She listened for Lankor's horse behind her and turned around when anything sounded amiss. Lankor rode with his hand gripped to the saddle horn and his body leaning back. His horse appeared to struggle under Lankor's weight. Zimp noted the strain and planned to rotate the horses later to give it a break.

The forest thickened and thinned at various places. The path Brok led them down declined in an easy slope and along a widened pathway. More than animals had used the path, Zimp thought. Parts of it were from trappers and hunters.

Birds of various kinds, robins and starlings, wrens and warblers, chirped and sang. A hawk screeched and flew past. Large game remained scarce, hidden from the band of misfits trudging through the forest.

When the earth flattened out, she announced that they'd rest and have lunch. She suggested they rotate the horses and Raik volunteered to swap with Lankor first. "I noticed it struggling on some of the slopes," he said.

"Grab some food. We'll rest for a short time and go on." She removed a large piece of bread and a pouch of blueberries from her pack and sat on a log. She saw Lankor drag a piece of dried, unrecognizable meat the size of his fist from his pack. He ripped a piece of meat off with his teeth. Raik and Brok both had meat as well, only Brok had bread with his.

Raik sat on the ground cross-legged, and Lankor plopped next to him. Brok leaned against a tree. "We appear safe so far," Zimp said. She glanced around expecting Therin to rush from between two trees at any minute.

"Safe," Brok said. "We're being followed. For the last hour."

"Therin?" Zimp said.

"He's keeping an eye on them," Brok said.

"Are they close enough to hear us?" Zimp said.

"No. Far enough away that we can't hear them, I'd say." Brok crouched down.

Zimp noticed that Lankor stiffened up with the news. "Do you suppose they have any idea?"

"Not at all," Brok said.

A few birds flitted into a bush at the edge of their small circle, then flew back into the woods. The birds startled Lankor.

"You've got to calm down and not look so ready to fight," Zimp said.

"Again you ridicule me," Lankor said.

"Might I make another suggestion?" Brok said.

Zimp cocked her head toward him. "What?"

Brok laughed and stood up. "You know, I'd be happy to follow you through the woods if you acted more like a leader. And, so you know, giving orders is not leading."

"I thought you had something to suggest. Is that it? You suggest that my authority is lacking?" Zimp said.

"I am the oldest man here," he suggested. "I slept under your wagon to protect you and Oronice. And now you're in charge?"

Before Zimp could answer Brok, Raik said, "Anyone concerned about our followers?"

"Good thinking," Lankor said.

"We don't act like four friends who are traveling together," Brok said. "So, for the captain's information, I suggest that we talk more." He glared at Zimp. "Maybe we could laugh and banter like we care about each other. They can't hear us at the moment, but they'll get braver. When they do, the last thing we need them to find out is that we hardly know one another, that we don't talk like we're friends. Right now we're traveling as though we're on a mission."

Zimp felt the blood rush to her face. Silently, she called on Zora. Had she been with her clan, she could ask Oro what to do. She looked from face to face and didn't recognize any of them. She knew little about Brok and she had witnessed one of his most sacred moments. She lifted her head and closed her eyes for a moment, blocking their faces from her vision. She took a deep breath of the forest air, earthy and clean. "You have thought this over and you're right." She would let Brok have his alpha male moment in the hopes that it would defuse his anger, and with the further hope that it did not fuel the anger of Raik or Lankor.

"What's that mean?" Lankor said.

"That we should talk and laugh as we ride. We need to look and feel as though we are out to see the land." She stood and walked over to Brok. She placed a hand on his shoulder and shook it, then patted it heartily. "We should be friends."

Brok bowed his head and offered Zimp a piece of his lunch. She declined, holding up her bread.

Raik laughed at them. "Keep that up and it will be funny, not familiar."

"Not much longer and we will get to a hollow where the mountains merge. We can follow that north and down toward Torturous Road," Zimp said.

"You've been through here before?" Brok asked.

"We are a traveling clan," she said. She stepped close to him. "Is Therin going to be all right out there?"

"He will."

"Do you think it'll appear strange having him in camp with us if we're being followed?"

Brok reached up and rubbed her back between her shoulder blades. Zimp tightened as he touched her.

"Just being friendly," he said. "And to answer your question, I don't know how it will look. Humans do keep animals around, but a thylacine isn't usually domesticated. Raik's family guessed right off that things were strange with us."

"We don't have much choice. We can't banish him." She thought for a moment and mounted her horse. "Will he be safe if we treat him like a pet we all share?"

"We can try," Brok said.

"Comforting." She pointed into the woods. "You lead."

Brok rode between trees and she followed. Behind her rode Lankor, and then Raik in the rear. Recalling Zora's most recent warning, she felt safe with Brok in the lead.

The path widened as they dropped into the hollow. Zimp

heard the rush of water a short distance to their right. In places, the path they took opened to the stony bank near the creek. They began to ride side-by-side, intensifying the need for them to act friendly in one another's presence. She rode next to Brok. "So, tell me a funny story, something that will make me laugh and act like we've know each other for a long time."

"Just talking will be fine. At least for now. If they get any closer this kind of talk has got to stop. They'll know we're unfamiliar with each other," he said.

"Well, that's because you just said so. If we continue to talk about our unfamiliarity, how will we become familiar?"

"What changes if we know each other better? Do we feel more sorry if one should die?" Brok said.

"You don't trust me," Zimp said.

"You helped me, Therin, and Breel a lot. And I appreciate that. I took an oath to the council, and I have to abide by that. But I don't have to believe that you're the right choice to lead us anywhere but into danger. You haven't shown me anything that would make me want to trust your knowledge of our situation."

"Fair enough," Zimp said. "Perhaps it's time that I show what I do know."

Brok looked at her in shock. His face softened after a moment. "I felt that," he said.

It was Zimp's turn to look confused until she heard Zora say, "As well he should."

There were things in The Great Land, Zimp realized, that even she didn't understand. The strength of Zora, even in the next life, was greater than Zimp had understood. Had something happened between them during the dance? She thanked her sister for whatever she had done.

The roar of the creek made it difficult to speak unless they yelled. Zimp heard the unrecognizable discussion that Raik and Lankor were having, but added very little to the noise by speaking with Brok except to say that they should cross the creek before going too much farther.

Brok halted his horse and when Zimp sidled up next to him, he leaned over toward her. "I haven't seen Therin for a while, only his footprints."

"Will he know to cross?"

"He'll double back and track us once he sees where we are," Brok said.

"There is something else bothering you," she said.

"Fewer birds. Fewer squirrels. I know it's loud sometimes, but that's not enough to cause the scarcity." Brok nodded as the other two got near.

"Are we crossing, my friend?" Lankor bellowed.

"You two enjoying yourselves back there?" Zimp said.

Lankor turned his shoulder toward her and bent at the waist in a respectful bow. "That we are," he said.

"Do you recall a place to cross?" Brok asked.

"It was many years ago," Zimp said.

Raik leaned in to listen, then sat back in his saddle. "While we were back there," he said, pointing up the hill, "I noticed a place just ahead where the land appeared to level out and almost ascend again. There should be a place there to cross. We might find a small pool."

"Good job," Brok said. "We'll ride on, then."

Zimp glanced at him and nodded her head.

"I'm glad you approve," Brok said.

Zimp turned back to Raik and Lankor. "Watch what you talk about."

"We know." Raik winked at her and a chill ran up her back.

Zimp would have liked to be in the top of a tree where she could feel safe and where she could see the farthest. Although she loved the forest as much as the plains, she wasn't as used to noticing the wildlife as Brok appeared to be. One thing she did notice, though, was anything that sparkled, and at one point just before coming to the pool that Raik predicted, Zimp saw several glints of sun against metal.

At the mouth of the pool, Brok walked his horse into the water and continued until the water rose to belly-deep on the beast. Zimp was next. Halfway across she checked on Lankor, who appeared to be having no trouble. Raik followed closely behind, almost pushing Lankor's horse into the water. Brok's mount stepped onto the shore at the opposite side and Zimp came up beside him. She turned and recognized Therin as he lept into the pool and swam behind the horses for a short while before overtaking them. He made it to shore before Raik could push behind Lankor.

Brok jumped from his mount and leaned to greet his brother. Therin shook his fur out and Brok backed away. Grabbing the saddle horn, Brok swung back into the saddle. "We'd better go quickly," he said. "Therin's nervous."

"We'll need to stop soon," Lankor said.

Zimp didn't know what to do, but felt she couldn't ignore the problem. She looked to Brok, then thought better of it. Brok wouldn't like it, but she turned to Raik. "Well, Flandean Guard, any suggestions?" The moment she said the words, she felt as though she were back in control of the situation. She didn't need to know what to do all of the time, but she did need to know who best to turn to.

Raik smiled. "Pull farther into the forest and away from the noise of the water. Then get off the path and travel through the thickest underbrush you think the horses can handle. They'll have to fall back because of the noise they'll produce. If we can find the smallest clearing within the thickest brush, we'll be able to hear them coming. One guard should be enough for the night."

"Brilliant," Lankor said.

Zimp nodded. "Very good." She motioned for Brok to lead on.

26

Racoons, opossums, owls, all chattered and hooted and moved in the forest at night. Other animals, like thylacines and bears, roamed the area. Nocturnal, scuffling, mating, hunting. Lankor listened to the magical voices of the forest as he relaxed against a tree in the deep chill of night out of reach of the fire's glow. He had never heard so much going on. He wondered if any of the sounds were the night play of doublesight.

What made one footfall and snap he heard strike an unnatural cord had little to do with the sound itself. All types of noises rose and fell around him. The trigger was that the other forest noises silenced. Lankor knew an attack was inevitable. The pursuers were on them. He threw a pebble at Raik's prone body and hit him in the chest.

Raik awoke and rolled onto his stomach in slow motion, reached out, and touched both Brok and Zimp on the face. Each of their bodies tightened. Each person found and grasped a weapon, ready for any signal.

Lankor waited. He knew that his bulk would create a strain on the ground around him. From his vantage point, Lankor watched as Raik rolled from and puffed up his blanket to look like someone still slept there. In a moment, the job completed, Raik crawled away, not on his knees, but on toes and hands, curving into the underbrush like a snake. He was one doublesight that embodied his beast image even as human.

Lankor vowed to remember that fact.

When a bush shuddered on the opposite side of the fire, Lankor heard someone call out in pain then heard the quiet thump of a body going down.

Brok and Zimp slipped from their rolls and crouched ready to fight, each holding a blade.

The attackers charged. There were only seven of them, and they were on Zimp and Brok in a moment, leaping over the last scrub between them and the two doublesight. Lankor waited to see what position the dusty attackers would take. One man in dark green and bright jewelry fell instantly, for as he hit ground in the clearing, Zimp sprang toward him, blade extended low and into the man's abdomen. Brok used the power evident in the charge of another man by grabbing an arm and pulling the man into the fire. An animal fur vest burst into flames.

The bandit screamed and rolled out of the flames scattering glowing coals. He had removed his vest and begun to rise, when Lankor's staff slammed into the back of his neck and lowered him again, knocking him out with one blow.

Lankor stood to see another man go down under Raik's sword. The remaining four men looked surprised when Lankor emerged from the brush. His heavy staff dropped another one who stood ready to stab Zimp from the side.

Zimp didn't miss the opportunity to catch another attacker by surprise and twirled in the air, reaching at the right moment with her scabbard to slice the man's throat. When Lankor turned, Brok had already taken the other two down.

In the half-light, the four of them stood with arms relaxed next to their sides. Raik slashed some of the brush away with his sword and walked into the clearing. Therin leaped near his brother and skidded on the slippery moss and pine needle floor, late for the fight.

Zimp pointed at Therin and said to Brok, "Would he know if there are more? Could he tell you?"

Therin lay down near his brother's feet.

"It appears to be safe," Brok said.

The man who Brok dragged into the fire moaned. Lankor walked over and grabbed the man by the front of his shirt and pulled him to a sitting position. The others gathered around.

Zimp leaned down in front of the dazed man. She reached up and slid several chains from the man's shirt. She lifted his wrist and on it were five bracelets. The man had a ring in his ear and two piercings in the flesh between his thumb and forefinger of his right hand. "Bandits of the worst kind," she said. "They don't steal. They kill and then scavenge."

"We're not even on Torturous Road," Brok said. "Is this what we have to look forward to?"

"These piercings on his hand mean something," Zimp said.

The man opened his eyes. He looked young to Lankor. "That is my killings, missy. You could be three."

"Not likely," Zimp said.

The man began to lift his hand and Lankor brought his staff down on it, cracking something.

"Ahh, you broke it," the man cried.

"I could have broken your neck. I'd suggest you don't move unless we ask you to." Lankor looked into Zimp's eyes. "Any more questions?"

Zimp appeared to be satisfied with Lankor's response, his obvious acceptance of her as leader. "We are sorry about your friends," she said to the man. "And we are sorry that we have to leave you."

Raik said, "They're not all dead. My sword only killed one. The other I knocked out. He'll be coming around soon too."

"There you are," Zimp said. "Your partner can set that arm, and you can be on your way. If we see you again, for any reason, you are dead."

The man turned his head away in answer.

"We might as well move on," she said.

As they stood over the man, the soft roar of birdsongs rose from the forest around them. A precursor to the rising of the sun, the sound filled every space that stood silent a moment ago. Beauty and annoyance entered Lankor's thoughts. He could no longer hear the movements of other animals.

"They'll quiet once the sun is fully in the sky," Zimp said.

He glanced at her.

"You looked bothered by the sound," she said.

"I was."

Raik left the group to round up the horses that had been tied a short distance away. He asked Lankor to retrieve one of the bandits from the bushes before the bandit awoke and went back on the rampage.

Lankor trudged through the underbrush where Raik had indicated the man would be located and almost tripped over the body. This was an older bandit. The space between his thumb and forefinger held six or more rings, and other rings hung from those six. It was the same with both the man's hands. A real killer. Lankor carefully turned him onto his back, grabbed the meat of his upper arm, and dragged him through the brush like a carcass. In the clearing, Lankor dropped the man near the younger one. "Your leader, I suspect."

The young man nodded quickly, but Lankor noticed something else in his demeanor that suggested the older man meant more to the boy. "He's your father, isn't he?"

"'Tis," the boy said.

"He'll be fine. Just sore for a while."

"Are you through?" Zimp asked. "Raik will be waiting with the horses." She had collected their gear and it lay at her feet. She picked up her pack and led them toward the horses, while Lankor and Brok picked up their rolls and followed.

Brok leaned in to Lankor. "At least she appears to know what she's doing."

"Shouldn't we have asked more questions of the bandits, though?" Lankor said.

"I might have. But then, I might have killed them all, too," Brok said.

"They deserve to live out their lives," Lankor said, an understanding his father had handed down to him, one that his clan believed. Had they not believed it, the underlying notion was that their own clan would be wiped out.

"Perhaps you believe that now, but remember that if it were up to them the doublesight would be no more." Brok pulled away. "Think about that," he said.

"Would you have us kill every human?" Lankor said.

"Every human that threatened the doublesight," Brok said.

"Not that I have seen it for myself," Lankor said, "but my father told me that even though the doublesight look strong in a compound like the council grounds, they are few. You should know that. You lived in Brendern Forest. We could not win an all-out war against the humans. Many of the doublesight would not even fight. Their religion forbids it unless they are attacked as we were this morning."

"Is that how your clan believes?" Brok said.

Lankor thought about the question. "My clan or me? I struggle with that question. I believe in life, yet I could see that I would kill until I was killed if my clan were at risk. When I am angry, there may be little room between the two beliefs. Other times, there is a chasm between them."

"This journey will help you to settle that confusion, my man. This journey will have you thinking about your own life and death as well as the life and death of our small group, your own clan, and the doublesight. I suggest you start to figure where your loyalties lie so that when the time comes, you can act with clarity of purpose." Brok patted Lankor's back as though he were a close friend.

Lankor felt the touch of someone wishing to manipulate his belief system.

Raik held the reins of the horses. They were saddled and ready.

Lankor wondered how he had prepared them so quickly, but dismissed the thought. A trained warrior could do many miraculous things, he was beginning to notice.

Back on the trail, the four of them attempted, once again, to talk as though they had known one another for years. Without actually having that contact, the conversation was punctuated with questions. Lankor felt uncomfortable with the whole exchange. It seemed forced. Yet he would use the time to truly learn about the many doublesight he had never met in his life. Riding next to Zimp, he said, "I am sorry that we didn't get to begin the day with a prayer." When she didn't respond quickly, he added, "Isn't that your clan's way? Are they not very religious?"

"Religion is a slippery word," she said. "People fight to

uphold religion. People feel that religion is right or wrong. We prefer to say sacred. To the crow clan, the land is sacred, the sky sacred, the water. To us, all things should be shared. Nothing belongs to one human, animal, or doublesight."

"You slit the throat of that bandit back there."

"He attacked us. If they had come in peace, we would have bargained or bartered, but I never would have killed. That is the difference between being a thief and a bandit in this land." She looked directly into his eyes, an intense stare, forceful and strong, touching and emotional. "To us, we are not thieves, but are taking what should be shared anyway. What we do helps the economy of the places we leave. No one understands that but us. As we ride away the vendors and artisans are visited once again. Money is exchanged. Mouths are fed."

"That sounds less like fact and more like rationalization," Lankor said.

"Believe what you will." She turned forward and said, "I noticed you didn't kill."

"There was no need. The threat was minimal when it began. Like you, I would have killed had it been necessary." He paused, shifting in the saddle as the horses began a decline. "The others had little problem. Brok said that he might have killed them all."

"Brok is angry. I don't blame him for that. Raik is a trained warrior. I expect him to kill." She turned her head, looking shy and vulnerable. There was a long hesitation. "We two are the more respectful of life, the balance. I only hope we can hold them back when the time comes. I wouldn't want to enter a battle we were not sent to enter."

"Is that possible with these two?" Lankor said. "They appear to listen to your orders so far."

"I don't feel as though they listen at all, but that they do what I say because that is what they might do on their own. Or that what I suggest doesn't matter to them. They have no feeling about it." She turned completely around in her saddle. "Even now, Raik has fallen back out of sight. Only Brok and Therin are behind us. You see, no one told him to become a rear guard. Perhaps he is separating from my authority this soon in our travels. I fear that a quick oath might not be enough when real danger sets in, when strategy needs to be set."

"We will see."

"And you?" she said. "Will you obey my orders? Will you take my lead?"

Lankor felt his chest tighten and his throat close. He did not speak right away.

"Exactly," she said.

"I was thinking," he said.

"You should not have to think about your allegiance to the cause, to our purpose."

"I don't," he said.

"Then your objection is to my ability to lead," Zimp said.

Lankor drew his horse around to go back with Brok. "I was just thinking," he said. Zimp said something, but he didn't hear the words clearly.

Lankor drew up next to Brok. "Did Raik decide to hunt for our supper?"

Brok's wide mouth snapped into a smile. "He said he wanted to be sure we weren't followed."

"Those two? One had a headache that would take days to clear and the other had a broken arm." Lankor struggled with his horse, which didn't want to ride so close to Brok's horse.

"Trouble?" Brok said.

"I'm getting used to it. Just sometimes these things don't listen."

Brok smirked. "Be a little easier on his mouth and he might relinquish to your guidance."

"Sounds like her," Lankor said, lifting his chin toward Zimp.

"She's quite a woman," Brok said.

"Do you have feelings—"

"No," Brok snapped.

"I'm beginning to understand why you might want her to see your skills."

"You know nothing," Brok said.

From behind, Raik trotted his horse next to Lankor and Brok.

Lankor gave him a questioning look.

"Taking care of a few things," Raik said.

"I thought you were just making sure we weren't followed," Brok said.

Raik glanced at Brok. "We're not now."

27

The small band of doublesight rode down the mountain, through the hollow, and north along the western edge of Brendern Forest. They were now in Weilk and had passed the turnoff that drove due west toward Weilk Post Stronghold. This meant that they already traveled along Torturous Road. It was obvious that many paths paralleled the road in mock recognition of the number of bandits and thieves and crazed killers who roamed the area.

They rode along a side hill, beyond a parallel path, and deep into the forest where they were to spend the night. It appeared to be an untraveled and safe place. Was that even possible?

Zimp glanced around as though sizing up everyone's energy. "Raik, could you take first watch and Brok second? I'll take third and Lankor can do morning watch again."

Raik knew that Zimp could sense the strength of his snake image. She could see the image if she paused and focused for a moment, but that wasn't necessary. She continued to pace the length and breadth of the camp as though she were unsure of her decision.

"Could I ch-change with Brok this evening?" Raik turned to Brok, "If that's f-fine with you?"

Brok dropped his pack from his horse and dragged it near the trunk of an oak. He shrugged his shoulders. "I could do that." He pulled his bedroll out. "What's the pattern of the bandits out here? When might they attack?"

"Not at all if we are far enough from them," Zimp said. "Not everyone gets attacked who sets foot on the road."

"You think a mile or so from the road is enough to deter b-bandits?" Raik said. He felt Zimp's anger rise at his words, but stood his ground long enough for everyone to have the chance to notice his strength and confidence.

"I didn't ask for this job," Zimp said. "If you have a better idea, I'd like to hear it."

Brok stepped between them and said, "I say we hunt a few bandits down and take over their camp. That wouldn't be expected. And, the fewer bandits we have to worry about the better. They're only human and would probably hunt us down if they knew we were here."

Raik pondered Brok's aggression and Zimp's reluctance for a moment, and almost reconsidered his own plans for the evening.

"What do you think, Raik?" Lankor stretched out on his blanket. Therin stood beside Lankor. The big man didn't look the least bit concerned about how close the thylacine stood. "Well? You're the warrior. Maybe we should consider what you think, especially in this territory." He nodded toward Zimp. "What do you think? We're headed into a rough town around the castle. He might be able to give us warning, at least. Make us aware of what we might expect."

"I wouldn't know," Raik said. He felt sorry he had brought it up. He meant only to undercut Zimp's already weak authority, play her reluctance to lead against her. He was on the spot.

Lankor stared at him.

"Are you looking into my beast image?" Raik said. "Isn't that considered rude where you come from?"

"You appear to be edgy tonight," Lankor said. "Your image is weaving and unsteady. What's bothering you?"

"I, too, sense an agitation," Zimp said.

Raik walked away from them. He knew that exposing his images would create conflict with the others. He was different. He hated that, and he felt that they mistrusted him. He'd show them. Even Lankor, whom Raik liked, was pressuring him about his images, about his natural movement. Had the dragon man never seen a snake before, a copperhead slipping through the grasses of The Lost?

Raik positioned himself behind his horse and made like he was caring for it. The wind through the trees clacked leaves against one another and whooshed along the ground. He didn't feel safe with the doublesight, but didn't believe they noticed until now. Why would he question her and bring attention to himself? The snake weaved before a strike. He knew that, but they obviously didn't.

A tightness built in him just outside the edges of his human body. Raik sensed the pull toward beast image like the gnaw of hunger against an empty stomach. For a moment he heard another voice in his head, but no words were said. The voice had a feel to it, the feel of his mouse image poking a sharp stick at his snake image. A sharp familiar feeling he never tried to explain, even to himself. He wished Bennek were there with him. His brother's words were calming and would take his mind from the hunger to shift images.

"You need help?" Lankor had crept up on him.

Raik jumped back and the horse stepped away as if afraid of the movement. "D-do I look confused to you?"

Lankor leaned back. "Not confused at all. Are you?"

"I need to be alone. You wo-wouldn't understand."

"Look, my little friend, we all understand." Lankor placed a hand at the horse's withers, and it calmed under his touch. "Care must be taken when and where we shift. This is not easy for any of us."

Raik, in a moment of focus, blurted out, "I have a double need. My copperhead hisses and hisses in my ears. It wants out." He looked at Lankor and saw that the man had no understanding of what Raik had just confided. "I wish one of them would d-die," he said.

"What can we do to help?"

"Leave me alone," Raik said.

Lankor turned and left. He stood near Zimp to talk with her. Raik could not hear what they said, but knew that they plotted against him. He had said too much.

Brok had spent some time laying out a variety of foods they had brought with them. There would be no fire this night. That was the good and the bad of it.

Raik took a deep breath and asked his mind to quiet. He often had to do that. He thought of his family, his boys. He knew that either Zip would kill Ka or Ka would slit Zip's throat in the night. That some day their beast images would overcome them, as his beast images were taking over his life. Bennek thought differently, but Raik knew the strain personally. The mouse would do anything to have the snake gone from its habitat and the snake would merely feed off the mouse and never think about it again.

"I'll take your watch," Lankor said. Again, he stood behind Raik.

Raik nodded. "Perhaps you're right. I am in n-no condition. But a warrior does n-not let his comrades down."

"We'll each take an extra few minutes. It'll be easy. We should be there for one another." Lankor reached for Raik's shoulder and placed a heavy hand on it.

Raik looked squarely into Lankor's eyes and nodded his approval. He followed his fellow traveler back to the circle of the camp and sat on the ground with his legs crossed. His mind hissed and raced and twisted. He could feel his own snake image, the aura of it, swaying. "Brull believes that I was the only mouse remaining in the doublesight. That is, until Ka was b-born."

"Dragons were believed gone, too," Lankor said.

"Something is going wrong with the doublesight, I fear." Raik picked at the moss in front of him. "We are on some sort of road to destruction. Either we will kill each other or we'll kill ourselves."

"Don't say that," Zimp snapped as though she believed Raik but didn't want to hear it said aloud.

Brok stood and they all looked at him. "I'm going to take some food and begin my watch early. Therin will go with me."

"Agreed," Zimp said.

"He knows. His b-beast image knows this is a dangerous place. It s-senses something," Raik said.

"Predator and prey doublesight live together in harmony. That's why we don't kill when we are in beast image. We play. We explore our animal side. We have fun with it," Zimp said.

"And that's how the humans, the singlesight humans, know which beasts are truly animal singlesight and which are doublesight. That is how they track the doublesight down and kill them." Raik paused. He noticed that he did not stutter through his last statement. He had no hesitation about what he said. "That is how it is done now that many of the predator doublesight have already killed off many of the prey doublesight. B-but things are changing. Prey doublesight are returning. Like me. And the doublesight that was wiped out, like Lankor's dragon image, is returning." Raik took a deep breath. The talk had quieted the voices in his head for a while. "What other horrible images have already returned? What might we truly run into? D-Demons? You don't understand as I do that we need to be willing to kill our own as we would our enemy, just as we must be willing to kill the humans who appear to be our only enemy. We may need to have the strength to k-kill ourselves for the betterment of the whole of doublesight."

"Don't say that," Zimp said.

"It is true," Raik said, sensing the depths of that truth like he felt none of the others would ever be able to feel.

"The doublesight have a right to live, too." Zimp scooped up a large piece of bread and pecked at it, nibbling the edge.

"All life may have a r-right to live, but at what expense to other l-life forms? We destroy trees and g-grasslands to build castles and villages," Raik said.

"That's different. Plants don't speak and move as we do." Zimp appeared to notice the mistake in her thinking almost as soon as she said the words.

Raik leaned toward her and said, "I can see that you are beginning to understand. What of the b-birds, small animals, insects that are destroyed for those villages?" Raik lifted his head high. "Even people die to build the greatest castles. Like Castle Weilk."

"The great land is large," Zimp said.

Lankor scuffled to a sitting position and crossed his legs.

He reached for a slice of dried meat and held it up. "We already kill animals to survive." He bit into the meat and ripped off a piece. "Buffalo," he said. "There are no longer any buffalo doublesight. Does that make it okay?"

"What do you want me to say?" Zimp said.

"J-just see our point," Raik said. "The great wars may have ended, but smaller wars have continued. We of this w-world kill one another. That is what we d-do. Perhaps there is no stopping us. With the doublesight spawning throwbacks, I fear things will only get worse."

"You sound as though you're on the side of the humans. Would you see all of doublesight go down?"

"I d-don't always know the answer to that. I see both sides. You m-must remember, my dear leader, that my family was already mixed between doublesight and h-human. I grew up knowing both sides of the argument," Raik said.

Zimp pushed into a standing position. Raik felt small below her. Crows were known to kill snakes. He felt the predator in her as well as in himself.

"You'd better select your side," she said. Zimp turned and took a few long and bouncy strides into the woods, in the direction of where Brok had gone.

"I see your point," Lankor said once she was gone from earshot.

"I thought you might, being raised in The Lost. It is wild there. You can't escape the killing or you could be killed." Raik let his head lean back so a breeze could cool his face.

Lankor's voice came through the sound of the breeze, a low and firm sound. "But I want our clan to live. Do you see the difference? I don't mind letting others live, the sacredness of life and all that belief that comes from my family. But, more than that, I want dragons to live. It is not possible for us to live without meat, without killing, but we don't have to wipe out another race entirely. Where is the sense in driving the doublesight into extinction?"

"I am a danger to m-myself. My children are a danger to each other. If you came upon me too quickly while I was in s-snake image, I could k-kill you with one strike." Raik waited for a response.

Lankor laughed. "You could slit my throat while I sleep, while in human image. We all have our personality, our nature. These bandits kill their own kind just to steal trinkets to buy other trinkets. What is the thinking in that killing? Is the killing of a species you fear any better reason than to kill for money or jewels? Or food and shelter? Or protection?"

"I think you are saying what I m-meant. We are killers. All of us. It will only get worse."

"I like you, my little friend. But I disagree that we should accept that we kill each other only to wipe out our fear. Fear, as my father has taught me, is personal. You must accept your own fear and deal with it. Getting rid of the thing you fear does not end your feelings of fear. If you fear your own two images, you must deal with it." Lankor bit off another piece of meat. "Kill only when you must and respect that which you kill."

"You sound a lot like my brother," Raik said.

"And that's a good thing?"

"Yes, very good. I'll admit that I don't always feel like I have control over my own thoughts and actions," Raik said.

"I'll watch for that," Lankor said.

They both laughed over the idea.

28

Brok scanned the area for a glimpse of Therin, but only heard his brother's faint footfalls. He knew that few others, doublesight or not, would be able to sense Therin's presence at all. Thylacines were natural stalkers, quiet and deadly.

Alert to his surroundings, Brok took a few steps and caught the scent of one of Zimp's candles. The crow clan doublesight woman fell from the sky, landing lightly on her feet. He caught the unusual odor long before he heard her. Stooping behind a pine tree, Brok began to take shallow breaths. He waited. Zimp did not call out.

He wanted to shift into his thylacine image, get a stronger sense of her purpose. An ache shot through his body, and a hunger gripped his thoughts. He had to catch himself before the shift began. To do this, he looked at his hand, reached for his sword and, in one smooth motion, rounded the tree and drew his weapon. Zimp faced away from him. He touched the shoulder of her cloak with the tip of his sword. "I thought I had first watch?"

Zimp sighed and said, "I heard you only when it was too late to do anything about it."

"That's the idea. What brings you out for a walk? Surely you weren't wishing a rendezvous with me?" he said. Brok lowered his weapon. He could see that she felt uneasy in his presence. "I'm not dangerous unless I choose to be," he said.

"That makes me feel better," she said, in an obvious attempt to lighten the conversation.

"You should. I have no interest in harming you."

"I came for a reason," she said.

"I don't trust either of the others, if that's what you want to know," Brok said. "I believe I told you that before."

She pulled a berry from a nearby bush and popped it into her mouth. "I think there is something wrong with Raik."

"He does appear to be the more volatile."

She cracked a smile. "Oh, you noticed."

"He disappeared—'fell back,' is what he said—to be sure we weren't followed," Brok said.

"By that old man and his son with the broken arm?"

"He didn't say. But when he returned I noticed a spot of blood on his horse's flank." Brok didn't wait for her to say anything. A response wasn't necessary. "He killed them," he said, knowing that Zimp was well aware where the conversation headed.

"Why would he do that?" Zimp said.

"They posed a threat," Brok said.

"To us? I can't imagine," Zimp said.

Brok shook his head. She had the distinct look of confusion on her face. The reason seemed obvious to him.

"What?" she said.

"They posed a threat to him. They know something about him." Brok stepped closer to Zimp, knowing that it made her even more nervous. Had Therin been close by, Brok may have brought him into the mix just for sport. Yet there was something about her that intrigued him. He wanted her to like him, trust him, but fought those feelings.

"That doesn't make me feel any better."

"I'm surprised he let me take his watch, that he allowed us all to stand watch for him. I expected him to protest," Brok said.

"You were going to follow him, weren't you?"

"Now you're catching on," Brok said. "I wanted to see how important it was to him. Maybe he took care of what he needed."

Brok watched as Zimp paced in a small circle. He stepped toward her.

She stared at the ground as though she were reading the

location of pine needles and leaves for an answer. She stopped and looked up at him. "He's a soldier. He'd see through your plan. He knows you're onto something and meant to side-step you." She laughed quickly. "He'll rest." She inadvertently reached for Brok's shoulder and he pulled back. "I'm sorry."

He shook his head. "It's all right." Then he reached out and took her hand. She didn't pull away as he had thought she might.

"We'll keep an eye on him. Don't let him fall back or separate from the group unless he clears it through me." She lifted her chin. "Can you do that?"

"Of course." He let go of her.

"Tell me something. Why didn't you kill those two yourself? It looked as though you wanted to."

"I just want to kill those who killed my family. I found that I have nothing against the others."

"Don't make it personal," Zimp said.

"It is personal."

"What of the doublesight?"

"That's personal on a larger scale, isn't it?" he said. "If I knew that they killed doublesight it might make a difference. If all they do is kill each other, why would I interfere?" He felt a great hand grip his chest as he breathed deeply. He gritted his teeth. "If I thought bandits were doublesight killers, then yes, I'd easily slaughter them all. You would too."

"I might for the sake of the doublesight. But it wouldn't be personal."

"I don't believe you," Brok said. He watched her walk away. Her red cloak stuck to the underbrush and held back while she continued forward. He heard the snap of the garment as it released. A breeze blew in from the north and chilled him. It was not as cold as when they slept at the crest of the mountain, nor as open. He listened for Therin and heard a soft panting twenty feet away. Had his brother listened to the conversation? Was he still able to? Brok snapped his fingers and kneeled. He waited for Therin to rush through the forest and sit before him. Staring into Therin's eyes, Brok questioned everything he had been taught, everything he had grown up believing.

Saliva dripped from Therin's mouth. The odor of fresh game lingered on his breath.

Brok reached out and rubbed his brother's ear. "You have no choice but to kill and eat game, do you? How must that feel to you, when before we only shifted to experience something other than our human nature?" He bent his cheek next to his brother's. He did not speak the words, but wondered, *When will that animal take over?*

With a wave of his hand, Brok sent Therin back into the forest to do what he would: eat, play, sleep. Therin never appeared to be out of energy during the day, so he must sleep somewhere during the night. Ever since the trip began, Therin has wandered off more than he stayed around. The thylacine brother padded off, a low whine trailing into the distant woods.

Careful not to snap twigs as he paced the periphery of their camp, Brok focused on his duties. The party of five were thrown together quickly, he felt. They were ill-matched and under-prepared. Too small a group for anything but secretly collecting information, yet too large a group, too mixed in personalities, to get the job done easily. He wondered what might be The Few's true purpose in sending them away? The most logical answer he could think of was that they were decoys. And he didn't like that answer.

Brok strolled in a twisting pattern around the camp. He particularly kept his eyes on Raik, who appeared to sleep uneasily for the first few hours. On Brok's fourth or fifth pass, he noticed that Raik had buried himself in his bedroll and calmed into a deeper, quieter sleep. Brok felt comfortable as he handed over his post later that night, and was satisfied to have the chance to sleep a few hours until daybreak. He pulled his blanket back with a shaking, tired hand and slipped under the cloth as quietly as possible.

The killing he had done wore on his thoughts as he fell off to sleep. His anger pushed him to kill, but the passive nature of his father and mother attacked his dreaming thoughts, reminding him of the commandments of life he grew up with. But it wasn't their world any longer.

A rough night with intermittent sleep patterns left Brok

drowsy in the morning. So, when he awakened to the sound of a slicing sword and snapping branches, he moved slowly. That sluggishness found him pinned to the ground. The bad teeth and acrid breath of a filth-ridden bandit stared too closely into his face.

As in a dream, Brok glimpsed the slow motion of a heavy staff slap into the side of the man's head. Some evil-scented drool slipped from the bandit's mouth, as he was jolted to the side, leaving Brok enough time to curl his legs and kick the man's chest, and pushing him away. A quick glance around and Brok could see that something wasn't right. There was no time to ponder, though. A young man came at him from the side and Brok was forced to swing his body out of the way. The man fell forward, a thin blade piercing the ground Brok had occupied.

A sharp growl and swift leap had Therin on the man. The jowls of the thylacine ripped at the man's throat, ending all voluntary movement.

Brok had never seen his brother kill. The wild animal inside Therin had taken over naturally. Nothing could have stopped him. Gaining his bearings, Brok traversed the short distance to his bedroll and snapped up his sword. The cold metal handle felt strange for an instant, then became a part of his arm as he swung it over his head in warning more than battle.

He stood, the blade at his side now. As he lowered his head, Brok let his eyes go soft. His peripheral vision captured the scene. There were only two bandits left to fight. One had cornered Lankor and the other rushed to help. Zimp lay a few feet from her sleeping area and Raik appeared to still be sleeping, his bedroll puffed like it was when Brok turned in the night before.

Therin, driven by instinct, leaped into the air for the attacking man. Lankor paused in surprise of an additional beast entering the fray. With luck the attackers broke pattern as well, allowing both Lankor and Therin to take down an opponent. One snapped a neck, while the other ripped out the throat of his opponent. Blood spit over the ground in a loud sputter.

Brok ran to Zimp and kneeled next to her. He noticed no blood. He lifted her head and she groaned.

Lankor lumbered over. "She'll have a sore head."

"Did you see what happened?" Brok said.

"She was on watch. I heard her call. When I opened my eyes three of them were bearing down on her. The closest one swung the butt of his scabbard across her head and let her fall." He poked at Brok with his staff. "You didn't even awaken."

"I've never slept so soundly," Brok said.

"That's not a good habit to get into on this trip."

Brok looked around. "I'm not the soundest sleeper though." He pointed to Raik.

Zimp turned her head into Brok's shoulder. "Oh."

Brok stroked her hair back from her face.

Lankor went over to where Raik slept, lifted his bedroll, and chucked it aside. A small mouse ran for the brush. As Lankor began to swing at it with his staff, Brok yelled for him to stop. At that instant, Lankor's face broke into recognition. "That lousy snake."

"Let him go." Turning back to Zimp, he said, "Get me some water."

When Lankor returned, Zimp had already opened her eyes. "What happened?"

"You warned us in time," Lankor said.

She made a painful smile.

Brok set the water pouch to her lips and she drank a few swallows. "Some leader," she said.

"We're fine," Brok said in a low, soft voice, his hand lingering for a moment on her cheek. "Another drink?"

She began to rise and sat up. "Where's Raik?"

"The little bugger shifted. His mouse image ran into the brush," Lankor said.

Zimp shook her head. "Damn the Gods." She rubbed her head and reached for the water pouch.

Brok let her take it and watched her drink. He had not noticed how smooth her skin was until touching it and feeling it for himself. Her hair felt thinner, finer, than it looked, as well. He had expected her black hair to be coarse.

"You're looking at me," she said.

"I want to be sure you're all right."

"I'm all right, now help me up." She reached for his arm. Brok took her hand and forearm and stood at the same time she did.

She let go of him. "I'm stable."

Brok turned around to assess the situation. Blood had been spilled in buckets. Therin lay in the center of the camp, panting. His muzzle dripped red and his shoulders were matted and damp with blood. He licked and lapped as he breathed. Brok noticed that Lankor also stared at Therin.

"Let's find Raik," Zimp said. "I want to know what's going on."

29

Lankor stared at Zimp, his staff heavy in his hands. She didn't look stable. Brok held her elbow to steady her. "Find him," she said.

Brok helped her to a sitting position. Therin rose to his feet with a start. "Bandits?" Brok said.

"Don't go far. Stay together." Zimp took a breath. "And leave Therin with me. I wouldn't want any accidents."

"He wouldn't..." Brok began.

"I'm not taking that chance. Now go," she said.

Lankor hefted his staff to his shoulder and led the way through the brush where Raik's mouse image ran. "I hope I don't step on him."

"That might be the best thing at this point," Brok said. "I think he skipped out last night. My guess is that he put the bandits up to this, but I don't know why." Brok touched Lankor's arm and stopped.

Lankor halted and turned in question.

Brok pointed. "Behind that tree. Can you hear him?"

Lankor nodded. Now that they stopped creating their own noise, the distinct sound of Raik's breathing came to him. "I'll go," Lankor said.

Brok stood fast.

Lankor parted brush that stood between him and Raik. He touched the tree's trunk and leaned to peer around it, seeing the last of a quick movement.

Raik coiled his body away at first and then looked up at Lankor. There was pain in his eyes. He lifted his arm to indicate blood oozing into his shirt. He nodded and the limp body of a bandit lay a few feet away. "Sh-should be the-the last of them."

Lankor gave him a questioning look and Raik turned his eyes away. "He cut you with your own blade?" Lankor pointed to Raik's knife, which lay conspicuously close to his leg. "What's going on?"

Brok came around Lankor. "What *is* going on, you two?"

Raik glared at Brok.

"Nothing yet," Lankor said, giving the little man time to think about what Lankor may have seen. "Let's go back to camp. I don't like leaving Zimp alone."

"She's with Therin," Brok said.

"Did you see how he ripped the throats out of those men?"

"I saw how you attacked them," Brok said. "Should we not trust you any longer?"

Lankor reached for Raik's hand and helped him up. "You and I might have a little talk later."

As they stepped into the small circle of the campsite, Zimp rose to her feet easily, recovered. "I want to know what you thought you were doing." She wore her cloak, which gave bulk to her thin body without obscuring her shape.

Lankor found her aggression interesting. Her words burst out with anger, but she leaned on one foot in a relaxed, almost softened stance. It took a moment for him to realize that she appeared as though her feathers were ruffled. He searched for her aura and a hazy outline of a crow's head perched over hers. The vision amazed him. Until recently, he had not seen another beast image in such a way. Trying to save the feeling, he attempted to focus on Brok and then on Raik.

"Stop your prying," Zimp said with a quick sweep of her arm toward Lankor. Her attention focused toward Raik again. "I mean it. I want to know what you're up to."

Raik raised his arm to indicate he'd been stabbed.

Zimp brushed his motion off with a shake of her head. "That's not a wound that would stop you from fighting. It's a scratch. I want to know how our best warrior, a Flandian Guard, would be the only one wounded from a surprise attack."

"Good point," Brok said.

Lankor didn't understand why, but he felt protective of Raik. Perhaps he was sorry for him. "A mistake in judgment," Lankor said.

"So you're back with us now? You aren't focusing on our beast images?" she said.

"We should all know what it's like holding to our human image at this point," Lankor pointed out. "Raik carries double that hunger inside him. If he shifted to his copperhead image and then back, his mouse image would be next. The human that occupies that time would be much less the warrior. We've all seen that lack of grace in him, even if briefly." Lankor waited for Zimp to think it over. He felt the sharp pain of betrayal. Yet, logically, he wasn't sure what was going on with Raik when he found him behind that tree. He did vow to himself to find out later.

Zimp sighed, then took a deep breath and clenched her teeth. "This time," she said to Raik. "You will not be out of sight from now on, or until I feel safe around you." To Brok she said, "Can you control Therin enough to cover Raik?"

Lankor knew already that Brok didn't like the way Zimp asked the question. For some reason, though, Brok didn't combat her wording or her insinuation, he merely replied. "Yes, he can do that."

"What about how that might look, us having a thylacine in tow?" Lankor said.

"Brok, you are the thylacine trainer. From now on, if we meet with anyone, you're it. I don't want anyone out of my sight any more." She looked at each of them in turn. "Got it?"

Lankor noticed that none of them looked directly at her, but all acknowledged her order in some way, whether with a nod or a word.

They prepared their horses for travel. Raik rode between them, Lankor taking up the rear. After only a few days he found that his buttocks still hurt from bruises, but by allowing his hips to be free and flowing with the movement of the horse, the overall ride didn't exhaust him as much. He relaxed into the saddle, balanced and almost comfortable.

Raik appeared to be less comfortable in his position. Every time Therin turned his head toward the snake image doublesight, Raik tensed. Not a fun ride for anyone.

Lankor felt sorry for him, but there was little he could do at the moment. Tensions in the group had peaked. All were guarded.

Brok and Zimp led the small group through the woods for two more days. There were no more early morning attacks, and they were all getting edgy with Raik. Even Lankor found himself suspicious. Toward the end of the woods trails, the five doublesight settled into camp for the evening.

"Tomorrow, early, we cross the short plain to Castle Weilk," Zimp said.

"You don't sound very happy about it." Brok slid his bedroll closer to the imaginary circle around a non-existent fire. His curly hair knotted into itself in locks. His cheeks pulled back into a broad smile as though he relished in the fact that she worried.

"It's not that," she said. "Things need to change, or at least appear to change."

"What's that mean?" Lankor said. "You have a plan?" If so, why had she kept it to herself? Wouldn't it be better had she asked for their thoughts? "Have you been there before?"

"Briefly. When I was younger." Zimp removed her cloak and placed it across her lap. She spent a moment to peer into the eyes of each of them, taking her time to make contact. When she got to Lankor he felt her hesitate and almost pull her eyes away. He knew that his energy pushed beyond his physical body. Was his dragon energy too strong for her? The long days of travel had him holding closely to his dragon image. He felt the shape of it pushing against his body, but more so against his face. His cheeks and nose, mouth and chin tingled with sensitivity. He knew from the sensation that he could break into beast image at any moment with one quick twist of thought. Pulling back from those feelings let her regroup and turn once again to look into his eyes. She said nothing about what had just happened.

"The old warriors wouldn't believe a woman could lead the group." She picked up a stick from the ground and pointed it toward Brok. "You'll lead. And don't get too caught up in ordering anyone around. Remember, we're friends."

Her eyes lifted to Lankor's once again. "You are my older brother. Like it or not, you've got to act a little protective of me. And honestly, this is not the type of place I would like to be left alone anyway."

"What about me?" Raik said.

"You stick beside Brok. You're a thylacine handler in training. Ask questions, but don't get cocky. Therin could tear you apart before you could shift."

"I d-doubt that," Raik said.

"He wouldn't have to," Brok said. "I would."

"You forget that I'm of the Flandean Guard," Raik said.

Zimp stuck her chin toward Raik. "I don't think you want to announce that here. King Belford held back your armies once. A single soldier..." she shook her head.

"I don't like this plan," Raik said. "We sh-should talk about it. And you didn't say what we're to do h-here. Are we to ask questions? L-look and l-listen?"

Lankor could see that Zimp was about to stand, but she held back. "You don't have any say in the plan. Perhaps you didn't notice, but since we kept you in sight we've had no trouble with bandits. I should let you act like a Flandean Guard. That might take care of some of our trouble."

"Coincidence," Raik said.

"Snake," Brok spit out under his breath.

"There's more," Lankor said as he kept an eye on Zimp's demeanor. "What is it?"

"We each must shift tonight." She threw the stick into Raik's lap. "You shift once."

"But I'll be useless if anything goes wrong."

"This is to make sure nothing does go wrong," she said.

"Is that wise?" Lankor said. "Not only would Raik be an easy target, we'd be left with one less sword."

"My other self can f-fight," Raik said. When the others looked surprised, he added, "Just not as well."

"Your other self? You refer to the human image before your mouse image as your other self?" Zimp leaned into her words, suspicious of Raik's reference.

Brok grew angry and lifted to a standing position using only his legs, both arms reaching into the air. "What's going on here? Are you saying that we have two different people to address?" He asked Zimp, not Raik.

Her head turned as though she heard something and everyone quieted. She shook here head and rubbed the back of her neck.

"Your sister," Brok said. "There aren't five of us, there are seven." He stepped back and asked, "What did she say? Are we in danger? Is Raik part enemy and part comrade?"

"Don't get so high on your horse, mister. We have no idea how wild your brother will get. He could turn on any of us, even you, at any moment." Again, Lankor noticed Zimp start to rise and then sit back down, as if trying to appear relaxed and in charge.

"Agreed. But he's safe now. And every minute I will know just how safe. I feel his energy," Brok said raising his hands, palms out, as though Therin's energy stood before him like a wall. "It's your turn. What did Zora say to you just now?"

Zimp blushed. She had been caught. Lankor realized that she'd been keeping a regular conversation with her sister all along. There was a pose that she struck and it finally settled into him what that pose was. He shook his head.

"Stop it," she said. "All of you."

"What more have you kept from us?" Lankor asked.

Raik leaned back on his hands, a glib smile across his lips.

This time when her muscles tensed Zimp did stand. She held onto her cloak with her right hand. Her shoulders slumped. "The truth," she said.

Brok whispered, "We're a decoy."

Zimp shot him a questioning look. "The truth about Zora. I'm still learning to hear her. Sometimes she speaks in riddles, sometimes so quietly I can barely hear her voice. I'm not always sure it's her. Other voices come in."

"The Gods have cursed us," Lankor said.

"I'm sorry. I was in training with Oronice. She is the Gem of the Forest. I'm afraid I'm nothing but a dull stone from the riverbed." She meant what she said, but Raik laughed at her analogy.

She turned on him. "Laugh, but you are a traitor to us all."

"Not me," Raik said in defense.

"The other you?" Brok said. He turned back to Zimp. "You haven't answered my question. Are we a decoy? Are The Few creating an army as we speak? Are we about to enter a war? A war we couldn't possibly win?"

"An honorable d-death," Raik said.

"A death all the same," Brok said. "And what of Breel?"

"She's safer with them." Zimp struggled with her own thoughts before exploding into words.

Lankor saw it coming and pushed his dragon image closer to the surface for protection.

"The only contact with this world that Zora has is through me and Oronice. She doesn't want to lose that contact." Tears welled in her eyes. "And Oronice is dying. I knew this before I left. Zora haunts me. She fears for my safety on this trip, and fears for my safety in your presence. She continually tells me to return to my clan, to shift and fly away, leaving you to whatever ends may come." Zimp let her tears fall. "She is frantic. I need her help, but it is becoming more difficult to gain any real knowledge from her. She warns me continually." Zimp lowered her head and took a deep breath. "Do any of you have any idea what it's like being tormented by your own thoughts?"

All three of the others said, "Yes," simultaneously, breaking the tension that they had carried the last few days.

Like a dam breaking loose, Zimp burst into laughter.

Brok reached for her and she rested into him. Her breakdown released his stress as well. He shook his head. "I fear that one day I'll awake and have to fight off my own brother."

"I can't keep track of which human image has which thought," Raik said. "Sometimes I fear that one is plotting against the other. There are days where I just want to die an honorable death." He kept his chin raised into the air, apparently open to share his feeling along with the others.

Lankor sat and let it all sink in. His shoulders relaxed, his mind released its tight hold on his thoughts. When he spoke, he used his hands to illustrate his words. "My beast image is grander and more powerful than my human image. It scares me. As I become tired or angry or emotional as I have these last few days, it wants out." He shook his head. "I want to let it out more and more every day."

Zimp wiped her eyes with the back of her hand. "Why send us anywhere?" It was not a rhetorical question.

Brok allowed her to step away as she gained composure. To Lankor, Brok looked as though he let her go reluctantly. "Are we a decoy?" he asked a third time.

"I don't know, but judging Zora's response, perhaps. There's one thing I do know. We are in real danger."

"I don't like it, then. My mouse image can't help us much. What if it's true and my mouse human is to blame for the attacks? Can we trust him?" Raik said.

"Don't you know?" Brok said.

Raik pushed his lips together. He stared directly at Brok. Then he shook his head slowly. "We have each bared a piece of our soul in this moment. That is my truth."

"We are cursed," Lankor said.

"We were told by The Few to return with information. If they are putting together an army, our findings will be important to the outcome of any war. They will gain strategic information." She nodded in apology to Lankor. "If dragons are the cause of this hatred, if the humans are being controlled by dragons, or if they are killing the doublesight out of fear of the dragons, The Few must know. Of all the cities in The Great Land, Castle Weilk will hold the answers. We must complete our mission. One of us must return to the Council Grounds." She hesitated. "Even if the rest of us die."

30

Oro felt safe propped between two of her own clan. "You should never come here alone again. We'll join you from now on," Storret said.

Storret remained the clan's most trusted guard and scout. Oro knew of his spying. She understood that Storret held more knowledge of the clan than most. And still he could be trusted like no other. And Noot, Zimp's closest cousin, played the part of kindness in the clan. He had become a symbol of all that was good in the world. Behind them walked Arren. Oro had diluted his power through two simple moves: sending Zimp with the reconnaissance party, and suggesting Storret as commander of half the army, while Arren stayed to protect The Few.

Oro missed her own sister who had died shortly after birth. Tintse had been weak from the start, but in death she was not weak at all. It was as though the balance had been set unevenly. If not for Tintse, Oro would not have become the Gem of the Forest. The same would be true for Zimp, once she learned to hear properly.

"You will not have my burden for much longer," she said to Storret.

"Don't suggest that you won't be with us," he said.

Oro looked into his face. "I will always be with you."

"He didn't mean it that way," Noot said. "We're here," he announced, and scooped the flap open for them to enter the council tent.

Only council members and a few others were present.

As if it suddenly became apparent to Noot that something important was about to happen, he asked, "Did you know about this?"

"I did," Oro said.

Storret nodded.

Oro let go of each of their arms and stepped forward on shaking legs toward the front of the council tent. She heard them talking behind her, but put the sound out of her head. She winked at Tintse, her image at least, as it faded into view against the dim light from overhead.

The small crowd separated to let her pass. Her legs moved slowly. She stared forward, marking her goal in her head. It would take time to complete what she was about to do, but she was ready. Zimp needed her.

Wellock welcomed Oro to the front of the group. He held out his hand and she gripped it with her own soft palm. "Oronice, the Gem," he said, bowing his head to her.

It had been years since she had heard Wellock speak her whole name. Zimp was never to know the truth about her grandmother, but here, in this place, with Zimp gone, Oronice felt re-anointed to her royal place with The Few.

"It is good to have you as our sage once again," Wellock said. "You are truly the Gem of the Forest."

"Not for long, my friend. Not for long."

Wellock reached out and put his arms around the old woman. "We will miss you."

"Zimp will need my help soon." Oro looked around Wellock. "Where are the boys?"

Wellock laughed and said, "They are late. Hammadin is strategizing and Crob is deep into his morning prayers."

"Am I early?"

"A bit, perhaps. It will give us time to talk." Wellock left his arm around her shoulder. "So, does your whole clan know of your decision?"

"No, but I'm sure they are suspect, by now. It is better that they allow for my decision. They understand that. We all must choose our time to leave. That is the way of the crow. It is not a social thing as in some clans, but a sacred one, even though dancing occurs at both. I'm just surprised they haven't noticed how fast my health has declined. I think they have taken care of me for so long that they've fallen into step with it."

"And who will inherit your home? Who will you suggest as your replacement? You know there are many questions yet to be answered," he said.

"The clan will know what to do about all of that." She glanced behind her. "Arren would like to be king of all clans, but I believe Storret, as a commander of one of the armies, will prove his worth through strategy and courage." She lowered her head. "I am sorry that this battling between us is happening again. Do we learn nothing from the past?" After a moment of thought, she spoke up and said. "And of course, Zimp will return as sage."

"There will be none like you, my good friend." Wellock's eyes opened wide. "Oh, here come my fellow guides."

Oro turned as Hammadin and Crob shuffled quickly through the crowd toward her. She immediately held her arms out to them.

Noot followed behind them. "I don't like this," he said to the two high members.

Hammadin grabbed Oro's hand and turned to meet Noot head on. "It isn't your decision. We are here to respect and support every clan in its traditions. And you should know to respect your own clan."

"Let me go to Zimp," Noot said. "She's my cousin. I have the ability."

Oro reached out to take his hand. He stood strong and sure. Funny that he had ignored how the journey had already begun for her. "Look at me," she said. "Would you have me stop the process now, mid-stream, and have to live the rest of my life as a weak old woman? You cannot tell me that you have not noticed my decline." She shook his hand as if to remove an answer from the motion.

"We've all known. We didn't want to believe it." He lowered his head. "No, I would not wish for you to remain like this." His eyes turned up toward her. "But I would care for you if you chose differently, even now."

"There are no other women ready to step up, to lead our clan or to council The Few." She looked over her shoulder. "You will be the first male to hold the post of High Sage until Zimp returns. The crow image doublesight need your voice."

Arren stepped from the crowd and objected. "Noot is too weak to become sage."

"Too peaceful, you mean. You, Arren, would have us galloping off to war before we find that there is one. We must plan and wait for Zimp and her group to warn us if the danger is great. Noot is not weak. He will hold the intention of peace and will stand strong to that intention." She turned back to address Noot.

"I will proudly serve The Few," he said.

"You, my friend, will lead us to peace or to victory with Storret's help." She let go of his hand.

Storret stood at a distance from them. He stared. Said nothing.

Oro had words for Storret, as well, but that was for later.

Breel reached from the crowd and took Storret's hand in hers. Oro smiled at Breel, even as sadness swept over the girl's face. Did she know the future as well?

Oro turned away from them all. "Let us begin."

Wellock took center stage and lifted his arms into the air over his head. Several people entered with torches and placed them at the four corners of the tent. Flowers and herbs were carried forward in large bowls and placed in front of Oro. Powders, liquids, and pastes were brought in on a flattened plank with hollowed areas for each substance. A short table and chair awaited her so that she could sit to perform the ritual.

Oro motioned for the torches to be put out. She lighted five candles that she pulled from her gown pocket, and placed them in the shape of a square with one candle in the center. She motioned for Crob to empty a flower bowl and hand it to her. With the bowl in front of her, Oro nodded to Arren, Storret, and Noot. The chanting began.

She focused on her work, gray hair hanging over her face,

nimble fingers pulling a pinch of this and two of that. Oro found the dried ground entrails of a squirrel and shoveled a fingernail full into the bowl. She pointed and Crob handed her the flowers. She shook them over her mixture. Pollen fell into the bowl and hovered over it, floating in the air. Moving the flowers over the candles, she shook them again and sparks flew, tiny pops and snaps joined the chanting.

Wellock and Hammadin stood behind Oro. She could feel their presence. In her own clucking and cawing, not the language of crow but a rendition of it, Oro fell into a meditation, a journey. Her hands became more animated as she scooped paste into the bowl, then one liquid and another in small portions. She was barely aware of which elements she used and which went unused. This was how true magic was done.

At one point she raised her palm near her head and Hammadin placed his palm against hers. Later, she did the same with Wellock. More mixing, more singing and chanting. Oro swayed and swooned. She reached for Crob and he kneeled to reach her. Their hands stayed close.

The other doublesight chanted, each in his or her own way. A symphony of sound rose from the council tent. A drumming began. A stomping of feet. Other sounds entered the tent, screeching and clawing at Oro's ears. She knew that she heard more than any of the others. She knew that half of her sensed the physical realm and half sensed the next realm.

Tintse flew into the tent, a mirage, a mist, fading in and out of corporeal reality.

One candle blew a sudden burst of fireworks into the air above Oro's head. Another began to flicker, then another blew flames higher than the rest. Oro lifted her chin. The center candle went out. She closed her eyes, shutting out one world and entering another. She sat straighter, taller, stronger. She shifted and entered the sky above the tent where she flew around it, first to the right, then to the left.

Tintse joined her and welcomed her.

The sisters played, rose into the sky, clutched their claws together, fell, separated, and flew off in joyful free-flight. Oro shifted back into her worn body. She knew that none of those present had seen the shift, for it happened in another place, another world. The chanting and drumming grew stronger and more oppressive. She slumped in her seat and whispered her own chant once again. Holding herself in two worlds at once, so close to death and to life, made her more tired than she had been when she entered the tent early in the evening.

Oro let a long slow breath leave her body. She forced it out toward the end so that more and more air escaped her lungs as if rejected. She fell forward and felt Hammadin and Wellock grab her shoulders. The chanting slowed. The drumming stopped. Three of the five candles were out. When all the chanting stopped, the silence fell like the silence of death. But death was not upon her yet. It would be another day before she moved over completely.

Crob lifted Oro's feet. Someone took her shoulders. She felt them pick her up and lay her on a stretcher. Crob grabbed two poles at Oro's feet and Wellock grabbed the poles at the old woman's head. Hammadin stood next to Oro as they walked toward the entrance.

She saw Rend's face as he came up to her and held her hand out for his. The stretcher stopped moving. She grasped Rend's hand and he placed his other hand over her forehead.

She whispered, "My dear, dear friend. I have always loved you, as you know. Now, stay close and I will take your courage and strength with me into the other world. I will deliver it to Zimp so that she may protect your son in both realms."

Rend shook his head and promised her that he would stay with her.

Oro glanced to his side and saw the glisten of tears in Mianna's eyes. "You have a wonderful mate," she said.

Mianna stepped closer and placed her hand over Rend's. "We'll both be with you."

Oro let go of Rend and Mianna by slipping her soft hand from theirs. She motioned for Crob to continue.

A small procession followed The Few and the High Sage to her wagon. Once the four of them were inside Oro sat up with some difficulty.

Arren, Storret, and Noot sat on Zimp's cot. Rend and

Mianna stood at the opening at the end of the wagon.

"Come in, come in," Oro said. "We'll make room for you."

When they were all settled, she began to speak as if still in a trance. Her eyes remained closed. She did not need to see them in order to speak. She conferred with Tintse as she spoke to her friends.

"Noot, the Peacemaker," she said in a shaky voice, "you are now the High Sage. You must hear me speak now and always. Listen closely to my voice as it becomes weaker in this world and stronger in the next.

"Storret, the Scout, you are to be commander of the doublesight's first army. You must train your army heavily. Hammadin will lead the recruiting outside our council gathering. There is a great change coming."

Tintse spoke wildly. Oro hesitated to listen. "Oh, my," she said. "You must train the doublesight to dance through battle. Whether human image or beast image, in the end, we must remember the other."

Oro took a deep breath.

Rend asked what he could do.

"You must stay with me until I leave." She took another breath. "I am tired. But Tintse is not. Some, some are the concerns of the other side. They care less about death. Note too, Noot, that they care less about us than themselves. I will begin to be the same."

"Nayman," she said to Rend and Mianna. "will be a second commander and will train a second army."

"But his foot," Mianna began.

"A commander need not fight. Nayman will be a compassionate leader. His courage is beyond that of most others. His life is always thought of second. He can experience joy in another's accomplishments. Yes, Nayman will lead also, but in a different way than Storret. The armies must train separately."

"He may not like this," Mianna said.

Oro opened her eyes in a small slit. "Often the best leaders are those who are reluctant to lead. They are much more careful of decisions."

"Like Zimp," Rend said.

Oro allowed a smile to appear and then disappear across her lips.

No one else spoke, and Oronice The Gem began to nod off to sleep. Tintse woke her and Oro's body jerked. She opened her eyes. The others sat around her, close and quiet. "You may go," she said. "Begin your duties now."

As the wagon emptied except for Rend and Mianna, Oro lay back down and began to enter sleep. Oro dreamed of battles, some won, others lost. She dreamed of Zimp and her small band of spies. A great field opened in her dream, clear and fresh, but not safe. "Zimp," she whispered. There was no reply. Had Zimp not meditated, not mixed herbs or chanted silently? "Zora," Oro said in despair. But there was no reply from her either.

31

The air lay dense across the small band of doublesight. Silence came to the forest as though an army crept toward them, but they knew differently. Each, in his or her way, was a part of the forest, a part of the animal kingdom. Each knew that the wildlife sensed what was about to happen.

Brok crouched onto his legs and shifted in a few breaths, annoying everyone.

Zimp jumped back as anger pulsed out of his body during the shift. What he had done was dangerous to them all.

Therin yelped and backed away from his own brother.

Brok slipped back into his human image as quickly as he shifted out.

Zimp yelled, "Never again!"

Brok stared back at her. "Afraid?" He spun around to leave, hesitated as if waiting for a thought, then swung around and pointed at Lankor in anger. "Your brother can protect you."

Lankor grimaced. "What did I do?"

"Nothing," Brok said.

"It's the best choice." Zimp knew why Brok got angry, but wouldn't announce it. The thought repulsed her. No matter how much she tried to feel comfortable around him, there was the constant image of Therin drooling or licking blood from his chops, which reminded her of Brok's beast image waiting to come out. He'd have to get used to the facts, yet now might not have been the best time for that to occur. "I didn't want to be in charge here," she said.

"You've said that b-before," Raik said. "I w-wish you'd stand strong or stand down. Your indecision makes me nervous."

"Okay," Zimp said turning and giving everyone her attention. "Fast shifts are only to be done in an emergency. We wouldn't want anyone holding too strongly to his beast image."

"Especially a thylacine?" Brok said.

"Anyone," Zimp said.

"Back him away," Raik said to Brok about Therin. "I'm next to get this over with. But remember, I'll remain like this for about half an hour.

"You'd better be on your best behavior," Brok told him.

Raik never stood. He leaned onto his back and with a deft pace shifted into his copperhead image. After fully shifting, his pink belly up, Raik rolled over. He coiled and stared at Brok and Therin. He uncoiled and slithered next to Lankor's leg.

Zimp shivered. She wondered if her shifting was as creepy as Raik's or as frightening as Brok's or Lankor's. What was it for them to see one another change shape, become part animal and part human, mold into another form as if their bodies were made of clay?

Zimp cocked her head and listened for Zora. Were the voices she heard really her sister or were they demons from the next realm? For the last two days she had felt exhausted from the hard travel. The voices came more often but were not so easy to decipher. "Danger," was one of the few words she heard. Danger at Castle Weilk or danger in our own camp? Zimp asked silently, followed by, "Who are you?"

Lankor shocked her into paying attention when she heard him begin to shift. The cracking and grinding of his bones grated against her thoughts. The odor of smoke from an ancient fire filled the air. The beaked face of the dragon protruded from Lankor's face, disfiguring it. Spikes like tree branches grew from his cheeks and along his head. Tattered wings and long single claws stretched ominously. A tail grew, scales and spikes protruded. Lankor stood for a moment and looked at the joint between wing and claw as if he didn't believe the change had actually occurred.

Compared to the shock of Brok's quick shift, Lankor's shift remained the most frightening Zimp had ever seen. She understood now how a single dragon doublesight might control whole hordes of humans. She also realized how reckless his first shift in front of the council had been. Dragons had great power, even in their shift. Lankor, if he chose, could scare a doublesight into singlesight if he changed quickly enough. After the shift, she wondered how conscious Lankor was of his human self, and how conscious was the dragon within him? She spoke slowly testing his understanding. "I have never seen you spit fire. I smell ash and smoke. Is that a truth or a myth?" She also wondered how such a large creature could fly, but upon closer inspection realized that his body was thin and emaciated. His ribs showed through his skin and looked as though they were just as spiked and dangerous as the spikes that protruded on the outside of his body. Did his skeleton cause him pain?

Lankor twisted from his standing position by coiling his body, snakelike, to the side. His great clawed feet followed after as though they needed to wait for the body to move first. The clawed wings scraped the ground and dragged through the brush.

Zimp saw how his wings would become tattered. Already the brush pulled at them just as they pulled at her cloak as she walked. Holes pushed through his wings, allowing light to shine through them in spots. In other areas a silvery scar stretched across the charcoal wings where the tears had healed.

Lankor's dragon image strained into an upright position and, facing a small bush that stood alone in the path, opened its mouth. A loud hissing slipped into the silence and a pop warned of the coming flame. Curling through the air, a white fog-like breath reached out. At first the fire appeared as a mist created from breathing on a cold day. By the time it touched its target, flames curled through the air and the bush burst into light, overcome first with white fire then blue and orange flames. After a moment, nothing but soot remained. A backwind scattered the gray dust.

Zimp and the others had retreated. The stench of fire coming from the depths of Lankor's body smelled vaguely of a dead carcass. The heat could have charred the hair on their arms. "I see," Zimp said in a weak tone.

Lankor returned to his human image and Zimp stepped closer to him. The idea of having a creature of such power in their group, or even on The Great Land, made her understand the complete horror people must have felt in the past. She could almost understand why the doublesight and humans might team against the dragons. Concern swallowed her thoughts for a moment. What if he joined the other dragon rather than protect their small party from its wrath?

Zimp's heightened sight allowed her to see the residue of his beast image all around him. The image receded with a calculated slowness, as if reluctant to give up its life for Lankor's. "We'll be able to remain in our human images longer, now that the hunger has been satisfied. In case we need to stay in Weilk a long while."

"Why would that happen?" Brok said. "Run into a few pubs and grapple with a few locals and we should know as much as they know."

"I have a feeling it won't be that easy," Zimp said. She looked around, then into the trees overhead. She took a deep breath. "My turn," she said. And with that announcement, Zimp felt her body energize and fold in on itself. It took concentration and will power and passion to shift. She had to feel her crow body before it could manifest. She could only guess what the others felt as she shrunk and shriveled into her beast image. Just before the change took hold in full, she leaped into the air, opened her wings and flew up into the trees overhead. She lifted higher and higher to near exhaustion, pushing against the thick forest air until she broke through the canopy and slid into the cooler night air above the trees. She glided in a wide circle, then dove below the thick uppermost branches of the trees. She cawed as though she had found intruders approaching. Yet the woods were silent, and that didn't set well with her. She struggled not to focus on why the forest appeared empty and tried to hold only to the fact. Too much focus brought her human image to mind. If she felt her human image too strongly, she'd shift, even in mid-air.

Zimp swooped toward the ground and once there decided to shift so that she could concentrate. She walked the path a short distance toward their camp. The area around them harbored no bandits. But why?

As she entered camp again, Brok spoke out. "Your warning, what did you see?" He held a sword unsheathed by his side. Raik had coiled ready for a strike, and Lankor's staff stretched behind his neck, both hands gripping it, one on either side.

"Nothing. I circled camp and there is nothing out there."

Brok slipped his sword into its sheath. "They know we're coming." He kicked at the path and narrowed his eyes. Swinging his entire body toward Raik he said, "Why do you think that is?"

The copperhead uncoiled and appeared to rest.

"We eat," Zimp said.

The three of them ignored Raik as they set camp and tended the horses.

Zimp pointed when she saw Raik move closer to the edge of camp. "There he goes," she said.

The snake lifted its head as it began to shift back. For a moment the copperhead held a small version of Raik's head. The rest of the shift increased in speed until he was whole.

"Therin could have eaten you," Brok said.

Raik smiled.

Zimp sensed that a different person sat with them. "How much of our conversation do you remember?"

Raik's eyes lowered as he shied from her attention. "Enough," he said.

She didn't like the shiftiness in his eyes and began to wonder about her decision concerning his single shift. "Will you be able to spend time with Therin and Brok without fear?"

Raik glanced at each of the others. "Not without fear." He swallowed. "But I'm a soldier in any form and will do what I am asked, for now."

"There is no 'for now' in following orders," Brok said. "If I have to spend that much time with you, I don't want to have to watch my back."

Raik shot a look at Lankor. "I saw what you did. Now we're talking about a warrior. If I were him," he said to the others, "I'd never be in human image."

"If I were him, I'd never want to be in beast image," Zimp said.

"Did you hear that we're not being followed?" Brok said. "No bandits. Again."

Raik's eyes glanced left and right. "You can't keep blaming me for that."

"Isn't it your fault?" Brok said rushing toward Raik and bearing down on him as though about to hit him across the face.

Raik sunk toward the ground. His shoulders visibly shivered, his jaw set. And with the swiftness of a frightened mouse, Raik pulled a blade from his boot, leaped up and struck at Brok, slicing the sleeve of his shirt and into his arm.

Brok yelped, the sound of a thylacine and Zimp feared he would change. Before she could yell for them to stop, Lankor's staff dropped between them. "Halt," he said.

The two men stood opposite one another. Raik shook and held his knife outstretched. Brok, calmer and less frightened, gripped his cut arm.

Lankor lifted his staff and let it push against Raik gently as the snake man stepped backwards.

Brok did not move.

"What did you have to do with this?" Lankor asked the shaking Raik.

Shock shot through Zimp, as Lankor had stood up for Raik all along. Had the little man gone too far in placing them in danger?

"At last, you notice his treachery," Brok said.

Lankor swung his staff in Brok's direction, causing him to jump backwards. "It's my question. Stay out of it."

Raik's eyes narrowed again, this time toward Lankor.

Zimp saw something familiar in his stare. Raik's face changed. The doublesight about to be a mouse actually looked different than the one about to be a snake. She had not noticed the nuances of change before, the rounding off of the chin, the tightening of the eyes, thinning of the lips. This man standing before her looked vaguely familiar. As she watched his face, his body changed too. Not a physical change as much as a change in stance and attitude. A slyness.

"The doublesight are animals," he said, causing each of them to look amazed.

"What?" Lankor said.

"The doublesight are reverting back into demons, mixed-beasts, anomalies." Raik laughed like someone frightened. "If the humans don't kill us, we'll kill each other." His head shook. "Or bear monsters instead of children." He pointed at Lankor. "Look at you. I can see the pain in your eyes. It's always there even before you shift. Your family has suffered enough. My family has suffered enough."

With his words, Zimp recalled the image of the man standing behind the archers who attacked her clan weeks before. "You!" she shouted at him. "You led the attack on our clan!" She rushed him and leaped at his head, casting his knife from his hand using her arm. She clawed at his face before Lankor had the opportunity to grip her shoulder with one of his hands and drag her away.

"It's personal now," Brok said.

Zimp turned on him, then. "You stinking, Godless beast," she said before catching her own words.

Lankor held tight to her shoulder until she twisted into him and pounded his chest.

Brok walked over to Raik and shoved him to the ground. Another step and he placed a hand on Zimp's head. "How can we help?" he said.

She could feel hate rising inside her. She turned on Raik again, but did not step away from Lankor. She heard the voice of Zora more clearly than ever before. Not a whisper. Not a mumble. "Do not kill him yet," she said, and Zimp felt comfort in her sister's final word.

Lankor shook his head in disgust. "Do you suppose they know that we're doublesight?"

"No," Raik said. "Only that we are coming."

"What shall we do?" Lankor asked Zimp, still holding her.

Her lips and cheeks tightened, holding back her anger, her

fear, her sorrow. "Well, my big brother," she said entering into her new role, "we carry on."

"You are a leader," Brok said. He rubbed her head.

"True doublesight do not kill other doublesight unless they pose a threat," she said to Raik. "*You* are not a true doublesight." Zimp pointed at Therin, the first time she'd ever addressed him directly, and asked, "Do you understand my words?"

Therin cocked his head and looked up at her in response.

Brok said, "I think he understands well enough."

Zimp said, "Watch Raik tonight. If he moves, eat him."

Shock crossed Raik's face. She felt a touch of satisfaction from his reaction.

"Let's eat and get a good night's rest," she said.

32

Lankor felt betrayed. He had stood up for Raik on several occasions because he had felt an unexplainable connection with him. He felt as though they had something in common. His judgment had been wrong. Raik's latest announcement proved just how wrong Lankor had been. That was his life story.

No wonder Rend's frustration always showed through whenever Lankor made a decision for himself. Both his parents and his brother treated him like a child, as though he was just about to do something stupid. They warned him to be wary of his actions, reminded him of his loyalties, and continually attempted to settle his rising passions.

No wonder The Few selected Zimp as leader, instead of him. She thought every decision through. She could listen to those she traveled with and then decide the next step in their journey while holding to an internal goal that she never released.

And, yes, he felt that he should have been selected leader over Brok or Raik: Raik, because he was a soldier and would always turn to fight his way through a problem, and Brok, because he boiled beneath his show of outer calm. Lankor wasn't fooled by the thylacine's feigned loyalty at all. Once that doublesight grew angry, it would be difficult to keep him from slaying anything in his path, especially if what was in his path was human.

He glanced around the camp. Each person held an image far

wilder than their human image. He understood why singlesight humans were fearful of the doublesight. Lankor sensed the animal in each of them, now that he knew its shape. He could pick these doublesight from a crowd with a simple shift in his perception. He'd always known he could do that while living in The Lost, but this extended knowledge amazed him in a way he couldn't explain. This newfound talent made him feel powerful and strong on the one hand, and innocent on the other. What other power might he gain? Would he someday be able to hear the dead like Zimp does?

Lankor became depressed about his own inability to judge people. Growing up in The Lost, with only dragon clan doublesight, had left him at a disability to live in The Great Land with other doublesight, let alone other humans. Did his comrades find him odd or quirky? Did they find him unsociable? Regardless of their attempts to banter and know one another, Lankor felt left out, alone, even among these brothers and sisters of the doublesight.

He slid a hand into a pouch from his saddlebag and pulled out a coarse and pitted rock. He rolled it between his fingers, and closed his eyes and recalled his homeland while the others pulled bread and jerky from their bags. He heard the lightness of footsteps and the sound of someone sitting beside him.

"What do you have there?" Zimp asked.

Lankor opened his eyes. He leaned on one elbow and Zimp sat close to him. He could smell her, the odor of scented candles, pine and peppermint.

She reached for his rock and he let her slip it from his fingers, touching hers for a long moment while doing so. The touch surprised him. She felt soft, almost feathery. The idea seemed strange but somehow accurate that she would feel that way to him, which meant that he must feel either scaled or like a thin piece of skin, like a bat's wing. Which was it?

"Is this from your homeland?"

"From The Lost, yes," he said.

Zimp shifted her weight and stretched one leg out in front of her as she slid her two fingers into the pouch she wore at her waist.

Lankor watched her leg and followed the length of it from her slender foot to her muscled thigh, to her thin waist. Her fingers removed a crystal of deep indigo with specks of gold. Even the dim light of evening caused it to sparkle.

"We sometimes find these on the beaches near the Belt of the Lakes," she said.

"Where you come from?"

"Yes, it's a small land mass that stands between the southern end of Western Stilth Alshore Lake and Diamond Lake."

Lankor cocked his head.

"Lissland," she said in answer.

He let her place it into his hand and it felt heavier than it appeared. Rolling it between his fingers, the stone sparkled and blinked at him. "Everything you own seems magical to me." He glanced into her face.

Zimp reached for the stone and returned his in the same motion. Her lips tightened and she made a quick nod of her head. She pushed to her knees, about to scoot over to her bedroll.

Lankor reached out and touched her hand. "Tell me, what do I feel like to you?"

Understanding spread over her face. Her eyes narrowed and her hand slid from his. She appeared scared to answer the question then opened her mouth to speak. "Your hands are soft and light, almost unbelievably so for a man who spends his life in the rough terrain of The Lost. But your chest is the opposite. You want to know if you feel like your beast image," she said. "And the answer is yes. Thick and hard. Again, the feel of your chest defies how it looks." She turned away and reached for her dinner.

"That was touching," Raik said.

Therin swung his head toward Raik as he spoke.

"I don't like this arrangement," Raik said.

Brok smiled at the snake, now mouse, doublesight. "I think my brother does."

Zimp patted her bedroll and stretched it smooth. She leaned back and rested her head. "When you're through eating…" she began.

Brok interrupted. "Take first watch."

Zimp didn't answer.

Lankor replaced his rock and lay on his back. He felt enclosed with the trees rising all around him. Even in their beauty, they were like bars of a cage. The wind blew motion into everything around him. He smelled the burned bush, which reminded him of his shift. He felt relaxed afterward even though he didn't get to fly anywhere as Zimp had. His shoulders rolled back and flattened along the ground. His eyes closed until it was time for his watch, and Zimp woke him with a soft whisper.

He opened his eyes and her face leaned close to his.

"You awake?" she said.

Lankor nodded and she backed away. "I don't think we'll have any trouble. We haven't lately," she said.

"I thought I had second watch," he said.

"After you fell asleep, I changed it." She smiled. "I know you like to see the sun rise."

"Better if there were a cliff nearby." He rose to a sitting position and quickly rolled his bed into a bundle and stuffed it next to his saddlebag. He reached in and grabbed some jerky, held it up so that Zimp could see it, and said, "Energy for my watch."

She made the sound of a whispered laugh then patted his shoulder. "Whatever it takes, big brother," she said.

As Lankor got to his feet, Zimp lay on her side and slipped her blanket over her shoulders. She fell asleep almost instantly, her breathing shallow and long.

Lankor's watch must have been the shortest of the three, because he barely made five rounds of the camp when the rising sound of the birds' morning song began in the distance. He had heard few nocturnal animals rustling around and concluded that this area, closest to Castle Weilk, must have been well hunted.

He woke everyone and they cleared the area in relative silence.

Once the horses were also ready for the morning's travel, Zimp pulled the group into a circle and lit two candles and set them on the ground. She pointed at each in turn, "A candle for peace and one for courage." She lit each of them. "Please, today's prayers must be your own and in silence." She lowered her head and opened her hands palms up.

Lankor thought about the day ahead of them, their trip thus far, the council and The Few, his travels with his family, his home, and the courage Nayman had when he needed it. Lankor asked for that courage, to risk his own life for the life of another. But instead of asking for peace, he asked to stay reminded to hold his power in check. The rest of the time he listened to the sound of the forest and felt the warmth of the sun.

After their short silence, Zimp pinched each flame out. The horses ready, the four of them mounted and rode toward the compound of Castle Weilk.

There appeared to be many roads and paths that led to the castle stronghold. Lankor and Zimp rode ahead and by mid-morning stepped into a broad and ravaged flatland. He could see fields off to his right in the distance. Small wooden shacks lifted like strange growths from the golden grain that grew there. Next to each shack grew sections of dark green, yellow-green, and an area that bore a blue haze, all coming together to create a patchwork of color.

"Those are the gardens of the slaves," Zimp said.

"Slaves?" Lankor questioned. "Slaves to what?"

She smiled at him. "There are economies built around the larger cities and castles. Those who are poor or incapable of greater things, those who have little talent, are loaned land masses to create a barely survivable existence."

"But they can leave if they wish, can't they?" Lankor had never experienced the truth of what he had just learned.

"Where would they go? How would they survive? They can leave, but would face bandits, wild animals…" she hesitated, "doublesight. They would never think of leaving. If they left, they could not return." She halted her horse next to Lankor's. "Here is how life looks in many cities," she said. Pointing to the farmers, she said, "The lowest class." Rotating toward the main roadway on her left, she slid her arm through the air indicating the wagons and carts entering the city in a long line. "A slightly higher class of poor are the skilled ones who hand-make goods such as utensils for cooking, for storing items, baskets, clothing of a higher quality, trinkets. Among these are traders who bring jewels and jewelry from far places. These are the ones who help to spread and mix cultures. You'll find the jewels of the sea and land and forest, collected from around The Great Land, all traded here. Performers come, too. Acrobats, singers, dramatic players. And high contests where warriors fight until death or humiliation, at which time they would rather be dead."

"And inside the city?" Lankor said.

"The owners of taverns, stables, Inns."

Zimp was interrupted by Raik who had ridden up on her and Lankor. "And whorehouses," he said. "What class do these women of sex occupy?"

"They are traders," she said. "They trade a moment's pleasure for a man's uncontrollable longings." She swung around in her saddle to look at Raik. "They makes a good wage for dealing with filth, don't you think?" She rode on and Lankor's horse stepped in beside her.

"And King Belford the Warrior?" Lankor asked.

"Top of the chain, as you might guess. He lives in Castle Wielk at the crest of the knoll." She grimaced. "It is his influence you'll see everywhere in the city."

"The scat at the top produces the stink at the bottom," Raik said from behind her.

She turned slightly to glance at Raik then over to Lankor. "For once he's right."

Lankor, the novice in the group, wondered how he'd be able to play the older brother when he had to ask his sister about everything that went on. He wouldn't be much help in knowing how to maneuver the city. But he'd come in good stead as manpower, or beast-power, whichever they might need at the time.

They crossed the trampled fields diagonally toward the city. Lankor felt conspicuous riding with these doublesight. They were to pretend to be traveling to see The Great Land. Why would such an odd group do such a thing?

An argument was occurring on the main road. Yelling ensued, and in a moment swords were drawn. Lankor watched as other vendors widened the space for the two, but continued on their way toward the short wall that surrounded the city and castle. Not wishing to be left behind or to be slow to enter the city, the men quickly gave up on their argument and ran for their carts.

There were multiple entranceways into the castle stronghold. Trails of people disappeared inside the walls. Loose groupings came from the woods northwest of the city, from due west, and from where Lankor traveled with his group. Having begun late, they were just now catching up to a few vendors coming from the southwest. He could see in the distance a line of people from due east as well.

"They are arriving here from the beaches of Weilk-Alshore Ocean," Zimp told him before he asked. "It takes a few days." She stopped short and peered into the sky.

"Your sister?" Lankor said.

"Maybe," she said. "I felt a terrible coldness in my chest."

"No words?"

"Sometimes there are no words to express what lies ahead," she said.

As they neared the castle, Zimp led them at a trot across the plain toward the main gate. "Mixing with the people will make it easier to be invisible."

Lankor and the others followed. He heard hoofbeats behind him. Therin pulled ahead of him at Zimp's heels. Her horse kicked out but missed and Therin took a wider berth.

In the distance, at the main gate, a confusion of carts backed up and one tipped. From inside the compound, seven armed soldiers barged through the onslaught of vendors and kicked into a gallop toward Zimp and her friends. She halted in front of Lankor and he rode up close to her. Raik and Brok flanked them, just inside Lankor's peripheral vision. Therin sat obediently near Brok's horse.

The soldiers stopped in front of the small group. They wore the crest of Weilk, a barbed blackberry bush wrapped around a trout. Five deep purple berries grew at one end. The insignia was said to be one of the more elaborate in The Great Land. Lankor didn't recall its entire meaning, but knew that the fish and berries were the foods that kept their warriors alive during the great battles with Sclan to the north and Flande from the far west.

The largest of the men pushed his horse slightly in front of the others. "You are not traders. What is your purpose here?"

Lankor waited for Zimp to answer. Her horse stood to the front of their group and the soldier had addressed her directly. She turned slowly to acknowledge Brok.

He hesitated, then rode around Lankor to stop near Zimp. "We are travelers of the land," he announced jovially. "We have never been in a great city the size of Castle Weilk." He pointed to those entering through the main gate. "It looks as though we're here at the right time, too. What is the purpose of all these people? Is there a bazaar going on? Will there be dancers and singers?" His tone grew more excited with each question, like a child on an adventure.

The soldier relaxed. "We heard of a small band of invaders, one being a Flandean Guard. Those westerners still believe we're at war with one another. If we find him, we'll throw him in the dungeons," the man said. He looked the five of them over, lingering on each as though sizing them up. When his glare landed on Zimp his eyebrows raised. "A pretty one, and with you men?"

"My sister does not leave my side since our parents died," Lankor blurted out aggressively.

"You needn't worry." The guard obviously noted Lankor's bulk. "I take no woman who would not have me." He leaned into his saddle. "But if she would have me, I would not complain." Several of the men behind him laughed.

Lankor noted Zimp's restraint.

"Keep the animal tied while inside." The soldier pushed his chin toward Brok. "You must be the owner. You have the same intensity in your eyes, the same look about you."

The man had no idea what he was saying. Lankor waited for Raik to be acknowledged, but the soldier said nothing. He hardly met Raik's eyes at all, glancing past him as though he was invisible. The soldiers turned around and the leader twisted in his saddle. "Slow down and take your turn entering the gate." He pointed at Therin and repeated, "Tie him now."

Brok threw a leg over his saddle. He searched in his

saddlebag. "Anyone have rope?"

Raik pulled a long cord from his saddlebag and handed it to Brok. "I know *I'll* feel more comfortable with him secured."

Therin twisted his head from the loop Brok made of the cord. "Therin, hold still," Brok said. He appeared to be having more trouble than he thought he would.

"Is he all right?" Lankor asked, knowing that everyone in the group understood the deeper part of the question.

"Therin!" The thylacine held still. Brok slid the cord over Therin's head. "He's fine for now." Brok patted Therin's head then looked up at the soldiers.

Satisfied, they turned and headed back toward the castle.

"I think it might help if we addressed Therin by name. Maybe pose questions to help him remain in analytical thought, you know?" Brok said.

Lankor and the others knew exactly what Brok meant. Therin might be slipping away, farther and farther into a beast singlesight. The thought of it reminded Lankor of his uncle, always to be a dragon, dropping slowly from the knowledge of being human. Eventually, his uncle would be banished outside the clan to live alone where he would not be dangerous. He would be chained. Dellin would have already lost knowledge of the doublesight and of the sacrifice he had made for them. Lankor felt a deep thickness in his chest, a pain he could not explain.

As the soldiers approached the castle in the distance, Zimp spoke to Raik. "You are lucky I had you shift only once. They saw no threat in you. But as you warned, they know of our arrival. If another group does not arrive today, we'll be watched closely."

"We'll be watched anyway," Raik said, pointing at Therin.

"And he'll watch you," Brok said. "This cord could be chewed through in a moment."

Raik said nothing. He shrunk into his saddle. "You can't keep me like this forever."

"Let's get inside," Zimp said. "It'll be easy to hide among all these people." She motioned for Brok to lead. "You've got to take over."

Brok mounted and advanced to the front. He wrapped the cord that held Therin in tow loosely around his wrist. The others fell in behind him. It took several hours of edging into the throng of people to make their way into the compound. Some vendors stopped at the gates and set up their carts, offering breakfast to the late arrivals.

Inside the walls, vendors set up their wares. It was market day, Lankor surmised. There would be no other reason for so many vendors to be there at once. The four of them dismounted and walked.

The noise was festive. Musicians played their instruments in various corners of the open central area. The stronghold appeared larger from the inside than the outside, with streets spoking from the central area toward a far off wall and another entrance gate. Castle Weilk looked to be a good distance away.

Brok led them deep into the grounds. He asked directions from several people who appeared to live inside the stronghold area. They'd point and Brok would lead the others closer toward the castle.

Lankor smelled the stable before they arrived. A blacksmith worked a pit of fire. As they stepped around a corner, the ringing of metal on metal pierced the air. A bargain was struck quickly and the blacksmith ushered out several young boys to lead the horses into stalls and to unsaddle them.

"We'll take our saddlebags with us," Brok said.

The heavy-set blacksmith pointed his hammer at Therin. "If you're leaving him, I have a cage in the back."

Therin whined and rubbed against Brok's leg. He understood those words.

"He'll stay with us for now. Everyone grab what's important and we'll find a place to stay for a few days."

One of the boys reached out to touch Therin. He growled and the boy yanked his hand back.

The blacksmith smashed his hammer onto a strip of steel and shook his head. "We don't like strange beasts here. If that thing ain't safe, you'll find it dead."

"He's safe," Brok said. "He just doesn't trust people. They're always threatening to kill him."

The man glared back at Brok. "Still, we'll want him in that cage tonight. And if by morning we find a man," he poked the hammer toward Brok, "like you, we'll keep 'im in that cage."

Brok nodded and swung around to leave, pulling Therin with him.

"What did that mean?" Lankor said.

"They are expecting doublesight," Zimp said. "I thought you said they only knew we were coming."

Raik said, "They heard nothing from me."

They dropped the conversation and mingled with the crowd for a while. Zimp leaned close to Lankor and spoke quietly into his ear. "These people appear to be tense about something. Even the children aren't running and screaming like I would expect."

33

Storret perched with his legs hanging over a high branch of a sugar pine, his back leaned safely against its trunk. The sun had already crested the eastern mountains, spitting sparks of orange along the treetops and into the lightly clouded sky. Feelings of frustration and pain, anger and joy, battered him in shifts. Just as he began to understand one emotion another shoved it aside and occupied his body. He had been noticed as an honorable clan member and talented warrior and leader. Why did it happen just when he met Breel, and why did Oro need to die for him to fulfill such an honor? And even though he felt that he was worthy of honor, what could he, as commander, possibly teach anyone? How much time was there to get ready? The singlesight humans had already attacked them once. Oronice had obviously sped up her journey to the next realm. The only thing he could think of that would encourage her to do that was that Zimp must be in grave danger, or was already dead.

The treetop cradled Storret as though it held a baby. He had spent much of his life in treetops overlooking The Great Land. As morning opened to another day, he allowed the brightness of the sun to cheer him on, to open his heart to whatever this world had for him. Another day. Another mystery as to what might happen. Each day could be an adventure if only one allowed it to be.

He would not make a plan for this day. When he arrived before his troops he'd look them over and decide on the spot what to pursue. He'd ask for their help to get them engaged. He'd praise each and every one of them, no matter what beast image they held. Each had his or her purpose, and that purpose would be met in a war of any kind.

A war. Had he really thought that correctly?

Doublesight were supposed to hold both beast and human life sacred. Why would they go to war? Legends foretold of great wars and how the Six Shapeless Gods disapproved and punished the beings that lived at that time by separating the humans from the beasts forever. So few doublesight were left on The Great Land after that. They were to be the reminder of what once was. Blessed were the doublesight. He laughed, mocking the idea that their lives had been blessed. In the last few decades, fear of the unknown had caused many humans to separate from their doublesight brothers. A few lords of the land acknowledged the doublesight and elected to accept them, but the singlesight humans, individually, could not be convinced. And laws were only obeyed in daylight and under watch.

As a reminder of just how blessed he did not feel, his crow image pulled at him to shift. As he leaned over to look down the trunk of the pine, his hand slipped from the branch he had been holding. His other hand flew up to grab a nearby branch to steady him. The fear of falling had come too quickly. His crow image got its way. The shift began before he could refocus. His body shriveled and folded into itself. He worked to keep his balance by shifting focus to his feet. Claws grew and gripped. Arms shrunk into black wings.

The change complete, Storret let loose his firm hold on his human thinking. It was there, but the urges of the crow were there also, competing for time, thought, life. This was the dilemma of the doublesight: wishing to be beast while human and wishing to be human while beast. Each person had his or her own struggles with sanity in this way.

Storret stepped into the wind and flapped his wings. He flew up and around the treetops once, then plummeted toward the forest floor. The quickness of the shift left him a little foggy in his thinking. His crow image held strong. Under that strength, though, was the human Storret. Always human first, Storret worked his way back into a semblance of control over the crow image. Instead of landing in a tree or cawing out a warning when he glimpsed the humans, he hit the ground behind a stand of scrub. He shook his head and ruffled his feathers. He focused on how he might organize his troops. He was back, full strength. It had taken longer than he would have liked and he reminded himself of the dangers of shifting too quickly.

Storret shifted smoothly back into his human self. Straightening his clothes as he stepped from behind the bushes, he greeted several of the men he would soon lead.

"Sir," one of them said, surprised to see Storret. The man held out his hand. "Floom," he said.

Storret gripped the man's hand, a totally human gesture. What image was behind that handshake?

Two more hands reached for Storret's.

Floom stepped aside. "My friends Sloat and Woss."

Storret shook hands with them as well. Strong, firm grips. Aggressive handshakes. They were predators of some kind.

"There are others in the clearing over here," Floom said, leading the way.

Storret recognized many from his own clan and smiled. Several nodded their heads in approval, making Storret feel better about the day. A wide variety of people were packed into the clearing, stretching into the woods as well. How many there were he could not tell. They talked among themselves in lowered voices, but the abundance of sound pierced the air.

Storret felt that he could tell one clan from another just by their human features. Tall or short, broad shouldered, curly hair reminded him of Breel and Brok. Thylacines? Were there also other predators? Wolves, hawks?

As he looked them over, his thoughts turned to Oronice. Although he trusted her judgment, he did not wish for her to die. There was much that she didn't say in front of anyone, and much that The Few held back as well. But Storret had heard enough concern in all their voices to know that the small army they were putting together would have to fight and that additional recruiting had already begun.

Judging from Oro's quickened departure, he suspected the rush involved Zimp and the small band of doublesight sent out to Castle Weilk. He raised his arms into the air and the crowd quieted.

"This is not the ideal training ground, but I assume many of you have already trained in some form of battle." A loud cheer went up and Storret saw staffs, swords, knives, and a few longbows lift into the air above the heads of those before him. "This is not what we are taught as doublesight," he said. Then he stopped. "But it is also true that we wished to survive." He could sense the shift in the emotion of those before him and thought that it was the most passive man who, when angered, puts up the most vicious fight. This, then, would be a bloody battle to the death. Numbers would not matter in the face of extinction.

The more he looked around, the smaller the clearing appeared and the fewer doublesight stood around him. "Eventually," he started, "and I know this may be difficult, but we'll need to know one another's beast image. If we are in battle and our brother should shift we don't want to be shocked into shifting as well. Remember, a fast shift makes you vulnerable to remaining in beast image longer and possibly forever, while a slow shift makes you vulnerable to immediate attack. Death, if you are in battle at the time."

Floom stepped out of the crowd and raised a hand. "Some of us practice fast shifts and have found a stability point."

Nodding approval, Storret smiled and rubbed his chin with his hand. "Perhaps you can teach us such a skill, my friend."

Floom almost leapt into the air. The lightness in his being tugged at Storret and he guessed a bird of some kind, a raptor. Wow, shouldn't a raptor be leading them into battle? No, he wouldn't question Ornice's decision. He would hold to his duty and post until otherwise removed.

"For this first hour we shall get to know one another. We are many, but not so many that we cannot learn who will fight beside us. Floom," he said, "you will walk with me and help to collect information. Before we shift, any of us, we acknowledge our beast image. I want to know what skills you have, how quickly you can shift and remain in human consciousness. Tell one another your names and your likes and dislikes. How difficult will it be for you to harm a singlesight? How much of an honor do you feel being selected to fight? While in battle, we must know the person next to us so that we are impelled to save their life as if it were our own. I want to know if you see yourself as courageous or cowardly." He lowered his head. Where did all that come from? How would he learn so much about them? He motioned to Floom to stand by him. "Begin," he said to the others.

Floom waltzed over to Storret, pride in his step. "Sir."

"A raptor, yes?" Storret said.

"Hawks. All three of us. In fact, there are probably twenty in all here." Floom lowered his eyes. "We know that you're a crow. Your whole clan. It's difficult to hide." A blush came to his face. "I'm honored to stand with you."

"Truly?" Storret said without thinking.

"Crows live in both worlds. They have no fear. I've seen crows attack all types of beasts. They never give up. And they are cunning and quick." Floom shook his head in amazement.

Storret had never seen himself in such a way, but listening to Floom reminded him of the truth. "Thank you. Now, let's see what we have to work with."

The two of them weaved in and out of the small army asking questions and discussing personal issues. At first it felt odd to be doing so, but Storret soon found himself growing more interested and closer to his men, and women. Many of the clans provided women warriors. Fox doublesight were equally matched, male and female. And there were rat doublesight, about fifty of them, a few eagle doublesight, and copperheads. Storret hadn't known before, but Raik must have been a copperhead, because his brother Galwit claimed to be one. Bennek stood next to Galwit and proudly announced that he was a singlesight human. "A snake charmer," he added.

Skill sets varied as well. They all claimed to be swordsmen, but some offered other talents such as archery and knife throwing. Hand-to-hand combat was the specialty of the fox doublesight, who were magical in their movements.

About mid-morning, a messenger worked his way through the crowd to alert Storret that Rend had requested his presence at Oro's wagon.

"I've got to go," he said to Floom. "Continue on."

Storret ran through the woods, a more direct route than any of the winding paths.

Rend had apparently heard him coming. The big man motioned for Storret to join them.

Noot, the High Sage, looked frightened, unsure, and confused. He would find his place quickly though. Storret had faith in that fact, even as he climbed inside the wagon and kneeled next to Oronice.

Oro's eyes opened into a slit. Her dry mouth wrinkled as she whispered. "You first," she said. "I will contact you first."

Confusion overwhelmed him. Why not contact Noot first?

Rend must have noticed. He leaned toward Storret and said, "She wants to have clear contact before she goes to Zimp. She fears that her granddaughter has not practiced enough, that she may become confused by what she hears."

"How she hears," Mianna corrected.

"How she hears," Rend repeated. "And what she may see. Do you understand this?"

"I do," Storret said. "But Noot?"

"He must remain a clear path for the other realm," Rend said.

Oro sucked in a deep breath and her chest heaved into the air. They all became still and awaited her last breath.

Rend motioned for the others to exit the wagon. He followed last, leaving Storret and Oro alone.

As the rear flap closed and Storret heard the last of the rustling outside as Rend and the others moved away, Oro eased out a long, slow aaahhhh, as though she were meditating. She created a sound passageway to the other realm.

He recalled at age six when his older brother taught him the first passageway. And now Oronice The Gem used it for her last shift, a realm shift.

Storret enjoyed the memory for a moment. He would miss

holding Oro's hand and dancing with her during ceremonies. He'd miss her scarred and scratchy voice, her wisdom. But there was something exciting about the new sense of her he was about to gain. He had had only a fleeting moment of such contact when his parents died, several days when his brother did his realm shift after a long illness. The more conscious the shift, the more available would be the inter-realm contact. That was unless you were lucky enough to have a twin. He wondered briefly why Zimp rejected the possibilities of what she was able to do?

Oronice's voice trailed off. Her chest sunk into the mattress.

Storret's eyes welled up. Was he unable to make contact? Did he need to concentrate in a special way that he had forgotten? He panicked. His daydreams of being younger had interfered with his focus. He had allowed Oronice to realm shift without being there for her, without listening for her. He had failed his most important task.

"Quiet!" he heard Rend say from nearby. But Rend had stepped away, hadn't he?

Storret stopped thinking. He quieted his mind.

"Better," he heard. Oronice had spoken.

Nothing he could have imagined could explain what happened next. If he had recalled his few days in contact with his brother, it would appear to be a sketchy, interrupted contact at best, for Oronice came through as though she sat with her lips next to his ear and her body touching his. In fact, Storret's entire body tingled as though he was being touched everywhere. His head felt an unusual pressure, and his ears shut down to all outside noise including the wind, the birds, the creak and snap of tree limbs as they scraped together, all of it stopped. He fell into a silence so complete that he questioned his own existence within it. Then he heard Oronice, a younger, more vibrant voice. He remembered the sound.

"Wait," she said. "Hold on to...wait."

There came the sound of someone taking a deep breath. He glanced at the dead body. Nothing moved. There was no other sound anywhere in existence. He could see in the physical world, but not hear. He only heard what went on in the other realm.

Her inhale stopped and again she exhaled, saying, "Ahhhh," in the other realm.

He could hear the sound of her exhale, and toward the end of her last breath, Oro said, "Oh, I see."

Storret waited.

"A birthing," she said. "I'm being born."

With her last comment, a loud flapping of wings came. He felt the air from the wild movement. He sensed a presence in the wagon with him, but was afraid to turn, to look around. He didn't want to lose contact. He didn't want to end that magnificent moment. He held his breath. The swipe of a wing touched his face. A clawed foot landed on his arm. Without moving, he used soft eyes to see Oronice, a young crow, perched on his arm. He was fully conscious of only the other realm. "Am I there with you?" he said.

Oronice laughed. "No. You are not even half way. But you've done nicely."

"What, what…"

"I was reborn as a crow image first. This is what makes contact difficult."

"Why can I hear you?"

"I'm not sure yet." She shifted before him. "Oh, that's why," she said.

"What?"

"Never mind. It's something I must sense." A young, and very beautiful, Oronice sat before him near the dead body of her older self. Her hand lay across his arm where a clawed foot had been a moment before. "You," she said accusingly, "could not imagine seeing me."

"Until I heard you," he said.

"Yes. Now listen to me closely."

34

The chamber wall stood a stark charcoal color against the yellow sunbeam that pitched through the one outside opening. King Belford the Warrior paced along the stone floor, scuffing his boots against the twisting grain in the hard river-stone surface.

"Calm down," Draklan said, making a smooth motion with his hand. "We'll find them. The double-beast will make sure of it."

"And what then? Kill them? Begin another war?" King Belford said.

"Your worry sickens me. Where is the fearless warrior who held off Flandean armies, who entered Sclan and left only ruins?" Draklan spit a glob of slime onto the floor in front of the chair in which he sat. The spit stretched and slid like a living thing across the stone.

King Belford stepped over it and continued to pace. "Why does it matter? Perhaps the warrior has seen enough death. Perhaps I believe there is no point to it. The doublesight threaten no one. They play inside their beast images like children. What harm?"

"What harm?" Draklan jumped to his feet. "You fool. It is not what they do now, but what they could do. You've seen the sisters."

King Belford's face wrinkled into disgust. "I have," he said lowering his head.

"They are the new doublesight being born. They have hate in their veins. They are the future of this world unless someone stops them." Draklan turned and stared at the wall. He spoke, not to the king, but to himself or someone deep inside him. "Only humans can stop them. Only pure bloods can put an end to this insanity, this hunger." He twisted on his heels, swung around with knees bent and head cocked, urging King Belford to agree with him. "Do you see?"

The king stopped pacing for a moment. His breathing became shallow. "What of you, then?" He waited but knew the answer and knew that Draklan would not say it. And what would happen to them all? Who or what might be left after such a war? "What is happening to The Great Land? What have the Gods allowed?"

"Fool." Draklan rushed past King Belford and stopped before the opening that looked out over the Weilk grasslands to the east. A line of wagons and carts appeared interspersed along the road leading toward the ocean. "The Gods," Draklan said, "have abandoned us all."

"It can't be true."

"Ah, but if not, what is this?" Draklan opened the way for his own shift to begin. He shook his head violently as a beak appeared and ruffled feathers pushed from his head and neck. He could feel each, like a pin-prick, form and grow from him. Draklan let a loud squeal out of his throat. He felt sick, about to vomit when the feathery growths turned to fur and his body took on a dense weight, a muscled thickness unlike any bird. He felt the pressure of legs, feet, and claws before another feeling of sickness came over him. Wings grew from his back, larger than any wings should grow. They pushed out and stretched above and behind him. Another weaker squawk escaped his beak as his tail slipped into form like a snake crawling from his body. Draklan felt every change as it occurred. His mind thickened even as the memory of his human image remained conscious.

Draklan let his claws protrude with a sharp scrape across the stone. He turned to face King Belford.

Transfixed in a frightened stare, the king stepped backwards and stumbled, catching himself before he fell.

Fury and sadness shot through Draklan's mind and heart. It was that look given him each time he shifted that caused his self-loathing. That fear in his father's eyes he knew all too well. His father's look of horror shaped Draklan's view of the world even before the sisters were born. He knew the wide-eyed stare. He knew how it felt to see such a shift, the fear and hatred behind the eyes. He had felt those emotions the first time he saw the sisters shift. He hated that he was seen that way as well, even though he felt the same hatred toward his cousins.

Draklan lifted a front paw and lashed out with his claws toward his father's chest. He never actually struck King Belford, yet each time he swung out the man reached for his sword as though Draklan were his opponent and not his son. Draklan's eagle eyes pin-pointed every movement and registered it, stuffing it into memory. He could anticipate his father's next motion just through noticing slight tensions in the man's body.

The gryphon turned around and walked away, letting his tail brush against King Belford's legs. This time his father did not move away. Draklan's continual taunting had become commonplace. He stood back from the window and glared past the procession and across the grasslands toward the horizon. He had never been to the Weilk-Alshore Ocean. Since birth, he had been sheltered until he could control his shifting. Only then could Draklan go on hunting trips with his father. Short trips. For the hunger for change grew quickly inside him, whichever image he held. As a human he longed to become beast, and as beast he longed for his human image. He felt that hunger now. The hunger to be normal, only one image not two, only one set of emotions. It was that hunger that drew against his sanity every day.

Heat from the morning sun caused the distance to ripple and shift, reminding Draklan of his double life. The moment between one image and the next was indescribably fluid, not land or air. The colors washed together, yet the focused accuracy tightened and contrasted into perfection. He could see farther, but discern no color. He could pick out a rabbit in the brush, but control his hunger for its flesh. The only hunger he could not control grew from his heart. Often that hunger first wished for his death, then to become human once more and never to change back into his gryphon image.

Draklan let his wings lower. He curled his head so that he could see his own lion's feet. Shifting back into human form took less time but left him exhausted. He sat on the floor of the chamber and drew in a great breath. He began to cry.

King Belford stood behind him and placed a hand on his son's shoulder.

Draklan turned into his father's legs and hugged them. It took immense energy to maintain the gryphon image. Not physical energy, but daunting amounts of emotional energy. And his first thought as a human, just before his shift completed, was of his mother's death. An angry child lashing out. The sound of his mother's broken neck, the slash of claws across her face. How she fell into his arms just as his human image became whole. Draklan cried for his mother's life, the tears doing double duty as they begged for death even though he knew his father would not do it.

"Come along, my son," King Belford said. He lifted Draklan from under his arms. Together they walked over to a long bench against the far wall and sat, the father's arms around the son's shoulders.

Draklan felt his energy returning. But anger kept him in check. The hunger to shift stayed hidden. "What has happened to us all?"

"Just as the doublesight are a reminder of our sins, The Great Land also reminds us by going through its own changes. War changes the face of all of us. It makes us evil, builds hatred where hatreds never blossomed before. We fear, my son. That is what humans cannot escape from. We fear whatever we cannot do, whatever we cannot see, and whatever lives differently." King Belford pulled his son closer. "I am tired of fear, yet I feel it rise inside me every day. What am I doing by allowing the sisters to live the way they must live? How long can I be partial to their feedings without losing my own sanity? I grow tired of allowing the killing to go on. I can only imagine what my brother must go through."

"I only wish for it all to stop," Draklan said. He straightened and shrugged to loosen his father's grip. "As long as the doublesight are alive there will be the potential for horrible beasts like the sisters. The gargoyles of the past are returning. The demons of history will destroy everything unless we stop it. I know that I am a doublesight, but I also know that what I say is true. We do not deserve to live if we are the downfall of The Great Land."

"Only some doublesight are dangerous."

Draklan leaped from the bench and walked to the center of the chamber before he turned toward King Belford. "I killed my own mother," he said pounding his fist into his chest. "That is dangerous enough."

"You were a child."

"Had I killed you in that same moment, your generals would have slain me on the spot. Had they seen me, even now…"

"Three generals have seen you. My brother, one of them." His father stood, planting his feet firmly and lifting his chin with bold abandon.

Draklan glared. "Yes, the father of the sisters. What would he say? That you and he are ruining your lives for the sake of throwbacks?" He spit the words as though they were vile creatures. "The other two are afraid of what I or the sisters might do if they said one word. Talk about fear." Draklan motioned toward the window behind him. "If your subjects had any idea what I was, what mother was, would they stay outside these walls?"

"They might."

"Out of fear, as you say. Out of fear and nothing more," Draklan said.

"Every human longs for what it feels like to shift."

Draklan shook his head. "They wouldn't want to know the pain. The doublesight spend their time battling their own longings, their own hunger. They are tormented, constantly at war with themselves."

"Not your mother."

"Silence!" Draklan's strength grew into anger. "Enough talk. Send out your men to find the doublesight before they know what I am, before they know who I am."

King Belford reached for his son as he walked past, but Draklan stepped backwards. Already the longing to shift into his gryphon image grew. What he did not say and could not say to his father was that his gryphon image had increasingly felt hunger for meat, even as he held back that hunger. He was becoming like the sisters, who craved blood and meat, something his mother had told him the doublesight did not do. He shook his head as he watched his father leave. It was market day. Better that the sisters be fed doublesight rather than picking off thieves or drunkards. No one would mind that a few doublesight disappeared into the castle chambers never to return.

35

Uneasy feelings settled into Zimp. The market grew rapidly in size but not in sound. Vendors looked suspiciously at each other while they set up their wares. Lankor crowded Zimp's space, obviously unsure of what attention a brother would pay to a sister. Then there were the voices she heard continually. Since she woke up that morning, Zimp heard the telltale whisperings of Zora, but also heard other sounds, louder, more directed.

As might be expected, crows flew over and around many of the carts looking for scraps of food, shiny objects to pick up. A cart owner dropped a coin and chased the crow that retrieved it. A few steps and the bird lifted easily into the air. Zimp felt jealous and had to look into Lankor's eyes for a moment, blankly but probingly, to hold back from shifting.

"What is it?" Lankor said, not understanding the look she gave him.

"You're too close," she said. "A brother might protect his sister, but he wouldn't stand that close to do so."

With a huff, Lankor straightened his back and placed his hand on his hip. He had left his staff with his horse in the stable, but held his pack under his arm.

Zimp noticed him fidget with his hands as though he didn't know what to do with them. She reached up and patted his shoulder. "A sister can get close to her brother, though." She saw confusion cross his face and felt a glib satisfaction.

Brok and Raik walked on opposite sides of Therin who pulled ahead of them against the taut leash line. Out the corner of her eye Zimp noticed that Raik held the leash. Brok must have done that to keep Raik in tow. A good idea.

The five of them walked for another few minutes, changed course down a side alley, and stopped in front of a small inn called The Hangover.

Zimp saw that above the sign ran a balcony jutting outward from the wall of the building. Enough space cantilevered above them for several people to sleep in the open air. She suspected that the space might rent cheaply after the rooms were full. Great logs ran diagonally from the balcony to meet the ground near the inn's walls. While inspecting the place, she heard a loud fluttering of wings close to her ears. Behind that sound one of her travel mates said something she didn't hear. She shook her head and took a deep breath.

"Well?" Brok said.

She turned with ease to look him in the eye. "I didn't hear you."

"Should Raik and I return to the stable with Therin? Do you think any inn would have a thylacine in one of the rooms?"

"Wait here and we'll see," she said. "Lankor, you get us a room."

She followed Lankor inside. The space opened to a dozen tables and long benches. Fifteen people, including a few Castle Weilk guards, sat in small groups talking and smoking pipes or sniffing smoldering pots of herbs. The thick air smelled of men and ale. Pine log beams stretched from one side to the other along the ceiling. Two staircases, one at each end of a long bar on the far wall, led to the rooms above.

Zimp held to Lankor's shirt in the back as he plowed through the room and weaved between tables. She heard moans and chuckles as she passed some of the patrons. One said, "Oh, yes," as she passed. She wanted to glare at him, but kept her eyes pointed toward Lankor's strong back. At the bar, Zimp came up close beside the big man.

"We'd like a room," Lankor said.

The innkeeper stood near a pail of gray water, dipping dirty mugs and plates in for a moment then removing them and setting them onto a shelf just below the bar. Many of the wet utensils still looked dirty as he lifted them out of the pail. He wore a torn shirt and pants that were long for him and frayed at the bottoms. A reddish scar crossed his face and appeared to run partway down his neck and into his open shirt. He had a round and hairy chest and belly, strong forearms, and a look of madness in his eyes. "You and the wife?" he said.

"My sister," Lankor said.

Laughter came from a table a short distance away. The innkeeper looked over at the men and turned back with a wide smile that glorified his green teeth. "Don't allow that kinda sex in here."

The men behind Zimp and Lankor howled.

Zimp reached over and squeezed Lankor's arm hoping to help maintain his calm. It worked.

Lankor turned to look at the men and let a great smile puncture his face. "No kind of sex will be happening with my little sister, I guarantee you."

The laughter subsided and several of the men turned back to their drinks.

A tinge of pride swept over Zimp unexpectedly.

"So it is, then," the innkeeper said. "I'm Budrill." He held out his hand.

Lankor took it and said, "Lankor. My sister, Zimp."

"Odd names." Budrill closed his eyes and cocked his head upward, thinking. "I'm good at names and would say that you aren't from the same part of The Great Land. Hmm. Zimp is definitely a southern name. Lissland?"

Neither Zimp nor Lankor made a move to answer him.

"My, my." He smacked his thick lips. "...was in the war, ya know? Ya wouldn't know it by lookin' at me." He slapped his round stomach. "Lankor is a Sclan name, sir, sure as I'm standin' here."

Zimp waited for Lankor to respond and when he didn't she started to speak only to be interrupted by his booming voice. "The war is what left us alone to care for each other," Lankor said. "It's what brought our parents together and what took them away." He held Budrill's stare.

"Sorry, my friend. A-many good families were torn apart." He slapped his palm onto the bar. "The two of you, then?"

"We are five," Lankor said. "Two others and our pet wait outside."

"What kinda pet? We don't allow nothin' dangerous..."

"It'll stay with us and never leave the room, even when we come down for dinner." Lankor reached around and pulled Zimp close to him. "A safe room."

Budrill blinked. "Our rooms bed three at best, and only if one sleeps on the floor."

"You don't want our money?" Lankor didn't give up.

"A room and a balcony for five might be as much as thirty clips of gold." He tapped his fingers. "You didn't say what kinda pet."

Lankor nodded. "A thylacine. We travel with two of the most talented trainers in The Great Land."

"They from Brendern Forest?"

"The master trainer," Lankor said.

Budrill shifted back and forth and was about to say no. His lips tightened as he glanced around the room. "I could fill those rooms quickly today."

Lankor leaned closer. "Forty clips then."

The man nodded. He walked to the end of the bar and retrieved a bluntly carved key and handed it to Lankor. He motioned to the stairs at the right of the bar. "Front of the inn, room with a seven scratched into the wood. The inn ain't responsible for nothin' stolen."

"I don't think we have to worry about that," Lankor said.

Budrill smacked his lips again. "Any trouble with your beast and I'll throw 'im over the side myself."

"You won't even know he's there." Lankor's voice softened and grew sincere. "Thank you."

Budrill cocked his head curiously, then wandered back to the end of the bar and his pail of water. He began to dunk mugs again.

Zimp turned and led the way back outside, the sun blinding

her vision for a moment. Squinting, she studied the alley, which led north and south several hundred yards. South dumped into the main road through the stronghold leading toward the castle proper. The northern portion split east and west. Most buildings lining the alley were two-story structures that stood thin and tall, unlike the inn, which was the longest building in the line.

"We got a room?" Brok asked.

"A room and a balcony." Pointing behind her, Zimp said, "Big boy here got Therin in, too. Nice job," she said, but she wouldn't look at him for fear that he might get cocky. She didn't need trouble handling the booming voice he used inside. That was a side of him she'd not seen and didn't want to draw on until she needed to.

"Who gets the balcony?" Raik appeared as though he already knew the answer. His eyes were big and his hand unsteady.

She didn't waste a moment in answering. "You and Therin."

"But we don't know…" Raik said, stopping his words as several guards walked out of the inn and trudged down the street.

Brok took the leash from Raik and made for the door. "I'll get him upstairs. Where's the room?"

Zimp motioned for Lankor to lead Brok, and for Raik to go next. She brought up the rear, but stayed close to Raik's back.

One group of men, and what looked to be two women – it was difficult to tell for sure – stood up and moved to a seat farther from Therin and Brok.

The stairs creaked as Lankor mounted them. Dust pushed from between the joints. Therin's tensely muscled body appeared to flow up the stairs at Lankor's heels.

Zimp thought that normally Raik would have floated up the stairs as well, his slight, wiry frame a mask of the warrior inside. But at this moment, he made small jumps up the stairs almost as though he were the small field mouse his beast image would expose. She had often noticed how beast and human became one, regardless of its present physical image. Raik's demeanor and movements exemplified her experience to its height.

She didn't like the smell of the room they were given, and

opened the thin door that led to the balcony. The short partition between each room's balcony space would be easy for a thief to crawl over. The flimsy door to the room had only one inside lock and could be broken down easily. No wonder the inn wasn't responsible for anything that might be stolen from the room. Luckily, Therin would be the perfect guard.

With everyone in the room, she saw that it would be a rough night. The balcony only had room for two. Whoever slept out there with Therin would have more space because of the animal's smaller body size, but they'd be subject to thievery. She turned around. "I'll take the floor in here."

Brok and Lankor said, "No," at the same time.

Zimp said, "You both need to be rested more than I do."

Lankor threw his pack down. "Not this time. I couldn't sleep in that short thing. I'll take the floor." He walked to the balcony. "In fact, if Therin will have me, there might be more room on the balcony for me."

"And I'm used to sleeping on the floor. It's good for my back," Brok said.

"Fine with me," Raik said.

Zimp shot Raik a sincere look to shut him up. She knew that Lankor missed the openness of The Lost and sensed that he had other reasons for wanting to sleep outside, personal reasons. To Raik she said, "You're off the hook, snake man."

Raik was insulted. "Don't ridicule me."

"These walls are thin, my good friends," Brok said. "I might be careful saying a lot of things."

"You're right." She reached for Raik's hand. "That was uncalled for."

Raik dropped his pack onto the other bed without acknowledging her gesture. "I'm not happy with this. I don't feel safe."

"Neither do I," Lankor said. "Something strange is definitely going on here. But at this point we don't have a choice; we have a mission."

Zimp unrolled her bedroll over the straw cot. "Can Therin be trusted while we get to know the stronghold better? I want to listen to the streets."

"You'll get nothing," Raik said.

"Then what do you suggest, we just sit in here stuffed together?"

Raik shook his head. "I suggest we rest for a few hours. Tonight's supper and a few hours of drink will bring about more talk than the vendors will offer during their greatest selling time. Unless you're bickering price, you'll get no attention. Tonight they'll be spending their take. A good day brings a good drunk for many of them. A good drunk brings a loose mouth. It can all be accomplished here, tonight." He bowed his head toward Zimp. "If you will."

"You lost your stutter," is all she said.

Raik turned away. "I know."

"We'll rest." She looked up at Lankor. "Can you get sleep with that sun out there?"

"Gladly," he said. He snapped his fingers to get Therin's attention, as though Brok's brother was a pet.

Brok let go of the leash and Therin lifted onto his toes and danced outside behind Lankor. On the balcony, he curled into a ball with his tail over his nose, looking comfortable in the afternoon sun.

In little time they were all settled and asleep, Zimp being the last to nod off. Each time she heard a voice, whether in the physical realm or the next realm, her eyes opened and she perked her ears. "Dangerous," she heard once. And another time, although the words were muffled, she thought she heard someone say something about gathering their things. Then she heard a loud voice in her ear that said, "Run." She popped up from the bed, disoriented and slow.

"What is it?" Brok said from the floor between her bed and Raik's.

"Nothing. One of those voices you hear just before you wake up."

Brok rolled to his side. "One of those voices you hear, you mean."

Zimp noticed the dim light around the balcony door. "How long have we slept?"

Brok got to his knees. "All right, all right. Sleep is over." He sat back on his haunches and shook his head.

Like a thylacine, Zimp thought. "The door," she said.

Brok reached out and shoved the door open a crack. The evening glow threw an orange light into the room. The sun, although it couldn't be seen, had not dropped below the horizon. Brok patted his stomach. "Dinner time," he said.

"Did you sleep well?" Zimp said.

"Very," Brok jumped to his feet and twisted his neck to loosen it. "Felt good." He shook Raik's bed until he noticed a stir. Then he shoved his bedroll to the side with his foot and opened the balcony door farther. "Hey, Lankor, dinner."

Zimp heard the big man get up.

"Ahh. The air is fresh out here. A comfortable sleep, a comfortable sleep," he said.

Therin whined for a moment at everyone's disruption.

"I'll bring some meat up for you later," Brok said.

Zimp heard Therin huff and imagined his head falling back onto his paws. She wondered what he was going through, the knowledge that he couldn't shift into human image, the confusion as to why, and perhaps the great sorrow knowing that he would never be in human image again. Therin never appeared to be angry about his predicament. Somehow he was able to take it in stride. Like an animal's sense that things just are as they are and no amount of thinking or analysis can change that. Yes, that was it. In beast image, even she had a strange sense that little could be affected. The weight of human image life fell away for a short time. Or loosened its grip.

"You're thinking again," Brok said. "Or hearing voices."

"Hearing voices? Are they loud?" Lankor poked his head around the door and squeezed through the opening.

"I was thinking just then. Earlier I heard voices. Not Zora. I don't know what I'm hearing."

"Oronice," Raik said. He had his eyes open wide as he lay on his side. "You knew she'd come to you."

Zimp shook her head. "I don't think so. Zora is my twin. I'm just hearing her through some kind of filter, a tunnel or cave. Something's muffling her sound."

"You don't want to face the truth," Raik said.

Zimp lunged toward him, stopped only by Brok's arm reaching out to take her shoulder.

"Think what you will. I'll think what I will," Raik said. "Are we heading downstairs? The place should be filling up. We need to get a corner table where we can hear clearly." Raik threw his blankets back. He stared at Zimp. "It might help if I were better prepared."

"We should kill you now so that you're not part of the problem," Zimp said. She shot her next look at Brok who she expected to say something about letting her personal feelings interfere with their mission, but he said nothing. Good.

"Not right now," Lankor said. "Let's go. Everybody ready?"

Brok sat on the floor to pull on his boots. Zimp and Raik followed suit from the edge of their beds.

Lankor held up the key and let them go ahead of him before locking the door. "Not that we need to worry," he said to no one in particular.

The place was half full with about forty people spread throughout the room. Raik scouted a corner table and the four of them sat together. Six to eight people could sit around one of the odd length tables. Lankor and Brok took the bench that allowed their backs to be against one wall. Raik sat at the head of the table against another wall. Zimp settled perpendicular to Raik, her back to the bar and other tables. Two other seats were available in the corner, one opposite Raik and one next to Zimp.

"What do we do now?" Lankor said.

Raik shook his head.

Lankor reached across Brok to point at Raik. "You might not last until she can kill you."

"I just love our friendly chatter," Brok said as a warning and a reminder.

Zimp couldn't see if there was any reaction from the people who were behind her at other tables, but she did agree with Brok. Things had escalated enough and she was part of the problem. Her nerves were rattled, her senses piqued.

Lankor pulled his arm back and a broad smiled crossed his face. "Just kiddn', my little friend."

A heavyset waitress with thick curled hair that hadn't been

washed in days approached the table. She wore a sack of a dress with a braided belt around her middle. "Yous eatin'?"

Lankor nodded.

"Five clips each," she said. "Seven if you washin' it down wit' ale."

The four of them pulled seven clips of gold from their pouches and pockets. Raik asked for water and dropped five clips into the woman's stained palm. Zimp wished she had requested water, but it was too late.

Once the woman walked away, Brok said, "I wonder what we're eating tonight."

"Meat and squash," Raik said. "Maybe bread with it."

Zimp looked at him.

"What? So I know what crops they were growing," Raik said.

"I've never eaten squash, or seen it. What's it like?" Lankor asked.

"Looks like a pile of dung, but tastes sweet," Brok told him with a smile. "Trust me. You won't like the looks of it, but you'll ask for a second helping."

Zimp hardly heard Brok's final words. They were already being drowned out by the sound of fluttering wings. She shook her head and placed her palms over her ears. "Well, well," she said so that she could listen to her own voice echo inside her skull. Perhaps that sound would be louder than the other. Perhaps that would bring her back to the table and the inn and the mission. She said it again, "Well, well."

Lankor reached across the table and squeezed her shoulder, bringing her back part of the way from the other realm. There was still an echo of fluttering in her head. She heard a familiar voice, then, but the fluttering was gone. "What?" she said.

A plate of food dropped in front of her.

Lankor jerked his arm away. "Eat," he said.

"All right," Zimp responded in a weak voice. Then she shook her head. "Maybe I'd better go upstairs."

"You need to eat," Lankor said.

Brok agreed, "Try."

Zimp let the sound of their voices retreat into the background as she began to shovel food into her mouth. In very little time, Lankor ordered another plate just as Brok had said he would. He emptied his ale mug as well and let it slam against the tabletop. Zimp sensed that the others were listening to the crowd, even though she could hear nothing behind her. She hardly heard her friends talking, getting only bits of a fake conversation. It all felt wrong and crazy to her at the moment. She lifted her mug and drank deeply from it. "Danger," she heard, but she'd heard that before, for days, and there had been no danger. She wanted to cry and felt an enormous rush of blood run through her body and into her face. Lankor's arm squeezed her shoulder again. "What's happening?" she said. The words came out of her mouth slowly. She could barely hear them now. "Listen," she said. "It *is* Oronice."

Lankor got up and came around the table. "Come with me," he said.

Zimp pulled away. "Did you hear me?"

"The ale has driven my sister a bit mad," he said.

Zimp noticed the quiet in the room and the eyes that were on her. A few castle guards got up from a table in one of the other corners.

Brok appeared magically at her other side. "We're leaving," he said more to Lankor than to Zimp. She was being pulled along between them.

The guards rushed around some tables, but Lankor, Zimp, and Brok passed through the front door well ahead of them.

"This way," Lankor led them down the street and up an alley.

Zimp ran with them, the physical motion bringing her back to the physical world. When she found her own feet again, the men let go of her arms. Twisting down another side street they stopped and waited.

The sound of men running got louder. When four of the guards turned the corner, their swords raised, they met with simultaneous blows from Lankor and Brok. Two of the guards were knocked to the ground. Zimp slipped her knife over the throat of a third. The fourth came down across Lankor's shoulder with the hilt of his sword. He was too close to do anything else, allowing Lankor to place his elbow into the man's ear with enough force to kill him. Brok grabbed the dropped sword of the man who attacked Lankor and dived in to kill the other two guards.

"We've got to get out of here." Zimp looked around. "Where's Raik?"

"The Gods have damned us," Brok said.

"No, I have," Zimp said.

"You never should have mentioned Oronice. I believe there were those in the room who know she's a doublesight. It is difficult to hide that fact." Brok took a breath. "I think you might want to let me lead the group. You are becoming unstable with all of your other-realm contact."

"I don't know," Zimp said. "Right now, we have to find Raik and stay out of the way. We may have to leave altogether. We may have lost our chance to learn anything."

Brok and Lankor looked at each other. "While you were blubbering, we were listening to conversations about what's going on here. But we have to hide for the night first. There has got to be a place we can stay."

"The stables," Lankor said.

"What about Therin?" Brok didn't wait for an answer. He slapped Lankor's shoulder. "I'm going back to get him. You two go to the stables and I'll meet you there soon."

"Raik?" Zimp said.

"He just became an enemy," Brok said.

36

"It's happening again," Zimp said.

Lankor grabbed her hand and felt the soft flesh of her palm against his rough skin. He hesitated a moment and looked into her eyes but they were already blank. He worried that, in her trance, she might be able to sense his feelings, the ones he fought to hide. But she didn't need to know how he felt about her. Not now. It would only complicate things.

He glanced up and down the alley and, convinced that no other guards were coming for them, pulled Zimp up the street, around a corner, and down another side alley in a loop that would deposit them at the rear of the stables.

She whispered words that made no sense, disconnected and jumbled. At one point she stopped Lankor and shook her head violently as though trying to dispel an insect from her ears. Despite her occasional confusion, Zimp appeared to be coherent much of the time, at least enough to run without his help. He held to her hand just in case she tried to veer off in another direction.

Lankor smelled the odor of hay and straw as they approached the stables. A horse nickered, and several others stirred inside their stalls. The two doublesight slipped through a crack in the rear door. Lankor sat Zimp on a stool and whispered for her to stay there until he checked the place out. She leaned against the wall and nodded.

He searched as quietly as he could around the stables. It appeared empty enough. He wished they had left Therin in the cage that stood on a wagon near one of the stalls. Then Brok would have had no reason to separate from them. He never should have allowed Brok to rush off as he did.

Lankor picked through the blacksmith's workspace. He found his staff and grabbed a poker sticking from a bucket near the anvil.

Saddlebags and packs hung on the stall doors. A horse inside one of the stalls came over and put his head over the door to sniff at Lankor's cheek. He patted its muzzle while pulling a strip of jerky from his saddlebag.

On his way back toward Zimp, he wondered why the smith would leave the stable so vulnerable. He ripped the jerky with his teeth. Coming around the corner of a stall, he saw Zimp sitting upright with her eyes wide and a look of surprise on her face. "It's just me," he said.

From either side of Zimp, guards stepped into the dim light. Each had a sword drawn, even though their numbers didn't warrant such readiness. One guard's dagger was held near Zimp's neck. Even a quick shift would leave her defenseless.

Lankor threw down the jerky and the poker he had grabbed for Zimp and hefted the staff into both hands. If he attempted a shift, he'd be killed instantly. The larger the beast the slower the shift, he thought, although he'd learned that wasn't true. He'd be slain before he could form the scales that could protect him. But, should he at least try to fight back with his human image? What of their mission? Someone had to make it back to The Few to report their meager findings.

"Hold there," he heard from behind. When he turned seven other guards advanced on him from the rear. Lankor took a few more steps toward Zimp and saw a young boy, obviously the stable boy, standing between two guards off to Zimp's left. The stable had been occupied when they arrived.

Zimp reached out for Lankor as he got closer, and he helped her to stand. One of the guards grabbed his staff. There were too many of them and Zimp would be too easy to harm had Lankor tried to fight back. He said a silent prayer that Brok had found

Therin and escaped.

Marched out of the stables and down the main street toward the castle, Lankor and Zimp were stared at. Vendors and their families, shop owners, other guards lined the road. "What's wrong here?" Zimp asked Lankor in an almost inaudible voice. "They are nearly silent. Like today," he said. A rumbling of voices and nothing more rose around them. The people whispered and pointed. They held their children close.

"They feel sorry for us. If they hated us they'd throw things, they'd yell insults." Zimp stumbled and one of the guards reached out to help her. She had a tear in her eye as she looked at Lankor again. "They are not afraid of us. They feel pity as though we have been cursed rather than blessed."

"Haven't we?" Lankor said. "In many ways we are the outcasts."

"Is that your deepest sense?"

He turned toward her. "It has been my life. Only now, when The Few need us, am I even allowed to travel outside The Lost. Even now, I am feared but useful against a greater fear, a dragon who kills, a dragon who is angry. A dragon, my dear crow-woman, who is not a dragon at all."

"What do you mean?"

"These people believe that the old doublesight that are coming alive are from Memory Tower. The burial grounds of the grotesque. The mass graves of gargoyles and demons that encircle the tower. The most feared doublesight, they believe, lives in the castle."

"They fear retribution if they torment us. It is hatred they feel. They are afraid to show it," Zimp said.

"Yes. If they show their true feelings, they might be the next to die. If there is any sadness in their eyes it is not directed toward us but toward themselves and their misfortunate lot to be here at all. But there is nothing they can do. This is their life, their livelihood," Lankor said as they approached the castle doors.

"What lives here?"

Lankor leaned close to Zimp. "A gryphon."

Zimp closed her eyes. Lankor felt pain enter his heart. She

didn't have to speak. He knew what she feared. It was the identical fear that Raik had, a fear that The Great Land had tricked them all, had turned back time. She feared that all the beasts of old were returning. The doublesight had not only been cursed once, but twice. She didn't need to say that the gryphon posed a threat to doublesight and humans alike. Fear fueled the fire of hatred, and hatred could be turned in any direction once it appeared in full strength.

At the castle, guards lined the halls. Lankor and Zimp were lead to a thin set of stairs that wound upward. One guard peeled off, drew his dagger, and held onto Zimp's arm as she mounted the first stone step. Her shoulders drooped and her head hung down.

Lankor sensed a similar invisible weight. The guard behind him had his sword unsheathed and at the ready. The only chance they had would be if they were left alone. That wasn't likely to happen. And even a dragon of his size couldn't pound his way through the stone walls around him.

At the top of the stairs, Zimp's guard dragged her through a hallway. She stumbled and shook her head. "No," she said.

Lankor noticed that the doors were wooden. He heard scuffling sounds behind some of them. The guard next to him said, "She's crazy like them all."

Another guard warned that guard to stand down. "Or you'll be gone by morning," he said.

Lankor's guard shivered and moaned. "Horrible creatures," he muttered.

The friend shook his head in concern.

Two doors opened ahead of them into a central chamber. At the far end of the room sat two throne-like chairs decorated in bright colors and swirling designs. A cushion of red cloth garnished each, and on the cushions sat two men, obviously father and son, their resemblances many.

As the guards with Zimp and Lankor flanked the doublesight, Lankor whispered, "Who are they?"

Zimp glanced at him, a blank look in her eyes. She didn't even hear his words.

The guards stopped about twenty feet from the thrones. One

must have been King Belford, the older of the two. He looked worn. Tired. Depleted of strength. His clothes hung loosely on his body from weight loss. Bags drooped under eyes surrounded by wrinkles. The other, the son, sat strong and healthy next to the father. Lankor didn't need to guess who had control over the castle, or who had their subjects fearful and wary.

The young man on the left sat forward in his chair. "Doublesight," he said in disgust. He held his position there, leaning toward his captors. "Your grotesque appetites and needs will no longer be tolerated in The Great Land."

"We are harmless and peaceful," Lankor said.

The guard poked his sword into Lankor's side until it hurt. "Silence."

The young man laughed and sat back in his throne. He brought one hand to his chin, and placed a single finger across his lips. "What nasty beast are you?"

Lankor remained silent.

"And your crow-friend," he said.

Lankor pulled away from the sword but another guard placed a sword near his neck.

"Oh, did I guess correctly?" The younger man stood. A long red cape fell around him. "She does have good taste for color," he said referencing Zimp's red cloak. "But it is rather torn and dirty. What was I to expect?"

He stepped down to floor level, about ten feet in front of Lankor. "And you? Are you the thylacine or the dragon?" He paced back and forth in front of Lankor and Zimp.

She lifted her head and Lankor knew what she was doing. It didn't take long either. Her connection to the other realm had been strong since before they arrived. "The gryphon," she said, confirming what Lankor had guessed, but also feared. The king's son was the threat. But why? As the King's son, he already had anything he wanted. And as a doublesight, why would he wish to wipe them out?

"It was only a matter of how long it would take for you to notice my etheric body, my friend, Zimp."

"Raik," Lankor said.

"How perceptive." The man snapped his fingers and three

guards brought Raik from a side door. His hands were tied behind him.

Raik flowed across the floor next to the guards. His head cocked to one side and his narrowed eyes warned of contempt. Lankor knew Raik's next image was that of the copperhead. "He brought us to you," Lankor said. "You repay him like this?"

"If he betrayed you, he'd betray me. You see, there are some doublesight that have hungers you can't imagine. Needs you would never understand." The man gritted his teeth and leaned with narrowed eyes at Lankor. Enunciating each word, the man said, "He. Can't. Help. Himself." He swung his arm toward Raik, pointing at him. "He's a demon, a gargoyle. I don't care what you *think* he is. He should not be alive. Pure doublesight do not have two images. Even he knows that. Ask him."

Raik took a step forward and said, "It's over." He began his shift. His head and body began to shrink. His ropes slipped from his wrists and he fell to his knees.

The king's son made a quick slice across the air and one of Raik's guards leaned back, slid a sword from its sheath, and sliced the sword easily through Raik's shifting neck. As his head and body fell forward they returned to their human image.

"His children," Zimp said in a semiconscious state.

"Stupid man." The son turned back to Lankor and Zimp. "His children are cursed too. You all are. Especially you," he pointed at Lankor.

"And you?" Lankor said.

"I will be the last. When I die, The Great Land will finally be rid of us all. No one will need to suffer any longer."

"In peace we do not suffer," Zimp said.

"Enough, Draklan," said King Belford. "Put them into the dungeon. Kill them. But stop this." He stood to go.

Draklan snapped his fingers again and several men dressed in robes came from behind the thrones to help the king depart.

"I believe his disgust of us came early today," Draklan said. He turned back to Zimp. "My dear beauty, you are the last of the peaceful, as you say, doublesight. You might recall that the doublesight have fought in wars before. They have killed before. You have killed as well."

"In self-defense," she said.

He hesitated as though he were going to stop talking. "Killing is killing. In self-defense. In hatred. In fear." His body lifted to full height and his shoulders tensed under some invisible strain. "In hunger for flesh? You have no idea what is being born, or what has been born to this land." He turned and his cape floated behind him as he walked away. "You might think I'm a horrible sight, but you haven't seen the truth of what the doublesight has brought upon us." He walked through a back door out of the chamber. Just before the door closed, he yelled out, "Show them!"

"To the holiness of the Gods," Zimp said. "Oronice has died."

Lankor noticed that her eyes were clear and her stance strong and upright. What had happened? And what did her words indicate? Before he could consider what she had said, three young women entered the room and stood before them. The three were dressed alike in thin robes of gray cloth. They appeared to be freshly bathed, their blonde hair light and soft. They were in their bare feet. One was noticeably pregnant. Possibly a second was also pregnant by a few months.

"He's good-looking," one of them said about Lankor. Her eyes were a stark and penetrating hazel color.

"Even the guards," another said.

The guard who stood nearest Lankor turned his head when she looked at him.

"But that's not why we are here," the first one said. "Draklan would like a small show before we eat."

With those words, the three sisters opened their robes slowly. Their naked bodies were smooth and white, their breasts round and firm. The only hair on their bodies was under their arms and between their legs where a puff of flesh and light colored fur stood out. Even as Lankor stared, he sensed they were about to shift.

37

Brok kept moving along the streets and alleys as though nothing was wrong, a vendor out for a stroll. He slunk through the streets in a great loop around the inn. Few others walked that evening, an occasional couple hurrying home as though the darkness would harm them, yet a small crowd had grown on the main street.

Hiding in a door well, Brok watched as Zimp and Lankor were escorted towards the castle. Thank the Gods Therin had not been left at the stables, or he may have been killed.

A light glow lay over the ridge of the mountain range to the west, the trees black against the evening sky. Brok imagined the sun, still visible in Brendern Forest, casting a sidelong glow through the underbrush. Breel came to mind and he prayed that she was well, that there were no more attacks on the council.

Shadows darkened the doorways and corners of the alleys as he glided over the dirt roadway. He heard voices from time to time, a couple speaking in low tones as though hiding their conversation. The king's son is what they discussed. What little conversation he heard from the people at the inn was enough for him to realize that one of them had to get back to the council and The Few with word of the gryphon. The Few would know that something terrible had gone wrong in The Great Land. They would know what to do.

He placed his back against an outside wall and leaned for

a moment as a man rushed by. Brok acted as though he were waiting for someone. While there he recalled the last weeks. His family had been slaughtered by angry and fearful humans. His brother had remained in his beast image because of the horror of attack. Brok gritted his teeth. He thought of Therin before the shock forced him into permanent beast image. Therin had always been the baby of the family, frightened of being in the forest alone, crying whenever something didn't go his way. Was it Brok's duty to go back to get Therin or to warn The Few? He had been sworn to the council. But it wasn't him they wanted, it was Fremlin, his father. Brok was only a substitute for a real hero, subjugated to the position of follower under a woman's command.

Brok closed his eyes and took a deep breath, letting it escape through pursed lips. He felt alone and scared. He leaned over and glanced down the alley in both directions. His mind recalled the beams holding up the balcony at the inn. Less than an hour and darkness would be secured. He could climb to the balcony and rescue Therin, but was there time for that? Would the innkeeper have already rushed upstairs to kill him while he slept, knowing that Therin traveled with doublesight? He needed a clear head to make the right decision.

Brok tapped his forehead and rubbed his hands along his sides. He thought of his father. Fremlin would find a way to do both, to save Therin and warn the council. Therin was his brother. He had to return, and there was no time to waste.

Brok jogged on his toes and could feel the thylacine waiting to escape the human image. Prancing down the street like an animal searching for a way out of a maze, Brok made calculated turn after calculated turn until he saw the inn. He stopped and began to walk slowly. No one stood outside or in the alley so he hurried to the beam that angled upward, and wrapped his arms easily around it. In very little time, he placed a hand over the top of the balcony wall and heard Therin growl. He must have been sleeping. Brok whispered, "It's me," and felt a wetness touch his fingers as Therin's tongue licked them. Just as Brok swung up, Therin jumped and placed his front paws onto the banister.

"I'll carry you down," Brok said.

Therin jumped back to the floor and turned to go out the door.

"You can't. They'll attack you down there."

Therin's head cocked.

Brok heard someone outside the door. When it opened, Therin yipped and growled and the innkeeper fell backwards trying to get out of the thylacine's way.

Therin dashed for the stairs and Brok heard all sorts of noise as people screamed and avoided the wild beast that was his brother.

The innkeeper sat on the floor and looked directly at Brok. "He's on the balcony," he said to someone behind him.

Brok had never swung his leg over, so he just lowered himself back to the beam and slid toward ground. Just as he hit dirt, Therin burst out the front of the inn. Brok snapped his fingers to get his brother's attention, and they both ran down the alley and turned toward the stables. He hoped it would be safe to go there now. He needed a horse. The yelling rose in volume as people from the inn ran into the alleyway. Therin's ears perked up at the sound. They were already around the corner with Therin in the lead.

Brok followed him around a second turn, then straight toward the stables. His brother stopped short of the door and sniffed. Brok sniffed the air as well, but could only smell the horses and the hay.

The hair along Therin's back stood straight up. He leaped into the doorway and landed with his legs spread and crouched in a ready position for attack.

A squeal rang out and a stable boy swung a poker toward Therin's head, catching him in the ear and knocking him to the side. The boy lifted the poker again. Before he could swing it, Therin leaped for his throat and tore it out. The boy fell backward. Therin stood on his body. A gurgling came from the boy as his body jerked and blood spit out of the opening in his neck. Blood fell from Therin's ear. He shook his head.

"You all right?" Brok said to his brother.

Therin lowered his head and ran over to nuzzle Brok's leg.

Brok dashed to one of the stalls and opened the door. He threw a bridle over the horse's head, looked at the saddle lying across a log at the other end of the barn, and decided against it. Back to Therin, he asked, "Can you run?"

Therin ran, but slowly, toward the front of the stable. Brok gripped the hair at the horse's withers and swung his leg over its back. "You'll have to try. We have to warn The Few." Brok rode the horse to the front of the stable beside Therin. The sun's glow had dimmed to an ember. A few minutes more and darkness would help hide them as they left the castle grounds. He had no idea how he'd make it through the gate he'd chosen to exit.

Therin sniffed at the air and his ears twisted to listen for voices. He must have heard something by the alarmed look on his face and his sudden dash for the street.

Brok followed even though he would have rather waited the extra minutes he thought would be helpful.

Therin jogged in small bouncy steps toward the front gate. Several guards noticed them coming and began to yell. Therin didn't stop.

Brok saw the men pull their swords, but Therin slipped under a cart that had been closed up for the evening.

"Where'd he go?" One guard ran behind the row of carts that stood near the gate.

Two other guards stepped forward to stop Brok. He rode up slowly.

"Halt there. No one leaves the castle grounds after dark unless they have…" The man turned his head when he heard the other guard yell out that it wasn't a dog but a thylacine. Surprise and understanding gripped the guard's face as he began to reach for his sword.

Brok slid his weapon from its sheath and came down on the man's head before the guard could lift his sword into the air. The other guard's sword had been drawn as well, so Brok slid off the opposite side of the horse.

Therin growled and Brok heard him attack. Something in the growl worried Brok though. Therin wasn't well.

From behind him, his attacker swung his sword at Brok's

neck, yelling, "Doublesight!" as he did so.

Brok blocked the attack and kicked at the guard's chest. The man fell backwards a few steps, long enough for Brok to crouch down and bring his sword up under the man's arm, nearly slicing it off. The man screamed in agony. Five more men ran from a nearby guard shack. They had not been ready for trouble and three were not fully dressed. But all five carried swords. Brok lifted the bolt from the gate and shoved, leading the horse through by its bridle.

Therin appeared beside him almost miraculously.

"Go," Brok commanded as he swing mounted onto the horse and rode off.

The guards crashed the gate open more fully and ran into the road screaming, their swords raised into the air.

It was too late. Brok rode away at a dead run. Therin kept up along side of him.

As it was late spring, the fields were not as high as they might have been. Brok rode through thick but short grain stalks. He planned to avoid Torturous Road and take his chances with the farmers and their families as he advanced toward Weilk Post Stronghold. The castle guards would not expect him to ride due south in the open rather than in the forest where he could hide more easily. His fear was for Therin and his horse. How long could either last?

A sense of duty filled him. The entire doublesight race could be in danger if gryphons and dragons were again populating The Great Land. He had to get back and tell The Few. He had to warn the doublesight.

Only stars lighted his way. The night sky, a beautiful canvas of constellations, opened to the great Weilk plains. Evening breezes bent the growth to the east, leaning and then straightening. He left a field of grain and dashed through a field planted with vines. Perhaps squash or melon grew there. The sound of his horse's hooves changed from the swishing of thin grass blades to that of the loose dirt mounded around the vines. The steady clomping beat matched the horse's neck and head as it rocked in slow motion.

Brok matched the rhythm of the earth, matched the heartbeat

of the land itself. To his left, Therin ran at full stride, but was falling back. Brok reined in a little to stay with his brother, who strode up one of the rows.

Brok smiled at his brother, and at that moment Therin fell and tumbled across several rows of the vines. Brok sat into the sway of the horse's back and jerked the reins. The horse stopped in three hops. Brok leaped to the ground. Foam fell from the horse's mouth. Its nostrils sucked in great chambers of air. Its head rose, and its feet continued to move as though ready to continue once Brok returned to its back.

Therin let out a quiet squeak and shook his head. He rolled to his stomach and tried to lift to his feet but fell over as though his balance was lost.

Brok rubbed the top of his head and along both sides of his jaw. Blood had caked at Therin's ear. Brok picked it off and said, "It's all right. We'll rest here for a while." He looked around and could barely see the silhouette of the castle in the distance. A farmer's shack stood at the southeastern corner of the field they were in, but nothing stirred inside. Brok bent to kiss his brother's head and Therin nipped at Brok's chin. "I can't leave you."

Therin panted and lay still over Brok's lap. It appeared as though the ear had stopped bleeding.

Brok continued to stroke Therin's side in a smooth, relaxed manner. Luckily, the horse ground-tied. After a short while it stopped shifting around the reins and stood quietly, turned toward Brok, waiting to be rescued. But Brok didn't move.

His heart ached with the memories of death, the fear of failure that crept upon him the longer he sat with his brother.

It was several hours before Therin awoke and tried to move.

Brok feared the worst for Therin and feared the worst for himself. Who might warn The Few if he were to die?

Therin got to his feet, but something was wrong. His movements were awkward, his balance off. He fell over after a few steps.

Brok noticed fresh blood on his leg. The ear had been seeping. He crawled to Therin's side. "Easy. We don't need to go anywhere." He lifted his brother's head and saw Therin's eyes roll back slowly. Brok shook him, but his eyes remained white.

"No, not you, not now." Brok slid under Therin's head and petted the sweaty fur along his side.

Therin coughed and his head relaxed completely. Brok watched as the thylacine lengthened and the head bore curly hair, matching Brok's. Hands and arms, feet and legs appeared as Therin's body shifted into its original human image. The beast image, no matter how permanent it appeared to be, could not maintain visibility in death.

Brok cried. Perhaps Raik had been correct. Being born a doublesight was a curse. Brok looked to the sky. Hours had passed. His ceremonial staff had been left behind. Only a parent can eat the heart of a child after death. There was little for him to do. He set Therin's head onto the ground, and began to dig a shallow grave under the stars.

More time passed, another hour. The dirt mounds were loose and easy to dig through. Brok rolled Therin's body into the grave and covered it over.

Standing next to his brother, Brok lifted his arms into the air toward the open sky. "I give my brother to The Great Land. May his arms and legs become the arms and legs of trees, may his feet and hands become the bushes, and may his mind join with the forest and live there forever." It was the only thing he could think to say. Brok fell to his knees. Remembering what crows believed, he said, "And if Therin now resides in the next realm, may he have peace there." He wanted to shift and smell his brother's scent for the last time, but the horse would run off in fear. So he let his beast image swell to a place where it was almost too late to stop a shift, then backed it off. He turned and the horse's eyes glared at him, wide and frightened. It must have sensed his near shift. As he walked toward the animal, it stepped sideways. Brok forced soothing tones and calm words, even though he wished to hurry. Taking one slow step at a time, he reached for the reins. As he closed in on them, he reached out and pulled the wary beast closer, then gripped a fist of mane and swung onto its back. No sooner was he on than the horse kicked the dirt behind him and raced onward.

Tears streamed down his cheeks. He wished Breel could have seen Therin one last time. She would have known what to say. Brok thought that he might have invoked the Shapeless Gods, but rejected the thought. Where were they? Had The Great Land fallen under natural rule? Were boundaries breaking down? Would the whole land revert back to the horrors of the past? Brok had never been to Memory Tower, but had heard that sickening beasts had lived there at one time. They created statues for themselves and their brothers until they died out and no other gargoyles were to be born again. That was supposed to include dragons and gryphons. What other horrible doublesights had been born? Was Memory Tower a breeding ground for monsters?

Brok tensed as he noticed that his mount slowed. He glanced behind him. The council had to be warned immediately. He rode off, and time collapsed within the rocking of the powerful beast he rode. The horse had only stumbled once and that was about an hour ago. Brok sensed the horse's fatigue as he pulled the reins and forced it to run toward the forest. His mount might have been less likely to run full-out through the woods, but Brok would feel more comfortable.

As expected, his horse slowed considerably as it approached the edge of the woods. It jumped a log and stumbled, catching itself to keep from toppling forward over Brok. The motion awakened Brok's mind. He couldn't be caught unaware again. He pulled up on the reins and lifted up so that he could see ahead. The woods were dark and his horse exhausted. He pushed on mercilessly, kicking the horse's sides. The hope was that the horse could see better than he could.

The grade ascended and the horse pushed with its hindquarters, letting out deep groans as it did so. Its neck was sopping, and foam dropped from its lips. Brok recognized the sound of its fatigue and pulled it around to tackle the mountain at a lesser grade. In an hour, the horse stumbled forward. This time Brok didn't try to keep it upright. He let it crumble to the ground.

Pushing off from its back, Brok induced a quick shift. His body pulled into itself, his snout grew long and, before he hit the ground, he met the surface with four paws. He continued to run up the mountain at the slight grade, but soon turned to take it straight on. Behind him, the horse lay still. He had no time to check on its safety, but he hoped that it would live.

38

The sword that was poised near Lankor's neck dropped to rest on his shoulder, and through the flat blade he could feel the shaking hand at the other end. It took his mind off the beauty before him, but only for a moment. The piercing hazel eyes of the three held his attention. The naked bodies enticed his interest, even the two who were pregnant. Then the sword that once pushed into his side dropped, clanging against the stone floor. The guard stepped backward. The other guards made no sound; if anything, they stood more transfixed and motionless.

One of the sisters stepped forward and pointed at Lankor's guard. "Later for you," she said and the man ran off, only to be stopped near the door.

Zimp turned her head away and bent to one knee. Her guard let go of her as she lowered and puked onto the stone, the horrible wretching sound filling the cavernous throne room. Zimp spit and cried openly. "Help me, Oronice," she begged, but from Lankor's view, she appeared to receive no answer.

The sisters all laughed at the same time. They let their robes drop and rounded their backs.

"Wings," Lankor whispered. If Raik's beheading hadn't caused Zimp to vomit, then what had she seen of these women's beast images that caused such an evacuation? The guard closest to Lankor shuddered as the sisters allowed a slow shift to begin.

First, their hair became grey and their faces pale, but no

beast was yet visible. Lankor waited almost out of curiosity for something to happen. Then, their feet narrowed and lengthened. Three claws protruded from the front, one out the back. Birds. But a large one, because their bodies had not shriveled like Zimp's had done. No, not birds. Lankor then caught the stench of their change, a body odor that reeked of human feces and urine. The sisters' breasts sagged under their own weight, and flattened. Their thighs became extremely hairy, as did their arms. Bent into a crouching position, scraggly wings, chipped and dirty with gaps of missing feathers, almost popped out of their backs. The once beautiful women shifted into hags. Horrible, stench-ridden hags with claws and wings.

Harpies, Lankor realized when his mind finally put it all together. He held back his own instinct to puke. He swallowed and stared. He placed a hand over his mouth and nose to ward off some of the odor. What he saw before him, what he stared at and could hardly believe left too many possibilities opened. Had Raik and Draklan been correct? Lankor lowered his head and peered at his own body. Was he an awful mutation returning to The Great Land?

"You, my lovely man," one of the hags said in a graveled voice, "are to be mine before long."

"No, he's mine," another of the sisters said while reaching out with her gnarled fingers and long dirty nails to scratch at her sister.

"Mine," the first one said stretching an equally nasty arm toward the other.

"Stop."

Lankor had not seen the man dressed in a general's garb enter the room. The man stood far to the side, his face worn as King Belford's had been. His stance, though, was stronger and more assured.

"Daddy," the sisters stopped fighting and almost fell into tears. One said, "We're horrible girls." The screech in her voice pained Lankor's ears. "Monsters," wept another.

The general was also in tears. "Enough," he said shaking his head. "My girls. My sweet girls. We will care for you later." He turned to go and drifted into a dark corner of the room.

The harpies huddled together. One spoke. "But I'm hungry," she said, and as though they had forgotten their father's presence, their tears stopped and their faces turned eagerly toward the captors and guards once again.

"Enough," the father said from the dark, not gone after all, but watching.

The three lowered their heads and began to shift. Their voices squealed and sang out in great pain. Their wings retracted with severity, cutting their way back into the harpies' backs. Blood dripped down one of the girl's sides. Each face clenched in its own torturous agony, eyes closed. Gravely voices became those of young women strapped and prodded by strange and invisible instruments. Tears flowed and more blood appeared at their feet as the claws turned in on themselves. One of the girls began to shake her head and scream, "No, let me die. Let me die."

The strangeness and pain evident in the room frightened Lankor. He didn't know how he might help. He looked to Zimp for answers, but again she was gone into another realm, her eyes shoved closed in either fear or in search of Oronice. Her head shook back and forth slowly to the rhythm of the harpies' cries.

The sisters huddled together on the ground, naked once again. The smoothness of their skin had been punctured. Blood seeped out and down their bodies. Their faces held to the pain, pulled back, eyes tight and teeth showing. They were not so beautiful now. They were frightening to Lankor, in a sad and pitiful way.

"Remove them," one of the sisters said in a weakened voice.

The guards who had remained with their captors reached out to Lankor and Zimp and pulled them away.

Zimp rose to her feet and followed in a slow stupor.

Fatigue had taken over Lankor's body and soul. His thoughts wandered. His muscles had drained of their strength in the presence of such beasts.

The guard shoved Zimp ahead and out of the room. The sisters cried openly, their voices echoing into the hallway.

Another turn and the guard forced Zimp down a set of stairs

that ran along the rear of the castle. She tripped and fell down a few steps. Lankor tried to rush to her, but the flat of a sword to the side of his face knocked him into the wall.

Blood appeared on Zimp's lip. Her guard stepped in front of her, swearing to himself. He drew her arm around his neck and continued on. Several flights more and they came to an opening. A heavy wooden door stood before them, flanked by benches. Four enormous men with broadswords looked up. Two guarded the door while the other two rested on the benches. The door was opened and the guards and doublesight entered the dungeon where low ceilings, dirt floors, and bone-chilling dank air welcomed them.

Lankor ducked his head. Although his human height didn't warrant it, his dragon image extended well beyond his human image. Regardless what Draklan had said, questioning Lankor's beast image, he must have known the truth. It would be impossible for Lankor to shift in here. He would be trapped at best, crushed at worst.

The guards continued deeper below the castle and the ceiling dipped even more.

Lankor's breathing became pained. He heard a cell door open and was thankful they weren't forced any deeper. Zimp was shoved into the cell first, and Lankor shoved after her. One guard bolted the door while the other looked on.

The guard who bolted the door said, "We didn't always feel this way about the doublesight. King Belford had taken one for a wife, you know. We had a greater trade from all kind over The Great Land. Times were good. Draklan turned one day and killed 'is own mother. Struck 'er, then ate her, is what I heard."

Lankor listened without a sound.

"Leave 'em, my friend," the other guard said. "Only the Gods know what this is about, and they ain't been here to stop it yet."

The guard addressing Lankor turned to go and Lankor cried out, "Wait. What about the sisters?"

"He don't need to know," the second guard said.

"Don't matter." The man turned back. "General Lansion is King Belford's brother. He was a great man and a great warrior and peacemaker." The man waved his hand in front of his face. "Don't care what you say; he was both. He and the king had been through many battles together. They both took doublesight wives. That was when the doublesight were revered. We had our own doublesight sages, doublesight families lived inside the castle walls. After the general's wife died, the doublesight saw what might happen and ran. It's said that they were throwin' monsters, too, and didn't want no one to find out."

"And Lansion's wife?" Lankor said in a tone that belied his curiosity.

"Come on. He don't need…"

"Mad. She went completely mad and leaped from the top of the castle. That's when it all began to get worse." The man placed a hand over one of the bars. "Tell you the truth, I think the sisters have tranced the general. Done somethin' with his mind. He ain't the same as he was. He feeds them human stock. He cares for them like they ain't the monsters they are." He turned once again. "That's why I won't look at 'em. Don't want to be called into them arms of death."

"Are you done? 'Cause I don't want to get caught with you talkin' like this."

"I'm comin'."

"Why?" Lankor said.

"The sages all believe it's coming from Memory Tower. Some evil is spreading from the graveyard up there, from all them statues of horrible beasts. It was once thought that a doublesight could only shift if the animal were alive. The images at Memory Tower is so strong, what if all you need is an image that *looks* alive?" The man looked Lankor square in the face. "The gargoyles is comin' to take over The Great Land."

Lankor watched them both leave. Were they that confident that there was no escape for him and Zimp? When he swung around and saw Zimp huddled in the corner, he wondered what good she would be. Perhaps they knew as well. He grabbed her shoulders and shook her. "Zimp, come out of it. You've got to come back."

To his surprise, Zimp's eyes lifted slowly and met his. He witnessed them as they cleared and became conscious of the physical world.

"Are we safe?" Zimp asked.

"I wouldn't say that," Lankor said. He slipped his thumb over the blood from her lip, scraping it off.

She reached up and touched the place he cleaned. "I hardly felt it."

"Lucky you. It looked as though it hurt pretty badly."

"And now?" She cocked her head.

"It's pretty dark to tell for sure, but it doesn't look so bad in this light."

"Light?" she said.

Lankor nodded, "Several lanterns where the guards stay at the other end of the hall.

"They left us alone. That means they believe we're trapped here."

"Yes, and I can see why," Lankor said.

"I couldn't break through, but you could if only…"

Lankor glanced around the room in dismay. "I couldn't shift in here. I can hardly stand being here in my human image."

"It is rather tight." Zimp stood and paced the room off. "How tall is your dragon image?" Then before he could answer, she said, "I know…lie down."

"What?"

"Lie down. Put your feet against the door."

"By the Six Shapeless Gods woman, you'll have me crushed to death," he said.

"Just try it."

Lankor lay on his back with his feet against the door. His head almost touched the other side of the cell, and the width was much less. He began to rise.

"Stay there," Zimp said. "Let me see." She walked along his body.

Lankor moved to his right to allow her enough light from the hallway for her to examine the situation. Now he understood what she asked of him. He held still and pushed his dragon image as close to shifting as he felt comfortable doing. He had to avoid initiating a shift.

Zimp stepped backwards until she touched the side wall.

"This will be close."

"Will be? I'm not in favor of it."

"We've got to try," she said. "That's the only choice we have."

"Brok will come for us," Lankor said without conviction.

"We can't even assume he's alive."

"We must," Lankor said.

"You'll either overpower that door, or we'll both be crushed," she said.

"Even if I do shove through that door, the hallway is narrower. What about the next door?" He sat upright and crossed his legs. "You may be crushed anyway."

She reached and touched the ceiling. "It's close," she said, "but I'll shift and stand between your wings. I'll have plenty of room if you don't flatten them out."

Lankor laughed. "You will, indeed." He shook his head and stood.

Zimp reached out and rubbed the back of his arm. "You can do this, big boy."

The sound of her confidence boosted his spirits. He went over to the door and shook it. The top hinge appeared to be the looser of the two. Shaking his head as he moved, Lankor lay back down, placed his feet high onto the door and stretched his arms over his head and flat against the opposing wall. "Climb aboard," he said.

39

Storret held his breath as long as Oronice held to her last breath. His eyes remained closed. When she let go of her physical body and entered the other realm completely, her throat rattled and her chest caved into itself.

Rend said, "She's gone," talking more to Mianna and Noot than to Storret, who began to let air escape through an open mouth. "Aaaahhhhh..." He held his tone until his lungs began to burn. When he stopped, he held his breath again for a short while then began to inhale. His mind let loose of the physical world enough to allow a moment of pure and complete silence to take over. He tried not to listen, but to hear.

Oronice's hand moved to Storret's knee.

He heard several of the others jump at the sight of Oro's dead hand moving so deliberately. He quickly shoved their surprise and fear from his mind and returned to the silence. The physical contact created a shamanic bond between the two where they could occupy the other realm together, the next realm at least.

Oro's voice came to him as a whisper, the sound of wind through trees or the passage of air over wings. "A great change has come. A great change. I see that death in the physical world strengthens the second realm."

Storret held to the sound of her voice.

"Death of the doublesight in physical reality will increase

the sensitivity and strength of the doublesight in the second realm. Death in the second realm strengthens the third. And so it is. And so it is. The other realms will always lead us to war."

Storret lowered his head, not wishing to acknowledge or to consider what she said, but only to listen and to record it later.

"Come," Oro said, and in Storret's mind's eye she appeared to him in crow form. "Crow image is strong now," he heard her say. She shifted to human image. "This is more difficult, but I will get better. In the next realm I will be human first again."

She reached for him and Storret allowed what he felt was his auric body to take her hand.

She smiled at him and then turned and they flew off together into a darkness beyond any he had seen.

He held fast, for he feared that, if he should let go, he would be lost in the second realm and could not find his way back. The journey had begun and Storret fought for his mind to stay silent, and equally, he fought for his mind to stay human. In the second realm, his crow image became strong just as Oronice's had.

The two of them floated through the dark space. Storret heard raccoons chatter and geese honk. He recognized other sounds as well: hawks, wolves, thylacines.

Light entered almost as though daybreak had occurred. The animals he had heard were nowhere around but he could feel the presence of their souls. Oronice waved as though she understood his thought and was expelling it.

Oronice pulled him close. They hovered over a great, tall tower surrounded by what appeared to be gravestones. A light snow had fallen and the tower appeared to be serene in the stillness, but something harrowing caused Storret to want to hold back and go no farther.

Oronice took his shoulder in her hand. She held him so that he could concentrate on the images below.

The headstones were not what he originally thought. Each wore a hat of snow that distorted their appearance from where he hovered above them. Slowly, the stones began to turn and look upward as though they knew that he and Oronice watched. Snow fell from their tops and Storret saw the gargoyle faces, each in its own unique sorrow or pain, each begging with its eyes to die. Somehow he knew that was what they begged.

"The Six Shapeless Gods turned these poor children into statues to remind us of our ill deeds. They were to look over The Great Land for eternity. But, the Gods become sloppy and detached from their powers. These stones held to the souls of the children they once were. Those children did not ask to leave and so did not leave completely. These souls are affecting the table of creation once again. They have forced their images into The Great Land once again. Soon, all manner of beast will come into being." Oronice turned and led Storret back through the darkness of the shamanic journey, and placed him back in the wagon beside her deceased physical body. "You have a question?"

"How do we stop this? How do we help them?"

"This battle against the humans is to save the doublesight clan, but you must also destroy the gargoyle statues and those gargoyles already set free by the pain of these poor children."

"The doublesight won't fight against themselves. We have been taught…" He recognized there was no need to finish his statement. She had shown him the truth. The difficulty was not to fight the human image only who attacked to kill, but to destroy the doublesight now being born out of the pain of those statues at Memory Tower. He must destroy the sacred Tower. Neither doublesight nor human would want that.

Oronice nodded. She shifted into a crow and said, "Go."

Storret fell over, exhausted.

Rend climbed into the wagon and lifted Storret's head. "Are you all right? You have been still for several hours."

Storret opened his eyes and saw that night had fallen around them. "Hours?" he said.

Rend nodded. "First you, and then Noot. He's been that way for a while now."

Storret could see Noot sitting on the ground outside the wagon. His legs were crossed and his hands placed on his thighs with the palms turned up.

Storret shook his head. "I need to get back to the troops. Let me know when Noot returns. We need to talk."

"Returns?" Rend said. "Where is he?"

Storret stared at the High Sage. "I don't know where she's taken him," he said.

Rend helped Storret down from the wagon. His face couldn't hide his confusion, but he didn't ask any more questions. "We'll bury the body," he said.

"No," Storret said. "We'll burn the body at sunrise. Leave her there and find Arren."

"Arren? I didn't think she trusted him."

"He will be honored to perform such services. It will show that we are on the same side," Storret said.

Mianna reached out and hugged Storret. She was his same height. "You were born to lead," she said. "I'm afraid what you may have been told, though."

"I am afraid as well," he said. He kissed her cheek and turned to go. He saw that Breel sat against a tree a short distance away. Her head hung to the side and her eyes were closed. Someone had placed a blanket over her.

Rend reached out to touch Storret's forearm. "She waited there for you."

Storret walked over to her and kneeled. He slid his hand along her arm and stopped where her hand rested against her thigh. He squeezed her hand through the blanket. With his other hand, he touched her leg, leaned slightly, and sat so that he could peer into her eyes.

Breel sucked breath into her lungs and awakened. She straightened her head and rubbed the back of her neck. "Not a good position to sleep," she said.

"You didn't need to wait," Storret said.

"I did too." She placed a hand on his cheek. "Are you all right?"

He shook his head. "Yes and no. I don't know what to do with the experience. I believe a part of me questions whether it really happened." He pointed toward the wagon. "I'm afraid of the implications."

"You will know what to do. Oronice does not make mistakes."

"I'm not worried about her making a mistake. I'm worried

about me," he said.

"You will not make a mistake." As she spoke her eyes searched his face as though she were trying to memorize it. "I have decided," she said, "to fight at your side."

"You can't do that."

"You'll find that I can be more cunning and ferocious than most of the men." She stopped. "I have no family now except you. How could you leave me behind?"

"I'm not sure..."

She placed a finger over his lips and he stopped.

Although his heart raced with the thought of his being her family, the situation could only complicate his position. Yet he knew that she was not mistaken in her self-confidence. And she would be the one person he could confide in completely.

She leaned into him and shook the blanket from her shoulder so that she could reach out with both arms to hold him.

Her hair smelled of dried pine needles and wind. Her strong arms reminded him of her strength. And his heart felt as though they were already connected with a thin cord that could never be broken. "You make my body sing," he said.

"I will never leave your side." She lifted to her feet, using his shoulder to pull herself up.

Storret caught the blanket as it fell from her. A moist heat escaped her body. He reached for her hand and rose next to her. "How many hours until daybreak?"

"Very few," she said. "You might want to check with Floom about yesterday. He sent word to wake him once you came out of your trance."

"It looks like I have a lieutenant."

Breel led Storret through the forest to where Floom and his clan camped. Many of them slept beneath a lean-to propped against a cedar. Their gear lay all around them. It looked as though they had a late dinner and went to sleep before cleaning up.

"They had a long day, too," Breel said.

"I hate to wake them this early." Storret walked around to where Floom slept on his side. When he reached out, Floom's hand came up and grabbed Storet's wrist, halting its movement.

Floom opened his eyes. "I am sorry. My reflexes…"

"No need to be sorry. Those are healthy reflexes to encourage," Storret said.

"You need only call out my name and I'll awaken."

"I'll remember that."

Floom let go of Storret's wrist and sat up. He took a deep breath. "We have much to talk about," he said.

40

"You're lying on your back," Zimp said.

"My legs are more powerful this way. I'm taking no chances," Lankor said. "Shift first. Your bird image could lie at my neck and be safe."

"They'll hear the door break loose. Someone has to answer if they inquire, so I decided to stay in human image. I'd like as much time to prepare as we can get." Zimp felt unsure of the plan even though it was hers. "I wish I could fit through those bars in my crow image. You wouldn't have to shift at all," she said.

"Do you get the feeling they were expecting us to arrive?"

"I wish I'd killed Raik with my own sword."

"And I with my own hands, but both are too late," Lankor said. He patted his chest. "Well?"

Zimp felt the weight of the air in the dungeon and could only imagine what Lankor must be going through. She heard a whisper and fluttering wings and tried to put both from her mind. She had to concentrate now. She had to help in their escape.

"Are you hearing things again?"

"Not now," she said. He didn't look convinced. Zimp kneeled next to him and placed her hands on his chest. She swung her leg over him and stretched her arms over her head and around his neck. "Will this be safe?" she said, her face against his breastbone.

He put his arms around her. "I think so."

"Then get to it. This is not exactly comfortable for me."

"I'm sorry to inconvenience you, but it was your idea," Lankor said.

"Don't remind me," she said. Yet Zimp snuggled closer to his chest and took a deep breath. She liked the way he smelled even after a few days, still a bit smoky from their camps and his last shift. She was concerned that the smell of fire would get much stronger.

"Get ready," he said.

Zimp let go of the back of his neck and slid her arms down to grab his upper arms. She gripped firmly and attempted to be as small as she could, lie as close to him as possible, although she felt confident that she'd have enough room.

The scent of smoke gripped her first, so she held her breath for as long as she could. She heard him groan with pain and his bones cracked. Holding so close to him, Zimp heard terrible sounds coming from inside his chest, as though his ribs were breaking one at a time. Regardless of the sound, Lankor's body expanded to several times its size. She could tell that he wanted to scream out, that he wanted to move. His heart rate tripled. His body became thick and leathery. She felt his wings slide over her back and head and she closed her eyes tightly.

His legs pushed against the door and his body slid backwards. She imagined his head bent and his shoulder shoved against the back wall. She let her breath out and tried not to breathe in, but she had no choice. She coughed and then fought the urge.

The door screeched as it was pulled from the wall. Then Lankor let out a great breath and the door broke from its frame.

Zimp heard the heavy wood and metal slide along the thick clay floor as it was pushed to the side.

"Hey? What's going on in there?" one of the guards yelled down the hall.

"This place is not safe. The castle wall just shifted," Zimp yelled back.

"Sounded like somebody dragging a body along the floor,"

the guard said.

"I don't care what it sounded like. This place isn't safe. You've got to get us out of here."

"Can't," the guard said.

"What are you going to do with us," Zimp said.

The guard growled, "Don't know. Nobody tell us nothin'." He banged against the dungeon hall door. "Now shut up."

Lankor had begun to shift back into his human image and let out a cough and groan.

As soon as she could, Zimp rolled off his chest and stood where the door had once been. "They can't see in here. It's too dark." She whispered to him and held out her hand.

Lankor waved her away and sat up. He didn't look so good.

"I had room to spare. I didn't even feel the ceiling," Zimp said.

"That scared the demons out of me," he said. "I could feel the ceiling. My wings and claws are scraped up from it. I won't be able to do that in the hall."

"And I can't fit between the bars at the end," she said.

"Great. We have more space to take strolls," Lankor said. He slumped over. "I don't have enough room. It scares me."

Zimp walked over to him. She ran her hand through his hair. "I'll find a way out."

"You do that or you won't be the only one hearing voices," he said.

She laughed. "You're funny when you're scared."

"Impending death can do that," he said.

She stood up quickly and walked to the door. She placed her hand along one of the bars. She turned around and asked Lankor, "Do you suppose the guards sleep?"

"What are you thinking? I'm not shifting anywhere in that cavern." He pointed toward the hall. "My ribs would snap like dried firewood."

"I'll bet if we can get one of these bars loose, we can use it to separate the bars on the outer door." She waited for understanding to kick in, but Lankor stared blankly back at her. "You're big and handsome, but you take a while to catch on."

"I'm handsome?"

"Don't get sidetracked. It's my turn to shift. I could fit through the bars if they were only a fraction wider. And you, my friend, are strong enough in human image to pry those bars. But first, you'll need to burn this door so we can get these bars out of there."

"I see now," he said.

"You can lie down diagonally. That will give you more room." She sat and leaned against the wall. "We'll stay quiet until they feel safe. They're on guard right now. When it's time, you've got to make it quick. If they call for more guards, we may be back where we started."

"I'm looking forward to it," Lankor said.

Zimp worried about Lankor. The cramped space affected his breathing and his body language. She sensed he held tightly to his own thoughts and that was why he made jokes. She told him to try to sleep to keep his mind off the closeness of the room.

Once he appeared relaxed, she shuffled down the hall to listen to the guards. Even if they didn't doze off, she felt that Lankor would have time to burn the door without disturbing them. From the corner of the door and wall, she could barely see one of the guards. He leaned back and listened to his friend, who complained about his wife. There were only two men there.

"Oh," the guard said, his eyelids heavy.

"Ain't nothin' a man can do. You get what you gets," his partner went on.

In about an hour, the complainer toned down to a mere mumble. The other guard's chest heaved as though he slept.

Zimp tip-toed back to Lankor and placed a hand over his mouth. "Shush," she said when his eyes opened. "Can you disintegrate that door with as little light as possible?"

"Fire produces light."

"I know that. So what *can* you do?" She looked around. "Oh, never mind. I'll think of something." She pulled her cloak from her shoulders and studied Lankor for a moment.

"What's that look for?" Lankor said.

"Remove your shirt."

"What?"

"I'm going to make a barrier between you and those guards so they don't see some great flash of light and wonder what it is," she said.

Lankor shook his head. He stood and began to unbutton his shirt.

She moved to help him.

Lankor stopped. "Please don't," he said.

Zimp backed away, her feelings hurt. "Then hurry."

Lankor finished and handed her the shirt.

She tied it to her cloak and walked down to the narrowest part of the hall. She stepped on one corner of the cloak and held the other against the ceiling just over her head. With her foot she scooted his shirt along the floor and placed a toe on it as well. She pulled the other end near the ceiling. Only a small gap was not covered. She lowered her hands long enough for her to nod for Lankor to begin, then she went back into position.

From behind the cloak, Zimp couldn't watch him shift. She could only hear the sound of his muffled groans and of his body scraping the floor as he changed form from human to beast. She sensed that he went through pain during each shift, but never as much as the harpies when they shifted. There was something horrible about their conversion, something cursed.

She felt a quick burst of heat and her cloak and his shirt glowed with a back-light for only a moment. The crackling of burned wood caused her to listen for the guards, but nothing stirred at the end of the hall. Once the area darkened again, she lowered the garments.

She had not realized how small the cell was until she saw Lankor's dragon image and how it almost filled the space. Enough fear and he could remain in dragon image. He would be trapped there, unable to move, lodged into the dungeon cell. Such a thing would drive any man, or beast, mad. The courage it took to shift twice impressed her. He had much more control over his beast image than she had thought. Perhaps more control than he knew, as well.

He shifted into human image and rolled onto his back, then lifted his arms and let them fall to his sides. A sheen ran along Lankor's muscled arms. He stood and turned toward her.

Sweat caused the ripples in his flesh to accentuate the curves and bulges in his arms. What strength those arms must yield. She caught her breath when he stretched to full height, and hoped that he hadn't noticed.

"You look tired," she said as she handed his shirt back to him.

"I am." He slipped the shirt over his shoulders, but didn't button it. Instead he reached out for the bars, exposed within the charred area along the door. He pulled one loose and charcoal fell to the ground.

"It's still hot here," she said.

"I tried not to allow very many flames," he said, "so I used as much heat as I could. That takes a lot out of me."

She felt her shirt and neck were wet from sweating. "That was very brave for you to do."

"The heat will dissipate soon," he said. He grabbed a second bar. "These will work nicely." He stood and looked down the hall. "It's funny, but I feel safer in this cell than I do in that hall."

"I can see why," Zimp said. She waited for Lankor to relax.

He held the bars in one hand and stared at the ground. After a few long, deep breaths he looked into her eyes. "Are you ready?"

"Let's go." She swung around and walked to the end of the hall with caution. She planted herself in the shadow created by the corner of the door and hall while Lankor lifted both bars and slid them between two of the bars on the outer door. Zimp closed her eyes and listened as pressure was applied, the bars scraping against one another, the metal emitting a low groan. She felt Lankor's hand on her arm and opened her eyes. The gap in the bars would be easy to climb through.

Zimp gripped Lankor's forearm with both of her hands. As her body shriveled she pulled him toward the ground. Her crow image pulled inward and made her feel like she would disappear soon. She placed a clawed foot onto his hand, and could feel his fear through his palm, sense his nervousness in the air around him. As he lifted her into the air, Zimp let her thoughts slip in and out of the other realm, searching, but for what?

She heard two distinct voices in her head: one was Zora and the other she feared that was Oronice's. It was done, then. Oro had left the physical realm and moved on. Her voice was the stronger of the two, confirming what Zimp had already known.

Lankor raised his hand near the opening in the door and Zimp hopped through the bars and glided to the ground. She ruffled her feathers. It felt as though someone touched her neck and back, running a finger down the length of her. Words entered her body, but not through her mind, not through her ears. The words felt physical, making themselves known at her wingtips and beak. How was that possible? Another crow appeared in front of her, between her and the guards. She cocked her head. It was Oronice. A second crow appeared and tried to push Oro aside.

"Zora," Zimp glanced toward Lankor, knowing that he could not understand what she said. He could hear only a cackle or warble leave her beak. But could he see the two crows that stood in front of her?

He pointed toward them. Or did he point toward the guards behind them? His eyes turned sad, defeated.

"Humans have made the doublesight impure," Zimp heard, or felt, from Oronice. "The statues must be destroyed. Set the gargoyle children free."

Zora pecked at Oronice. "What are you saying? Bring the doublesight home." She hopped closer to Zimp. "This is the true realm, not the physical. Come here with us. Join us."

"No," Oronice began to shift. Zimp knew that she'd have to shift too in order to understand what Oronice had to say. But she wanted to talk with her sister, as well, and didn't want to abandon her.

One of the guards stirred behind Oronice and Zora. Zimp pushed her attention toward human thought. Zora's image faded slightly, but Oro's remained clear throughout her shift.

As Zimp gripped her human image fully, Zora was gone.

"Listen to me," Oro said.

"But how?" Zimp said.

Oronice placed a finger over her lips to shush Zimp. "They cannot see nor hear me. But they can hear you.

Zimp glanced around the room, purposely ignoring Lankor. "I know. It is as though the walls and air are speaking and not me. You can feel my words in your hands. They are physical. Feel this," Oro said, "you are in great danger."

Zimp stepped back. The words hurt her chest, her heart. The lantern flickered and a shadow swept over the chamber accentuating the darkness that lay waiting for the fire to go out.

"The souls of the gargoyles from Memory Tower have grown strong. They are pushing through to the physical world. Entering through the weakest links, through humans. But only through humans who have taken a doublesight mate. The strength of knowing your beast image is strong. A human's yearning to know a beast image makes them weak. The two..." Her voice faded.

"Oro," Zimp said.

One of the guards sat upright and opened his eyes.

"Zimp," Lankor said, desperation in his voice.

Oronice disappeared before Zimp's eyes. But her grandmother's words spread throughout the chamber. "Some doublesight must die. Storret, Storret knows," were Oro's last words.

By now the guard had pulled his sword and lumbered toward Zimp. "How did you get out here?"

She stumbled backwards.

Lankor stretched his arm through the bars but couldn't reach the guard. "Hey," he yelled.

The guard turned long enough for Zimp to shake the visions from her head and tackle him at the knees. The sword came down and cracked against the floor waking the other guard.

Zimp ran her hand along the guard's calf and found a dagger, her weapon of choice. In an instant, she pulled the blade from its sheath and let the blade glide up along the guard's thigh, cutting an inch deep as it went.

He screamed and leaped back, shoving her away.

Zimp fell against the door, rolled to her back, and kicked with both feet to jar the bolt loose.

Lankor pulled the door open and stepped into the guards' chamber.

41

With only a few days of training after getting to know one another, Storret felt that he and his army were totally unprepared. He had discussed his concern with Breel and Floom several times, but they both reassured him that things were as they were meant to be. The men and women would sharpen their talents whenever time permitted. Although most doublesight had been brought up to be passive, they learned battle tactics as a defense, and would call on those tactics when necessary.

Since Oro's death, Noot wandered the camp visiting each of the two bands of makeshift warriors. He appeared to be dazed much of the time. He spoke very little and would walk off while spoken to.

Storret knew what contact with the second realm was like and understood how it could affect a man in such a way. What worried him was how uncommunicative Noot had become. He didn't remember Oronice ever being that removed from physical reality. What if the man couldn't handle the strain of living in two worlds at once?

"You have enough to be concerned about," Breel said. She stood next to Storret as he stared down one of the forest paths after Noot.

"Will he be all right?" Storret said.

"That is not for either of us to be concerned about. Do you

trust Oronice? Did you not return unharmed?"

"Yes, but I was taken on a journey and brought back. Oronice held my hand the whole way. I'm afraid Noot has been left to fend for himself in a world where the values and beliefs of our physical world may not apply. I can only guess at the struggle he must be going through." Storret reached for Breel's hand. "I feel that Oronice has left him alone so that she can go to Zimp."

"May the Gods watch over them all," she said.

Storret squeezed her hand in agreement, then let go and turned toward the clearing where his men practiced offensive and defensive moves using swords and staffs. He stepped around several men who sparred in front of him. "Rats," he said. "They are many, but they are not so easily taught. And they are not aggressive fighters until they are cornered."

They walked on and came to another clearing where about twenty people, men and women alike, practiced hand-to-hand combat.

Storret knelt down and Breel followed suit. "I am always mystified by the movements they make," he said. "Watch as they circle. Watch their feet and nothing else."

Breel stared for a moment and turned to him amazed.

Storret smiled at her.

"It's like their legs disappear and reappear in a different place. Their stance changes to match that of their opponent, at which time the opponent's stance changes," she said.

"Now watch only their arms and hands," he said.

"It can't be," she said. "They are fighting. But, I also see them kicking. How can their legs be in the air and on the ground at the same time?"

"I can't even keep track of their punches. I've tried. They are either extremely quick or their bodies come in and out of the physical world," Storret said. "I talked with one of them the other day and he's not even sure how it's done. They learn the practice from childhood. They call it the art of dance." He stopped and thought for a moment. "Oro said to dance into battle. I plan to lead with them." Stroking Breel's curly locks, Storret asked, "Have you ever watched foxes in the woods?"

"No," she said.

"They can appear and disappear in an instant. I can't explain it, but you can't actually watch them for long without losing track of their movements."

"Too bad we don't have an army of them," Breel said. "Too bad they can't teach the others how to dance."

"Except that they can't do the same with a weapon in their hands. Somehow a weapon ties them more solidly to this world. They are fast. And they're tricky. But it's not the same."

"Will we battle against the humans as humans?" Breel said.

"Both. I've ordered our fighters to shift if that would help them overcome their opponent or help them to escape. Shifting in battle is dangerous at any time. Too fast and you may never leave your animal image; too slow and you're dead before the shift is complete. I've taken the suggestion of Graap, the leader of the rat doublesight. What they do is surround a small group of their fellows and maintain a barrier between them and the battle. Once shifted, the rats can scurry off to safety, run up the legs of the attackers, all sorts of things. It's something that was handed down as a strategy. If we did such a thing for the bird clans, they could fly into the air and return with a wider view of the situation. Strategically, that would give us the advantage."

Breel placed her hand on Storret's shoulder. "Brilliant," she said. "You were right when you said we'd learn something different from each clan."

They stood and turned back to the path. Small practice battles were going on in several clearings, the only places where they could get large numbers of people together. Storret and Breel passed a place where the copperheads fought. Bennek battled alongside of them. His movements were smooth and hypnotic, a snake charmer with the movements of a snake.

"We should meet at noon to discuss mixing the doublesight up for the second half of the day. We shared a lot of battle tips just in the differences we witnessed." He turned to Breel. "I'll let the north half of them know. Would you tell the southern group?"

She kissed his cheek and jogged off to the south.

Storret watched her leave. He wished she'd stay with Arren and The Few, and hunker down at the council grounds, but she was determined to follow him into battle. And she was one of the best swordsmen he'd ever met. Fremlin had taught all his children well.

Storret reached Floom's group after rounding a grove of wide-based cedars. He stopped short and watched as the hawks practiced shifting while in battle. He shook his head. They were faster than any doublesight he'd ever witnessed. And they appeared to be totally conscious of their human image when they snapped back. The only problem he saw was that the hawks were a little slow to get airborne from the ground.

"Storret." Floom waved him over.

"What do you think? I'm sure we can help to train other doublesight to shift more quickly. It's a mental practice we've learned as children." Floom's eyes were bright and eager. "It's quite simple really, but does take a little practice."

"We'll talk about it at noon, in my camp around Oro's wagon."

"I'll be there," Floom said.

"One thing I noticed," Storret said.

"What's that?"

"Who will protect you until you get into the air?"

Floom grinned. "We're not as quick to fly off as crows, if that's what you mean."

"I wasn't trying to say…"

"I know, I know." He turned around and yelled, "Sloat, Woss, Bresh, show Storret how we get skybound."

Sloat, Woss, and Bresh stopped battling long enough to separate from the other hawks. The three of them set a pose and began to fight. Quickly, Sloat stepped to the side, grabbed Woss's free arm and shifted. Woss's arm lowered only slightly from the weight as he continued to swordfight with Bresh. Bresh purposely tried to strike at Sloat, but Woss's strategy changed from offence to defense as he protected the bird. Suddenly, Woss bent at his knees, struck at Bresh with his sword, and pitched Sloat over his head and into the open air.

Sloat flew into a low branch of a nearby cedar and waited.

Floom said, "Well, what do you think?"

Storret stood transfixed, looking up at Sloat. "Amazing. If

you could teach us all to shift like that, we'd frighten the souls right out of the humans." After saying humans, Storret stopped short. He lowered his head.

"I know that sounds terrible. We are all human first. What we must do pains me as well." Floom motioned for Sloat to return to practice, then said to Storret, "What has made us so horrible that we must be killed like animals?"

"Even we kill animals for food," Storret said.

"The Great Land has many mysteries, many horrors, and many pleasures," Floom said.

"There are times when I don't want to experience them all."

"Me as well, my friend, me as well," Floom said.

"Noon," Storret said, before leaving. A short distance down the path and Breel came running toward him. "Hurry. This way."

Storret ran to her and grabbed her arm. "What is it?"

"One of the foxes tried a fast shift during battle and appears to have remained in beast image."

Storret turned back, ran until he felt Floom could hear, and yelled for the hawk image doublesight to follow him and Breel. In a moment, a hawk flew over their heads. Turning into the clearing, a band of foxes kneeled in a circle. "Spread out," Storret said as he rushed into the circle.

Floom dropped to the ground and shifted into his human image.

"What do you do?" Storret asked him.

The fox image kneeled on the ground, shaking. A fox in human image had a hand on the animal's back and another hand stroking its head and neck.

Floom stared for a moment. "For us, you must start before you shift. You must concentrate and repeat…"

"Repeat what?" Storret said.

"It's simple, really, we repeat the name of a loved one. Someone special. And we imagine them in human form while doing so. I don't know, but somehow that keeps us firmly connected to our human image even during a quick shift. Coming back is easy then."

Storret looked to the person stroking the fox's head.

The man closed his eyes. "She's my wife," he said.

"What's your name?"

"Radmal," he said.

Storret looked around. "Everyone, stare at Radmal, repeat his name over and over. Detail his face as you do so, imagine someone you love. Feel the love that..."

"Seana," Radmal said.

"That Seana has for her husband." Storret closed his eyes and recreated Radmal's face in his mind. He allowed the love he felt for Breel to fill his heart. Then he began to repeat out loud, "Radmal, Radmal, Radmal..." in the sweetest voice he could make, as though he loved Radmal as much as he loved Breel.

Soon the other foxes and Floom and Breel were whispering Radmal's name as well.

Storret placed a hand over Seana's head and willed the vibration of his words and his heart to move down his arm and into her. He entered the other realm more easily than he thought was possible. In that realm he stood beside Seana and whispered in her ear. Over and over, Storret chanted in two realms. The others chanted Radmal with feeling until one of the foxes interrupted the chant. "Look."

Storret opened his eyes and Seana's arm was human.

Her legs lengthened. Her hair grew longer as the redish fox fur stretched. Her smooth cheek twitched in the pain of the shift.

Tears streaked down Storret's face. Several of the foxes cried openly.

Floom shook his head as though he couldn't believe it. "What have you done, my friend?"

"Thank you," Storret said to Floom. "We must all learn this. Why it was not part of all of us I do not know." He turned to Breel and she collapsed into his arms.

Seana reached for her husband.

Radmal held to Seana with one arm and reached his other across her body to grip Storret's hand. Nothing was said.

"Could we do this for Therin?" Breel said.

Storret's chest tightened into a fist. Floom answered before Storret was forced to. "It will be too late," he said.

"We could try," she said. "You didn't think this would

work."

Floom turned his eyes from her. "If that would make you happy," he said.

"We'll do everything we can," Storret said.

As the group began to break up and Seana rose to her feet, several rat doublesight scurried into the clearing. "Come quickly. A lookout has spotted a thylacine running this way."

"Therin," Breel screamed out. She ran after the doublesight, following them northward.

Storret turned to Radmal. "Rest. All of you," he said, then ran with Floom after Breel.

Just north of the practice clearing, rat doublesight lined the path with swords ready. "Is that him?" Storret asked Breel, even while pulling his sword from its sheath.

"No. It's Brok." She ran toward her brother and kneeled for him to leap into her arms.

The thylacine panted. Its chest heaved. It let out a yelp and a short growl as Storret stepped closer.

"He's not shifting," Storret said.

"He is," Breel said. "Slowly though. He's exhausted, but I can feel the shift occurring."

Storret stood back with Floom and the others as he watched Brok twist and stretch during the shift. Legs stretched and became arms. His torso expanded and contracted as he heaved. A human cough escaped his mouth even though Storret couldn't see his head, which was cradled in Breel's arms.

"Oh," she said with relief. "He's fine."

She looked back at Storret, who was forced to say what she couldn't say, "Where's Therin?"

Brok pushed into a kneeling position and held to Breel's shoulders. "Therin's dead," he said between breaths. "He saved my life. He retained human thought to the end. I know he did."

Breel cried, turned away, and fell to the ground.

Storret went to her.

Brok looked at him in question. But when Breel climbed into Storret's arms, Brok's expression turned to understanding. "It is a time of sorrow, I know. But we must move soon. Castle Weilk harbors a mad gryphon, the king's son."

"King Belford? A gryphon?" Floom stepped forward.

Brok nodded. "Not a dragon. And they've captured Lankor and Zimp."

"How did you escape? What happened to Raik? Where's he?" Storret said.

"Raik is a traitor. He's probably leading them to you at this very minute. I escaped because I went back to save Therin."

"And then he saved you," Breel said.

"Family first," Brok said. "Now, I stay with you."

42

Lankor held a bar in each hand. The look of surprise on the guards' faces was enough for him to know that they either saw in his face or sensed in his stance that there was no turning back from this battle.

Zimp crouched near a bench behind them all.

Lankor blocked a swing from one of the swords that came at him from the side. The ceiling hung much too low to get a good overhead swing, and Lankor sensed the awkwardness of the guard's attack. They were at the disadvantage.

Lankor placed his swing across the back of one guard's neck, the bar cracking bones loudly. That guard down, Lankor brought both bars together in front of him on either side of the second guard's jaw line. Another fatal blow. Blood gushed from the man's mouth as his knees gave out and he slumped to the floor.

Lankor swung around and reached down for one of the swords. He handed it to Zimp. "Who in the name of the Six Shapeless Gods were you talking to?"

Zimp's eyes filled with tears. "Oronice is dead."

"You knew that before."

"But I saw her. I felt her words. They were everywhere in this room." Zimp's lips quivered.

"What'd she say?"

"I don't know."

"But, if you heard her…" Lankor picked up the other sword from the ground.

"I felt her words in my chest and arms. Along my neck. It was about Memory Tower. The souls of the statues are pushing through to this realm."

Lankor stopped moving. What was she saying? What did it mean? "You're hearing too many voices from the other realms. You haven't been able to decipher them up to now. Why do you believe this story?"

"It's not a story." A fire appeared behind her eyes. "You don't trust it, do you? You don't trust me."

"It doesn't matter." Lankor pulled her up by her elbow. "We've got work to do. I'm not waiting down here for another second."

Zimp stopped him. "Is there a human in your bloodline?"

Lankor couldn't answer the question. He performed a quick memory search and found no answer. "I don't know."

"You could be one of them," she said. Then she reached out and hugged him, squeezing his body close to hers.

Lankor felt his heart race and the blood run to the surface of his body. He loved her touch, but it wasn't right. He didn't want to like it at all. What if one of them died? There was no time to consider anything but their mission. Draklan and the three sisters were a threat to The Great Land, a threat to the doublesight. A war could wipe out their race. It must be stopped now.

Lankor shoved her away. "Your visions are getting in the way of your sanity. We've got to go." He led the way through the next hall. The walls in some areas brushed his arms on both sides of his body. He felt the fear of death rise inside him. It slowed his progress.

Zimp's hands touched his back. "Keep going."

They heard guards talking near the entrance to the dungeon. Another passage broke off to the right. Lankor pivoted on one foot and flattened his back against the wall. "I don't remember another door."

"I do," Zimp said.

Lankor had been so preoccupied by the pressure of the walls

and ceiling that he walked with his eyes closed much of the way to their cell. He felt ashamed. Zimp was not to be trusted to know what was going on. He should have paid closer attention. "Now what?"

Zimp charged toward the door and yelled out, "Hey, your friends back there might need some help."

Lankor held back.

"How did you get outta there?" a guard said. The door bolt rattled loose and the door opened. "Get her!"

Lankor heard several men run into the opening. He jumped out and ran to take position in front of Zimp. They would never get past him. Still holding one of the bars, he slammed the first guard in the ear and lifted his sword through the crotch of the second guard as the man tried to step over the first. The third guard turned to run.

Lankor bent down to move the men from his path. Zimp hopped over him, rolled across the floor and rose to her feet a short distance from the running guard. She placed her knife between his shoulder blades and he fell forward with a splat of flesh against stone.

Lankor caught up with her. "They don't waste many guards down here," he said as he led the way up a set of winding stairs, leaping three at a time. Near the top, he stopped and listened. He recalled the hall the stairs emptied into. Its width would be welcome, and the height of the ceiling double that of the lower chambers.

Zimp squeezed past him. "Let me," she said as her body shriveled and turned black. Her crow image flew toward the opening at a steep upward angle.

Lankor kneeled on the steps to allow there to be room overhead. He felt as though the ceiling was already upon him and that his movements were continually stymied. He edged up two more steps and was about to stand when he heard Zimp whisper that the hall was clear.

He broke into the open space and spread his arms and closed his eyes. A tingling sensation spread across his skin, like being unchained or let loose from a small cage. He twirled once around. He wanted to howl with delight.

"Lankor," Zimp whispered louder.

He opened his eyes and saw her at the end of the hall about to mount a second set of stairs, the ones that led to the great chamber where Draklan and King Belford had first greeted them. As he passed a room to his right, Lankor caught a glimpse of something inside and stopped to investigate it.

"No," Zimp ran toward him. "Don't look in there."

At the door, Lankor placed his face against the bars and in the far corner a child dragged its snake-half across the floor. The little girl's smudged and dirty face looked sad. She had been crying. Lines of clean skin streaked down her filthy cheeks. She propped herself up on her hands. She looked frightened. Her eyes asked him, why?

Lankor had no answer for her.

She began to shift.

Zimp stood at his side and pulled at his shoulder. "Come on. We must go now."

He jerked from her grip, unable to turn away from the girl's eyes. He watched as her mouth opened to scream but only a hissing sound came out. New tears fell and her face tensed against what appeared to be immense pain and a need for understanding. Her head fell forward onto the floor, where it thinned and stretched into a copperhead's upper torso, but the snake's tail that was there a moment ago grew and filled in. It split into the spindly legs of the sweet little girl whose other half stared at Lankor a moment ago.

Then the snake's head did something totally unexpected. It turned on its own body and struck at the thin legs. The mouth opened wide, the head swaying as though trying to empty the poison from its fangs.

Lankor could see where it had struck at itself many times. Pairs of tiny holes lined her legs. He reached up and took the bars in his hands and shook them.

The snake's head swung around and began to shift back into the girl, brown hair growing from its tiny head.

He let his arms drop.

Zimp stood close to him and placed the back of her hand against his neck.

The little girl hissed at him.

Recalling what Zimp had said in the dungeon, he asked, "Am I one of them? Is my clan a throwback?"

"Not if there are no humans in your bloodline. Dragons were one of the original creatures designed by the Six Shapeless Gods." She pulled at him to move on.

"Raik and Draklan are right, aren't they? Something horrible is happening to the doublesight."

"Only when doublesight and human mix. Oro said that it has to do with the souls of the gargoyle statues," she said.

"Can you be sure? Is your connection with the next realm that secure, that fluid, that clear?"

She stared back at him and shook her head. "But I'll find out."

"What do we do now?" he asked. "Fight for the doublesight so that they may live, or accept the horror that lies before us and..."

"We don't give up," she said. "We stop this insanity right here. And we start with Draklan."

They moved to the next door and against Zimp's instruction, Lankor glanced into the cell. This time a hairy beast with wings like the harpies and the face of a fox slept in the corner. It curled its head between its legs.

"Please," Zimp said.

"I'll kill them all," Lankor said. "How can they allow this to go on?" He charged toward the stairs and again took them three at a time.

Zimp ran behind him.

Lankor burst into the hall at the top of the stairs without caring if anyone was around. His lungs burned as he stopped to allow Zimp to catch up.

Guards outside the throne chamber yelled out when they saw him. Three of them advanced and one ran for help. Each of the guards had a long spear and a sword. They charged Lankor with the spears held side by side.

Lankor pointed to a window to the right of the guards. "Get out of here," he said to Zimp. "Fly to the council grounds and tell The Few."

"I fight with you," she said.

Swinging his sword over his head, Lankor let it loose and the guards dived out of its way. He ran forward and grabbed the closest spear, gripped it firmly and yanked it from the guard's hands. Like a staff, he swung the blunt end into the head of the guard next to the first, then pulled the spear back and rammed it into the chest of its original owner.

The third guard thrust the tip of his spear at Lankor, ripping a hole in his shirt and drawing blood along his shoulder.

Lankor tried to duck and while doing so, Zimp slid across the floor and stabbed the guard's shin, toppling him over.

Other guards rushed from both sides of the chamber entrance.

"Run," Lankor said.

Zimp began to dash toward the window when the chamber doors opened and Draklan's voice boomed for them to stop.

The guards held still, lowering their weapons to their sides.

Lankor nodded toward Zimp to continue toward the window, but she held fast to her position. He couldn't tell if she failed to see him nod or if she listened to Oro's voice coming from another realm.

"Let them enter," Draklan said.

The guards stepped to the side and allowed Lankor to walk forward.

Draklan jumped from the throne where he had been sitting, and landed at the base of the few stairs. King Belford stood to the side and screamed for his son to stop. "Not here," he said.

"You've no doubt seen the Sisters' children," Draklan said. "Don't be concerned. They seldom live long." Lankor watched as Draklan's eyes drank in the size and shape of the expansive throne room and calculated something dark and secret.

Lankor charged forward. His mind raced with the images of the children in the cells and the truth of their births. Anger surged through his veins. He held fast to the spear he had commandeered from the guard. Before him, Draklan crouched down. Was he reaching for a dagger? Was he taking a fighting pose? Would he soon dash to the side or leap upon Lankor? It took him a moment to realize that Draklan had begun to shift.

Already the man's body grew in size while shifting in shape.

Lankor dropped his weapon and spread his arms to his sides. His dragon image shoved forward as though nothing stood in its way. He screamed out, attempting to shift faster without losing his ability to remain in human thought. Bones felt and sounded as though they cracked. Wings stretched to his sides.

But Draklan had shifted faster. He lifted onto his lion's legs and ran toward Lankor, who could not turn away until his dragon image had fully shifted into existence.

Zimp screamed from behind him and he heard her footsteps as she ran away.

Draklan ran into Lankor, who fell backwards as he completed the last of his shift. The gryphon's head pulled back ready to strike with its eagle beak.

Lankor swiped the air in front of him with the claw at the end of his wing.

The gryphon reared back.

Lankor blew fire toward it. The beast was gone. The dragon image rolled to its stomach and pushed into the air. Although the chamber was large, there was little room to fly. Lankor's mind grew stronger and weaker with human thought, careful not to begin a shift or he would be killed in an instant.

The chamber had changed color. Dragon eyes were so different than human eyes that the strangeness of the world took a few moments to get used to. The walls burned red and the people were blue. He glanced around to find Draklan. The gryphon held to a corner of the room. Somehow Lankor knew that the eagle eyes could pinpoint any target to attack on his dragon image. He had a choice. He could spit fire or fly. The gas in his chest that allowed both to happen had been diminished only slightly by his first firey attack on Draklan. Lankor lept off the ground, circled the chamber, and closed his wings close to his sides. Facing the gryphon in the corner, he dropped straight toward the floor. Blue men scurried out of the room, yelling in a language he couldn't understand. Before he splattered into the stone, Lankor opened his wings, caught the air and glided down. His dragon image naturally bowed forward, a shape that wouldn't allow him to bend backwards and look into the air very well. Spitting fire would steal his ability to fly and maintain a strategic position. He approached human thought with too much effort, considering how to fight the gryphon, so he fell back into dragon mind. The dragon reacted to Draklan's movement toward it, spewing fire half the distance to the corner.

Draklan eased into the air with several flaps of his wings and flew around the chamber.

Lankor turned but had to watch the beast using peripheral vision. With two great flaps of his wings, he lifted into the air to meet Draklan head on. The two beasts crashed together.

The gryphon's powerful legs clawed at the dragon's chest, tearing at the leathery plates. It screeched like an eagle diving into a lake.

Lankor swung his spiked tail around and into the gryphon's side, slashing a huge gash along the fur. The dragon also struck out with its spiny beak, shaking his head from side to side, slamming into the gryphon's powerful beak and head.

The two fought in the air and fell together onto the floor.

Stunned by the fall, Lankor's human thought struggled to hold tight as animal instinct took over. The huge beast spun around and searched for its opponent. Great pain struck his head from behind. He felt blood ooze from the wound. Before he could turn around, a sharp claw caught hold of a wing and ripped at it. Lankor lifted and swung his tail and caught his attacker in the shoulder, throwing the gryphon to the side. The dragon turned and clawed the air in front of him as he attacked the limping beast. He checked the feeling of fullness in his chest and made a sudden choice to use the gas to throw a fireball.

The gryphon's fur burst into flames. Draklan began to shift. Was he dead or forcing the shift to escape his burning fur?

Lankor heard the men shouting behind him and turned. There must have been a thousand crows attacking the guards who were throwing spears and swinging swords to stop them. Lankor's human image gripped his mind and held tightly. He dropped to the floor to duck from the flying spears. Before Lankor's shift was complete, Draklan was on him once again, hands wrapped around his neck.

Before Lankor could catch his breath, a crow gripped Draklan's shoulder and pecked at his face. Draklan fell backwards and several other crows attacked him.

Lankor completed shifting into human image and ran for the closest downed guard. He pulled the sword from under the man, swung around and rushed to where Draklan fought the crows from his face. The crows flew off as Lankor approached the struggling doublesight.

Lifting the sword over his head, Lankor hesitated before bringing it down on Draklan. There was something in the man's eyes that stopped Lankor short. What was it?

Draklan lay back onto the floor. His body relaxed with abandon. "Thank you," he said, as Lankor's blade struck his chest.

43

Zimp flew toward Lankor and landed on the floor near his sword blade. He looked down at her. She cocked her head and pushed her human thought forward until a shift began. The excited sound of the crows all around her changed as she shifted, until she heard only the cawing of birds.

"Who are we now?" Lankor said.

"We are doublesight." Zimp took his sword hand, slipping her fingers around his grip.

"I'm surprised the sisters are not here," he said.

Zimp shook her head, recalling a recent image. While collecting crows, Zimp had looked into a chamber where there was movement. One of the sisters shifted while making love to the obstinate guard who had brought them to the castle earlier. The sister had begun to eat the guard during the act. "They are feeding," she said, ashamed at what she had seen and what she knew of their lives, their children. She swallowed. "We'd better go. Follow me to the rooftop."

"But the guards?"

Zimp smiled. "I'll bring help," she said as her form began to change. She took to the air, her mouth open, announcing for some of the crows to follow her. She made one circle around the chamber before Lankor ran for the door.

Most of the guards were too preoccupied warding off attacks by crows, several at a time to each man, to follow Lankor. In the hall more guards had gathered.

Zimp dropped from the air, chasing after a bald man who turned toward Lankor. She clawed the slick top of his head. When he reached to knock her away, Lankor slapped the man with the side of his sword and toppled him out of the way.

She flew to the side, hoping her friend would follow her, but Lankor didn't appear to know which crow she was. Just as in the physical world. Why should she expect anything different? She yelled for other crows to follow her up the stairwell that led to the top of the castle.

Lucky soldiers relieved of the attack quickly picked up their weapons.

Zimp circled overhead until Lankor followed the mass of birds toward the stairs, driving two unprepared guards from the entrance, and leaped up the steps in an all-out run.

Zimp flew over his head and escaped onto a broad landing, the early morning sun lifting fog from the yellow-green fields. She perched on a ledge and looked off to the east, toward the Weilk-Alshore Ocean, which was too far in the distance to see. Other crows perched around her. She pushed for a shift, then heard a noise. As she turned, she began her shift, which slowed her movement considerably.

A guard had stayed behind and ran out from the single room attached to the landing by a broad wood door.

It was too late for Zimp to reverse her shift. She stared and tried to move as the man lifted his sword over his head. Without reason, the guard's motion stopped, and he let go of his sword. It clanked to the floor. When he fell over, a look of surprise on his face, Lankor stood behind him.

Zimp completed her shift and dropped to her knees.

"You should be more careful," Lankor said.

"Why, when I have my own dragon-boy to save me?"

He laughed.

"It's good to hear you laugh," she said.

Lankor said, "Your friends can't keep them back forever. What's next?"

"Oronice is drawing me toward Memory Tower."

"I was afraid you'd say that."

"I'll watch as you shift," she said, reaching for his sword. "We're flying?" His face lit up. Zimp looked over the edge. "You wanted to walk?" She smelled the strong odor of fire and smoke, and stepped back. His shift frightened her as much as the first time, and she was a doublesight. No wonder the humans couldn't take it.

She wondered briefly, as he groaned and stretched his wings to his sides, how he felt about his ancestors being killed off by humans and doublesight alike. Was that why he ignored her advances? Did he retain a historical distaste for other doublesight?

Lankor lifted up in front of Zimp, a magnificent being of unbelievable strength and power. Who wouldn't fall in love with him? She couldn't help herself from wondering about his beak and bird claws. Were they, was he, an original dragon as the Six Shapeless Gods had first designed? No other flying animal had feet and looked reptilian except statues of other types of dragons. Were those dragons the mutants and Lankor of original stock? She believed that was so, whether because of her love or because of his appearance, it didn't matter to her.

She did a slow shift as he looked on.

The noise in the stairwell got louder with human voices. Three men ran onto the landing and stopped to stare at Lankor. He spun around and glared back at them, bowed, and turned to go. He stepped onto the landing wall, and fell into the light of the morning sun.

Zimp followed him toward the mountains.

*   *

Several hours later, the sisters heard of Draklan's death and went to see his body, which had been taken to his chamber. Their father, General Lansion, escorted them.

King Belford the Warrior stood over his son, his head and shoulders rolled forward in sadness. He had dressed in full uniform, ready for battle. The king did not look up as his brother entered the room, but said, "This is what he wanted."

General Lansion stepped close to King Belford and placed a

hand on the man's shoulder.

"You wish to comfort me, but there is nothing in me left to comfort." The king turned. "I loved and hated him. Found joy and fear in his existence."

"I know, my king."

"Do you fear us?" one of the sisters said and then quickly giggled.

The other two giggled after her.

The general turned to them and they quieted.

"What have we done?" the king said.

"We have kept our children alive," General Lansion said.

"Is this life? Is what they suffer life?" He spun around and pointed at the sisters. "Do you feel as though you're living? Is it not painful to shift? Do you not wish to die while it's happening? Are you ashamed? Do you fear for your own children?"

The pregnant sister ran her hands over her stomach and began to cry at his outburst. Her voice as she spoke sounded sweet, yet like an autumn wind had a definite chill to it. "I hate you both," she said evenly. "I hate what you have created – me, and my hunger not unlike yours. A hunger for flesh at any cost, flesh in all its functions. When I shift there is nothing but hate and hunger and I don't care what I produce. Is that how it was for you, Daddy? You didn't care what we would be, only that your hunger was satisfied?"

"No," he said. "That was not how it was. I loved your mother."

She hissed at him and he shut up.

"I love what grows in me. When I'm in human image and pregnant, I love it. When it is born..."

"Stop it," her father said.

"What will you do now, Daddy?" She stepped closer to him and her two sisters reached to stop her, but she shook them off. "Now that Draklan is gone? He knew how to care for us. He alone could stomach it. What will you do now? Now that our only friend is dead?" Her anger pushed her over the edge of change.

Her sisters gasped as she screamed out in pain. They knew that every shift felt worse than giving birth, worse than self-hatred. The pain stretched through her physical and emotional bodies. It was astral and ethereal.

She dropped her robe and let her body shift while naked.

Her father yelled out for her to stop, but there was no stopping what she had started.

Her shift kicked off shifts in her sisters. All three whined and screamed, their bodies twisting slowly in pain. Blood dripped from their bodies where wings appeared and where legs broke into bony claws.

The pregnant sister leaped onto her father, scratching at his face and neck.

King Belford called for the guards. He stepped backwards into the arms of the other two sisters. He yelled again.

As General Lansion slid to the floor, bloodied and weak, his daughter began to morph back into human image. She cried and yelled, "Daddy!" repeatedly. "I'm sorry. I'm sorry!"

King Belford looked on, a dazed blankness in his eyes.

"You did not kill him, did you?" one sister said. "Because we need his army. We need to live."

"But I hate being like this," the pregnant one said.

"We are the future of this world."

"We are awful."

"Only in their eyes. In my mind, we are only different. Stronger," she said. "We must stop the dragon and the crow."

*   *

Lankor relished the sensation of flight. The open sky became a large playground as he twisted and swooped. He couldn't help enjoying the flight toward Memory Tower.

The color of the morning air had turned green and purple. The smoky smells allowed the scent of growing fields to linger lightly as he breathed.

A hundred crows flew with him, all around him. They were noisy at first, but flew quietly now, staying out of his way as he rolled or dived.

A small voice nagged at him to stay the course, yet his dragon image thought to let the play last as long as it could. The dragon felt powerful and alive. It felt invincible. Whatever lay at Memory Tower could not possibly threaten him. What could jeopardize the doublesight now?

Lankor's human thought held tightly for a moment, long enough for him to wonder which crow was Zimp. He hoped it was the one flying closest to him. He glanced over and could have sworn that it winked at him. Then he nodded and slipped into background thought again.

The flight placed more strain on Lankor's dragon image than he would have liked to admit. He seldom strained the dragon's body by flying so many hours. He began to tire. He played less as he flew and found that he looked for ways to ride the wind using his wings, twisting them enough to produce lift. Soon he would have to return to human image. He searched out a place of safety just north of Memory Tower. He needed rest now.

Curving his legs forward, Lankor aimed for a rocky crag, bared of snow by the wind blowing over the ridge. Beyond the crag, the ground appeared flat and open as well. A few trees grew to the south and north, blocking the winds. Lankor touched down, the snow cold on his clawed feet. His wings shivered as he pulled them close to his body.

Crows landed all around him noiselessly. The soft fluff of snow fell from a branch to embrace the silence of the place with movement, but no sound.

Lankor gritted his teeth and held back the pain of shifting. Steam escaped his mouth. He breathed deeply the cold mountain air. He bent to touch the snow with his hand. He had seldom seen snow in The Lost and never this much.

"Beautiful, isn't it?" Zimp said from behind him.

"Yes," he said, "beautiful and cold."

"That's not always the case. In the sun it can become quite warm even with all this snow around." She peered into the east. "Perhaps later today."

"I didn't know where else to land," he said. "I was so tired from flying that I was afraid I'd shift if I thought about it too much."

She laughed then said, "No wonder you were tired. Were

you trying to impress me?"

Lankor turned away from her gaze. "I seldom get to play like that. It was such a beautiful morning. I couldn't help it."

"How much control does your human image have while you're a dragon?"

What did she mean by that? he wondered. Was she suggesting he was like Draklan or the sisters? "I've never killed and eaten flesh while in dragon image," he said. "Does that answer your question?"

"I didn't mean that."

"You did. You can't help but wonder if I'm a throwback to a previous time, a time of monsters."

"That's not true," she said.

As she stepped toward him Lankor retreated from her. "I am not a monster," he said, "even if I am a throwback. My only hunger is to play." He thought for a moment. "I feel powerful. I feel...well, magical and amazing, inspired, but never hungry for flesh." He waited for her to speak and when she didn't he said, "Do you believe me?"

"Yes," she said. "I can sense in you a childlike playfulness that anyone could love. I never felt threatened by your dragon image, even though watching you go through a shift can be frightening."

"As frightening as watching the sisters?"

"I feel great pity for them. They cannot help themselves. Their needs are gruesome and grotesque, but they are instinctual as much as conscious. No," she answered him. "They are much more frightening because of the horror that lives inside them."

"What are we to do now?"

"Stay the night and plan how to destroy those lost souls wishing to escape Memory Tower," she said.

"I don't understand," he said.

"Neither do I. Not yet. But tonight I enter the other realm." She took slow steps toward Lankor. "Will you stay with me tonight? Will you protect me while I'm gone?"

Lankor flowed with his heart's desire and reached for Zimp's hand. He lifted it toward his chest, pulling her closer. His mind raced and questioned his actions. He stared into her face, traced her lips with his eyes, and then met her eyes squarely. He hesitated and she leaned closer. "I'll protect you like a brother," he said, patting her hand affectionately.

*   *

The night had been long. Brok woke several times, upset about the loss of his brother.

Storret also awoke. He went to Brok's side, arriving to comfort Breel more than Brok.

Storret feared what had to be done. He secretly hoped there would never be a war. Since Brok's return all that had changed. After Brok's private meeting with The Few, Storret, Nayman, and Noot were called in to strategize. Storret and Nayman were to give up part of their army to Brok. The Few had asked both Storret and Noot about Oronice and both of them expressed danger and concern with Memory Tower, although Storret felt that Noot appeared to be disconnected from the physical world as he explained his thoughts.

Hammadin had ordered that Storret and Nayman march first on Memory Tower and then join Brok, who would enter Castle Weilk to free Lankor and Zimp and to kill the gryphon Brok had told them about.

"King Belford must be heart-broken and torn from bearing such an unfortunate offspring," Hammadin had said. "I feel it is not what he would have wished for."

"Unfortunate offspring," Storret whispered.

"What did you say?" Breel reached for Storret's hand.

He looked up. "Nothing. Just something Hammadin said last night."

Brok rubbed the back of his neck and down his arms.

"Are you rested?" Breel said.

"Enough for what we need to do," he said.

"I've dispatched Floom to separate a third of the men to you," Storret said.

"I'll kill them all," Brok said, hardly listening.

"There is but one menace at Castle Weilk," Storret said. "A war with the humans would not be wise. Nayman and I will do battle only if we must. You must consider doing the same."

"They didn't kill your entire family," Brok said. He glanced at Breel, "Almost."

Storret thought to say something else, to disagree. He could suggest that Brok not be allowed to march on the castle. But The Few had spoken and he trusted that they knew what they were doing.

Storret reached for Breel as he stood.

"I'll stay for a little while, if you don't mind," she said.

Storret nodded, and against his own wishes he said, "You may choose to march with your brother."

"I'll march with you," she said. "But we will meet up in a few hours."

Storret felt a rush of happiness. If Breel fought beside anyone it should be him.

"We'll win this war," Brok said.

"May the Gods bless us all," Storret said.

END

ABOUT TERRY PERSUN

Terry Persun has been writing for a living for over thirty years, and has written in many genres. He has been a board member & the agent and editor liaison for the Pacific Northwest Writers Association since 2004. He also teaches the craft of writing at conferences, writers' groups, MFA programs, etc. He and his wife live near Seattle and he has three grown children. His books have won several awards, he's an Amazon bestselling novelist, and his novel *Doublesight* was recently made into a **Kindle World**. For more information, visit www.terrypersun. com and follow him on Twitter @tpersun.

Other works by Terry Persun

Fantasy Novels in the Doublesight Series
Doublesight
Memory Tower
Fugitives
Gargoyle
Science Fiction Novels
Hear No Evil
Revision 7:DNA
Backyard Aliens
Cathedral of Dreams
Techno-Thrillers
The Killing Machine
The Humanzee Experiments
Mystery/Suspense
Mistake In Identity
Man by the Door (romantic mystery)
The NSA Files (a shaman detective novel)
The Voodoo Case (a shaman detective novel)
Historical Novels
Ten Months in Wonderland (during the Vietnam War)
Sweet Song (after the Civil War)
Mainstream Novels
To Our Waking Souls
The Perceived Darkness
Wolf's Rite
Giver of Gifts
Deception Creek
The Witness Tree
Poetry Collections
Blues and Beyond/Sentences (with Gerald Braude)
And Now This
Every Leaf
Barn Tarot
Problems with Opaque
Nonfiction
Tell Don't Show: How to successfully break the rules of fiction
Guidebook for Working with Small Independent Publishers
Make Money Writing

Made in the USA
San Bernardino, CA
03 July 2017